Cursed with a poor sense of direction and a propensity to read, **Annie Claydon** spent much of her childhood lost in books. A degree in English literature followed by a career in computing didn't lead directly to her perfect job—writing romance for Mills & Boon—but she has no regrets in taking the scenic route. She lives in London, a city where getting lost can be a joy.

Born in the UK, **Becky Wicks** has suffered interminable wanderlust from an early age. She's lived and worked all over the world, from London to Dubai, Sydney, Bali, NYC and Amsterdam. She's written for the likes of *GQ*, *Hello!*, *Fabulous* and *Time Out*, as well as a host of YA romance, plus three travel memoirs—*Burqalicious*, *Balilicious* and *Latinalicious* (HarperCollins Australia). Now she blends travel with romance for Mills & Boon and loves every minute! Find her on Substack, @beckywicks.

FROM FRENCH KISS TO FATHER

ANNIE CLAYDON

A RIVALRY IN PARADISE

BECKY WICKS

MILLS & BOON

First published in Great Britain 2026
by Mills & Boon, an imprint of HarperCollins*Publishers* Ltd,
1 London Bridge Street, London, SE1 9GF

www.harpercollins.co.uk

HarperCollins*Publishers* Macken House, 39/40 Mayor Street Upper,
Dublin 1, D01 C9W8, Ireland

From French Kiss To Father © 2026 Annie Claydon

A Rivalry in Paradise © 2026 Becky Wicks

ISBN: 978-0-263-41981-8

01/26

MIX
Paper | Supporting
responsible forestry
FSC™ C007454

This book contains FSC™ certified paper
and other controlled sources to ensure responsible forest management.

For more information visit www.harpercollins.co.uk/green.

Printed and Bound in the UK using 100% Renewable Electricity
at CPI Group (UK) Ltd, Croydon, CR0 4YY

FROM FRENCH KISS
TO FATHER

ANNIE CLAYDON

MILLS & BOON

CHAPTER ONE

THE CONFERENCE CENTRE in Warwickshire was—just another conference centre. Dr Pearl Johnson was looking forward to discussing an aspect of neurology that fascinated her, but she wasn't reckoning on finding any friends. Learning new things, considering different ideas from colleagues who were interested in the complexities of the human memory, would be more than enough.

And then Dr Henri Auclair detached himself from a knot of people, all busy getting to know each other on the large terrace outside the bar area. 'Pearl! I was hoping I might see you here. What a pleasure.'

'Henri! I didn't expect you to come all the way from Paris. How are you?'

'First things first,' Henri chided her, his blue eyes flashing with humour.

'Of course.' Pearl took his outstretched hand, leaning in for a kiss on both cheeks. Henri's gentlemanly charm had been the foundation of a firm friendship, which had seen her through a very dark time.

He'd been working at the London hospital where Pearl had taken her first, uncertain steps into her speciality training. Henri had taken his role as her mentor seriously, helping her to negotiate the challenges of a budding career and then stepping in when her personal life had fallen apart. His office had been an oasis of calm, there for her to talk if she wanted, and Henri had been one of the *good guys* who reminded her that not all men were like her ex-husband.

'You have any news for me?' Henri was always tactful; he was asking how Pearl was making her way in the world, after escaping the violence and coercive control of her marriage.

'Only that my life's good. Settled now.' And safe. Pearl could finally sleep at night, protected by the shelter of locked doors and the reassurance of only ever associating with trusted friends after work.

Henri nodded. 'That obviously suits you—you look well. Nathalie and I are turned upside down...' He took his phone from his pocket, tapping on the screen and then handing it to her. Pearl caught her breath.

'These are Francine's twins?' Henri and Nathalie's Christmas letter had proudly announced that they had become grandparents.

'Yes. I'll be able to spend more time with them soon. I'm planning on giving up my role as head of department, and working only three days a week.'

'That sounds wonderful. You *must* have more photographs—are you going to share?'

Henri chuckled. 'Of course. Over an aperitif this evening, perhaps. Now is a time for introductions.'

Pearl met new people, new patients, every day but that was in the controlled environment of the hospital. She'd put the introductions part of this week out of her thoughts as a slightly unwelcome necessity. 'You're here as part of a group?'

'My colleague has gone to fetch some coffee.' Henri

scanned the group of people clustered around the drinks counter. 'There he is...'

Pearl felt the muscles in her jaw tighten around her smile. Henri was gesturing towards the most gorgeous man she'd ever seen, who was currently manoeuvring a small tray through the crowd. Doctors didn't usually come in such beautiful packages.

He's married—or maybe he's vain or has terrible breath... Anything to break the mouth-watering spell of his looks and reduce him to someone who didn't make Pearl regret the decisions she'd made. Living her own life meant avoiding romantic entanglements, and this man looked exactly the kind of person who would be easy to become entangled with.

'He's one of the *good guys*,' Henri murmured, leaning towards her. 'In case you were wondering.'

'No, I...' Pearl decided *not* to admit to wondering anything, as that implied a measure of interest. 'Doctors are all the good guys, aren't they?'

Henri shot her an unconvinced look, but had clearly decided not to press the point. 'So they tell me.' He moved towards a free table and sat down, holding his arm up to attract the man's attention.

There was still time to run. If she did that then Henri would undoubtedly start to worry about her. Pearl sat down in the seat next to his, ignoring his small nod of approval.

Close up, the man was just as attractive as she'd feared. His eyes were dark blue, almost violet, the unusual colour softening the strong line of his jaw. His suit screamed casual, laid-back, and he wore it with the kind of indifference that suggested he didn't really care whether people were looking at him or not. And the way he moved...

Pearl wasn't going to think about that, because the combination of controlled power and grace was unthinkably fascinating.

Henri was all smiles. 'Dr Pearl Johnson, may I present Dr Luc Belange.'

Luc was staring at her. Probably because she couldn't help staring at him. Henri gave them a moment, and then smoothly resumed his introduction. 'Luc specialises in clinical neurology and is a colleague from Paris—' he turned to Luc '—and Pearl specialises in surgical neurology and is a much-valued colleague from my time in London.'

'Nice to meet you.' Luc's voice was just perfect, like honey flowing over her senses. And he spoke very good English, with only a trace of a French accent. 'You travelled up from London this morning?'

'Yes. You?'

'We caught an early train from Paris and then drove here. I'm staying on next week, to visit family.'

'You have family here?' Luc had just said as much, but it was all that Pearl could think of in the way of polite conversation.

'Yes, my mother's English. She was teaching in Paris when she met my father.'

Pearl swallowed hard. 'Which is why your English is so good?'

'My mother always spoke English at home.' Luc smiled, setting the tray down on the table in front of them and putting one of the empty cups in front of Pearl. 'I'll go and fetch another cup.'

'I'll go…' Maybe Luc didn't hear, or had decided that he wouldn't argue, because he was already on his way back to the counter.

* * *

Pearl was perceptive and thoughtful, with auburn hair which shone in the sunshine and dark eyes that brimmed with warmth. And as the week wore on it became apparent that she had a quick mind and a playful sense of humour. Luc's late wife, Camille, would have liked her and he imagined that she would have laughed at his hesitation, telling him that it had been six years and he was allowed to move on. But knowing that Camille wouldn't have wanted him to grieve this long was one thing. Believing in a world where loss wasn't an inevitable consequence of every gain was quite another.

But he and Pearl could spend time together. They could discuss the morning's sessions over lunch, and argue about the finer points over dinner, leaving Henri to indulge his gregarious nature and cover the rest of the room. And maybe it was Henri's obvious pleasure in their friendship that allowed them to trust each other.

Or maybe it was the chemistry between them. It was that heady, inescapable fusion which told Luc that Pearl wasn't idly straying across boundaries when her questions became personal as they took an evening walk together in the grounds of the conference centre.

'You said that you live alone now. Have you ever been married?'

'Yes. For five years.'

'Me too. Just for a year, though. Things didn't go so well.' Pearl quirked the corners of her mouth down. 'It turns out that the happiest day of my life was the biggest mistake I ever made.'

'How so?' Luc knew that if he asked it would lay him open to Pearl's questions, and he never spoke about the day he'd lost Camille. But maybe Pearl was the person he'd been waiting for—a virtual stranger who seemed to know him so well. Someone whose warmth might melt the ice that formed in his veins whenever he thought about that day.

'My ex-husband was...' She shrugged. 'There were red flags that I didn't see, or maybe I just didn't want to see them because I loved him. On the evening of our wedding, when we were finally alone, he told me that he had a plan for us that would make us both happy...'

Luc frowned. 'You had any input on this plan?'

Pearl laughed suddenly, but there was no warmth in her smile. 'Thanks for asking. No, I didn't. I'd just started my first year of speciality training, which was demanding, but if there was a thing out of place, anything not done at home, it provoked a long tirade about how I wasn't putting my marriage first. Things got worse—I needed approval to spend time with my friends, which was never given... You get the picture?'

Luc nodded, feeling suddenly helpless. If he voiced all of the protectiveness that was forming in his heart, maybe it would sound too much like the coercive control that Pearl had experienced.

'In the end...it was Henri who came through for me. I should have known better than to tell everyone at work that the spiral fracture in my wrist was due to a fall. Every doctor knows that they're caused by twisting rather than impact.'

'Yeah, that's a red flag.' Luc ventured an agreement. 'Was telling them that a cry for help?'

'I think so. One that Henri heard. He wasn't my direct boss as I was on the surgical side and he was the head of clinical neurology. But he saw there was something wrong and stepped in. He and Nathalie helped me leave, but then…my ex-husband wouldn't accept it and for a year afterwards he'd turn up wherever I went. Henri helped me install new high-security locks in the flat I'd found, and they helped me sleep. Things got better, my ex finally lost interest in me, but I took the locks with me when I moved on and bought my house.'

She shot him a wry smile. As if this was all one of those things.

'I'm so sorry that happened to you, Pearl. I can't imagine how it must have felt—' Luc fell silent as Pearl suddenly stopped walking.

'I don't want you to try. It felt awful, and I was blaming myself and feeling that maybe there was something I could have done. I think differently now.'

'Then may I imagine all of the strength that's taken?'

This time Pearl really smiled. 'Yes, you can do that.' She took his arm, and started walking again. It must have taken a lot for her to tell him this, but now Luc understood.

'My marriage was different. My wife died, in a car accident, six years ago.'

'I'm so sorry, Luc.' He felt her grip tighten on his arm. Some people felt that the words were everything and used them to back away from the realities, but Pearl wasn't *some people* and she was holding on to him. Grounding him.

'She was coming to meet me for lunch. I was sitting outside, with a coffee, and she crossed the road… A van turned out of a side street and hit her.'

'You saw it happen?'

'I… It happened in front of me, but I didn't really *see* anything. The cafe was just around the corner from the hospital and there were several other doctors there. They had to pull me away—I was begging her to get up and telling her she was okay, even though she'd died on impact.'

'Shock. Your heart can't take in anything your head is telling you.' Pearl turned her gaze up to him, and he saw tears in her eyes. They said more than anything, and suddenly it was possible to voice the one thing he'd never spoken about.

'She was pregnant. We'd only found out two weeks previously and hadn't told anyone yet.'

One tear rolled down her cheek and Luc brushed it away. Pearl nodded, in an unspoken understanding that no words of consolation would mean so much.

'It gets better. Time heals.'

She nodded. 'Yes, I suppose so. Although it doesn't make either of us any less lonely.'

Two people who could no longer bind themselves to words like *relationship* and *commitment*. But as they walked, they were moving past the silence, past thoughts of things they couldn't change. Knowing that Pearl was just as wary of stepping out of her comfort zone and into a relationship as he was gave Luc the courage to ask for her friendship.

'I won't be at the closing lunch tomorrow. I'm driving Henri over to Stratford-upon-Avon. He's got something on at the weekend and wants to get an earlier train. I don't suppose you'd like to come along and catch a performance of Shakespeare in the park? If I can get tickets...' He left the invitation hanging, as if Pearl's answer hardly meant anything to him. But he hadn't been able to stop thinking about the idea.

Pearl's hand flew to her mouth in mock horror. 'You mean play truant from a long and boring lunch, where everyone drinks one too many glasses of wine? What if it rains?'

Luc chuckled. 'I won't run for cover if you don't.'

'So you're an old hand at ignoring the weather. In that case, count me in, I'm definitely coming.'

Their suitcases were in the boot of the car, and they'd both checked out of the conference centre. As they waved Henri off at the station, this seemed like venturing into a new world. Pearl had entered into the spirit of the afternoon, replacing her smart suits with a summer dress that was accessorised by a waterproof jacket with a hood. Luc rented a groundsheet, and brought along a bottle of sparkling fruit pressé and a punnet of strawberries.

They went through the ritual of choosing a place to sit, not too close to the wooden stage, but not too far away, either. *A Midsummer Night's Dream* was the ideal production to watch in the open air. Mischievous fairies and sprites appeared from behind the trees, making their way to the stage through the audience, and when one of them brushed his gloved hand against Pearl's cheek and then ran away, she let out a cry and moved closer to Luc. Even here, surrounded by the delights of a magical summer's afternoon, Pearl was a little on her guard.

But she wasn't immune to the magic. Her face was shining as she sprang to her feet, applauding the bowing actors. As they gathered their things up to leave, she turned to him.

'Thank you for sneaking away from that tiresome lunch with me. I had such a good time.' She flashed him a mischievous look. 'I've been missing wonderful adventures lately...'

'Me too.' He could let the feeling go. Go back to his

life, with just this memory. But something about the look in Pearl's eyes told him that he didn't need to. 'It's still early…'

'We could go and get some dinner at the place Henri suggested.' She paused, frowning. 'How come Henri always knows the best places to eat, wherever he is? Does he have some kind of culinary radar?'

'I wouldn't be surprised.' Right now, the only thing that Luc cared about was that he and Pearl were together. 'Shall we go and check it out?'

It had all happened as effortlessly and naturally as floating downstream. The country hotel was away from the tourist bustle of Stratford-upon-Avon, had five-star reviews for its restaurant and an open-air terrace for a warm evening. Pearl had called ahead to book a table, which wouldn't be ready for an hour, but they were welcome to spend their time exploring the splendid gardens of the Tudor manor house.

Luc ducked under an arched entrance, into a passageway between two hedges. 'It's a maze. What do you think? Right or left?'

'Left.' Pearl didn't want to go the right way. Not tonight…

They meandered along snaking pathways, making no effort to find their way to the centre, because it was enjoyment enough just to be together. Pearl slipped her hand into his and felt Luc squeeze her fingers.

'Do the rules still apply here, Luc? The ones that say love is an unfaithful friend and we should never speak to it again?'

He thought for a moment, gazing down at her. Pearl knew what his answer was from the look in Luc's dark blue eyes. 'I think…they may not. Everywhere else they do, but perhaps this is our very own midsummer night's dream.'

She could almost see the fairy faces. Hear their voices when the breeze rustled the leaves. But when she reached up, skimming her fingertips against Luc's cheek, and he kissed her… Then there was only him. Warm and gentle, but with a deep vein of passion that told her he wanted the same thing she did.

'Shall we stay? Just one night, when there's no past to answer to?' She nestled against him, feeling the strong reassurance of his body.

'I like that thought very much. Let's go back and I'll find out if there's a room available…'

A man who knew less about the complex workings of desire might have cancelled their dinner booking and ordered room service instead. But Luc had more finesse than that, and he smilingly told Pearl that they had plenty of time to enjoy all of the pleasures the hotel had to offer. As they talked over dinner, a night spent together became more than just an impetuous dream.

They strolled arm in arm through reception, then walked up a grand old staircase which creaked with every step. When Luc let them into their room, Pearl couldn't help catching her breath in delight.

'A four-poster bed! I've never slept in one before.'

'You want to sleep?' The curl of his lips told Pearl that sleep was the very last thing on Luc's mind.

'Not before we've made this real.' Pearl reached up, running her thumb across his lips, and Luc took her in his arms and kissed her. All of the passion that had been simmering for the last week began to boil in her veins, and Pearl tugged at his jacket, and then his shirt. Then it was his turn to unzip the back of her dress and pull it from her shoulders.

His body was strong, beautiful, and Pearl couldn't take her eyes off him. The touch of his fingers made her shiver, and the feeling of his skin against hers made her burn. Luc was a present and generous lover, holding her safe in his arms as he touched and explored, searching for the caress that pleased her the most.

And when she melted into a body-shaking orgasm he followed her rhythm, keeping the feeling going. Finding new ways to arouse her. Suddenly, once just wasn't enough. It never had been.

'Will you do that for me again?' He murmured the words and Pearl felt a tide of new desire crashing over her.

'Just as long as you know that I'll be turning the tables on you…'

Luc chuckled, his kisses moving down her neck to her breasts. Now that she'd given a little piece of herself to him, their connection had deepened and he seemed to feel her pleasure more keenly. 'I can wait…'

When they drifted downstairs for a late breakfast in the deserted restaurant, Luc appeared thoughtful. Pearl sipped her coffee, reminding herself that other people's feelings weren't always her fault, despite what her ex-husband had tried to teach her.

He seemed to shake off the silence, looking up at her suddenly. 'I'm sorry. Last night wasn't what I expected.' Luc's slow smile told Pearl that it had been better.

'You mean…not just a way of getting through the night?'

'No. It was never that, Pearl. It was special but it can't change the past. I was just wishing it could.'

Pearl wished that too. 'We're good together, Luc, but we can't make a go of things. I'd be fighting you all the way. Wanting my space, afraid of losing control over my life again. I like you far too much to want that for either of our futures.'

He chuckled. 'And I like you far too much to try to wrap you in cotton wool in an attempt to shield myself from loss. That's too close to taking control for my liking.'

Or for Pearl's, but Luc was too generous to mention that. 'As long as we both know that, we could stay a little longer, couldn't we? Is there anywhere you need to be before Monday morning?'

'Nothing I can't easily postpone.' His smile told her that Luc was just as tempted as Pearl was. 'And we just walk away afterwards? Never see each other again?'

'It's a small world, and we both specialise in the same area of medicine. I'm not going to run and hide if I happen to catch sight of you at a conference again, or in connection with work.' She smiled at him. 'We just draw a line under this. We won't get in touch, or arrange to meet up again, and I won't cross-question Nathalie to find out how you're doing. Call it a way of keeping this weekend safe. One thing that will never change, and we can't lose.'

Luc's gaze met hers. The decision was already made and Pearl felt a sweet rush of anticipation. The dream hadn't ended yet.

It had been two days and two nights. They'd explored the hotel's gardens together and dined in the restaurant. Talked about anything and everything, and made love like enchanted beings who knew no limits. Two precious days that had taught Pearl that she *did* know how to give her heart to someone, despite everything that had been missing from her marriage. But they both knew that the only thing that had made it possible was that it couldn't last. On Sunday afternoon, they packed their bags and Luc drove Pearl to the station.

'Are you sure I can't take you back down to London?' he asked.

'Quite sure. Let's not make two hours on the motorway the last thing we do together.'

Luc nodded. 'No goodbyes, then...'

'And no looking back.'

Pearl kissed him one last time. And then she got out of the car, and hurried for her train.

CHAPTER TWO

Paris, two years later

PEARL STOOD OUTSIDE the hospital, taking a moment to gather her courage. The sweeping arches of the building, which stood at the far end of a large courtyard, made it seem an unlikely centre of medical excellence, but she knew that inside it was very different. A new hospital had been built within the shell of its much older predecessor, taking advantage of all of the latest technologies and medical techniques.

The conference had prompted Henri to formalise the friendly relationship he'd fostered between the London and Paris hospitals. Both sides had benefitted from the resulting information exchange, but Pearl had made a point of not contacting Luc directly, and he'd never contacted her. Their time together had been safely locked away, in a place where neither the past nor the future could touch it.

She'd never forgotten Luc, though. And now that everything had changed for her, she needed to see him again. When the chance of a week's visit to Paris had come up, and her head of department had asked Pearl whether she'd like to go, she'd jumped at the opportunity.

She'd waited, counting the days until there was just a week to go. Then written a carefully worded email to Luc, saying she'd be taking two weeks' leave and combining her visit with a holiday, and that perhaps they could have dinner together. He'd responded with just two lines, but they were written with all the warmth Pearl could have hoped for. He was looking forward to working with her, and wondered whether he might show her around the hospital when she arrived. It was a departure from their agreement, but Luc seemed comfortable with it, and Pearl needed to speak with him.

And now she was here. Terrified and uncertain, knowing that the next three weeks were more important than she'd let on to anyone.

Just do it, Pearl. Her legs responded, carrying her forward across the courtyard. The glass doors of the arched main doorway slid back, and she found herself in a soaring modern reception space.

She saw Luc waiting for her by the main desk, his tan and the lines of his casual suit making him look for all the world as if he were on holiday here himself. He was no less handsome than she remembered him—probably more so, since she'd made a conscious effort to forget that part of the equation.

'Pearl. I can't tell you how much I've been looking forward to seeing you.'

'Likewise, Luc…' It was impossible not to respond to him. Not to look up into his blue eyes. There was a moment of awkwardness, as they both tried to negotiate a handshake and a kiss on the cheek at the same time, and then Luc's smile settled the matter. It was going to be two kisses, one on each cheek, done without hesitation or embarrassment.

'This hospital. It's beautiful… Is it all like this, or just the entrance?'

He smiled, clearly proud of the place. 'Some parts have more of the old, and others more of the new. Henri's not here on Mondays and Fridays, but he says that you're keen to have a look around and given me a long list of things I absolutely must show you.'

Pearl felt the beginnings of panic crawl up her spine. She *had* told Henri that she was keen to see the hospital, but it had taken all of her courage to make this first step and she needed to catch her breath before the second.

'I thought it would just be a quick tour. I don't want to put you to any trouble—you must have other things to do.'

'I've managed to clear my diary, for most of the morning at least.' His brow puckered in a frown. 'Unless of course you need to be somewhere else.'

Pearl had known that this would be hard, and that it might well get harder. The chemistry was still there between them. All the feelings, and all of the memories. But the last two years had taught her something about surviving things that felt impossible. The shortest way was through, even if around seemed easier at the moment.

'That's really nice of you, thank you. I have my laptop with me and have been collecting some case studies and discussion points from my colleagues, which I'll copy over to you. I'm hoping to spread my five working days over the three weeks I'll be in Paris, to give you a bit more flexibility in arranging meetings.'

'That works for you?' Luc shot her a surprised look. 'It would certainly help us, particularly with some of the group meetings, but don't you want to spend some of your holiday out of the city?'

'No, I want to stay here, in Paris.' This was exactly where Pearl needed to be. 'If you're happy with the arrangement, then it's what I'd prefer.'

Luc smiled suddenly. 'That's great. Perhaps we'll be seeing a little more of each other than I'd expected.'

Somehow Pearl had managed to stay calm and friendly, and that seemed to have put Luc at his ease as well. Maybe a case of *if you can do it, so can I*. They'd played that game once before in the heat of a warm night. He'd whispered the words to her and they'd slowed the pace, enjoying each exquisite moment until it was impossible to hold back any longer...

'What do you think?' His raised voice suggested that he'd caught her daydreaming, and Luc must have some idea of what *that* was all about. Pearl felt herself redden, looking around the light, airy therapy room which artfully combined all of the possibilities of the new with the tranquillity of the old.

'Wonderful.'

'You agree with me?' Warm mischief shone in Luc's eyes. Clearly he wasn't in a mood to help her out.

'It's my first day here—I agree with everyone.' She jutted her chin a little as she looked up at him, daring him to enquire any further.

'That's one approach.' He smiled, opening the door for her, and Pearl stepped outside into the corridor. She looked right and left, wondering whether she was supposed to know which way they were going, and Luc finally came to her rescue, leading her towards the exit of the neurology department. 'In case you were wondering, we're on our way to the library.'

Pearl nodded. 'To look at...books?'

Luc shrugged. 'I suppose we could. I happen to be the director of library services for the hospital and I'd like to show you what we've been doing there.'

'I didn't realise…'

'It's an honorary position—I don't get paid. It's more than a hobby and slightly less than an obsession.'

'A vocation?' Pearl smiled up at him and he shook his head.

'That's a little too sombre. A passion, maybe…'

And beneath that urbane, charming exterior, Luc knew all about passion. Pearl tried not to think about it. 'And what made you choose a library?'

Her question went unanswered as the buzz of a vibration sounded and Luc took his phone from his pocket. 'Sorry—I won't be one minute. I have to make a call.'

Pearl's French was good enough to understand that he was needed elsewhere, and she assumed that '*Les urgencies*' meant that he was going to A&E. 'You have to go?'

'Yes. I'm sorry…' He shot her a querying look, obviously surprised that she'd understood. She hadn't been able to translate a single word of the things he'd whispered in her ear two years ago, but that had been okay. They sounded wonderful, and kept what was about to happen next as a surprise.

'Someone with a stroke? In A&E?' She was showing off now.

'Yes, I won't be too long. Perhaps I could point you towards the coffee bar on the way?'

'Or perhaps I could observe?' At some point Pearl was going to have to get used to communicating with Luc on a working basis, and the sooner she did that the better it would be. 'I won't get in the way but I'd be interested to see your A&E department in action.'

'Yes, of course, you'll be very welcome.' He guided her out of the department and towards a bank of lifts, one of which opened as they approached. 'I'm not usually the only person to call in neurology, but the patient in question and his wife are here from England on holiday. The A&E staff have tried to get information about what happened and when, to help assess whether clot busters are an option, but our patient isn't able to speak and his wife doesn't speak any French. So rather than call a neurologist *and* a translator, they decided to call me.'

'One of the dangers of being far too useful.'

He nodded, moving swiftly out of the lift and through a network of corridors. 'Your French has improved since I saw you last.'

'When I knew I was coming here, I got an app that's supposed to teach you French in ninety days. That gave me the basics, but actually watching a French cop show on TV with the subtitles on was pretty useful.'

Luc chuckled. 'Yeah, I can see that. There's nothing like hearing a language spoken to become fluent. So you could arrest me in French, if you put your mind to it?'

Pearl couldn't help laughing. However hard she tried to fight it, Luc was the nicest guy she'd ever met. And as his gaze met hers, the feeling that they shared just one thought sent shivers down her spine. What might they have done together with a pair of handcuffs…?

This would ease. She'd be able to look at him without her thoughts melting into a sweet mess of memories of what Luc could do to her, and what she'd done to him. She had to, for their daughter's sake.

Luc had been looking forward to seeing Pearl again. He hadn't been able to entirely stick to his promise of not looking back, but his memories were his own and he had no control over his dreams. Knowing that Pearl was out there, living her life, had brought him a measure of peace.

He'd hesitated when she'd emailed him about dinner, but two years was enough to put their weekend together firmly in the past. And showing her the hospital and the library that meant so much to him was a temptation he couldn't resist.

But when he'd seen her, walking towards him in a summer dress that filmed around her legs and a pair of comfortable canvas shoes, he'd felt his heart beating an urgent rhythm in his chest, as if it had something important to say to him. Luc had clearly overstepped his authority when he'd promised himself that this meeting would be as friends, but he suspected that Pearl had too.

She seemed uneasy and awkward in his presence. They'd begun to slip back into the easy to and fro that had been there almost from their first meeting, but he'd caught several glimpses of her embarrassment. Maybe working together wasn't such a bad idea; it would give them time to find their feet, and move on to become colleagues and friends.

Luc walked quickly through the busy A&E department, finding the cubicle number he'd been given. Inside a man who looked to be in his sixties was lying on the couch, clearly agitated and with the telltale drooping of one side of his face. A woman was sitting next to him, trying to soothe him.

The nurse who was with them handed Luc the notes and he nodded, telling her that he'd take things from here. The first thing he needed to do was to reassure Mr and Mrs Wells, who both looked very stressed.

'Hello, I'm Dr Luc Belange, and I'm a neurologist. My colleague, Dr Pearl Johnson, is visiting us from London and would like to sit in on our consultation if that's all right?'

'Oh!' Tears suddenly started to course down Mrs Wells's cheeks. 'Thank you. Thank you. You speak such good English. My husband's the one who speaks French and I'm a little lost. The other doctor… He wrote a note.'

Mrs Wells was clutching a piece of paper as if her life depended on it, and Luc took it gently from her hand, reading it.

'This says that he's gone to arrange an urgent scan for your husband, to check what's going on, which is exactly what we need. And that Mr Wells is allergic to NSAIDs.'

'Yes, that's right. Thank you, I wasn't sure whether he understood what I was saying.'

Luc consulted the notes. 'Yes, it's all here, written down under Allergies. What are your husband's symptoms?' He glanced around at Mr Wells, and saw Pearl standing on the other side of the bed. She knew as well as Luc did that their patient might not be able to speak, but could be understanding everything that was going on, and her smile radiated comfort and reassurance. Luc could do with that kind of getting-in-the-way for every one of his consultations.

'His throat swells up and he can't breathe.'

Luc nodded. 'Then you're right to be concerned. I'll add that to the notes, to make sure that everyone knows that this is important.'

'That's a relief. Thank you, Doctor.' Mrs Wells smiled at her husband. 'It's all written down now, Don.'

Mr Wells looked across at him and nodded. Luc scanned the sheets of paper in front of him and saw that there was no indication of the time when he'd been taken ill. 'We'll need to know when you first noticed that your husband had symptoms and what they were.'

'We'd decided not to have breakfast at the hotel and

walked to a cafe that we'd found and rather liked. That was around nine thirty, and we had coffee and croissants and then…' A tear rolled down Mrs Wells's cheek. 'Then Don just stopped replying to me.'

He heard Pearl clear her throat and turned to look at her. She was standing next to the bank of monitors, and Luc saw that Mr Wells's heart rate, which had previously been a little high but within acceptable limits, was increasing.

Pearl wasn't licensed to practise here, but the hospital had authorised her to talk with patients and practitioners. Luc had relied on patients' friends and relatives to translate before, if no one else was available, and as far as he was concerned asking for her help was well within his remit.

'I need to go and fetch some medication. I'll be one moment… Pearl, perhaps you'd sit with Mrs Wells while I deal with that?'

The smile she gave him told Luc that Pearl had made exactly the same calculation. Something stirred in his heart, and he ignored the buzz which accompanied the discovery that the same synchronicity that he and Pearl had experienced once before seemed to have followed them out of the bedroom. Luc went to fetch the medication Mr Wells needed, and returned to find that Pearl had sat down beside Mrs Wells, clearly intent on obtaining a timescale for the morning's events from her.

'So would be fair to say that this happened at around ten this morning?'

'Yes. That's right. And I remembered—I'd seen it in an advert—FAST.'

'That's great. So you looked for specific symptoms?' Pearl was gently getting the information they needed, without putting words into Mrs Wells's mouth. 'What was the first that you noticed?'

'Face...' Mrs Wells recited the first word from the acronym. 'His mouth was drooping on the left side just as it is now.'

Pearl nodded. 'And Arms...'

'His arm—the left one—was just hanging at his side. I asked him if he was all right and he tried to speak but it was so slurred that I couldn't work out what he was saying. That's number three, isn't it? Speech.'

'That's right. And did you notice any of these symptoms before that?'

'No, I didn't. He was absolutely fine when we left the hotel, weren't you, Don? And he was talking to me as we ate breakfast.'

Luc looked around, wondering if Pearl was writing all this down, and saw that she had a notebook propped on her knee and was scribbling furiously with a pencil. Wondering why he'd even bothered to doubt her, he went back to his own job, noting that the medication he'd administered to decrease Mr Wells's heartrate was taking effect.

'And so you...? What happened next?'

'I called the waiter and he phoned for an ambulance for us. They arrived really quickly and were so kind, but they didn't speak much English and I didn't know what to do...'

'Of course not. But you've given us the information we need to know and you acted quickly, which can make a real difference. The *T* stands for Time.'

'Ah yes, that's right. Isn't there some medicine you can give to reverse the stroke?'

That was the hardest part of their job—the note of hope that sounded in Mrs Wells's voice. Pearl met it head-on, without flinching. 'You might be thinking of clot busters. They can be very helpful but only with certain kinds of stroke and in particular circumstances. Dr Belange will make a decision about whether they'll be right for your husband, and will be taking various different things into consideration, such as the results of the scan. And also the information you've given me, which is very important. It's a real help that you've remembered everything so clearly.'

She'd explained everything, carefully and kindly. Hope was sometimes an uncertain bedfellow of honesty, but Pearl had this just right. Luc could see in Mrs Wells's face that she trusted Pearl, and he added his own words of reassurance.

'Your husband's in good hands here, Mrs Wells. We'll be making sure that he gets whatever he needs.'

A knock sounded on the door of the cubicle, and the A&E doctor appeared. He'd arranged for the CAT scan to be done immediately, and Luc agreed that he should accompany Mr Wells to monitor his condition and make sure he understood all that was happening to him.

'We can't go with them, but Dr Belange will be there to explain everything,' Pearl reassured Mrs Wells. 'There's going to be a wait, so perhaps we should find a coffee shop where we can sit comfortably for a while.'

She didn't need to do that, but Mrs Wells was obviously grateful for Pearl's offer. 'You know where the cafe is?' Luc asked her.

Pearl returned his smile. 'I think my French is up to asking the way if I get lost.'

'Okay. Remember not to tell everyone that you're a police officer and to lay down their weapons for starters. That'll just cause panic.' It was a joke, but Pearl took it in just the way it was intended, turning to Mrs Wells and rolling her eyes.

'Don't listen to him. I've been brushing up on my French by watching cop shows on TV…'

Mrs Wells grinned suddenly, turning to her husband, whose crooked smile showed that he understood too. Pearl shot him a get-you-back-later glance that made Luc's heart thump and then turned, waiting for Mrs Wells to tell her husband that she'd be there with him again as soon as she was allowed, before ushering her from the cubicle.

Luc had reviewed the test results and made his decision. He'd explained everything to the couple, showing Mrs Wells the English language consent forms that he'd printed off, which she signed on her husband's behalf. Clot busters were administered less than three hours after Mr Wells had shown the first symptoms of the stroke, and Luc was confident that they'd make a significant difference to his recovery. He'd be kept under close supervision for the next few hours, and Luc had instructed the nurses in the neurology ward to call him if they had any concerns.

Then the afternoon was their own. Almost as soon as they walked out of the department, Pearl regained her nervous, jumpy air. He'd thought that working together had broken the ice between them, but it appeared that it had only temporarily relieved the symptoms of something deeper.

'What's next? The library?' The painful uncertainty in Pearl's eyes broke all of Luc's resolve. They'd promised to draw a line under their weekend together, but Luc couldn't think of anything else that might be bothering her and they really *did* have to talk.

'Yes, unless there's somewhere else you need to go.'

Luc shook his head. The only thing he wanted right now was to find out what was bugging Pearl. He led her out of the main building, and across the rear courtyard, to the library. They hurried through the large, central area with its book-lined galleries under a high, vaulted ceiling and then up three flights of curving stone steps. Then he opened the door of his office, and ushered her inside.

The central gallery of the library was spectacular, but Luc had clearly been in a hurry to be somewhere else. Pearl followed him, wondering what could possibly be any more splendid than the rooms he was striding through without so much as a second glance.

'This is my office…'

Pearl caught her breath. The bright room had high, arched windows and the desk in the corner seemed like an afterthought in the large space.

'This is gorgeous, Luc. I think it's bigger than the ground floor of my house.'

'I was thinking of moving in here—it would be handy for the morning commute. But when the staff and volunteers want to work without interruptions, they usually commandeer the conference table.' He gestured towards two sofas on the other side of the room, set in front of an ornate fireplace. 'Sit. Would you like some tea? There's a kitchen right next door, in case I ever feel the need to hold a dinner party.'

'A cup of tea would be nice. Only if you're making one for yourself.'

Amusement showed in his eyes. Maybe he was remembering that one weekend, when neither of them had any hesitation in asking the other for anything. But Luc said nothing, and was gone before Pearl could think of anything to add.

The room was too big, its architecture too ornate to take in all at once. In contrast, the clean lines of the modern furniture added an understated elegance to the space. Everything was neat and tidy, and Luc's desk was clear, save for a laptop and a phone. This would be a great place to either work, or relax. Or just to take shelter from a world that was sometimes too complicated to bear.

Luc returned, with two cups of tea and a plate of biscuits. Pearl took a sip from the mug he placed on the low table in front of her, the quiet of the room suddenly seeming oppressive. Luc had left his tea on the table between them, and was sitting on the sofa opposite her, regarding her thoughtfully.

'Are we okay, Pearl?' His question was almost a relief.

'Yes. Yes, we're okay.'

Luc didn't seem convinced. Maybe she'd answered a little too glibly. 'I wouldn't like to think that anything I've said, or done, makes you uneasy.'

'No. Really, there's nothing. It's good to see you, Luc.' The words that came tumbling out were clearly not very convincing; Pearl could still see concern in his eyes. 'There was something I wanted to discuss and I thought I'd ask you if you were free for dinner. And if you knew a good place where we could go. Somewhere quiet…'

'Or we could save ourselves five or six hours of—' Luc shrugged '—whatever this is. And talk now.'

He knew that something was up. And the naked honesty they'd once shared was beating at the doors of her consciousness, demanding to be let in. Pearl took a breath. Now was the time, whether she liked it or not. And whether Luc liked it or not…

'I brought someone with me, to Paris. Someone I'd like you to meet. Her name's Celeste…' Her courage failed her. Maybe Luc would put it together from that, ask all the right questions. But he just looked perplexed.

'Celeste Helena Johnson. She's my daughter.' She could see a spark of something in Luc's eyes. He was moving in the right direction…

'How old is she?'

'Fifteen months.' They were so close now that Pearl couldn't help putting an end to the uncertainty. 'She's your daughter too, Luc.'

CHAPTER THREE

CELESTE HELENA JOHNSON. Fifteen months. Luc didn't have to count them; he knew exactly how long it had been since he'd last seen Pearl. Almost to the day, although he'd been trying not to think about that.

Every emotion that he could name, and a few that he couldn't, was crowding into his heart. Pearl was trembling, looking at him intently, and all Luc could think of was the obvious question. Why hadn't she told him before now?

'I know this is a shock, Luc. Celeste is your child, and if you want to be sure—'

He held up his hand and she fell silent, her gaze searching his face. This was one question he could ask without any hesitation. 'Are *you* sure?'

Pearl nodded. 'Yes.'

'Then why would I doubt you?'

Tears spilled down Pearl's cheeks. 'Thank you.'

It had been a good start, but anger and loss were still gripping him and they wouldn't let go. If he could trust her, then why hadn't there been one single moment when Pearl felt she could trust him in the last two years?

The feeling of loss was overwhelming. He'd already lost the promise of a child, and now all he could think of was the fifteen precious months, when he could have been there for Pearl and their baby.

'Luc…?' Pearl was reaching out to him and he couldn't respond. He got to his feet, walking over to the window and staring out. Trying to direct all of his questions somewhere else and not at her. Pearl didn't deserve this; from what she'd told him she'd been married to a man who was jealous and unstable. This was all she knew about the realities of a relationship, once the fairy-tale part was over.

'I should go and see how Mr and Mrs Wells are doing. I'd like to organise for her to stay with him tonight… I want to talk, but it's best we do so uninterrupted.'

'Don't do that, Luc.' When he turned, Pearl was pressing her lips together, looking at him thoughtfully.

'Do what?'

'Make excuses in order to take a little thinking time. I'm not going to crumple if you tell me what's on your mind. I don't do that anymore.'

'Then what's *your* excuse for not telling me before now? You didn't have to come all the way to Paris—you could have just picked up the phone. Is that so very difficult?'

His words hit her hard. Pearl's cheeks reddened, and he saw tears in her eyes. Luc was raw with questions and couldn't keep a lid on his emotions. But he couldn't bear to be the guy who hurt Pearl with words that came from a place of loss.

'We *will* talk, I promise you, just not now. I can't talk to you now.'

She nodded, leaning forward to take a piece of paper from her bag. 'Here's my mobile number. Maybe we'll speak soon.'

'You can count on it. I'll call.'

She nodded, putting a fat manila envelope onto the table. 'This is for you and… You don't have to look at it.

I'll just leave it so that you can.' Pearl was on her feet and heading for the door before he had a chance to ask, and maybe it was better not to. He should let her go, and trust that they could start again and get this right the next time.

And then she was gone. Luc walked over to the sofa, sitting down, and taking his phone from his pocket to transfer Pearl's number into it. Then he laid his fingers on the envelope.

He knew he was going to look, and he may as well dispense with the agonising over the decision and do it now. Inside there was an A5 photo album, with soft covers, and Luc turned to the first page with trembling fingers.

The little girl was wearing a pink sweater with dungarees that were a little muddy around the knees. Dark blonde hair and blue eyes. She was standing in the sunshine, a riot of flowers in the background, and Luc supposed they must be in a local park. He stared at the photograph, trying to take in every detail. Celeste's eyes were the same colour as his...

He took a breath and turned to the next page of the album. Pearl was kneeling down, one arm tightly around her daughter and her other hand stretched out to feed several mallards which had ventured close to the edge of a pond. Celeste was reaching out towards the ducks, her face shining with inquisitive glee. He could almost taste the pleasures of a sunny afternoon, where everything was an adventure.

Someone else must have taken the photograph. A friend or maybe even a lover... That afternoon didn't belong to him and all he could do was look at a memory of it. Luc could feel tears on his face, and he closed the album.

This little girl...she was the child that Luc had thought

he'd never have after he'd lost Camille. He'd never forgotten their child, never missed the passing of the years and how that small, precious speck of life might have grown. Even though he'd missed the first months of Celeste's life there was much more to come, and Luc knew he had a lot of love to give her.

He needed to get a grip. Do whatever it took to get his head straight so that he could be constructive when next he spoke to Pearl. And he needed to do it now, before he drove her away.

Pearl ran down the stone staircase, holding tightly onto the handrail in case her legs really were going to give way. By some miracle she managed to find her way out of the library, and she took a deep breath as she hurried across to the main building. She could read the signs well enough to find her way back to the main entrance, and she ran across the courtyard and onto the pavement.

Not far enough. She could feel tears on her face and if Luc was about to leave the hospital in a rage, then he'd find her. She hurried to the nearest corner, and then walked part-way down the road, ducking into a coffee shop and indicating to the waiter that she wanted to sit inside, at the very back. She tried out her French on him and he brought her a coffee just as she'd ordered it.

What was the worst she'd expected? The worst was easy, but she hadn't really expected Luc to tell her that he didn't care and wanted nothing to do with Celeste.

Second worst? All manner of things. She'd known this would hurt Luc, and that he'd be angry. She knew that he had every right to challenge her about her long silence and that it would take time to process something this big. What she hadn't foreseen was her own reaction. It was all very well to tell herself that her ex-husband was in the past and she'd never have to deal with his anger again. But Luc's anger had frightened her, even though she knew that he was different in every respect.

She'd panicked and given him an incomplete account of what had happened. And the pain and confusion in his eyes had hurt her more than anything Luc could possibly say or do.

But it was done. Luc had said that she could count on seeing him again, and she had to trust him. Hold her nerve and let him take whatever time he needed.

Nathalie hadn't asked about her morning, just admired the flowers that Pearl had bought for her at a stall by the entrance to the metro station, and observed that Celeste loved playing in the sandpit almost as much as Henri did. Then she'd ushered her out of the back door, to go and see her daughter.

Celeste was engaged in filling a bucket with sand, and then tipping it back out again, while Henri was completing a rather more ambitious project. Pearl took off her shoes, sitting down with them and taking her daughter on her lap to hug her. Suddenly she could breathe again.

'Did you tell him?' Henri asked, not taking his gaze from the castle.

Pearl sighed. Perhaps it had been too much to ask that Henri wouldn't guess. 'So you worked it out.'

Henri turned, sitting back from the sandcastle. 'Maybe it's just a coincidence that her middle name also belongs to one of the characters in *A Midsummer Night's Dream*. But the colour of her eyes does rather give it away.'

'Thanks for pretending you didn't know. And yes, I

told him. Luc's…processing.' Pearl kissed the top of Celeste's head, feeling a tear roll down her cheek.

'Hey. None of that. Did I tell you that Luc's one of the good guys?'

'Yes, you did. But even the best guy would be forgiven for wondering why it took me so long to tell him.'

'I expect you had your reasons. I can think of one very good reason why you wouldn't want to get involved with anyone again. It must have taken a lot for you to come here.'

It had. And if Henri understood then maybe Luc would too. 'He's had a lot to deal with as well. I can't begin to imagine the tragedy that Luc's had to face.'

Henri nodded. 'Nor can I. But this is why I believe that he and you can work things out. You both have—' he waved his hand, trying to summon up a word in English '—humanity for each other.'

Pearl couldn't think of one English word that summed that up, either. 'It's a nice thought, Henri. I'm not sure that either of us showed much humanity for each other today. We argued, it was my fault…'

'If I know Luc at all, he'll be counting the ways that it was *his* fault. This is what happens—you argue and then you forgive. Although forgiving yourself seems to be harder than forgiving him.' Henri always had been perceptive. That was what made his outspokenness so challenging sometimes. Pearl smiled at him.

'Whatever. We're going to talk some more.' Pearl wondered if she should ask Henri whether she really *could* count on it, and decided he probably wasn't in a position to comment on the unknown. 'I don't suppose you could check up on him when you go to the hospital tomorrow? Surreptitiously, if at all possible.'

'Of course. And I'll make sure that he's not retreating to that library of his and brooding.'

'Is that what he does?' Pearl wondered whether the library meant more to Luc than she'd thought. Perhaps it had been the place where he'd mourned his wife and child.

'We all have our ways of dealing.' Henri had always been particular about not sharing other people's secrets, and Pearl had been grateful for that when they'd worked together. 'If he's not dealing, I'll persuade him to take some time off.'

'Thanks, Henri. I'm so grateful for all that you and Nathalie have done for me.'

'And I am grateful for my marvellous new friend.' Henri smiled, turning his attention to Celeste. 'What will you do, now that my castle is finished, *chérie*?' He waved his hand at it.

The little girl slid from her mother's knee, regarding the castle solemnly. 'She's going to knock it down, Henri…' Pearl knew that look.

Henri chuckled as Celeste took a step towards the castle, looking at him to see what he would do. He nodded, smiling at her, and she took another step.

'This is why we get along so well. She is of an age when she likes to knock things over, and I am of an age when I build them up again.'

'So *that's* what you've been doing today, is it?' Back here, with Henri and Celeste, things didn't seem to so bad, although Pearl was still worried about how Luc was doing. But she'd promised to give him time, and she had to wait.

CHAPTER FOUR

LUC HAD MADE sure that Mr and Mrs Wells were settled, and that the hospital's translation service would send someone to see them this evening, in case there were any more questions to be answered. He'd managed to get through his afternoon clinic by distancing himself from everything but the needs of his patients, but that only postponed his agonised restlessness. Luc caught up the sports bag he kept in his office, and went to the gym to let off a bit of steam.

After forty gruelling minutes on the treadmill he'd come to two solid conclusions. First of all, Pearl needed to talk. And secondly, he needed to listen. Neither of those things were going to be easy. But as he'd doggedly taken his body as close to exhaustion as he could, he'd caught a glimpse of the place of trust they'd shared. The weekend where nothing had seemed impossible, and where Pearl had quietened his fear of loss for a while.

Fresh out of the shower, and before he could change his mind, he called Pearl. She answered her phone on the second ring.

'Hi. Pearl…?'

'Hi. Thanks for calling me, Luc.' Pearl's tone sounded warm. Hopeful.

'I just wanted to say that I'm sorry. I shouldn't have said those things…'

'Apology not accepted, Luc. You should have said them, and I want to answer all of your questions.'

Luc took a breath. 'I really want to listen. At any time that suits you.'

'This evening?'

Luc would sleep a great deal better, and perhaps Pearl would too. 'That would be great. Where are you staying?'

There was a short pause. 'Let's meet up in the court-yard outside the hospital, on one of the benches. At about seven o'clock? I have someone who'll watch Celeste.'

Luc wasn't going to ask. Either Pearl wanted to keep him away from Celeste, or she wanted to keep him away from where she was staying. But he was done trying to jump to conclusions when he didn't have all the facts.

'That's good for me. On one condition, though. You allow me take you back to your hotel afterwards. My car's in the library car park.'

'That's kind of you, thank you. I'll look forward to seeing you.'

Luc had been sitting on a bench in the courtyard outside the hospital since half past six, and was just wondering whether he should have fetched coffee, when he saw Pearl walking towards him with two takeaway cups. She sat down next to him, handing him one.

'I was hoping to get here before you. You must have been very early.' Pearl seemed nervous but she was smiling.

'I was just thinking that I should have brought coffee. I guess that's given us both the opportunity to show that we're serious about this meeting.' Calling it a meeting sounded a little formal, but Luc didn't want to call it a date. 'Would you like to go somewhere else, or shall we stay here? There's a terrace outside the library with seating but that gets busy in the evenings during the summer.'

'This is fine. Shall we go over there?' Pearl indicated a row of benches that were away from the main thoroughfare, and Luc nodded, getting to his feet. They had somewhere that was public enough, and yet private enough, a warm evening and coffee. So far, so good.

'Henri and Nathalie didn't know I'd had a baby, Luc.' Pearl started to talk as soon as they sat down. 'I booked a child-friendly hotel, which provided everything I needed for Celeste, so I could pack light and come on the train. And I have a place for her in the hospital crèche for days when I'm working here.'

'Right…' Luc wasn't sure where all of these explanations were going, but he'd promised to listen.

'They turned up at my hotel yesterday morning, and… Well, obviously they found out about Celeste.' She shrugged. 'You can hardly ask a fifteen-month-old to go down to the coffee bar for half an hour and pretend they don't know you. I said that we were fine where we were, but they wouldn't have it. They already have cots and high chairs for their grandchildren…'

She looked so miserable that Luc couldn't stop himself from coming to her aid. 'I know what Henri and Nathalie are like. They were probably counting on persuading you to stay with them anyway, and once they found out you had a toddler with you, you wouldn't have stood a chance.'

Pearl flashed him a grateful smile. 'No. I didn't. They wouldn't hear of Celeste going to the hospital nursery, either. When I left to get the metro this morning, Henri was already making sandcastles for Celeste in the sandpit they have in their garden.'

One more thing he'd missed. But Luc was becoming

more and more determined to make his own memories with Celeste. 'She'll be better off with Henri and Nathalie than in the nursery.'

She nodded. 'Yes, she will. You understand, then?'

Luc thought for a moment. 'Of course. I still have questions, though.'

'About why I waited so long to tell you? We'd agreed that things would never work between us in the long-term and... I wondered how you might react.'

Whether he'd be angry? He had been. Not for the reasons that Pearl seemed to think; it hadn't occurred to Luc to wonder why she'd broken their agreement. Just the opposite, he'd wondered why she hadn't...

'Is this about us, Pearl? Or someone else?'

She straightened her back, defiance showing in her gaze. This was the Pearl that he wanted, the one who looked him straight in the eye.

'I wanted it to be about us, but... You're not my ex-husband and you never will be. If I'd found that I was pregnant with him, then I would have run and never looked back, to protect my child. But this is different. You have a right to know, and protecting Celeste means giving her an opportunity to know her father.'

Luc had heard when Pearl had told him about her ex-husband, but he hadn't really understood the consequences, which she still lived with. 'I didn't appreciate just how much it took for you to come here and tell me. I hadn't thought about what that meant to you. All I was thinking was what it meant to me.'

She nodded. 'I was working my way around to telling you and I would have, but...'

'But what?' Luc reached for her hand. He could see now how hard this was for Pearl and comfort was the least he could offer. When she looked up at him, her face full of all the agonies of uncertainty that he'd been feeling, Luc wished he could offer a great deal more.

'I developed early-onset pre-eclampsia. It was managed at home for some time, but I spent almost a month in hospital before Celeste was delivered at thirty-four weeks.'

The sudden flash of concern, the thought that he would have done everything and anything to avoid losing them both, told Luc exactly why Pearl had kept silent. 'And you thought I couldn't deal with that? Because of what happened to my wife?'

'You've already been through too much, Luc. Celeste and I were always well monitored and cared for, and I knew that it was far too much to ask of you to be there for us. There was nothing you could have done, we just had to wait.'

'And you're both all right now?'

She nodded. 'Celeste was given extra support at first, but that was really only a precaution. She's never had any problems due to having been born a little prematurely.'

'And you?'

'I'm fine. It took a couple of months for my blood pressure to go right back down again, but the cure for pre-eclampsia is delivering the baby.' Pearl's smile became a little brittle, as if it was exhausting her. 'Can you understand, Luc?'

'I understand that it was always going to be difficult, for both of us, and that you shouldered it all on your own. I can't say that I like that, and I certainly don't feel very proud of it. I'm in awe of your bravery, though.'

Pearl's eyes filled with tears. 'It wasn't brave, to leave it for so long. After Celeste was born and I was feeling confident about travelling with her I kept putting things off, wondering about the right thing to do. But I knew it was your right to know, and when my head of department offered me this trip I said yes, because then I wouldn't be able to back out…'

'Hey. Listen to me.' He squeezed her hand, trying to reassure her. 'What's done is done. You took care of Celeste and that's what matters. We're going to stop talking now, and you're going to go back to Henri and Nathalie's and hug your little girl. I'm going to go home and look at the photographs, one more time. Which are wonderful, by the way. I'd really like to meet her, and get to know her. When you're ready.'

Her gaze searched his face. 'I've stolen so much from you, Luc. Too much time…'

'If I give that to you then it's not stolen.' Luc still felt the loss, and the wrench was almost physically painful. But he made himself do it, knowing that the regret was something he could bear. 'Do me one favour. Let me get you a taxi home…'

'I can get the metro. I know the way.'

'I'm compromising already.' Luc smiled down at her. 'If I take you then you'll be wondering whether to ask me in or not, and I'll be wondering whether to say yes. So I'll spare us both that by getting you a taxi, because I want to know that you're back at Henri and Nathalie's safely.'

She leaned over, kissing his cheek. 'Is this the first compromise of many?'

'Probably. But that's for tomorrow to take care of.' Suddenly there *was* a tomorrow. And however fearsome it seemed, he was going to be equal to it.

Luc had promised to call her at about five the following day. Pearl's phone rang on the dot of five o' clock and she grabbed it, barely letting it ring once.

'Who's that? Did I just pocket-dial?' His tone was playful, and clearly Luc had been having a good day. Pearl had too. Yesterday had been hard but it had cleared a lot of the worries that had been burdening her for so long.

'I was just thinking of you. Perhaps that's why my phone rang.'

Luc chuckled. 'What do you say we give in to what's obviously fate, and go for coffee, or something to eat?'

'I think we're going to have to. What time?'

'Any time that suits you. Why don't you settle Celeste down to sleep and then give me a call?'

That was nice of Luc. He was making his expectations clear, and removing the uncertainties of wondering whether she should introduce him to a potentially tired and fussy toddler.

'That sounds great. About eight o' clock, then.'

When he drew up outside the house, Pearl was waiting for him. And so was Henri, who stood in the light of the open doorway as she hurried down the path.

'Nice car!' Luc had just got out of a shiny, dark blue two-seater.

He shrugged. 'No room for a child seat. It may have to go.'

'Mine has a child seat. You could use that if you visit us in London...'

They were both taking a lot for granted, but suddenly that seemed okay. A much-needed splash of optimism.

She turned to wave to Henri, who waved back and then closed the door. 'That didn't feel at all as if I'm sixteen and being watched down the front path by my dad.'

Luc chuckled. 'If he's trying to work out whether I'm the type to go too far with you, then he's left it a little late... I assume they do know?'

'Henri didn't admit to it until yesterday afternoon. They'd noticed that Celeste's eyes were the same shade of blue as yours, and Henri reckoned that her middle name was a bit of a giveaway.'

'Helena?' Luc waited for her to get into the car and closed the door, taking his time in walking around to the driver's seat, but when he settled himself behind the steering wheel he still seemed puzzled. 'Does Henri know something that I don't?'

Pearl shook her head. 'After Helena in *A Midsummer Night's Dream*. I thought it was a pretty name, and it's a reminder that she started out surrounded by magic.'

Luc's smile told her that he liked the thought. A lot. 'It's a really good name. And Celeste?'

'It's my grandmother's name. I spent a lot of time with her when I was little, and she was great. Such fun and very wise.'

'So her name was perfect for your little girl.'

'For *our* little girl, Luc. Celeste is a French and an English name.'

His hand brushed at his face and he leaned back in his seat. 'It means a lot, Pearl. That you remembered me when you named her.'

She'd always kept her reasons for choosing Celeste's names private. They were all about a future that Pearl couldn't have, but that she wanted for her daughter.

'Why wouldn't I? It's who she is, a part of you and a part of me.'

He nodded. 'It matters to me, though. That you acknowledged it.' Luc reached forward, starting the car, and Pearl settled back in her seat, happy for him to have the last word.

The small square, five minutes' drive away, was edged

on just one side by the road, and on the other three sides by shops, cafes and restaurants. The lights strung in the trees at the centre gave a fairy-tale look that seemed suddenly very appropriate. Luc walked over to one of the cafes to buy coffee and crepes, while Pearl saved one of the tables under the trees for them.

'I've been thinking, and there's something I want to say.' Luc reached across the table, squeezing her hand in a gesture of reassurance.

'I'm listening.'

Luc gave her a smiling nod. 'I'd love to be able to say that you should have called me when you found out about the pre-eclampsia. But in truth... I would have dropped everything and come to England to take care of you. Waited on you hand and foot and done my best not to let you out of my sight. That wouldn't have been what was best for you after all you'd been through with your ex-husband, and it would have driven me crazy with worry.'

Pearl nodded. She'd thought the same.

'Maybe we would have got through that, and maybe not. Even though I wish you'd let me try to be the person you needed, you made the decision the best you could and I stand by that.'

'Thank you.' Pearl took a sip of her coffee. If she needed proof that Luc wasn't like her ex-husband, then here it was.

'I really want this opportunity to get to know Celeste. To be a proper father to her, not just someone who turns up for birthdays and at Christmas. I want to help you make decisions for her, be there when she needs me... Is that something you feel comfortable with?'

'It's what I want for Celeste and—' Pearl ventured the admission '—what I want for me, too.'

His blue eyes were so like Celeste's. And right now they were dancing with light.

'Paris isn't so far from London, a bit more than two hours by train. We can work something out which allows me to see her on a regular basis. Grow into a role of co-parenting with you.'

That was more that she'd dared to expect. But with Celeste's future at stake, Pearl had to be practical. 'Luc… I'm sorry but I have to ask…'

He nodded. 'Ask. This isn't the time not to.'

'You've already lost so much. I love that you feel you can be so committed to Celeste, but I'd understand if that was too difficult for you.'

Luc was taking time to think about his answer, and that was what Pearl wanted him to do. 'This sounds crazy…'

She smiled. 'This isn't the time to worry about how our answers sound, either.'

'I haven't even met Celeste yet, but I can't help loving her.'

'That's not crazy. When I was first pregnant I couldn't feel or see her. But she changed everything for me, and I loved her. You understand that, don't you?' He'd felt the unquestioning commitment to the promise of a child once before.

'Yeah. There's no choice, is there? Whatever the cost. But you and I—we do have a choice. We made it two years ago, for all the right reasons. To support and protect each other.'

This was everything she'd wanted. And yet it felt like a final recognition that she and Luc couldn't be together. It was the right thing—the only thing—to do and Luc had been braver than she was in acknowledging it.

'I see what you mean. And you're right, we owe it to

ourselves and each other to make our relationship work for us both.'

He nodded. 'Are we good, then?'

'We're not there yet, Luc.' She smiled. 'We've got a lot to work out, but I'm fast coming to the conclusion that we can do it.'

'We have time.' He sat back in his seat, smiling. 'So how's your coffee?'

She took a sip. 'Very good. We must come back here again.' She opened the cardboard takeaway box that contained the crepes. 'And these look nice too…'

When they'd arrived back at the house, Pearl couldn't send him away. She'd asked Luc whether he wanted to come inside and look in on Celeste with her, and he'd agreed immediately. Nathalie had answered the door, and when Luc bent to kiss her cheek she'd given him a tight, wordless hug before steering him smilingly to the bottom of the stairs.

There was a night light on in the spare room and Celeste was fast asleep in her crib. Looking just as angelic as Pearl might have hoped for Luc's first sight of their daughter. He bent, picking up her teddy from the floor, putting it carefully back into the cot.

She couldn't bring herself to tear him away now. Pearl motioned to him to sit down in the comfortable chair next to the cot, and left him alone.

Half an hour later the baby monitor relayed Luc's goodbyes to his daughter, whispered fondly in French. Then he appeared in the doorway of the sitting room.

'You'll stay for some iced tea, Luc?' Nathalie got to her feet.

'Thanks, Nathalie. Another time? I'd like to go home,

take my shoes off and feel overwhelmed…' He shrugged, grinning at her. 'And I have to be up early for work in the morning.'

In the hushed melee in the hallway, Nathalie and Henri had said their goodbyes and tactfully left Pearl to see Luc out. She hung back, not sure of what to say. She wanted Luc to reassure her, but maybe that was too much to ask of him.

Or maybe she could be the one to take the initiative. 'Do you think you could get off work a little early tomorrow? Say four o'clock?'

Luc chuckled. 'That won't be a problem. I'll have finished my clinic by then, and Henri was bugging me this morning about taking some time off. I'm sure he'll cover for me.'

'What do you say I bring Celeste up to the hospital? Then we can go somewhere, maybe…?'

'I'll ask him now…' Luc started forward, grinning, and Pearl caught his arm.

'It's late and you should be on your way. I'll mention it. Text me when you get home, eh?'

'Of course. It won't be too late for you?' She shook her head in reply. 'In that case, I'd better hurry…'

Pearl resisted the temptation of iced tea, and made her apologies to Nathalie, saying that today had tired her out. She spoke to Henri, who said that covering for Luc for an hour or so would be his pleasure, and took her phone upstairs with her. She switched it to silent mode, and quietly got into bed, listening to the sound of Celeste's steady breathing. She was wide awake now, and waiting for Luc…

Pearl woke still clutching her phone, as tightly as Celeste hugged her teddy bear to help her sleep soundly. She and

Luc had texted for an hour last night. There had been no urgency about the conversation; they'd just passed a little time together, and their talk had gently lulled her to sleep…

She switched the phone back on, checking that she'd ended the conversation with a *goodnight*, rather than just falling asleep on him. She could hear Celeste in her cot, awake and babbling to herself.

'Good morning, sweetheart.' Pearl pulled herself out of bed, going to give her daughter a morning hug. 'You're such a good girl, letting Mummy sleep in…' Pearl glanced at the clock on the bedside table. It wasn't exactly late, but it was a little less early than usual.

Henri had already left for work, but it was nice to have some company for morning coffee, and Nathalie insisted on watching Celeste while Pearl took a long, luxurious shower. Then they discussed their plans for the day.

'I've agreed to take Celeste to see Luc at four, for a couple of hours. We're going to meet at the library.'

Nathalie nodded. 'You must see the library—it's an important place for Luc.'

More than a hobby and less than an obsession. Pearl hadn't taken much notice of her surroundings the other day, but today the library seemed to be a place she needed to see more of if she wanted to get to know him better. And despite the feeling that they knew everything there was to know about each other, there was still a great deal that Pearl didn't know.

CHAPTER FIVE

PEARL HAD LET Celeste sleep in her cot for a little longer than usual this afternoon so that she wouldn't be tired and irritable later on. The little girl looked unbearably cute in her best blue dress and Pearl clipped her hair off her face with a matching bow.

'There. Ready to meet your daddy?'

Celeste didn't react to the word. She didn't know what it meant. Pearl had made things more difficult for everyone by waiting so long, and allowing her daughter to start exploring a world that didn't have Luc in it. But she had an opportunity to make things right now...

She was at the library a little early, but Luc was already there waiting for her, standing on the steps that led up to the main doors. She waved, bending down to the pushchair to point him out to Celeste as they approached. Luc waved back and Celeste regarded him solemnly.

'Hello.' Luc smiled a little awkwardly and then squatted down on his heels. 'Hey, Celeste.' He was keeping his distance, giving the little girl space until she wanted to come to him. But when Celeste pointed at him his grin broadened. He pointed back and the little girl wriggled in her pushchair, wanting to get out and find out what all of the fuss was about.

'Perhaps we should go somewhere private?' Not for

Celeste's benefit, but for Luc's. Someone was going to notice that adoring gaze of his.

'Not on my account.' He got to his feet, grinning. 'She seems to like it outside and there's a terrace at the back where we can sit for a while.'

If that was where Luc wanted to go, then that's where they'd go. Ever since they'd been in France Celeste had been soaking up new sights and sounds like a sponge, and she was sure to find something of interest to her anywhere. Luc led them around the perimeter of the building to a paved area with tables and chairs.

'This is nice. Somewhere for people to take a break?' There were several groups of what looked like students, talking animatedly.

'Yes, when I took over, the library was a very much a place for quiet study. It still is mostly, but we've made a few changes. This is a nice place to sit in the summer and we've allocated some areas as places for discussion and group learning. We're setting up a computer centre as well. Most people use their own laptops but we also have terminals with subscriptions to various online resources and libraries.'

Luc found a place for them in the shade, watching as Pearl lifted Celeste from her pushchair. She was a little shy, but not in one of her clingy phases, and she'd clearly decided that Luc was someone she wanted to take more notice of.

No one of any age could resist that smile of his. He squatted down on his heels, letting Celeste walk towards him, and she laid her hand on his knee to steady herself. 'Would she like a drink?' He glanced up at Pearl.

'Ask her.' Pearl had seen Celeste react when Luc mentioned the word *drink*.

'Celeste… Would you like a drink?'

The little girl nodded. 'Drink…' Clearly she was under the impression that Luc might have some juice concealed about his person, because she stepped a little closer, grabbing at the lapel of his jacket and sliding her hand into his pocket.

'Hey! We're not pickpockets today…' Celeste ignored her and Pearl didn't have the heart to lift her up out of mischief. She was just going to have to reinforce the idea that going through people's pockets was only okay if they were friends. 'Sorry. She does this.'

Celeste pulled a shopping receipt out of his pocket, looking at it carefully and then putting it back again. Luc was clearly delighted with the whole procedure, and ignored Pearl. She could see several vending machines, inside the glass doors that led into the building, and looked inside the bag on the back of the pushchair for her purse.

'I'll get them…' Luc was clearly in a dilemma over how he was going to reach the vending machines, while still allowing Celeste to continue her investigation of his pockets. Pearl decided it was time to take charge and picked her daughter up. Celeste reached for Luc and she delivered her into his arms.

He was all smiles, asking the students on the next table to keep an eye on the buggy, and then leading the way across the courtyard to the vending machines. Pearl picked a carton of pure orange juice, and he felt in his pocket for change, letting the little girl down to help him slide the coins into the slot and then collect the carton of juice from the dispenser.

Everything was magic to him. Everywhere that Celeste looked, everything she reached for. He'd get tired of that soon enough, but for the moment Pearl was just glad that

Celeste was in one of her investigative moods, and willing to include Luc in her adventures. 'I'll get the coffee. She'll walk with you if you hold her hand...'

Luc did as instructed, slowly walking Celeste back to their table, and Pearl got two coffees from the vending machine, following them back to their table. By the time she reached them, Luc had unwrapped the straw and taken Celeste on his lap to drink from the cardboard carton.

It was just what she'd wanted for Celeste. She didn't know now that this was her daddy, but if he stayed around long enough she'd get the idea. They had to start somewhere, and Pearl reckoned he *would* be there for Celeste. Not all the time, but enough to show her that she was loved. Feeling a little jealous of her daughter was wildly inappropriate, and she should stop that right now.

All the same, the smiles that Luc lavished on Celeste, the care with which he allowed her to explore while keeping her safe from the world... Pearl would never have that from Luc again. But if the thought hurt, it was a small price to pay for the one thing she really wanted. Celeste would know her father, and Luc would know his daughter, and nothing should get in the way of that. Attempting the impossible and trying to make a relationship that was any more than friendship with him was a necessary sacrifice.

'She's very adventurous. Interested in everything.' Luc smiled at her as she put the two cups of coffee down onto the table.

'She has her moments. But yes, if she's got something to interest her, she's generally very happy.' At the moment she was focusing on her drink, and Pearl hoped she wouldn't spill any of it onto his shirt.

'Dr Belange. Sorry to intrude…' A young woman from the next table approached him, speaking in French. Something to do with information sharing and memory issues.

Luc was one step ahead of her and suppressed a smile. 'This is our visitor, Dr Pearl Johnson, from London. And her daughter, Celeste.'

The young woman turned to Pearl, giving her a broad grin. 'Hello…' She launched into a fast-spoken stream of words, clearly trying to make as much of this opportunity as she could. Her name was Marcheline and she was something to do with Neurology…

Luc smilingly held up his hand, switching to English. 'Marcheline's in her first specialist year in the neurology department. She's heard about your visit and is very keen on helping out in whatever way she can.'

'Ah. I look forward to seeing more of you…' Pearl tried out her French and Marcheline nodded, grinning broadly.

'Your little girl is beautiful.' Marcheline waved and Celeste obligingly waved back, letting go of her carton of orange juice. It was just as well that Luc had been steadying it for her and the whole lot didn't go into his lap. Parenting lesson number one—Celeste tended to drop things when something else claimed her attention.

'Thank you. Paris has given us both a warm welcome.'

'And I'll let you know what we're planning—as soon as we've finalised dates and times.' Luc grinned at Marcheline. 'It's great to know you're so interested.'

Marcheline nodded, shaking Pearl's hand with a smile and going back to her friends on the next table. Pearl lowered her voice. 'Did she want to know about my visit or the baby?'

Luc chuckled. 'Knowing Marcheline, she probably heard us speaking English and wanted to know about your visit. She's a very bright young doctor, and she's ambitious. It's not unusual to see parents bringing their children here—it's something I want to encourage, as long as they stay in the communal areas and don't disturb anyone who wants to study. Libraries should be at the centre of their community, don't you think?'

Pearl couldn't disagree with that. 'What made you choose a library, though?'

'I suppose it would be more accurate to say that it chose me. It took me in when I needed a place to go and I decided there were things that I could do with it. Back then, the post of director was a one-year tenure and you had to be one of the medical staff at the hospital.'

'So...there's no need to actually know anything about libraries. Or books?'

'There's a need to know about study and fulfilling patients' needs, but I think we all have that in common, don't we? There's a librarian who runs the place on a day-to-day basis and I liaise with her.' Luc offered the drink to Celeste again, and she grabbed at the straw.

'You said that your tenure was only for one year?'

'It was when I started. But I made a few changes, attracting more people to use the library and gaining some extra funding. The hospital board extended it indefinitely and I've been doing the job for five years now.'

Five years. That must be...

'You said that you'd needed a place to go...?' Pearl couldn't think of another way of asking. She didn't even know whether Luc would *mind* her asking. They were making the rules up as they went along.

He turned his gaze on her, clear and steady. 'Yes, that's right. I used to come here when I lost my wife, because I couldn't bear to go home in the evenings.' His fingers rubbed Celeste's arm, as if to reassure her, but the little girl didn't understand and was much more interested in her drink.

'I'm sorry. I didn't mean to overstep my boundaries.'

'Don't be. I think overstepping boundaries is exactly what we need to do at the moment. And it doesn't make the library a sad place for me. It's just the opposite.'

Was this why Nathalie had told her she needed to see the library? Maybe Luc had a commitment to it that was nothing to do with gorgeous architecture, or the pursuit of learning.

He looked down at Celeste, shaking the drink carton he was holding. 'All gone?' The little girl nodded, pulling it from his grip and spinning it across the table. Pearl caught it, flattening it and putting it into her empty coffee cup.

'There's somewhere I'd like you and Mummy to see…' Luc was addressing Celeste, but since there were no boundaries Pearl guessed it was okay for her to overhear.

'Celeste…' Pearl called to her softly. 'Let's go.'

Celeste understood that, and slid off Luc's lap, stamping her feet to indicate that she was ready even if no one else was. Luc stood, taking a draught of his coffee while Pearl tried to put Celeste into her pushchair. She wriggled and kicked in a sudden show of obstinacy.

'It's not far, if she'd prefer to walk. Fold the pushchair, I'll take it…' Luc took another gulp of coffee and then collected up the cups from the table. They set off, meandering towards the door that led into the library.

'I won't take you through the central reading area—it's a bit much to expect her to keep her voice down. But we'll be fine here…' He led them through a panelled corridor, unlocking one of the tall timber doors at the end and ushering them inside.

'This is lovely…' There was something familiar about the highly polished library table and the ornate chairs around it. The wooden cabinets that lined the walls and the library steps that gave access to the top shelves. Pearl looked around, trying to recall where she'd seen this room before.

'You recognise it?' Luc was smiling.

'Yes, but I don't know where from…' Pearl stared up at the vaulted ceiling, decorated with a moon and stars motif. 'I remember now, I saw it in a film. Something about treasure hunters?'

Luc chuckled. 'That's right. They were here for two weeks filming, a few years ago. We had to close parts of the library but it paid for some restoration work on the shelving that we badly needed to do. We sometimes hold concerts here in the evenings, and talks on topics of interest to encourage people from outside the hospital in.'

'And this space wasn't used before?'

'It didn't exist. The room was here, with the bookcases, but the library steps and the table and chairs were in other parts of the library. And the books were all in storage. They're old volumes that are only of interest to historians and a few medical students who are thanking their lucky stars they don't have to practise in the eighteenth century.'

'And you gathered them all together. You've done all of this in five years?'

'Hardly any of it. I was just the guy who wouldn't take no for an answer from the hospital board. Our librarian and clerical officer did most of the real work, along with a large posse of volunteers.'

Somehow Pearl doubted that. From what she knew of Luc, he would have rolled his sleeves up and been working harder than anyone.

'It's been worth it, though. This room is just lovely and so atmospheric.'

Celeste had been looking around the room, wide-eyed at yet another new place. She tried to manoeuvre her way between two chairs to get under the table, and Pearl headed her off. 'Not under the table, sweetie.' Perhaps she was a little young to really appreciate her surroundings. Then Luc led her over to one corner of the room.

'You see these? They're very old, but you can touch them if you want.' He sat on his heels, running his fingers over the smooth leather bindings of a row of books on the bottom shelf, and Celeste mimicked him, touching them carefully.

'This one's not very interesting, and it's quite wrong in its conclusions about the treatment of renal failure. That one has some splendid drawings but they're not wholly accurate...' Celeste didn't understand what he was saying but she knew that all of Luc's attention was on her. And maybe those blue eyes, so like her own, were drawing her in.

'What about this one?' Luc hooked his finger behind a third book, pushing it so that it stood out from the others. Celeste ignored it, and Pearl bent down, seeing that the binding was different.

'What's this, Celeste? Shall we take a look?' Pearl pulled the book out a little further, and saw the brightly coloured cover of a children's book.

Celeste took the book from the shelf, and sat down on the floor, while Pearl opened it for her. It was a board book, and the first page showed a watercolour picture of the Eiffel Tower, with a boy on a bicycle at the front, a dog trotting beside him. When Pearl moved the slider underneath, the boy and his dog travelled from one side of the thick card page to the other.

Celeste chuckled, batting Pearl's hand away so that she could try for herself. She made the boy move back and forth across the page a few times and then Pearl encouraged her to turn to the next page, which featured the boy and his dog, standing in a flower market. Celeste tried swiping her hand across the bottom, and when that didn't work she found the button in the corner, and pressed it. A tinkling tune sounded and she leaned over, pressing her ear to the picture and chuckling.

'What a beautiful book, Luc.'

He nodded, a little awkwardly. 'I hope she likes it.' Luc seemed suddenly unsure of himself.

'Look at her face, Luc, she *loves* it,' Pearl chided him. Celeste was struggling to turn the page, and Pearl helped her with it. The next picture was of the Louvre Museum and Celeste found the slider that made the boy and his dog appear from behind the glass pyramid.

'Good. I wasn't sure what to get. I picked the one I liked the best.'

This must be hard for him. Not knowing what Celeste liked and disliked, and clearly wanting to please her. 'You're doing fine, Luc. By the way, did Henri mention dinner tonight? Nathalie told me that I should be firm and insist you come. Henri's working late and will be giving us a lift home.'

Luc chuckled. 'I took a rain check when Henri asked. I reckon it would be best to take things slowly for starters. But I'll be sure to let Nathalie know that you applied maximum pressure on her behalf if she says anything.'

He was probably right. They'd be eating after Celeste's bedtime anyway, and there was no reason for Luc to be there then. 'I appreciate that. Since I'll be here tomorrow, in my guise as fellow neurologist, then perhaps I can persuade you to come then? You could spend an hour or so with Celeste and eat with us.'

He grinned suddenly. 'Nice tactics. Nathalie will be very proud of you. I won't turn that offer down, but tell Nathalie I'll bring something for dessert.'

'Will do. I'll mention that there was no talking any sense into you...' Pearl paused as Luc's phone beeped and he took it from his pocket.

'Sorry...'

'A patient?'

Luc shook his head. 'We have a volunteer looking after the front desk this evening, and he's not sure where everything is. This won't take a minute.' He dialled a number.

'Hi, this is Luc...' He listened for a moment and then launched into a complex set of instructions in French, which seemed to include a few rights and lefts, along with several wrong turns. Finally Luc nodded. 'Yes, that's it. No problem, thanks for your help...' He ended the call and put his phone back into his pocket.

'You know where all of those books are, without even looking?' She'd recognised the names of several well-known scientific authors who wrote on a diverse range of subjects.

He smiled. 'If you promise not to laugh...'

'I'm a neurologist, with a special interest in how memory works. I won't laugh.'

'I have a mind palace, which helps me to remember the library catalogue. Since it's situated here in the library then I've been able to include pointers to where each category of books is located in real life.'

Pearl frowned, trying to get her head around the idea. 'That sounds very complicated. Wouldn't it be easier just to sit down and learn it by rote?'

'Yes and no. Because the creative part of it is that you associate things you want to remember with things that mean something to you on an emotional level. It's broadly similar to the some of the memory techniques we use with our patients, associating memories with physical objects. Pick a topic…'

'Um…pharmacology. Dermatological agents.'

He smiled. 'I'm glad to hear you're making it easy for me. That's…right at the far end of the reading room, in the gallery. Second stack. You want to check?'

Pearl glanced at Celeste, who was playing happily with her new book. 'I'll have to take your word for it for the time being. Assuming that you're right, this doesn't look quite as dramatic as it does in films.'

Luc shrugged. 'I could ham it up a bit, if it makes you feel better. But actually mind palaces date back to Ancient Greece. As I said, it's a process of associating visual clues with information you want to remember. A bit like a mnemonic is a word or letter clue.'

'Okay… And how does that work in practise?'

'We'll start with a small mind palace…'

Pearl grinned. 'Maybe a mind semi-detached. In Surrey.'

'Perfect. You're getting the idea of this—it's all a matter of imagination. You start with a room that you can visualise easily, don't tell me what it is, it's personal to you. And a list of things you want to remember.'

The image of the hotel room they'd shared floated into

her head. Pearl could almost see it, she'd thought about it so many times. 'The periodic table. I never could remember that at school.'

He took out his phone. 'Neither could I, so I'm going to look it up.' He glanced at Pearl as she raised her eyebrows. 'Mind palaces don't make your general memory any better—they're a technique of getting the most out of what you have.'

'So, start in one corner of the room, and place something there which you can associate with the first thing you want to remember. Use your emotions and your imagination, I find you can remember it better that way. First hydrogen.'

A hydrogen rainbow, reflected up onto the ceiling by the door. 'Okay.'

'Next helium. Place something that reminds you of helium in the room, next to the hydrogen. A balloon, perhaps…?'

'Hey. This is *my* mind palace…' Pearl grinned at him. A red, heart-shaped helium balloon, set free to float gently up to the ceiling, would do very well.

'That's the first two, then. Just keep adding to them, a few at a time, until you have the lot. And of course it helps to go back to the beginning every now and then, just to fix the order of things in your memory. The associations aren't so difficult if you choose them yourself.'

'And that's all there is to it? What if I run out of space in my room?'

'Then you go to the next room. Or walk out into the garden or down the street—the route you take is up to you. Before long, you'll find your "mind semi-detached" becoming a mind palace.'

'And…the library's your mind palace?'

He nodded. 'I have one at my apartment as well, which helps me remember my weekly shopping list. Much more efficient than having to write it and I never forget anything that I need.'

Pearl nodded. 'I'm going to go away and think about this. And reread the part of the talking points you sent me which covers helping people remember things by association. I assume you included that so that we could discuss all of this later.'

'Yes. Only in more scientific terms, perhaps.'

Pearl rather liked the idea of having her own palace. Filled with things that meant something to her. But for Luc, maybe there was a deeper connection. One that linked the library to his most precious memories.

She glanced at Celeste, who had discarded her book in favour of investigating how easily she could slide up and down on the polished wooden floor. The attention span of a toddler wasn't going to keep her amused for much longer.

'We'll talk about this again. I think we should probably be going soon. I don't want to keep Henri waiting too long, and it would be good to get Celeste home and settled down before her bedtime.' The last few hours had flown by, and the disappointment that showed on Luc's face echoed in Pearl's heart.

'Could I have… Would you mind if I took a photograph?'

Pearl had wondered whether he would ask, and was glad he had. She picked Celeste up, hoping that the little girl wouldn't cling to her when she tried to give her to Luc to hold. 'What about one with you?'

He looked down at Celeste, his face brimming with warmth. The little girl reacted by reaching for him, and grabbing hold of his shirt. As soon as she was safely in Luc's arms, Pearl fumbled for her phone, stabbing at the shutter button in the hope of catching the moment between them.

'I like that one.' She flipped through the photos, finding one where Luc and Celeste were looking at each other, and showed it to him. By accident she'd managed to get a perfectly composed picture of the two of them together.

'That's really nice…' He flipped through the other photos, some of which were of the floor, and got to one where Celeste had grabbed hold of his ear and Luc was grimacing. 'I like that one too. Will you send them to me?'

'Of course. I'll text you later?'

'Thanks. I'd like that.'

He walked them back out of the library, and Pearl settled Celeste into her pushchair, giving her the new book to hold. 'We've got to go now, Celeste. Say bye-bye.'

Celeste held up her hand, scrunching her fingers. 'Bye-bye-bye-bye…'

'See you soon.' That was a far too ambitious phrase for Celeste, but she made Luc laugh by waving her new book at him. *Let's not look back* was out of the question. Pearl knew that she would, and that Luc would be standing, watching her go.

Henri was waiting for them in his office, and Celeste waved her new book at him as well. He got to his feet, slinging his jacket over his shoulder and picking up his briefcase.

'How was your afternoon?'

'Really good. I have a very nice photo of Luc and Celeste together.'

Henri nodded. 'Will you show me?'

Pearl handed over her phone, and Henri flipped through the photographs, smiling when he came to those he liked. 'So Luc took you inside the library? It's an interesting place.'

'Yes. Very interesting.' The books, the stunning architecture and the historical treasures paled into insignificance next to Luc's relationship with the library. He'd mourned for his wife there, and Pearl wondered how many of his memories of her were still there, wandering the corridors of his mind palace.

CHAPTER SIX

LUC LAY ON his bed, holding his phone up in front of him. He and Pearl had texted their goodnights, and he hoped that she was sleeping now. But he hadn't been able to resist one last look at the photographs she'd sent, and there was no going back from that. Now he couldn't tear his gaze away from them.

A child. Someone who might depend on him. Who might need him.

That was terrifying enough, but Luc reckoned he wasn't the first to wonder whether he could be equal to the responsibilities of fatherhood. And he knew exactly what he needed to do next.

But Pearl… She was a beautiful enigma. They were so right for each other, on so many levels, and yet they both had very good reasons for not stepping out of their comfort zones and into a relationship. They'd understood that, right from the start, and it would be foolish to lose their heads and deny it now.

But however many reasons there were for him and Pearl to be friends, co-parents and nothing more, Luc still couldn't stop himself from thinking about what it would be like if they were a proper family. Not just bound together by their child, but bound to each other by love.

He threw the phone down onto the bed, and got undressed, then slid under the duvet. He hadn't expected to see Pearl again, and certainly never expected this second chance to be a father. He shouldn't let go of that, for impossible dreams would fade if he refused to acknowledge them. Now was the time to start building something that would last.

'We're going to do this properly,' Luc announced when Pearl walked into his office the following morning.

'And a good morning to you too.'

He felt the muscles of his jaw relax. 'Sorry. Good morning.' Luc elaborated a little on the theme. 'Looks as if it'll be a nice day today.'

Pearl's hand flew to her mouth, in mock astonishment. 'Luc! You even threw in a reference to the weather. I'm overwhelmed.'

'The French talk about the weather as much as the English. In my experience, anyway.'

'That explains why there's such a lot about various kinds of weather on my app for learning French.' She grinned at him, planting her hands on his desk and leaning towards him. 'So what are we going to do properly, then?'

'Henri told me that he thought I should take some more leave over the next couple of weeks and I said it wasn't necessary. I texted him this morning and told him that I was wrong. We need time to work things out, Pearl.'

She nodded, sitting down in the chair on the other side of his desk. 'I don't disagree that you should take some time off, Luc. But can't we do happy things? Maybe take Celeste out for the day together or spend some time getting to know each other better? Then perhaps the working-things-out part will just…work itself out.'

If Pearl wasn't likely to misinterpret the gesture, and

think she'd done something wrong, Luc would have put his head in his hands at his own short-sightedness. She'd was right: this wasn't a project; they were parents. And losing sight of the pleasures was… Maybe that was just his way of keeping everything under control. Disconnecting himself from the joy of spending time with Pearl and Celeste, because it was too hard to think about losing them.

'Can we compromise? Put some time aside to discuss the practicalities, but make sure we don't lose sight of why we're doing this, either.'

'I agree. You're right, we do have to look at how things are going to work in a practical sense, but I don't want you to stretch yourself too thin. This hasn't been an easy week for you.'

Or for Pearl. But she forgot all of that in her concern for him. Luc tried to ignore the feeling of warmth that was creeping up on him. Although maybe he should just bow to the inevitable, and accept that it happened from time to time, and he couldn't do anything about it.

'So if I take some of the time off in lieu that I'm owed, you'd be up for a few days out? I'll ask Henri to finalise your meeting dates so that we know where we are with that, and we can go from there. There shouldn't be any problem with taking a few days off at short notice. I generally manage to find an excuse not to take the time back and the HR department are always nagging me about it.'

Pearl was smiling, nodding her agreement. 'I think we're going to be good at this, Luc. Organising how to be parents together…'

Pearl had thought that having a child was the best thing she'd ever done, but also the hardest. But Luc was coming a close second at the moment.

She understood his point of view and agreed with it. Neither of them had any choice about loving Celeste, but they did have a choice about their relationship with each other. Being lovers had worked for just one weekend, and only then because they knew that they would part.

She couldn't give up the life she'd made for herself, and trust in the frail promises of commitment. And Luc belonged here, in a place where he was at peace with his memories. But it was hard not to touch him. Not to think about him when she was alone at night. How it might feel to be able to find her safety in his embrace.

And she couldn't stop wishing. Loving the good times together. Adoring his blue eyes and the way that Luc was smiling at her right now.

'It's all sorted.' He put his phone down on the desk.

'Yes?' Pearl couldn't do anything about the thrill of anticipation that quivered through her, either.

'Henri's going to firm up all the dates for your meetings today, so you know where you are with that. And the head of department has okayed time off whenever I want, which makes me feel suddenly dispensable.'

Pearl laughed. 'That's the thing, though. You're completely indispensable to Celeste.'

And to her. But Pearl wasn't going to think too much about that.

Luc had prepared her for this afternoon's meeting by extending her French vocabulary to include several medical terms and words for useful concepts, and correcting her pronunciation. The gathering had been organised in one of the splendid meeting rooms in the library, and Luc had arranged coffee and soft drinks, laid out on a white-clothed table.

'This is nice.' Pearl looked around. 'It takes us out of the doctor-patient dynamic.'

Luc nodded. 'We have a lot to teach our patients, but they have a great deal to teach us as well.'

'This is something I want to take home with me. Our previous head of therapy was very good, and he got results, but he never forgot that he was in charge. He retired at Christmas and we have a new person who's much more interested in finding ways to create different kinds of relationships. I suppose having this place helps.' Pearl looked around her. 'Just the architecture seems to value the people in it.'

'I never thought of it quite like that.' Luc considered the idea for a moment. 'But I think it's really just a matter of attitude. We have to be firm, because people with brain injuries need a secure framework and a lot of encouragement, particularly to start with. But the people you're going to meet this afternoon have done a lot of hard work, and deserve to be listened to…' He turned as the door flew open.

'Ah, Marcheline.' The young woman who'd spoken to them yesterday appeared in the doorway. 'Ready to take some notes?'

'Yes… Sorry I'm late. I got caught up with a patient Dr Auclair was dealing with. Have I missed anything?'

Luc chuckled. 'No. Get yourself some coffee…'

When the patients and their families began to arrive Pearl felt more confident in chatting to them in French. The group all seemed to find strength in supporting each other, and it became obvious that Luc had allowed himself to become a part of that too.

'Did your little girl like the book?' asked a middle-aged woman who'd accompanied her husband here. Luc stepped in, with an unneeded translation and a very-much-needed explanation.

'I called Marie on Tuesday morning, and asked if she knew of a bookshop close to the hospital which had a good children's section. Marie works in publishing and distribution so she's the person we all turn to for advice on the best new releases. The quality of my Christmas and birthday presents has improved enormously.'

'Ah.' So Luc hadn't shared his true reasons for wanting a child's book at such short notice. 'Yes, she loves it. It was a good choice.'

'Marie's been working part-time since her husband was injured last year. But he's doing very well and she's thinking of increasing her hours.' Luc had returned to speaking French and was speaking slowly and clearly, glancing at Pearl every now and then to make sure that she was keeping up. She nodded, and smiled at the woman.

Everyone drank coffee for a while and chatted, and then it was time to sit down around the large, round table. The atmosphere was friendly and supportive—those who needed time to speak were listened to patiently, and when one man told Luc that mind palaces were overrated, and that he had a mind garden to help him remember what tasks he needed to do every morning, everyone laughed. The technique didn't work for some people there, but it did for others, and no one had any hesitation in giving their opinion. Luc smilingly mentioned that every brain injury was different, which prompted universal agreement, and Marcheline typed furiously on her laptop, getting everything down for future reference.

'I can't believe that no one's thought of this before.' Pearl turned the key ring over in her hand. Shapes, colours and words marked out which key was which, and when Luc had produced it from his pocket, several of the group had showed how they'd customised theirs to meet their specific needs.

'I imagine a lot of people have. We were able to put it into practise because we had access to a 3D printer. I can dig out the templates for you if you're interested.'

'I know where they are—I can get them,' Marcheline offered, and Luc nodded. When the meeting had broken up, and people had stayed to talk, she'd made sure to introduce herself to everyone in the room, shaking hands and listening to what people had to say.

'Thanks, Marcheline. And thank you for all of your help this afternoon, you've done a really good job.'

Marcheline grinned broadly. Maybe those blue eyes of Luc's made his praise even more gratifying. 'Thank you, Dr Belange. Is it okay for me to clear away the cups…?'

'No, leave that. I'll be looking forward to seeing the write-up of your notes, so you can tell Dr Auclair that you're busy with that if he wants you to do anything first thing tomorrow morning.'

'I could do them tonight…'

'Yes, you could. Or you could go home and do whatever it is you do when you're *not* working. Some things are urgent and others can wait.' His tone was firm enough to make that sound more than just a request, and Marcheline nodded, gathering up her things and leaving.

'There are times she makes me feel very old and jaded.' Luc started to gather the cups, stacking them onto an ornate wooden trolley that stood beside the drinks table. Everything here was a thing of beauty, even the most utilitarian items.

'You're not jaded, Luc. You get through twice as much

as Marcheline, in half the time. When she settles in a bit, she'll learn the knack of appearing unhurried.'

He chuckled. 'Yeah. You remember when you were a brand-new doctor, trying to impress?'

She remembered being a brand-new doctor, and a confused wife, trying to please everyone and failing miserably. Unable to understand why her ex-husband had changed since their wedding, and shouldering the blame for it all. Feeling her whole life begin to shut down, when it should have been opening up with new opportunities.

'Yes. I remember.' Something in her tone must have betrayed her, because Luc turned suddenly.

'I'm sorry. I didn't think… I know that must have been an unbearably difficult time.'

'I got through it, with a lot of help from my friends. That's all in the past, now.'

Don't change, Luc. Please *don't ever change.* The thought spun into her head before she could stop it.

He put a pile of cups down onto the trolley, walking over towards her. His bulk seemed suddenly warm and reassuring, and his face was full of tenderness as he took the cups she'd collected from her hands.

'It's okay to have to stop and take a breath every now and then, Pearl. Nothing's ever *all* in the past.'

'I wish it were. I don't want Celeste to be fearful…'

'Then it's up to us to teach her. You're doing such a good job there, and I'm planning on learning from you.'

'You say a lot of very nice things, Luc.' Her hand strayed to his arm in a motion that started out as gratitude and ended up as something else. His hands were full and he couldn't return the gesture, but something ignited suddenly in his gaze, and Luc didn't move. Her fingers were barely skimming his shirtsleeve, but they were no strangers to the eroticism of taking their time. Luc knew just how to take a moment and make it into delicious longing for the next.

The door opened, and she instinctively jumped back. Pearl wasn't aware of Luc moving, but an empty cup crashed to the floor between them.

'Sorry to startle. I was wondering whether you were finished here and were ready to go home.' Henri breezed into the room, as if nothing had happened. Pearl reminded herself that actually nothing *had* happened. She'd touched Luc's shirt, which was hardly going to raise any eyebrows.

'We're all done, apart from the obligatory broken cup,' Luc joked and Henri smiled. 'Unless you want to break the saucer that goes with it, Pearl?'

She laughed. 'That's okay, you can even things up next time you hold one of these meetings. We'll be with you in a moment, thanks, Henri.'

CHAPTER SEVEN

HENRI USUALLY CAME into work early and left a little early to avoid the rush hour. He'd told Pearl that it was just a matter of fifteen minutes and a carefully chosen route, which made all of the difference, and they were making good time. Luc was sitting in the front passenger seat of the car, his eyes fixed on the road ahead, obviously keen to see Celeste again.

'What's this?' Henri had turned into one of the side streets that Pearl recognised as one of his short cuts, and suddenly come to a halt. Luc wound down the car window, leaning out to speak to the gendarme who was standing in the middle of the road, blocking their path.

Then he reached inside his jacket, pulling out his hospital tags, which still hung around his neck. 'We're doctors...'

The gendarme waved them through, and then stepped out into the road to stop the car behind them from going any further.

She heard Luc's sharp intake of breath as Henri turned a corner and then stopped the car. Up ahead a large lorry was angled across the road, blocking it completely. A badly damaged car was wedged tight against the side of the cab, and a second gendarme was trying to get a woman with blood streaming down the side of her face to sit down on the steps in front of an open front door. The lorry driver seemed to have escaped unscathed, and was sitting on the steps outside another doorway, talking to several people who had obviously come out of the building to help.

The woman let out a long, wavering cry and appeared to be struggling with the gendarme. Luc was out of the car already, running towards her, and Henri made for the boot to fetch the medical kit he kept there.

The woman was screaming incoherently, reaching towards the car. Luc took her by the shoulders, speaking to her and she seemed to calm a little. 'You are a doctor? My child… Please help my little girl…'

Pearl ran towards the car, peering through the open driver's side door. 'Luc… Luc, there's a child in here.'

The anchors for the car seat must have come loose in the impact of the crash, and in the footwell behind the passenger seat she could see the side of a booster seat along with a pair of feet, one bare and the other still wearing a pink sandal. She leaned in, trying to gauge how to get to the child without causing any more damage in the smashed interior of the car.

'Let me…'

She felt Luc's hand on her shoulder and automatically moved out of the way.

He climbed carefully into the driver's seat, pulling a lever on the passenger seat and folding it forward, while his other hand steadied the booster seat. Then he leaned over, obviously trying to gauge the condition of the child.

'She's sustained facial injuries. I can't see their extent. Her breathing's very shallow… She's still strapped into the seat—I think I can lift it out with her in it.'

'Okay. Tell me what you need.' If the child's airways

were obstructed then they had no choice but to risk moving her.

'Get Henri to find out if any of the offices along here have a medical kit with resuscitation equipment.' Luc's voice was measured and calm, but that only indicated how serious the situation was.

She ran, stumbling towards Henri, who left the woman in the gendarme's care and came to meet her. Pearl delivered the message and Henri nodded.

'Leave it with me.'

When she got back to the car, Luc had managed to lift the booster seat clear of the footwell, and turn it ninety degrees so that the little girl was lying on her back, in the seat. He slid it towards the open door of the car, and Pearl took its weight as she carefully moved it out of the vehicle. Luc followed, taking the seat from her and looking around for Henri.

He'd enlisted several people to help him and they were moving from door to door. Pearl saw a woman, on the steps of a building further down the row, call to Henri and they exchanged a few words. Then he turned, beckoning to them to bring the child over, picking his own medical kit up as he went to meet the woman.

Inside, they were directed into an office, where the woman had unlocked a large cupboard. She lay a foil blanket down on top of the carpet, and while Henri inspected the contents of the cupboard, Luc lay the child down on her side, still strapped into her car seat. He opened Henri's medical kit, passing a pair of gloves to Pearl and she started to examine the little girl.

'Her airways are obstructed...' Pearl performed a finger sweep of the girl's mouth which did nothing to alleviate the problem. Her lips were beginning to turn blue.

'I think she has a broken jaw and…there's a lot of swelling here. My only option for a child of this age will be a needle cricothyrotomy. Henri…?' The ambulance was taking too long, and this was their last option.

'Right…' Henri quickly checked the shelves of the cupboard. 'Yes, we have what we need. They keep a medical oxygen cylinder in storage here, and the office manager has gone to fetch it.'

'Okay, we need to get her out of the car seat and lay her flat…' She glanced at Luc and he started to unbuckle the straps while Pearl carefully supported the child's head and neck, ready to lift her out of her seat. 'Will you give me your confirmation that you agree with my assessment of the situation and that I should proceed with a needle cric?' Pearl wasn't licensed to practise in France, but the Good Samaritan laws required her to do what she could to help in an emergency.

'I agree.' Luc spoke quickly. 'Henri?'

'Likewise. Go ahead, Pearl.'

Now she needed to work fast. 'Henri, antiseptic swabs, please, and a local anaesthetic if we have one. Luc, I don't need your help at the moment so if you need to go and see how the mother's doing…'

She felt Luc's hand on her shoulder, in a wordless expression of support. Pearl leaned over the little girl, carefully isolating the cricothyroid membrane, and Henri handed her the antiseptic swabs.

It was done. Pearl had worked quickly and carefully, finally attaching an oxygen cylinder to the improvised air delivery system. Henri had opened then closed the air valve and they'd seen the little girl's chest rise and fall.

Pearl had secured the catheter with tape, and sat back on her heels.

Ten minutes later, the ambulance arrived, after having fought its way through the rush-hour traffic. The little girl and her mother were transferred quickly, the one aim being to get the child to the hospital, where she could be treated. Pearl, Luc and Henri went to sit in the car, watching silently as the street began to clear.

'Why did those people have an oxygen cylinder in the office?' Luc asked finally.

'One of the directors of the company has asthma. It's part of their emergency plan for her,' Henri answered. 'Let's take all of the luck we can get, and hope for a little more.' The child had more surgery to go through when she reached the hospital.

'Yeah.' Pearl saw the side of Luc's face tighten with stress. 'About that…'

'I know… I'll let Nathalie know that dinner together is going to have to wait until another day.' Henri started the car, turning in the road and nosing his way back past the police barriers. Then he swung the wheel, heading back to the hospital.

Henri had dropped them outside the hospital, and then continued his journey back home to help Nathalie with Celeste. Pearl had hesitated before getting out of the car, and Henri had told her to go.

'Celeste will be all right. Nathalie and I will be fine too. We have plenty of practise in handling whatever a toddler chooses to present us with. There's only one person who really needs you now and you should be with him.'

'Thanks, Henri.' Pearl got out of the car, running across

the courtyard in front of the hospital to catch up with Luc, and slipping her hand into the crook of his elbow.

'It'll be a while,' Luc observed. 'They'll probably be setting her jaw and they'll need to stabilise her airways as well. That's at least two hours, probably more.'

'I couldn't let you wait on your own.'

He frowned. 'I don't want to be the reason for you spending less time with Celeste.'

He was important too. Luc was a part of their family and… Pearl didn't know how to put it into words. That what she felt for one didn't take anything from the other. Luc probably wouldn't accept that, anyway; he was so determined to be a good father and nothing else.

'I'm here now. It's for me too.' Pearl's concentration, the professional detachment needed to keep her hands steady, were beginning to wear off now. Two small feet, one with a battered pink sandal… The image resurfaced in her head and wouldn't go away.

She felt Luc's arm around her shoulder. Pearl tried not to flinch in surprise, in case he thought he'd done the wrong thing. It was exactly the right thing—warm and comforting.

'Shall we wait in the library? I'll get coffee and we can go to my office and dust some books. I have any number of boxes of books which need to be dusted.'

His voice was warm and comforting too. 'Yes. I'm really good at dusting, particularly books.'

Luc chuckled. 'One thing you should know. Never— ever—say you're good at dusting books. Not when I'm around…'

He'd left her in his office, and gone to get the coffee. Luc was a while, and when he came back he had news. The little girl had arrived at the hospital and was in surgery. That was the best they could hope for at the moment, that she still had a chance for life.

When Luc had told her he had books to dust, he hadn't been joking. Pearl followed him along the corridor to a large room, which was clearly the book hospital. On one side, there was a long bench, with workspaces and tools that probably hadn't changed much since the library had been built.

'That's intensive care, is it?' Pearl could see several books in various stages of deconstruction.

'Yep. We have partnerships with several organisations that teach book restoration, and there are volunteers who do the easier tasks. Over here we have the minor injuries unit, which is what I'm allowed to do.' Luc moved over to the other side of the room, where stacks of boxes were lined up on a series of shelves. He picked up a box, and Pearl took the next in line.

'Careful, that's heavier than it looks…'

She'd just found that out. Pearl smiled and ignored Luc's warning, following him back to his office.

He laid a thick cloth over the polished surface of the conference table, and took several boxes of tools and bottles from a cupboard. This was clearly something of a ritual, slow and careful. One that felt comforting after the rigours of the day.

'First thing to do is finish our coffee.' He walked over to his desk, picking up their takeaway cups and handing Pearl hers. Luc finished his in one swig and spun the cup into the bin. Pearl took a gulp of hers, and followed him back over to the table, where he was busy laying out two sets of tools.

'First of all you take the book out of the box and look at it. Try not to start to read, or you'll get distracted…'

'That's easy enough—they're mostly in French, aren't they?'

He chuckled. 'You're perfect for the job, then. Feel free to come back any time you like…'

Luc showed her how to brush surface dust from the books, then wipe with a dry cloth and finally apply a special cleaning solution. There was a wide range of books, many of them modern and some older, and if they were damaged they put them aside either to be replaced or for the restorers' attention.

It was repetitive work, which required a degree of concentration. Pearl was beginning to see how the library had taken Luc in, and given him respite from his grief. Given him something to do, while his mind worked to regain its balance. And now, in Luc's mind palace, his memories of his wife were inextricably linked with the library.

After more than two hours of careful work, they'd cleaned and sorted three boxes of books. Then Luc's phone rang. He glanced at the caller display and answered quickly. This could only be one thing and, coming so soon, it was either very good or very bad news.

He was listening carefully to someone on the other end, but Luc reached over, taking her hand. Finally he smiled, and ended the call.

'Good news.' He gave her the thing she really needed to hear first, waiting for Pearl to breathe a sigh of relief. 'The break to her jaw wasn't complex, and it was a straightforward thing to repair. They've converted the emergency cricothyrotomy to a tracheostomy, which they're expecting to reverse as she improves. And her surgeon would like to know who did a textbook needle cricothyrotomy, working on the floor of an office.'

Pearl laughed with relief, feeling a tear trickle down the side of her face. 'That's good…very good…and a nice thing to say.'

'It's well deserved. Don't ask her to say it again, because she doesn't believe in too much praise for anyone. And the little girl's name is Jeannie…' Luc's voice broke with emotion.

There was always something. For Pearl it was a pink sandal, and for Luc… 'It's a pretty name.'

He nodded, getting to his feet and walking to the window, seeming restless and unable to stay still. Pearl followed him, touching his arm hesitantly. Wondering if he'd push her away…

Luc turned, his gaze burning into her. She curled her arms around him, hugging him, and felt his chest heave. His arms were around her now, holding her tight, not allowing her to step back and pretend that this was a fleeting thing. It wasn't. It felt as necessary as breathing at the moment.

'Hey… I appreciate the company this evening.'

Pearl smiled up into his blue-eyed gaze. 'It's my thing. Book dusting.'

'Yeah. It really is.' They didn't need to talk about it. Every doctor faced these moments. Every parent did. They were just facing it together.

He was holding her less urgently now, and Pearl laid her head against Luc's chest. As soon as this became something that they both wanted, rather than something they needed, they'd both be stepping back. And she needed it for just one moment more.

He held her for more than one moment. Maybe it just

seemed that way, because Luc had the ability to stretch time when he wanted to. But Pearl knew that he *was* going to let her go, and he did it with just enough regret in his face to let her know that this hadn't been a mistake.

'I should get back to Celeste. She *should* be asleep by now, but just in case…' Pearl turned away from him, starting to tidy up the books she'd been cleaning. Wondering if that might get her thumping heart under control.

'Leave that, I'll sort them out tomorrow. What are you up to?'

'I thought I'd have a day out and explore Paris with Celeste. Nathalie insists that it's a pleasure to look after her, but she's done so much and I'd like to give her a break. We can drop in after you've finished work, or to take you to lunch?'

'That would be nice. How's Monday looking?'

Pearl hadn't thought that far ahead. 'Nothing. Well, something probably, but I don't have any meetings so I may count it as a holiday day, instead of a workday.'

'Would you like to go to the zoo? The zoo here is great—the animals are housed in biozones, which represent their natural habitats as much as possible—and they have space to roam. Celeste might like it?'

'I dare say she will. I'd love it…' Pearl turned to him. 'It's okay for you to take Monday off?'

He nodded. 'It'll be less crowded. Perhaps we can just take things as they come at the weekend?'

Luc was so careful, still. Not wanting to overwhelm Celeste, or push himself, but obviously keen to see her. 'I'll call you. We'll find something nice to do.' She picked up her bag, searching for her phone. 'Do you have a number for a cab company?'

'I'll take you. My apartment's only ten minutes' brisk

walk and I'll go and pick up my car and meet you back here. That'll be a lot quicker at this time in the evening.'

Maybe it was the hug. Those brief moments they'd taken for themselves and no one else. Pearl wanted to walk back to his apartment with him and go inside, maybe let him show her around. Perhaps stay for coffee...

'Okay, thanks. Should I wait here, or at the front of the hospital?'

'Come and sit on the terrace, where we went with Celeste. There's a slip road that runs past it, and I'll pick you up there...'

CHAPTER EIGHT

THE LAST FEW days had been an exercise in sunshine and relaxed pleasures. Celeste was getting to know Luc and they were becoming firm friends. He didn't spoil her with endless presents, but always brought something he thought she might like. He handed a selection of fruit over to Nathalie for everyone to enjoy, which meant that Celeste got her first taste of sweet apricots. And he always had something in his pocket, like the bubble-blowing kit, which he entrusted to Henri's care as they all sat in the garden together.

But Monday was going to be for just the three of them. Luc arrived at eight in the morning, and he and Nathalie swapped car keys.

'I have the convertible, Henri!' Nathalie danced around the kitchen. 'And I may not give it back…'

Luc chuckled at her delight. He had Nathalie's compact SUV, which had a child seat and a boot roomy enough for a folded pushchair, and clearly felt he'd done better from the bargain.

As soon as they entered the zoo, Celeste was in explorer mode, stretching in the pushchair to see around her. Luc was looking down at her, his brow creased.

'May I take her out of the pushchair and carry her? She'll be able to see better.'

'Why don't you ask her?'

He smiled, squatting down next to the pushchair and leaning forward. 'How do you feel about biodiversity and animal welfare, Celeste?'

Celeste wriggled in her pushchair holding her arms out towards him, and Luc grinned. 'Okay. We'll talk about that a bit more later.' He loosened the harness, lifting her up in his arms, and Celeste babbled with joy, twisting around to take everything in.

'How do you feel about a baby carrier?' Luc was going to get an elbow in the eye any minute now.

'Shouldn't you ask her?' He grinned, jiggling Celeste up and down to calm her.

'No, it's your decision whether you think you can carry a wriggling toddler around all morning. It's not bright pink, by the way...'

'Shame. Although that does sound like a plan.' Luc submitted to the process of loosening and tightening straps, until Celeste was secured firmly to his chest in the carrier, still waving her arms and pointing.

She was wide-eyed when she saw the giraffes, chuckling when they bent their long necks to and fro. The zebras, by comparison, left Celeste unimpressed, but she laughed when meerkats reared up on their hind legs to look around. And the penguins were her favourites. She wanted to watch them do everything, from marching around in groups, to sliding into the pool to swim.

They finally managed to leave the penguins to their own devices, and walked towards one of the food kiosks. Suddenly Luc stopped, cradling the back of Celeste's head with his hand. 'I think she's asleep.'

Celeste had curled her arms in front of her, and was

sleeping soundly against Luc's chest. An instinctive tug of emotion made Pearl catch her breath.

'Yes, she's worn herself out. It's almost time for her nap. We'll put her in the pushchair and she can sleep while we get something to eat.'

'She'll be all right?'

'Yes, she'll be fine. She just needs to recharge her batteries for an hour. She can have something to eat, and then she'll be ready for more.'

Pearl unfolded the pushchair, tilting the seat back, and Luc laid Celeste carefully down in it. The hood shaded her from the sun, and she slept soundly.

'Now I know what people mean when they say "sleeping like a baby".' He grinned as he sat down, putting their food on the table.

'Sometimes that means waking up crying every hour or so.' Pearl had been so determined to show Luc the good parts, make him want to be a dad to Celeste. Maybe she needed to at least acknowledge that life with a young child wasn't always like that.

'So you're admitting that she's not a little angel all the time?' Luc smiled at her. 'I'd worked that out.'

'She's a little angel. Just a bit of a grumpy one sometimes. Or one with a stomach ache, or a new tooth that's bothering her.'

'I don't just want the good parts, Pearl. In fact, the parts I want the most are when she's a grumpy angel, or when she's sick or hurting. I really want to be there for that.'

Pearl removed the lid from her coffee, taking a sip. She'd thought about how Luc was beginning to bond with Celeste, but it had never occurred to her that the little girl might have wriggled under his defences. They seemed so impenetrable.

'You're talking about the scary parts? When you're frightened for her?'

'I'll admit that I might not be too good at those. But they're the parts that matter, aren't they?'

Pearl took another sip of her coffee, allowing his words to sink in. It had taken time for her to come to terms with the thought that having a baby would change her life in ways she couldn't imagine. But Luc had thought about all of this, once before.

'Do you mind, Luc? That the child you planned to have with your wife isn't here? It's just us, instead.'

He leaned back in his seat. 'I mind that I lost that child. I don't forget it, or my wife, but I've done my grieving for them. Celeste is my child too, and she's not a replacement or a second-best. She has all of my love, just as the child I lost did. That's the way it is with children, isn't it?'

'Yes, I suppose so. I just wondered if you felt torn, sometimes. It would be okay if you did...'

He shook his head. 'I don't. And you don't have to save all of the good parts about being a parent for me. I don't want to miss any of it.'

'There might be some things you want to miss, Luc. Seriously...'

'Like what?' He smiled suddenly. 'Name one thing that you think I can't handle.'

This was Luc all over. He could talk about the sad and sensitive things, but he knew how to lift them both out of them as well. Pearl thought for a moment.

'When she's sick in your best shoes. Actually *in* them, so that you don't notice for a week.'

'Bring it on.'

'Refusing to go to sleep. Crying until she's red in the face and your heart breaks for her.'

'I can handle it. Probably not that well, but this is what we're there for, isn't it?'

'Well, yes. But that doesn't make it any easier. Harder actually… Okay, what about going through your pockets and tearing up the receipt for the faulty coffee grinder you were going to take back to the shop?'

'That's just adorable, though.'

Pearl laughed. 'You're going to be really sorry you said that. Fate's going to cycle around when you least expect it to, and pay you back.'

His gaze found hers and suddenly everything in the world was okay. How did that happen? They could be there for each other and listen, but they both seemed to know the right moment to turn it all around and laugh at the world. Pearl spun the lid from her coffee across the table at him and he threw it back.

'So what do you think the odds are that we'll be visiting the penguins again this afternoon?'

'High. Very high.'

Luc nodded. 'Bring it on, eh?'

'Yes. Definitely.'

They had gone to see the penguins again, and it seemed that Celeste had learned a new word. They'd almost reached Henri and Nathalie's house when Luc heard her intone mournfully, behind him.

'Pin-gin.'

'Oh, sweetie…' Pearl turned in her seat. 'We'll see penguins again.'

'Pin-gin.'

Luc turned the wheel, slowing as they passed a parade of shops. 'I can't bear it, Pearl.' He spotted a parking space, and manoeuvred into it, then took a note from his wallet. 'It's not spoiling her, is it?'

'What isn't?'

'The toy shop over there does lots of nice cuddly toys. I've been in there to get things for Francine's twins. They'll probably have a…a winged Antarctic creature.' He took a note from his wallet, pressing it into her hand.

Pearl laughed. 'Right. No, I don't think it's spoiling her, and you can give her whatever you like. I'll go and have a look, shall I? You stay here and try not to mention any black-and-white things we may have seen recently.'

'Okay. Thanks.' He turned to Celeste, who turned her wide, innocent gaze onto him. 'Mummy will be back soon. And in the meantime, we're not going to mention zebras.'

'Pin-gin…'

Pearl returned three minutes later, holding a paper carrier bag, which she put into the footwell in front of her. 'I *really* like that shop. I'm going to have to go back there before I leave.' She smilingly put the change back into his hand. 'Perhaps you could tell her that the thing in the bag stowed away and came home with us.'

'You want me to lie?'

'It's make-believe, Luc…'

Make-believe or not, it was definitely magic. He made himself wait until Celeste was settled in the high chair in the kitchen and Nathalie had given her a drink, then showed her the contents of the bag. 'Look who came home with us, Celeste.'

'Pin-gin!' Her face lit up and she cuddled the toy. Nathalie admired the penguin, and Henri delivered a pot of tea to the table, while Pearl fetched the cups. Luc sat down, and for the first time in years it felt as if he'd come home.

* * *

It seemed that the hard part might be over. Or, at least, Pearl hoped that it was. On her free days, Pearl brought Celeste into the hospital and Henri filled in for Luc if necessary to allow him a longer lunch hour. When Pearl was working at the hospital, Luc brought her home and spent time with Celeste in the evening.

She was sharing experience from her own hospital and learning from therapists and patients here. With Luc's help, her French was improving, and she was starting to understand all of what was said to her, although she stumbled over her replies sometimes. And working with Luc was a pleasure that Pearl hadn't anticipated. He was measured, friendly and patient, and he knew the importance of giving people hope.

She was working in the library, waiting for Luc to be ready to leave, when her phone vibrated in her pocket. 'Are you ready to go?'

'No, I've just been called by A&E. I'll be half an hour at least.'

'May I join you?' Pearl had learned a lot just by watching people, and Luc never minded introducing her to his patients and asking if she might observe.

'Of course. I'll meet you there.' Pearl heard the ding of an arriving lift as Luc ended the call.

When she arrived in A&E Luc was talking to one of the doctors who worked there, and from the set of his jaw things weren't going entirely as he might have hoped. She hung back, waiting for him to finish the conversation, and Luc turned to her.

'It's someone we know, Gabriel Bernard. Really nice guy, he has prosopagnosia and short-term memory loss due to encephalitis about five years ago. We worked with him quite intensively over the first few years and he's made a lot of progress.'

'Acquired prosopagnosia? I'd be interested to meet Gabriel. I haven't seen many cases...' Face-blindness wasn't a memory issue; it was an inability to process visual information, but meeting someone with this rare condition was well within a neurologist's remit.

'He's not actually here for the neurological conditions. He has a cut on his arm that required stitching. The doctor who saw him didn't want to let him go until he'd been seen by a neurologist because Gabriel couldn't give him any details about how the accident happened.'

'Do you mean the doctor wasn't able to take account of his neurological differences, or that he's genuinely concerned?' Many of Pearl's own patients were hampered by the attitudes of other people who couldn't, or wouldn't, take the time to understand.

'Most likely a bit of both. He's only just qualified, and is new here, so he wants to cover all of the bases. Which is fine by me. I'll probably just need to make sure Gabriel's all right and then discharge him.' Luc looked at his watch. 'Do you want to go? By the time I've finished here the rush hour will be starting and going for the metro now will probably be a great deal faster.'

Pearl allowed herself one stab of longing for her child. 'It's okay, I'll stay. The bargain I make with myself is that if Celeste's happy and well cared for then I can be a few minutes late every now and then. If she needs me, that's the time I drop everything and run.'

Luc nodded. 'Must be difficult. If you had a patient on the table...' It seemed that he was starting to feel the instinctive tug, and it conflicted with Luc's commitment to his patients.

'I work very hard to make sure that doesn't happen. That she's always well cared for at the times I can't leave work.' That was one more thing that she and Luc were going to have to navigate. He would be a long way away from Celeste for much of the time and would be relying on Pearl to be there when their daughter needed someone.

Luc nodded, his worried look giving way to a smile, and he led her through A&E to one of the cubicles.

Gabriel was a young man, dressed with all of the style that the Paris streets could muster. His linen jacket was slung over the back of the reclining seat he was occupying, tanned fingers drumming on the inevitable planner that most people with memory loss carried. The only clue to why he was here was the bloodstain on one rolled-up sleeve of his shirt, and the dressing on his forearm. He looked up at Luc and Pearl with an enquiring smile, clearly not recognising Luc.

'Hi, Gabriel, it's Luc Belange. How are you?'

Gabriel got to his feet, grinning and holding out his uninjured arm to shake Luc's hand. 'Nice to see you. I feel fine. Did they call you?'

Luc nodded. 'They were right to do so. We want to make sure you're well before we let you go. This is Dr Pearl Johnson She's a neurologist, visiting from a hospital in London. Are you happy for her to stay while I examine you?'

'Of course.' Gabriel turned, shaking her hand with a smile. 'Face-blindness and short-term memory loss.'

'But what's your name?' Pearl asked him. For all his charm, all that self-assurance, he'd clearly learned to expect that his neurological conditions were the first thing that anyone noticed about him.

Gabriel's smile broadened. 'My name is Gabriel Bernard. And it's a very great pleasure to meet you.'

'Sit down, Gabe.' Luc gave him a relaxed smile, bringing the focus around to the information he wanted. 'What do you remember about how the cut on your arm happened?'

'I was stressed out, thinking I should go to the hospital. I remember that.'

Luc nodded. 'Okay. Do you remember falling or banging your head?'

'No, I don't think so.' Gabriel's gaze followed Luc's moving finger without his having to be told and then he submitted to Luc's probing to see whether he had any bumps on his head.

'No nausea, disorientation, drowsiness or dizziness. I do have partial short-term memory loss, but we knew that already.' Gabriel grinned over Luc's shoulder at Pearl, and she couldn't help smiling back.

'All right, smart guy.' Luc gave up on his examination and sat down opposite Gabriel. He was the patient who tested every doctor's mettle—the one who knew as much, if not more, about his own medical condition as they did.

'I know that you don't want to go through all of this. I'd be impatient if someone from A&E started to go through the symptoms of a concussion with me. You know how important it is, though. Would you prefer it if we didn't care?'

Gabriel gave a wry smile, shaking his head. 'Don't let me stop you from that—you know I appreciate it.'

Luc finished his examination, and then waited while Gabriel wrote down the main points he needed to remember about caring for the cut on his arm. 'Will you be seeing your girlfriend tonight?'

Gabriel consulted his day planner. 'Yes, she has a late meeting but she'll be home by about seven. We're getting married next year, so strictly speaking she's my fiancée now.'

Luc beamed at him, shaking his hand. 'Congratulations! I'm so pleased to hear that.'

'Thanks. I got the ring made, to my own specifications. I'll always be able to recognise her by it.' One of the characteristics of face-blindness was that people could often recognise clothes and jewellery when they couldn't distinguish faces.

Pearl smiled. 'That must make it so special to her.'

'Yes, it does, actually. And to me.'

'Make a note to tell her what's happened and that you're to call me on my mobile if you have any worries. Just to be on the safe side.' Luc added a final thought to the list of instructions.

Gabriel nodded. 'Thanks, Luc. And thanks for being here.'

'My pleasure, as always. You can find your way through to patient information service desk, in reception?'

Gabriel shot him a grin. 'No problem. The nice thing about hospitals is that they signpost everything.'

They said their goodbyes, and Pearl noticed that Luc couldn't help watching as Gabriel navigated his way out of A&E, smiling cheerfully to the woman behind the desk as he went.

'He's…one of a kind, isn't he?' That was the only way that Pearl could think of to describe Gabriel.

'Yes. He was lucky to come through the encephalitis as well as he did, but he's made the most of that luck. He has a blog, where he talks about face-blindness and how people can help. There's quite a community of regular contributors and it's worth a read.'

'Thanks, I will. Are you ready to come and see your daughter now?' Pearl smiled up at him.

'Yes.' Luc was suddenly all movement, chivvying her towards the exit. 'I've been ready for that since I said goodbye to her yesterday...'

Time was running away with Luc, and one week had turned to two so quickly. At this time next Sunday, Pearl and Celeste would be back home, and Luc would be missing them like crazy. But a future was beginning to form for the three of them.

Pearl was curled up on the sofa in Luc's apartment and Celeste was on Luc's lap, watching as he drew. The beeswax crayons and large drawing pad that he'd left on the coffee table for her to find hadn't sparked her interest, but as soon as someone else picked them up and started drawing, she was fascinated.

'Pin-gin.' Celeste pointed to where she wanted the penguin, and Luc nodded.

Pearl chuckled lazily. 'She's winding you around her little finger, Luc. Show her who's boss and draw a giraffe.'

'*Don't* teach her how to say *giraffe*. I've only just worked my way up to doing a half-decent penguin.' Luc started to draw and Celeste leaned forward, watching him. 'You're sure the apartment's okay?'

'It'll be great. Open plan's not a problem, and your spare bedroom is more than enough room for us. If she's sleeping close to me it means I don't have so far to go if she wakes up at night. All you really need to do is go through the list I printed out for you, and lock away anything you don't want broken.'

Celeste pointed to another empty space on the paper, leaving him to decide what to draw this time, and he started to draw a tree.

'Okay. I'll prepare for a hurricane.'

He grinned and Pearl smiled back. It would be a hurricane that was well worth any amount of trouble if it felt like this.

'I'm still feeling guilty that you'll be doing most of the travelling, Luc. If it gets too much for you we can always do what I suggested.' Pearl had been very flexible over arrangements for access, and they'd agreed that two weekend visits a month would be a good place to start. She'd been willing to travel over to France for one of those weekends but Luc had vetoed the idea, saying that it was far more difficult for her to travel with a toddler.

'If you're happy with my coming to England twice a month, then I'm happy. It's about two and a half hours from the centre of Paris to the centre of London on the train, and I can work on the way if I need to. Bring Celeste over here for a couple of holidays every year—that's more than enough for you to do and much less disruption for her.' Luc hadn't shifted on that point, even though Pearl had protested. He hadn't expected her to offer him the option of staying with her, in her home, but that would make things even easier.

'I'll be sure to do that. I'd really like her to feel that Paris is her home as well as London. This idea of you speaking to her in French, and me speaking in English...'

'It worked for me, and does for a lot of other people. I never felt confused by the two languages as a child. My mum just spoke English and my dad spoke French. I used to wonder why most of the other kids at school couldn't speak English.' Luc had been delighted with Pearl's commitment to Celeste's French roots, and that his daughter would have all of the opportunities that he'd had.

It was a bargain built on trust, and that was difficult for both of them. But they'd already come a long way, and Pearl seemed as committed to making it work as he was.

'Henri and Nathalie don't mind babysitting for Celeste on Thursday?'

'No, they were fine with it. What are you planning, Luc? You know I only have a limited wardrobe to choose from, I had to pack light to get everything into one case to bring on the train with me.'

'You'll be fine. It's a come-as-you-are kind of thing.' He kissed the top of Celeste's head. 'Don't wait up for us, will you, sweetheart.'

The little girl waved him away in an obvious warning that she'd wait up if she wanted, and stabbed the paper in front of her with her finger.

CHAPTER NINE

LUC WAS DETERMINED to make a few memories. A few for Pearl to take home with her, and some for him to keep. He hadn't shared his memories for a while now, but Pearl and Celeste had changed all that. He'd asked Henri if he could fill in for him for the afternoon, and called for Pearl at half past twelve. She might have been standing behind the front door, because she flung it open as soon as he reached the porch.

'You've taken the top off your car!' Nathalie had appeared in the hallway, along with Celeste, who was clutching Mr Pin-gin. 'Look at the car, Celeste.'

'Oh-uh.' The little girl added her own opinion, and Pearl bent down to hug her daughter.

'Bye-bye, sweetheart. See you later.'

'Bye-bye...' Celeste pulled at Nathalie's hand, obviously ready to concentrate on more important business.

'You might need to borrow a headscarf.' Nathalie nodded towards the hall cupboard. Pearl shot her a grin and selected one from the large pile that Nathalie kept there.

She fixed the scarf over her hair, grinning as Luc opened the passenger door of the car for her. Pearl turned to wave to Nathalie and Celeste, and the little girl finally entered into the spirit of things, dropping Mr Pin-gin and waving.

'Where are we going?'

'You can't leave Paris without seeing some of the sights. I thought we might take a tour…' The idea obviously pleased Pearl, and Luc started the car.

The route began with a tour of the narrow streets of Montmartre. Then on to park a few streets away from the Arc de Triomphe, and take the foot tunnel to the centre of the huge roundabout. Luc had brought along his camera, and they took a few tourist snaps, before going back to the car.

Then, they moved on to the Eiffel Tower. Luc had already bought tickets, and before they boarded the elevator they took vertigo-inducing photographs of the tower.

'Oh!' Pearl made a grab for the skirts of her dress as they stepped onto the open-air walkway at the top. Luc took off his jacket, offering it to her, wondering if Pearl would accept the gesture, and she smiled and thanked him. She slipped her arms into the sleeves, and did up the bottom button, which was enough to keep the top of her dress under control and free up her hands for the binoculars he'd brought with him.

'I can see the hospital…' She swung the binoculars a few degrees to the right. 'Which way is your apartment?'

Luc put his arm around her shoulders, guiding her view back to the left. 'Should be about there.'

'Ah yes! I can see the park at the end of the road…' He could feel her excitement, leaking through the fabric that separated them, and Luc took one moment to appreciate it before he stepped back.

They traced a winding path through the city, handing the camera back and forth between them to take photographs. After a stroll along the banks of the Seine, they stopped for cafe crème, drunk under a flapping sunshade.

Then it was time for one more memory. Luc took a route back to the hospital which took in as many of the sights and sounds of Paris as possible. He parked in the library car park, and Pearl got out of the car, taking off her scarf and folding it into a neat square before putting it into her handbag.

'Just one more thing. Our latest project.'

'You have a project here? Along with all the other things you have going on at the hospital?' Pearl smiled up at him.

'It's just an idea at the moment. We've had a structural survey done as well as a health and safety assessment, and there are builders there who are investigating the possibilities for us. If the hospital board decide to go ahead, and they all seem enthusiastic, then we'll have to get a dedicated project manager in. This isn't something an amateur like me can handle. Come and see what you think.'

He led her into the library, and along a little-used corridor. The door which led to the basement was unlocked, and when he opened it, Luc could see that the lights were on. There was a small vestibule which contained several metal cupboards and he opened one, finding a hard hat for Pearl and one for himself.

'It's a precaution. We have people working down there, so it's subject to the rules and regulations concerning building sites.'

'It's not a catacomb, is it?' Pearl looked a little alarmed at the thought.

'No, the catacombs are much deeper, and to the south of here. This is just at basement level, and there's plenty of light down there. But if you'd prefer not to go, we'll give this one a miss…'

'No! As long as the lights are on, I want to see it.'

'Okay. If it's not to your taste, just say the word…'

It seemed that Pearl's inquisitiveness was getting the better of any fears she might have, and she dismissed the suggestion. All the same, Luc held out his hand as he made his way down the narrow stone steps and felt Pearl's fingers, holding on to him tightly. But when they reached the bottom, she gasped.

'Luc! This is amazing!'

'You like it? It's called an undercroft, which is really just a traditional name for a vaulted basement.' He looked around the large space with a new appreciation of it. The vaulted ceiling was supported by pillars, which resulted in a set of interlocking arches that curved through the space in a complicated geometrical pattern. The overall effect was one of quiet dignity.

'I love it, Luc. It definitely *should* have a different name, to mark it out from the ordinary.' Pearl left his side, wandering among the arches to look up at them. 'It's so beautiful.'

She was so beautiful. Like a waif, appearing and disappearing behind the wide stone pillars. An ethereal being, who would dissolve if he reached out to touch her…

Then a clatter sounded from the far end of the space, its echo dispelling the fantasy. Luc made his way over to Bertrand, whose dusty overalls and solid frame were very definitely part of the practical world. They shook hands, and Luc turned to see Pearl drifting over towards them.

'This is a colleague of mine, Dr Pearl Johnson. Pearl, this is Bertrand Allard. He's the building foreman, dealing with the project.' He introduced them in French, and Pearl smiled, holding out her hand.

'Pleased to meet you.' Pearl's French had improved a

lot in the last weeks, and although she still had a notice-able accent, she could get by in most situations. 'This is a beautiful place.'

Bertrand looked around, maybe seeing his surround-ings anew, as Luc had. He nodded in quiet satisfaction. 'It's a very good example of this kind of structure. There are quite a lot of them in this district, and this one is dry and in very good condition.'

'It seems so—' Pearl frowned, obviously groping for the right word '—as if it floats.'

Bertrand nodded. 'Yes, it does. But the way it's engi-neered gives it enormous strength. The more load you put on a structure like this the stronger it becomes.'

Pearl looked a little confused, and Luc wondered whether it was the language or the physics which was confounding her. He could translate, if not entirely ex-plain the combination of forces. Bertrand settled the matter by interlocking his fingertips, then sliding them together, as if a weight had been laid on top of them.

'Ah. I see, thank you. Like a staircase that floats?' She made an upward spiralling motion with one finger.

Bertrand smiled broadly. Despite the language barrier he seemed to have finally found someone who under-stood him. 'Exactly.'

'What's through there?' Pearl pointed to the darkened antechamber that Bertrand had just emerged from and he waved his hand dismissively.

'Just another basement. Reinforced-concrete construc-tion, installed in 1911, it's of no interest.'

Pearl glanced at Luc, and he translated the words for *reinforced concrete* into English, guessing that this was the part she didn't understand.

'Ah. I won't go in, then.'

'I'll be there tomorrow, with a construction team.' Bertrand turned to Luc. 'We might be doing some drilling, but I doubt very much you'll hear it upstairs. It won't be for long—we're just taking a few samples.'

'Those are the ones the structural engineer recommended?'

Bertrand nodded. 'Yes, we have her go ahead on it.' He turned to Pearl. 'I'll leave you to take a look around, miss. No one else comes down here, so enjoy this place while it's all yours.'

'I will. Thank you.'

They wandered for a while, and then Pearl sat down on a stone bench which circled the broad pillar in the centre of the space. Luc went to sit down next to her but Pearl was running her fingers around the edge of the slab, and leaned over to examine something.

'Have you seen this?'

He bent down to see what she'd found and saw pair of initials, carved into the stone. 'No, I've never noticed it before. It must have been done by someone who worked on this. You'd have to have the proper tools to make these indentations.'

'I suppose so. This is so special, Luc. It would make a wonderful peaceful place to read and relax. Think a little, maybe.'

'Yeah, it would.' Luc turned the corners of his mouth down. 'I think the hospital board are looking to have some return on the investment required to clean it all up, though. Someone suggested a cafeteria. My plan is to try and persuade them to use it for the kind of function we have upstairs, which does bring in an income and allows it to be used as a quiet space during the day. I think it's special enough that it would attract people, if we smartened up the staircase.'

'Yes, definitely. I'd imagine that it's protected, isn't it? Something like the equivalent of a listed building in the UK?'

'Yes, the whole library is a *monument historique*, which is much the same thing. But you could fill it with tables and chairs, and a free-standing service counter, without touching the fabric of the place.' He shrugged. 'Whatever happens, I'll make sure that nothing's lost.'

Pearl got to her feet, taking his arm. 'In that case, I'm happy to move on now, because I know it'll be safe and sound the next time I visit. Did you have anywhere else in mind, or is this your grand finale to a wonderful afternoon?'

'Are you hungry? We'll get something to eat and then there's one more stop to make…'

Pearl hadn't asked where they were going, and Luc seemed intent on keeping every new place, each new thing, a surprise. He parked in the small space outside his apartment block, leading her to the lift.

When they reached the top floor and he let them into his apartment, it seemed a little different. When she and Celeste had been here during the day the open-plan space was bright with sunshine, but in the early evening, it seemed more intimate. The moon was beginning to rise in a darkening sky, and Luc switched on the lights over the deep counter which separated the kitchen space from the living area.

She perched herself on one of the high stools, watching as he busied himself in the kitchen. Luc set some blinis to warm in a pan, and started to take tubs and packets out of the refrigerator.

'Can I help?'

'No…' He turned suddenly, giving her a dazzling smile. 'I have all of this timed. I'm hoping to impress you by throwing together a starter in three and a half minutes.' Luc grabbed a knife, starting to chop a small bundle of chives.

'You've already set the bar pretty high, Luc. This afternoon's been perfect.' That wasn't the best part about it. Luc had obviously put some thought into it all and gone out of his way to make it perfect. That was what was sending shivers down her spine. 'Should I time you?'

'No. Don't do that.'

'Close my eyes, then? In case you drop anything?'

He chuckled. 'Yeah. That actually might be very helpful…'

Pearl laughed, putting her hands over her eyes. She could hear the sound of him turning the blinis, and then the rattle of ice. Then the sound of something being put onto the counter in front of her…

'No cheating.' She could feel Luc close, murmuring the words. Making *this* perfect as well.

There was the sound of utensils clattering into the sink, and then the sharp smell of lemon…no, lime. More arrived on the counter and then Luc's voice again. 'You can look now.'

There was champagne on ice, along with sparkling water and slices of lime. In front of her, a platter full of blinis spread with cream cheese, half of which were topped with salmon and a single chive, and the other half with caviar. Pearl caught her breath.

'Luc, that's beautiful. I've never had caviar before…'

He grinned, sitting down on a stool on the other side of the counter. 'That's why I did smoked salmon as well. I know you like that. Caviar can be an acquired taste, but to my mind it's never too late to start acquiring it. Will you try some?'

'Definitely...' Pearl laid the two small side plates out in front of them and Luc reached for the champagne. 'Don't open a whole bottle just for me, Luc.' She knew he wouldn't be drinking, because he'd be driving later on.

'You're sure you don't want any? You could always take the bottle with you for Henri and Nathalie to finish up.'

'No, let's drink it together, another time. When we have something to celebrate. What are you having?'

'Sparkling water with a little lime. Goes well with the richness of the caviar.'

Luc poured the water, adding a twist of lime to each glass, and Pearl chose a blini from the platter, taking a small bite. 'It's...interesting.' She sipped her water then tried a second bite, allowing the flavour to develop before she swallowed. 'Actually... I think I'm already beginning to acquire the taste for it.'

Pearl didn't have to ask whether he was enjoying her voyage of discovery as much as she was; there was no faking his smile. They took their time over the starters, and then Luc brought a large charcuterie platter from the refrigerator, cutting slices of artisanal bread to go with cured meats, cheeses, dips and vegetables. It was a perfect way to end a day that had been full of so many sights and sounds.

They ate with their fingers, talking and laughing as the room around them grew dark. Then Luc cleared away the remains of the platter, putting the dishes into the dishwasher.

'Did you mention to Nathalie a time for when we'd be back?' Pearl wanted to stay here with Luc, for just a little longer.

'I said we might be very late. I had it in mind to take you on a night river cruise along the Seine to finish off with. We still have time to go there or I have strawberry tarts in the fridge…'

Pearl caught her breath. 'From the bakery you fetched them from the other day?' Luc *knew* she couldn't resist those and grinned, nodding.

'The cruise sounds lovely, but you're not playing fair with strawberry tarts. Maybe we could do it another time—I can take you on a night cruise along the Thames and we can see which one we like the best.'

Luc raised an eyebrow. 'A competition, eh? Tower Bridge at night is hard to beat, admittedly, but I see that and raise with the Eiffel Tower.'

'Okay, I'll see your Eiffel Tower and raise with Big Ben. *And* the Houses of Parliament, naturally.'

'Of course. I have the Louvre Pyramid up my sleeve.'

'And I have the London Eye, tucked into my dress…' They were both laughing now.

Luc opened the fridge door, taking out a box. 'I'll put these on plates while I'm thinking about what to do with my winnings.'

'Not so fast, Luc. I may have to throw in a day trip on the river down to Hampton Court. We could take Celeste. It'd be her first ride on a boat…'

'Now *you're* not playing fair.' Longing flickered in Luc's eyes as he put a plate with a strawberry tart in front of her.

'As soon as you let me know that you're coming, I'll book the tickets.'

Luc nodded as he sat down opposite her, picking up his fork. 'That would be great. Thank you.'

She should take a step back. Finish eating, then maybe stay for coffee and then thank Luc for a wonderful afternoon and let him take her home. But she only had two more days left in Paris and Pearl wanted more. She really shouldn't take it, but she couldn't help herself…

CHAPTER TEN

THE FOOD HAD seemed like a good idea when he'd ordered it from his favourite delicatessen, but it had been a mistake. Luc should have seen what had been growing between them and taken Pearl to a restaurant. But he was here now, alone with her.

That was okay. They'd move to the sofa, drink their coffee and then he'd bring the evening to a close, leaving behind all of the things that might have been. But when he took her empty plate from in front of her, and added it to the stack in the dishwasher, he heard Pearl's stool scrape on the floor behind him. He turned to see that she was on her feet, making her way around the counter.

'Shall we have our coffee over there?' Suddenly space seemed to be closing in on them. Pushing them together. When Pearl caught his arm, he was trapped, unable to move away from her gaze.

'I want to thank you, Luc. I came here wanting impossible things, that you'd forgive me, and accept and love Celeste. And you did it all. I hope you know how much that means.'

'Do you know what it means to me that you've been nurturing our child all this time? Keeping her safe and helping her to grow. I should be thanking you.'

She reached up, and he felt her fingers on his collar.

Such a light touch, but he was unable to move. Pearl stood on her toes and kissed him on the cheek. 'Would it be so wrong for us to take something for ourselves?'

She was asking him? That was the question that had been tormenting Luc, ever since he'd first seen her. 'We made our bargains, Pearl. There were good reasons for them.'

'Yes, there were. We wouldn't do well together, and it's best that we lead our own lives and work together as co-parents. Does that stop us from being together tonight? We've done it before.'

And despite everything, all of the regrets and the times he'd longed for Pearl, Luc couldn't think of one thing he'd do differently. She couldn't heal every wound—no one could—but she'd given him a measure of peace that he hadn't had before.

He kissed her. That was the only thing that made any sense at the moment. Luc could feel the soft pressure of her body against his, see the light in her eyes. It felt intoxicating but he'd never been more sober in his life.

'You have condoms?' She made the practicalities sound like a delicious come-on. Something that forged wild dreams into realities.

'Yes. One packet, which gets replaced every time its shelf life runs out...' That sounded like passion too. An honest admission that he'd been waiting for her. That his heart had defied all of the promises they'd made, and always hoped that they might find their way back to each other.

She kissed him again. The sweet taste of strawberries still lingered on her lips. 'Are you telling me that you're a starry-eyed dreamer, Luc?'

If he was, then he was going to catch those dreams

again. Even if it was just one more time. 'We have hours before the world wants us back. Will you spend them making love with me?'

'All of them?' Pearl was smiling, knowing that Luc would hold out for a *yes*. Making him work for it.

'Every minute. Maybe you'll count them out for me…' He wrapped his hands around her waist, lifting her up so that she could sit on the countertop. That extra few inches brought her face-to-face with him.

Pearl wrapped her arms around his neck. 'That sounds nice. Or maybe I'll make *you* count them out.'

'Maybe you will. I'm open to the suggestion…' Something was up. Pearl had slowed things right down, and maybe she was having second thoughts. Then he saw her glance to one side.

The windows. Luc had become used to spending his evenings with the lights of Paris for company and didn't think twice about it. They were on the top floor and this block was the highest in the street. You'd need a helicopter and a pair of binoculars to be able to see inside. But Pearl was obviously struggling to be comfortable with them.

'Wait…' He kissed her cheek, his fingers caressing the side of her face in a promise, and he walked along the line of windows, closing the shutters over the lower half of them. Then for good measure, he turned the latch for the deadbolt as he passed the front door. It was stiff from lack of use, and made a satisfying *clunk* as it engaged.

'We're on our own, Pearl, apart from the moon.' He nodded towards the sky, which was all that showed through the tops of the windows. 'This is a safe place for you—it always will be. Whatever we choose to be, whatever we choose to do.'

She caught his shoulders, pulling him close again,

whispering in his ear. 'Yes, Luc. To making love until we've both forgotten how to count...'

He put his hand behind her back, sliding her closer on the counter. He could feel her bare feet against the back of his legs and wondered briefly when she'd taken her shoes off. That might have been some time ago...

Luc knew what turned her on. He whispered in her ear, one arm holding her tight against him, the other hand skimming the material that covered her breast. Telling her that he wanted to share each rush of her pleasure, every moment of calm. Hearing her sigh, feeling her body react to his touch.

'You can have that later, Luc. I'm not in a mood to give you the choice just yet.' He felt her legs tighten around him as she unbuttoned his shirt. Her fingers exploring, turning heat into an uncontrollable fire. Luc swallowed down a cry, and felt her hand move to the button that secured the waistband of his chinos.

'Pearl...!' Her name tore itself from his lips.

'That feels good?'

'What do you think?' Her assertiveness had spun him into a whole new world of pleasure. Their weekend together had been all about tenderness, about finding connections that they'd never thought would survive their parting. But they had and now they were like explorers, setting out for the horizon to see what lay beyond it.

'Enough waiting, Luc. You need to show me your bedroom. Right now...'

His gaze never left her face. Luc's eyes were the things she loved the most about him, although his obvious arousal was coming a very close second at the moment. He scooped her up in his arms, carrying her to the bedroom.

There was one moment of calm when he sat her down on his bed, closing the shutters over the windows and returning to kneel down in front of her. 'I know your body's changed.' He smoothed her hair back from her face, kissing her. 'It's been busy doing valiant and wonderful things, which is such a turn-on for me. This is a new adventure…'

That was Luc all over. If there was an elephant in the room, he talked about it, honestly and without embarrassment. It made her brave, too, and when he kissed her, Pearl felt just as beautiful as she had two years ago. More so—she'd been away on a valiant journey, but now she was back.

And this was one of the most adventurous things she'd ever done. Feeling the urgency in his movements as he undressed her. Hearing his breath quicken as she tore off his shirt, and propelled him back onto the bed. The touch of his skin against hers as she climbed on top of him.

This time she understood more of what he was saying when French started to take over. New flatteries and new secrets. Luc couldn't hide anymore and when he begged for her, Pearl knew.

When she rolled the condom down in place, his body shivered in a sigh. Checking it left him helpless. As she guided him inside her, Pearl felt something roll over her. The first murmurs of a surrender that would claim both of them.

'Don't back out on me now, Pearl.' He laid his hands loosely on her hips. Waiting for her to take the initiative. She squeezed the muscles that cradled him and he groaned, his body arching beneath her.

Then she knew. Wherever they went next, she would be taking them there…

* * *

They'd both needed to rest a little after the first explosive orgasm, which had spread like wildfire between them. But two years had been a long time to wait, and there were more fantasies to explore.

He'd used his fingers and tongue to claim her again. Then whispered words had turned into long, slow love-making. Pleasure ebbed and flowed between them, changing again as Luc finally showed her his own assertive side. Their weekend together had been like a fairy tale, something they'd purposely kept away from their everyday lives. But this was so much better, because it was real.

She clung to him as they lay together, her gaze fixed on the numerals of the clock at his bedside. They'd have to go soon.

'Hey…' A tear had trickled down her cheek, and slid onto his chest. 'Are you telling me that you regret this?'

'Would you mind?'

He wrapped his arms around her. 'Yes, I'd mind. I'd mind a great deal more if you *didn't* tell me.'

Pearl stretched up to kiss his cheek. 'I don't regret one thing about this evening. I'm sorry that it's almost over. We have to go in another…forty minutes.'

He turned, looking at the clock. 'My associative memory isn't going to let you go so easily. I'll have to move some of the furniture around next week.'

'Okay. I'm getting the message. You're moving on but you're not going to forget. I think that's what I really needed to know and it's what I'm going to do.'

He kissed her. That was what she needed too.

'Let's not allow the clock to have the last word, eh? If we go now, we can take a drive through Paris at night, on the way back.' There was something rebellious about his smile.

'You mean if we don't follow the clock's rules, you won't have to have a harsh word with it when you get back?'

'I mean that I won't be tempted to drop it out of the window.' He sat up, taking her with him. 'I'll find where you've scattered your clothes, if you collect up mine.'

He put his jacket around her shoulders when they reached the car, and took the route they'd followed this morning. On the dark streets of Paris, the breeze seemed to blow away the burden of regret, leaving only the pleasures of the day.

When he drew up outside Henri and Nathalie's house, Luc turned to her. 'Thank you for today. I'll always remember it.'

'Me too. Thank you Luc.' Pearl leaned over to kiss his cheek before getting out of the car. He watched her to the door, waving when she turned before closing it behind her.

'You look tired after your late night,' Nathalie observed as Luc walked into the kitchen. He'd promised to pick Pearl up today so she could spend the day at the hospital, finishing and collating the report of her visit.

He smiled, sitting down at the kitchen table, where Henri was giving Celeste her breakfast. 'It was a really good afternoon and evening. We took some great photos. There was one of Pearl in your headscarf in the car with the Eiffel Tower in the background.'

Pearl puffed out a breath. Seeing Luc again hadn't been as much of a challenge as she'd thought. He was relaxed and noticeably free of morning-after embarrassment. 'I look very 1950s.'

Nathalie laughed. 'Any time you want to borrow my car, Luc… I don't mind taking the convertible.'

'It's a deal.' He was smiling and relaxed.

This was a side of him she hadn't seen before. Luc treated sex as one of life's pleasures, something that didn't need to be talked about, and didn't require guilt. Her ex-husband had talked about it all the time, and Pearl had felt guilty about her silence. Her disappointment that he'd no longer seen any need for her pleasure after the wedding. Her lies when he'd decided it was time for them to have a family and she'd taken her contraceptive pills to work and kept them in her locker, instead of the bathroom at home, because she couldn't bear to bring a child into their relationship.

Last time she and Luc had been together it had been a fairy tale. Something that Pearl could tell and retell to herself, but was divorced from the everyday. It was a different life, one that she might have had. This time, it had been a few short hours, limited by all the things that kept her and Luc apart. But it had been real.

He said goodbye to Celeste, picking up Teddy and putting him back next to her in her high chair. Then he waited for Pearl to give her daughter kisses and cuddles and say bye-bye before walking out to the car with her.

'Did you get some sleep?' The top of the convertible was still folded down into the boot, and Luc was waiting for Pearl to knot Nathalie's scarf securely over her hair before he started to drive.

'I crept upstairs like a teenager, and went to sleep as soon as my head hit the pillow. You?'

'Much the same. Only without the teenager part.' Luc

started the engine. 'I'm going to be busy this morning, but would you like to meet up for lunch?'

'Yes, that would be nice. I thought I'd work in the library this morning. I'll be there whenever you're free.'

'Okay.' He took a right turn that Pearl wasn't expecting and she threw him a querying look. 'If we don't get a move on, we'll be caught in the rush hour traffic. This is one of Henri's best short cuts...'

Pearl *had* got some work done this morning, along with a little daydreaming. But when Luc walked into the small meeting room that she'd found for herself, her report was finished.

'All done.' She closed her laptop, smiling up at him.

'Nice one. Perhaps we can have some sliced pears and yoghurt with Celeste this evening to celebrate. Or we could have coffee and a sandwich from the food truck on the terrace...'

'Or we could really push the boat out and do both?'

Luc chuckled. 'Sounds like a plan...' He fell silent as a rumble sounded from somewhere. A vibration as much as a sound, and the glass shade of the lamp in the centre of the table rattled in sympathy.

'What was *that*?' Pearl looked around the room but everything was just as it had been.

'I don't know. Downstairs...' Luc's almost physical connection to the place hadn't let him down. He knew that the sound was coming from the basement, as surely as he'd know if someone dropped something on his toe. 'Why don't you stay here—I'm going to check it out.'

Or she could go with him. The shadows that had fallen across his face told Pearl that this was something out of the ordinary, and he was concerned. She got to her feet, following him through to the doorway that led down to the basement, waiting while he unlocked it.

'I thought you were going to wait for me...'

'I decided not to.' Her words prompted a slight shrug and a flashed smile. One of the things she liked about Luc was that he never expected her to do as he said.

Although maybe, just this once, she should have. Luc handed her a protective jacket, along with a hard hat from the cupboard, before leading her down the stairs to the undercroft.

Everything seemed just as it had been yesterday. Then an eddy of dust began to trickle into the space on the other side of the undercroft, from the opening which led to the second basement.

'Stay here. Really.' Luc's tone was more urgent now.

'Bertrand's been working there, hasn't he? If someone's hurt...' Pearl wasn't going to argue with him and started across to the other side of the undercroft.

Luc caught up with her, moving her firmly out of the way so that he went first into the square antechamber. It was dark in there, and he pulled his phone out of his pocket, switching on the torch to look carefully around the space before moving across it to a door which must lead to the main part of the basement. It opened easily, and they were confronted by darkness and dust.

A light came on from a phone somewhere inside. Pearl felt Luc's hand searching for hers and caught it, clutching it tightly. Now wasn't the time for false bravery; darkness made her panic...

Bertrand's voice sounded as they made their way into the basement. 'Charles... Hugo...' Bertrand was making a roll-call, and she heard grunted replies that the first two men were okay. 'Yvette... Yvette?'

There was no time to wonder where the woman who hadn't answered was. Pearl heard something fall in the darkness, and ducked instinctively. Bertrand's voice sounded again, telling everyone to get down, and she felt Luc pull her to the ground. His body curled protectively over hers as the rumble of something heavy falling turned into a thunder. She felt, rather than heard, herself whimpering with fear and then Luc's hand found hers, holding it tight.

CHAPTER ELEVEN

JUST HANG ON. It's going to be okay. If the noise around them had allowed any words of comfort, then perhaps that's what Luc would have said. Pearl repeated the words over and over again, squeezing his hand to reassure herself that he was there.

The crashing sound seemed to last for a long time before silence fell, broken only by the sounds of movement and curses.

'Are you okay?' Luc's whispered words sounded like those of a lover. Someone who'd protected her through a storm.

'Yes. You?' She'd felt him flinch when the noise was at its peak.

'Yeah…'

Pearl didn't believe him. She forced herself to release his hand. 'You're sure?' She ran her hands across his shoulders and then down his back. As they reached his waist, she heard Luc catch his breath.

'It's okay. Something hit me, but there's no damage done.' She felt him move, and the reassuring press of his body lifted from hers.

'I'd rather you let *me* be the judge of that…' Suddenly a powerful arc light flashed on, and she blinked as her eyes adjusted to it. Luc was on his feet, and he bent to help her up, wincing slightly.

'I'm okay. Really.' He called across in French to the dust-covered ghosts beside the light. 'Bertrand. Is everyone all right?'

'Yvette is hurt,' Bertrand answered and Pearl saw two other men gravitating towards the centre of an area where part of the concrete ceiling had fallen in.

'Wait, lads…' Bertrand was keeping his voice low but his tone was firm and insistent. He moved to one side, switching another light on and directing it towards the ceiling.

It went against every instinct, but this had to be their first concern. The men's bravery in searching for their workmate would count for nothing if they were caught in another fall of concrete. The ceiling to one side of the basement had completely collapsed, running from the back of the space through to the door they'd entered by. Pearl felt suddenly sick as she saw the mess of rubble, just yards from where she and Luc had been standing.

'Will it hold?' Luc had reached Bertrand, skirting carefully around the area where the ceiling had collapsed.

'Yes. The first fall was mainly plaster, and then that area of concrete came down. There's nothing more up there apart from the joists of the floor above that, and they look undamaged.' Bertrand swung the light towards the mess of rubble below it. 'Yvette… Yvette…'

A woman's keening cry sounded, and Luc moved towards the far end of the rubble, stooping down suddenly. 'I need one man to help me and another to go with Pearl to see if there's a way out of here. Keep an eye on the ceiling, Bertrand, and warn us if anything else looks as if it's about to collapse.' He started to scoop dust and small fragments of concrete away from the edge of the pile.

That sounded sensible. Apart from the bit about her going for help, because that was clearly because Luc wanted her out of a potentially dangerous environment. But he was busy, and before she could protest, Bertrand had directed one man to help Luc and another to go with her.

She could go and fetch help, then come back again. Luc couldn't stop her from doing that, and Pearl wasn't going to leave him alone down here. She pulled her phone from her pocket, switching on the torch to guide her as she followed the workman towards the door. He started to shift the debris away from it, his movements haphazard and panicky. Pearl hurried towards him, knowing that they needed to take care.

'Hey.' She caught his arm and when he straightened Pearl saw that even though he was tall and seemed strongly built he was just a boy, his face streaked with dust and tears. 'What's your name?'

'Charles.'

She could see now why Bertrand had sent him with her, leaving the other, older man to help Luc. Charles was too frightened to be of any use with the injured woman, and Bertrand wanted him safely out of here too.

'Charles, I'm Pearl. And I'm…' What was the word in French? Pearl managed to dredge it up from somewhere. 'I'm scared too. We'll work together, yes?'

Charles nodded, straightening a little. 'Yes.'

'That's great. First thing is to clear that…' She didn't know the words for a mess of rubble, either, but she pointed and Charles understood.

They heaved a large lump of concrete out of the way,

and then cleared the smaller pieces of debris that were blocking the bottom of the door. Charles had found his sense of purpose now, and they worked quietly and carefully. Finally Pearl got to her feet.

'That's enough.' They could open the door a little way, and see what was on the other side.

'Okay…' Pearl pulled at Charles's arm, moving him back. She turned the handle, carefully opening the door by an inch.

Nothing. Just darkness. Pearl took out her phone and turned the torch on, gingerly opening the door a little further so that she could see. The whole of the ceiling in the antechamber had collapsed, and a sheet of concrete had slid down and was lying at an angle across the entrance to the undercroft.

Crying might be an option right now. One that Pearl wasn't going to take. She took a photograph of the concrete slab, and checked her phone for reception before closing the door and turning to Charles.

'No service?' Charles's voice sounded remarkably steady.

'No, and that way is—' Pearl couldn't think of the word for *blocked* '—closed.'

Charles took his own phone out of a pocket in his overalls, switching it on and holding it up. 'I've got nothing.'

'Okay.' Reassurance was difficult enough in English, let alone French, and Pearl grabbed his arm and smiled. That did the trick. 'Come with me.'

She made her way back over to Bertrand, Charles following her.

'You can't get out that way?' Bertrand asked.

'No.' Pearl showed him the picture on her phone and Bertrand shook his head.

'We can't dig through concrete.'

Charles spoke up. 'Our phones don't have service, either.'

Bertrand pursed his lips. 'They must know something's going on down here. Someone will have called the emergency services. All right, lad?'

'Yes, boss.'

'Go and fetch another of those arc lights, then. When Hugo's finished, we're going to make safe space, where we can sit and wait, and the more light the better.'

'He's finished now. I'm going to help Luc.' Pearl wasn't sure whether doctor outranked foreman, but as far as she was concerned it did when it came to injuries. 'And what's the matter with your hand?' Bertrand was cradling his left hand against his body, but she could see that the fingers were bleeding and already swollen.

'Yvette first. I can manage the light with one hand.' Bertrand turned to Charles, clearly considering the matter closed. 'Hurry up, lad, we're going to need those lights today, not next week…'

Luc knew that he couldn't keep Pearl away. Sending her to get help was fair enough—that was the one most important thing that they needed and someone had to go. But she was still here, which meant that there was no way out, and there was an injured woman to care for. Pearl had made the obvious clinical decision and was picking her way across the rubble towards him.

When she'd ducked, Luc thought she'd been hit by the falling concrete. He'd pulled her down, trying to shield her with his own body. When something had struck his back, all he'd been able to think of was that it hadn't hurt Pearl.

He could justify wanting to protect her by saying that she was the mother of his child, and that Celeste needed Pearl more than she did him. But the things which came before he was able to rationalise it all didn't lie. All of his instincts, every thought and every action, had been intent on protecting Pearl. It felt like love. Something he couldn't admit to, but which had governed his every move.

And now he could smell flowers in a dusty underground vault. And he was sure that his back hurt a little less because he could see Pearl's smile.

'Hey. How are you?' she asked in French, and Luc assumed that the question was for Yvette.

'Not too bad. The doc's going to get me back in shape.'

'Yes, no problem,' Luc agreed with Yvette, sitting back on his heels to look up at Pearl. Normally he'd take a step away from a patient at this point but there was no way he was leaving Yvette unattended.

'So there's no way out?' Luc switched to English, not wanting Yvette to hear what he was saying.

'No, there's a block of concrete across the way into the undercroft and Bertrand says we can't dig our way through. There's no phone reception, either.' Pearl gave an almost imperceptible nod in Yvette's direction. 'Injuries?'

'She has a broken arm, possible cracked ribs and a probable fractured ankle. I've examined her for any spinal injuries as well as I can and if we're not going to be getting out of here soon I think our first priority should be moving her to the safest, most comfortable place we can.'

Pearl nodded. 'I'll go and see if I can find something that will work as an improvised stretcher.' She glanced up at the space above their heads. 'Is that the underside of a floor that I can see above us?'

'Yeah, probably. What are you thinking?'

'Just that if the concrete's blocking the phone signal then maybe here will be better.'

Of course. 'Why didn't I think about that?'

Pearl gave him an intoxicating smile. 'Because your mind was on your patient…'

Things were starting to move. Bertrand reckoned that the safest place for them was in the area where the ceiling had already collapsed, and Pearl suggested that one of the metal doors from a line of storage cupboards might serve as an improvised stretcher to move Yvette. Charles and Hugo set about removing the door, while Pearl inspected the contents of the cupboards.

Luc glanced at his phone, feeling his heart beat a little faster as one bar flickered on and then back off again. Maybe he could get a little closer to the underside of the floorboards after they'd moved Yvette, but in the meantime… He looked down, smilingly reassuring his patient that everything was in hand.

Everyone was working quickly and quietly. One of the cupboards had been used to store dust sheets and furniture covers, which Pearl reckoned she could fold together to provide a warmer and slightly less uncomfortable alternative to the concrete floor. Hugo and Charles were clearing a space for Yvette, in the area that Bertrand had indicated was safest.

'We have to move you, Yvette. It won't be as comfortable as a stretcher, but it's just a few metres.' Luc smiled at Yvette as Pearl cut a strip from one of the dust sheets to serve as a strap for the makeshift stretcher.

'That's okay. Whatever you need to do, Luc.' Yvette grimaced.

There was no need for any conversation between Luc and Pearl; they both knew exactly what was needed. Together they rolled Yvette onto her side, supporting her head and neck, and then back again onto the door. Pearl secured the dust sheet around her waist as Luc positioned Charles and Hugo at two corners of the door. Then smoothly, carefully, they lifted it and carried Yvette over to the place that had been prepared for her.

'All done. You did great.' Luc grinned at her. 'You can breathe now, if you like.'

Yvette let out a quavering sigh, a tear rolling down her cheek. Luc took her hand, leaning forward to brush the tear from her cheek. His tenderness couldn't conceal the facts from Yvette; she was hurt and they had no way out of here, but they were helping her to be strong.

'I'm going to see if I can get my phone to work. Pearl will stay with you.' Luc disentangled Yvette's fingers from his.

'I'll go…' Pearl suggested. Luc was clearly a comfort to Yvette and he should stay here with her.

'Your French might not be up to our shopping list. And anyway, this woman has a grip of steel—it's only fair that you share the hard work,' he joked and Yvette smiled.

He had a point—she could probably summon up the words for all that they needed for Yvette, but couldn't rap them out as quickly or clearly as Luc could. Pearl nodded, sitting down on the floor next to Yvette and offering her hand. Yvette took it, curling her fingers lightly around Pearl's.

'Is this what he means by a strong grip?' She leaned forward, murmuring to Yvette.

'This hurts as much as when I had my son. In different places…' Yvette whispered quietly. 'You have kids?'

'A daughter. Squeeze a bit tighter.' Pearl nodded as Yvette tightened her grip a little. 'What's your son's name?'

'Marcel. He's five. He's with my sister...' Tears appeared again in Yvette's eyes and she seemed to be struggling for control.

'It's all right.' Pearl turned, motioning the men away. 'If you want to cry then do it. We're twice as tough as they are.'

'Only twice?' Yvette smiled suddenly.

'Three times...'

She could hear Luc talking behind her and prayed that this was the much-needed telephone call to the outside world. He let out a low groan of annoyance, and Pearl turned quickly, glancing behind her. He was standing on a pile of fallen concrete, as close as possible to the ceiling, and seemed to be redialling. Pearl held her breath, and then he smiled and began to talk again.

'Good news. Luc's talking to someone.'

Luc had breathed a sigh of relief when the call had gone through to the phone in the library upstairs and Marthe, the librarian, had answered. He knew that she'd be writing down everything he said, and that his messages would get to the right people. He'd turned his head once, just to get one, much-needed glimpse of Pearl and the call had cut out, but when he'd tried again the call had gone through.

He'd ended the call, leaving Marthe to get on with what she needed to do. Pearl was sitting beside Yvette and the three men were standing in a tight knot a few metres away, making a show of not listening to what was being said by the two women. He knelt down next to Pearl, beckoning the men over.

'The emergency services are already here and they're working to get us out.' That was the first thing that everyone needed to know. 'They think that they can take up the floorboards and that there'll be a big enough gap to get some medical supplies down to us in the meantime.'

'That's great.' Pearl was sharing her approval of this good news with Yvette, but she turned for a moment and flashed him a smile, which reached all the way into his heart.

'Can we call out for burgers?' Charles spoke up.

'Nah, you have to be trapped for a while before you get burgers. We'll be out before then.' At least, Luc hoped they would.

'I'll buy you one, lad. At that place you're always talking about.' Bertrand spoke gruffly to Charles but with obvious approval.

'After you've had an X-ray done on your fingers.' Luc turned to him. They'd had to concentrate on the most important things first, but he'd noticed straight away that Bertrand was hurt as well. 'Come and sit down, and let me take a look at them.'

He gained another nod of approval from Pearl. Those sweet moments were keeping him going. Giving him the strength to believe that they could push back against the tragedy that seemed always to be just around the corner. Showing him that she'd be walking out of here with everyone else, and that he wasn't going to lose her.

CHAPTER TWELVE

THE PEOPLE UPSTAIRS were obviously working cautiously for fear of disturbing anything and causing more of the ceiling to collapse. But they must have rolled back the carpet in the place he'd indicated to Marthe, and before long light started to filter down through the dust in the air. For all the world like a break in the darkest of clouds.

Slowly. Carefully. Everyone was quiet, listening for signs of activity above them. Watching the light above them grow as the rescuers carefully removed one floor-board and then the next. Bertrand was sitting with Hugo and Charles, one arm in the sling that Luc had fashioned from a piece of dust sheet, and Yvette seemed to be drifting, exhausted by pain.

'I don't suppose you know where her phone is, Luc?' Pearl asked him.

'I think this is hers. I saw it on the ground when I went to make the call.' The screen was cracked but he'd salvaged the phone almost automatically, putting it down in the pile of odds and ends that were collected at the end of the improvised bed.

'Thanks.' Another one of those smiles that he was fast learning to depend on. 'Let's hope it's still working...'

She switched the phone on, and Luc saw immediately

what she was up to. The handset was still locked but a picture of Yvette with a little boy was visible.

'Yvette.' Pearl murmured her name, rubbing gently on the back of her hand, and Yvette's eyes fluttered open. 'Look what we found.'

Yvette took one look at the picture and smiled. 'Marcel.'

'That's him, is it? He's a beautiful boy.'

Yvette nodded, her gaze fixed on the picture.

'You'll be seeing him soon, Yvette. We're getting there.'

'We are…?' Yvette seemed increasingly disoriented, and Luc knew that Pearl was trying to concentrate her attention. He craned around, glancing at the photograph.

'This is at the Jardin des Tuileries?'

'Yes…'

'Did you take Marcel to the museum?'

'No. He's too young to enjoy that. The funfair. Last year…'

Luc nodded. 'Ah yes, of course. Which rides did you go on?'

Yvette was more focused now, and started to haltingly recount what they'd done that day. Pearl took her own phone out, showing Yvette a picture of Celeste, and Yvette smiled murmuring the four numbers of the pass code to her own phone. Pearl got the message, unlocking the phone and then asking whether she might open the image gallery so that Yvette could see more photographs.

She must feel this. Luc had known about Celeste for less than three weeks, and still this place made him long to hold her. Pearl must be experiencing that a thousand times over, but still she was holding back her tears, and helping Yvette to concentrate on the photographs of her son. Luc turned away from them, making a silent promise that he'd do whatever it took to make sure that Pearl and Celeste were reunited.

'Dr Luc…' He heard Charles's insistent whisper. 'Look, they're sending us something.'

He turned to see a tightly packed bag being lowered through the hole in the ceiling. Pearl had looked around too, and he quickly grasped her hand, giving it a gentle squeeze.

'We're getting there…'

The look in her eyes told him that she knew. They weren't just one step closer to getting out of here; they were two steps closer to each other. To a time when a touch, or a sigh, meant everything. Back to a place where Celeste wasn't the only thing holding them together, and all they'd needed was each other.

Then Pearl's gaze suddenly focused over his shoulder. 'Luc! It's swinging.'

He turned around to see the bag gently swinging back and forth, the rope threatening to graze the sides of the hole in the ceiling. The rescue party had stopped lowering the bag in an effort to steady it and Luc hurried over towards it, reaching up. He could just graze the bottom of it with his fingertips, but it was enough to steady it.

'Another five centimetres…' he called up, seeing a man's face above him, leaning through the legs of the gantry that spanned the hole. He signalled to someone, and the bag dropped a little, just enough for Luc to get a good hold. 'Got it,' he stated, and the bag started to move downward again.

He called up to the rescue party, then carried the bag back to Pearl, laying it down on the floor and unzipping it. She was all smiles now, as excited as a kid opening her presents at Christmas, and Luc sent up a silent thank you to whoever had packed it so well. They had all the medical equipment they needed for Yvette, and there was even a small inflatable mattress tucked into the bottom of the bag, which Luc handed over to Hugo and Charles to deal with. He turned his attention to the slim emergency lantern, switching it on so that he could read the labels attached to the medication that was packed in a plastic box.

'You'll be feeling much more comfortable soon, Yvette. Just hang on for a few moments more...' Pearl reassured her as she opened a packet of antiseptic wipes, handing one to Luc and scrubbing the dirt from her fingers with another. Then she donned a pair of surgical gloves, clipping a pulse oximeter onto Yvette's finger and then checking her blood pressure and nodding in satisfaction.

'Not bad, Yvette. I think mine's higher than yours at the moment. I'm going to listen to your breathing and press gently on your chest...' Pearl was checking all of Yvette's vital signs as quickly and efficiently as if they were working in a well-lit consulting room, with a couple of nurses in attendance to help her.

'Good. Well done.' She turned to Luc, switching to English. 'How do you say that I can hear a few signs of a cracked rib but her breathing sounds good? I don't want to get that wrong.'

He relayed the information, and Yvette nodded and smiled back at Pearl. 'I'm getting to like your terrible accent.'

So was Luc. Pearl stumbled over words at times, but she always made sure that she was understood. And her smile reached beyond the boundaries of language, connecting her with the people around her. She shot Yvette a cheerful grin, and sat back on her heels to finish writing her findings down on the small notepad that had been tucked into the webbing at the top of the bag.

It was his turn now. Luc went through the necessary questions that needed to be asked before administering analgesics, and repeated back the type and dosage for Pearl to write down. She understood the value of double-checking everything in these conditions as well as Luc did, and they supported each other without having to be asked. They waited for ten minutes for the pain relief to begin to work, and then carefully immobilised Yvette's arm and ankle with inflatable splints. Charles was ready with the inflatable mattress and they lifted Yvette gently, slipping it underneath her. Then Luc turned his attention to splinting Bertrand's broken fingers, while Pearl tucked the blanket around Yvette.

'Thank you.' Bertrand let out a sigh. 'That feels much better.'

'Good. It's only temporary and when we get to the hospital they'll take an X-ray and go from there.'

'And give me another round of painkillers?' Bertrand chuckled. He'd refused the ones that Luc had offered, saying that he needed to stay sharp. Luc had reluctantly agreed, knowing that Betrand's structural expertise was valuable to them right now, but persuaded him to accept a half dose.

'Is what I gave you not working? Pain isn't going to help you stay sharp, you know.'

Bertrand shot a steady-eyed, thoughtful look in his direction. 'It's working. I'm fine. I'm just looking forward to a hot bath and a long snooze after all this is over. Same as you, no doubt.'

Luc nodded. He was looking forward to different things. Being able to take Pearl somewhere on their own, and hold her. Seeing her re-united with Celeste. Being able to curl his arms around the two people who were more important to him than anyone…

Nice fantasy. Which was broken by Charles leaping to his feet.

'Steady on, lad. Quiet and careful.' Bertrand reminded him. He'd impressed that need on everyone, as a precaution against dislodging any loose debris.

'Sorry, boss. Can I go and get it?'

Bertrand eyed the smaller bag, which was descending from the hole at greater speed than the last one, and didn't seem to be as prone to swaying back and forth. 'All right. Move quickly but carefully. Anything falls from that ceiling and you leave the bag and get yourself out. You hear me?'

'Yes, boss. I hear you.'

Luc watched as Charles moved towards the bag. Pretty much everything that was going to collapse had already done so, but Bertrand had given Charles a set of rules to follow which would reassure him and stop him from panicking. The lad brought the bag back, setting it down next to Luc.

Inside there were two large thermos flasks, and some paper cups, along with several bottles of water and a handful of energy bars. Someone had even thought to add a nonspill cup for Yvette. On the top was an envelope, marked Important, and Luc took it out, scanning the contents.

'What do you think?' He passed the letter over to Bertrand, who read it.

'Yes…yes, I reckoned this might be what they'd try to do. I doubt any of us would fit through that hole in the ceiling, and making it bigger is going to involve messing with the space that's safest for us. If they think that they can clear the passageway then that's a much better option, even if it might take a bit longer.'

Luc nodded. 'Thanks. That makes sense to me as well. We need to transport Yvette as carefully as we can. I'll let Pearl know…'

He allowed himself to glance across towards Pearl. She'd carefully cleaned Yvette's face with one of the wipes, and had turned her attention to her hands now, talking quietly as she did so. It was a level of tenderness and care that doctors didn't get a great deal of time for, but which could be just as effective as anything that they could prescribe.

'One minute…' Bertrand brushed his sleeve, and Luc turned back towards him. 'We'd like to visit Yvette, please.'

They were sitting approximately three metres away from her. Luc wondered if he'd been clear enough in his reassurances to the men. 'She's in no danger, Bertrand. She has broken bones and a cracked rib but she's responded well to treatment.'

'Yes, we know. We're a team and we stick together. The lads would just like to tell her that she'll be out of here soon and sit with her for a while.'

'Okay. Sure. She's not to drink anything apart from water and don't give her anything to eat, either.' Luc hadn't come across this before; people were generally more than happy to hand their workmates over to the emergency services' care when they were injured. But then he'd never been trapped in a basement before, so his experience probably didn't count for much.

'Right you are, Doc. Thank you.'

'That's so nice of them.' They were sitting only three or four metres from Yvette, but speaking in English gave

Pearl a feeling of privacy and intimacy. One that she so craved at this moment.

Luc nodded, smiling. 'Yeah. Bertrand said they were a team.'

The three men were sitting in a semicircle to one side of Yvette. Relaxed, talking and joking quietly between themselves. Charles was holding the no-spill cup, ready to hand it over when Yvette wanted to take a sip, and she was lying quietly, watching them.

'That really matters. People just being within reach...' Maybe Luc didn't know that now Pearl had a chance to think, memories were flooding back, almost overwhelming her. Maybe he shouldn't know.

He put his arm around her shoulders. Casually, almost, as if he were just a friend. As if last night had just been a crazy dream and hadn't really happened. It seemed a long time ago now, and Pearl needed him right now.

'You did all the right things, Pearl. Never missed a beat. Now you're shaking.'

Was she? Pearl hadn't realised. She took a couple of breaths, wondering how it was possible to stop trembling if you weren't aware of having started.

'You've never heard of medics setting their own feelings aside to enable them to do what they need to do?' Her voice was barely more than a whisper.

'Yeah. We do it all the time. What did you set aside?'

This was Luc all over. He didn't miss things, but he wasn't confrontative or blaming. It was what made him so easy to talk to.

'Oh, being trapped in a basement. Not sure whether the roof's going to collapse on top of you.' That was an obvious answer and it was so much easier than the truth.

'Bertrand thinks not. Neither do the structural engineers who are working to get us out.'

'They *would* say that, wouldn't they? You can't tell me that you're not a little bit worried.'

Luc nodded, taking a sip of his hot chocolate. 'No, I can't tell you that. If you want me to accept that's what there is to it, then I will.'

Luc wouldn't ask any more, but it was clear that he knew there was more to it than that. Suddenly Pearl was tired of all of the times she'd told people that she was okay, and they'd believed her.

'So I'm not as good a liar as I used to be?'

He didn't flinch. 'You mean when you were abused? Fighting for your life? Probably not.' Luc didn't pull his punches, but he never let her feel that he didn't understand.

'Do you know what made me leave my ex?'

'When he broke your wrist?'

Pearl shook her head. 'No, that was when Henri found out what was going on. I didn't leave until six weeks later. I'd accepted an invitation to a family get-together on a Saturday afternoon, and my ex didn't want me going. He locked me in the basement for the whole weekend. It was dark and pretty cold down there—he'd switched off the power at the fuse box.'

She felt his arm tighten around her. Holding her close and safe from danger. 'Why didn't you tell me that? When I brought you down to see the undercroft.'

'It's not so much being underground. I can deal with that. It's being in the dark…' Pearl could feel herself trembling now. Her fingers were reaching for him, all on their own, and she couldn't stop them.

'There's something you need to know.' He turned, curling his other arm around her in a hug. Pearl looked towards the men sitting with Yvette and he tipped her chin back to face him. 'I don't care what anyone else thinks. Do you?'

'No.' Pearl leaned against his chest. 'They can think whatever they like.'

Luc nodded. 'There was never any question about my leaving here before you did. Now that I know this, I won't be letting you out of my sight, either.'

He couldn't promise that. Maybe he'd be hurt, maybe some of the others would be hurt and that would require them to split up. But Luc didn't seem to care; he was promising anyway. And somehow, Pearl believed him.

'I don't want to cramp your style, Luc.'

'Then you'll just have to keep up, won't you?' He smiled at her, brushing tears that she wasn't aware of having shed from her cheek. Pearl snuggled against him, feeling his chest rise and fall as he held her.

'Maybe we should just pretend this is a temporary wobble. And that I'm over it now.'

'Nah. This is just fine, Pearl. We need to get through this together, and that's exactly what we're going to do…'

Luc had been as good as his word. He'd held her for a while, and then they'd gone together to see how Yvette was doing. She'd relaxed in the company of her workmates and he'd decided that they could stay for a little while longer, as long as they didn't tire her out. Then Luc had taken Pearl by the hand, leading her back to the spot they'd made their own. It was a long wait, but he was there with her for every moment of it.

Two hours later everyone was suddenly watchful as

scraping and muffled voices sounded behind the door. Then a voice called down from the hole in the ceiling.

'Someone get the door for them, please… Just open it and then step back.'

Luc was on his feet, but he didn't move. Pearl nudged him forward. 'Go, Luc. Don't worry about me, just go.'

She was too late; Hugo was already picking his way towards the doorway. He stopped outside it, clearing a space so that it would open fully and then retreated back the way he'd come.

'What's happening?' Luc's voice betrayed a note of frustration. He was a driving force, someone who led rather than followed, and Pearl could see from his face how much his inaction had cost him. Maybe she shouldn't have allowed him to make that promise, but at the time she'd needed him so badly.

'I don't know. The slab of concrete that's blocking the way through to the undercroft is still in place. We can't get past it.' Hugo was as mystified as everyone else.

'Stand back from the doorway, everyone. Wait for us to come and get you.' The voice sounded again from the opening above their heads, and Luc called back up to say that everyone was clear.

The sound of hammer blows came from behind the concrete slab, and showers of dust and debris began to trickle downward from the top. Bertrand frowned.

'If they're going to try and break that up, we may as well all sit down. It'll take a while.'

No one was listening. Pearl kept her gaze on the slab, and two slightly larger pieces of concrete fell through onto the floor. Then she saw a face, peering through the gap that had been made at the top of the slab.

This wouldn't do. If Luc wasn't going to move, then

she had to. Pearl shook his hand from her arm, walking carefully forward into the doorway.

She caught her breath. The person peering through the gap was a woman, and when she saw Pearl her face broke into a broad grin. 'Hi there. I'm Maisie. Stay where you are. I'll be with you in a minute…'

Maisie disappeared for a moment and two heavy boots slid through the opening and dropped to the ground, followed by a thick protective jacket. Then a pair of legs and a woman's torso. Maisie was wearing a climbing harness, her weight supported by ropes which prevented her from falling to the ground on their side of the concrete slab as she wriggled through the opening.

Luc slipped past Pearl and hurried forward to help Maisie, almost getting kicked in the face for his pains. He grabbed her socked foot, cradling it between his hands to give her some purchase and received a muffled 'thanks'. Maisie levered herself through the gap, then called through to the team on the other side.

'Thanks, guys. You can let me down now.'

The ropes began to play out, and Luc reached up, catching Maisie by the waist and guiding her down. She unclipped the karabiners, and released the harness, then sat down to put her boots back on. Luc collected her jacket, helping her into it before they walked through into the basement.

'Hi there. It'll be a little while before we can move that slab, but we're making good progress on the other side. In the meantime I'm here to help get everyone ready. How's the woman who's been injured?'

'She has a broken arm and potentially cracked ribs, maybe a fractured ankle, but she's comfortable and her condition is stable. She'll have to be moved carefully,' Luc replied.

'Great. That's good. The main hospital is sending us through a stretcher and my guys will pass that through to us as soon as they can. Keep an ear out for them— they'll be letting us know what's going on any minute now. Any other injuries?'

'We have someone with two broken fingers.' Luc switched back to English. 'Is that a Canadian accent I hear?'

'Yep.' Maisie might be petite, but she had a huge smile. 'You're from…?'

'Paris. This is Pearl, she's a doctor from London.'

'Oh, hi, Pearl.' Maisie gripped Pearl's hand briskly. 'I've swapped mountain rescue in Ontario for a six-month attachment to the Paris Fire Service, where I've been learning a *lot* about underground rescue in a city setting. And I simply *love* Paris…' Maisie turned as a muffled voice sounded from the other side of the concrete slab.

'We've got a vacuum mattress and a basket stretcher that'll fit through the hole. What do you reckon?'

Pearl glanced at Luc and he nodded. 'That'll be great. Just what we need.' The vacuum mattress would wrap around Yvette, and help to keep her safe and comfortable as they transported her, while the basket stretcher was easy to manoeuvre.

'Right then.' Maisie turned towards the doorway, switching back to French to call to her colleagues. 'Guys. Send them through, will you…'

It hadn't taken long to finish clearing the antechamber. The men on the other side of the concrete block were concentrating on breaking it up so that the pieces could be hauled out of the way, and Charles had volunteered to help Maisie on this side.

'Nothing like being rescued by a pretty woman to turn a lad's head,' Bertrand had confided to Pearl. 'He'll probably get over it.'

'And if he doesn't?' Pearl understood the appeal. She didn't do a lot of crawling through holes in the course of her work, but the days when she felt that she'd made a difference to someone were always the best.

'Then he'll be doing a difficult job. You can tell me about the rewards, can't you?'

Pearl nodded. Following Luc down the steps and into the darkness had taught her something. She could be brave—but she knew that already. Leaving her husband, surviving the aftermath of her marriage. Having a child alone and protecting her from a world that Pearl couldn't bring herself to trust. That was one thing.

Luc was another thing entirely. She'd worked with him as if she were his right arm and he was hers. Believed him when he'd said they'd get out of here. Loved him, because that was what it took to feel that being by his side was the right place for her. Even though she was frightened, and every last one of her instincts was telling her that she had to get back to Celeste.

Even now, watching him talk to Yvette, explaining how the vacuum mattress would work and reassuring her... Even now she loved him. Maybe she still would when they finally climbed to safety, and could breathe fresh air and feel the sunshine. What would happen then?

CHAPTER THIRTEEN

LUC WAS JUST going with the flow now. He knew what needed to be done and how to make Yvette comfortable and safe for the journey out of here, and he did it. Never once allowing himself to lose sight of Pearl.

He didn't have to work at that. They'd been like the graceful arches of the undercroft, in perfect balance and rendering each other stronger. In a world where there was only this place, they could have loved each other. But Celeste was waiting for them. Depending on them for everything. And he couldn't bring himself to risk not being there for her.

Luc had told himself that he would have given up everything for his wife and his son, and he'd grieved over never having been given that chance. Never having had the opportunity to take the force of an oncoming vehicle himself and leave them unscathed. But he could do that for his daughter. He could let everything stay as it was, co-parenting with Pearl and allowing Celeste to take the best of them both. He and Pearl might be made for each other in every way that Luc could imagine, but acknowledging that would be a hard road for them. Too hazardous to contemplate when they had a child to think of.

The rescuers were still clearing a way through but they were making obvious progress. Everything was being done quickly but carefully, with the aim of avoiding panic, and Maisie had taken on the role of coordinating everyone. She caught Luc's eye, coming over to sit down with him next to Yvette.

'We should have a clear path out soon. I want Yvette to go first. A couple of our guys will be carrying the stretcher, and you'll be with her in case she needs anything along the way.'

'No…'

Maisie glared up at him. Clearly that hadn't been a request.

'Pearl's just as qualified as I am, and Yvette trusts her.'

'And you want her to go first?' A gleam of humour showed in Maisie's eye.

Of course he did. Luc had made Pearl a promise. 'I'm a doctor, Maisie. I want us both to be where we can be most useful. I can go with Bertrand.'

'Okay. Right behind Yvette, then.'

Luc chuckled. 'You could try that if you want. He's the boss and he won't be going anywhere until his guys are out. I'll make sure he's okay and keeping up.'

Maisie pursed her lips. 'Okay, that's fine with me. Any other touchy-feely doctor priorities you want to tell me about?'

'Nope. Any cuts or bruises you want to tell me about, tough guy?'

'Tough girl, if you don't mind. Don't imagine that I haven't seen that you're moving as if something's hit you right there.' Maisie jabbed her finger in the direction of the left side of his back, and Luc couldn't help confirming her suspicions by flinching back. 'Are you okay?'

'It'll hurt in the morning, but it's just a bruise. I'm fine to do whatever I need to now.'

'All right. Have it your way.' Maisie got to her feet, walking over to where Bertrand was sitting and squatting down on her heels to talk to him.

When Maisie formed them up in a line, ready to go, Pearl almost turned his plans on their head. She caught his eye, a look of protest on her face, and gestured in Maisie's direction. Luc broke ranks and strode over to her.

'We need you to look after Yvette.'

'But…' Pearl could clearly see the sense in that, but all the same she shot him an imploring look.

'I should stay with Bertrand, and he won't go ahead of Charles and Hugo. But trust me—I'll be right behind you all the way.' Luc allowed himself one moment of vulnerability. 'Please…'

Pearl's gaze met his. Her smile told him that she understood now, and knew Luc wasn't breaking his promise to stay with her. It didn't matter that they'd be a few metres apart, they'd be doing this together.

'Okay. See you on the other side.'

'Count on it.'

Temporary lighting had been strung up in the antechamber and the large, jagged lumps of concrete seemed even more forbidding than they had in the half-light. No one dared look up, and Luc could see Pearl ahead of him, shielding Yvette's face with her hand, as the men bearing the basket stretcher manoeuvred their way carefully over the uneven ground. Charles had lost his bravado, and he saw Hugo lay his hand on the lad's shoulder. Even Bertrand was silent, struggling alone with his fears, but he was keeping up and they'd be out of here soon.

When they reached the undercroft, it felt as if the worst was over. Bertrand sent a few words of encouragement forward to Charles, and Luc saw the boy's back straighten. They waited, while the stretcher was manoeuvred up the stairs by the rescue team, and Luc was rewarded with a glimpse of Pearl, walking through the door and into the library.

He climbed the stairs, making sure that Bertrand was steady on his feet, and holding firmly onto the banister. They walked silently along one corridor, and then another, emerging into the sunlit entrance to the library that seemed at the moment to be full of ghosts. The rescue team was covered in pale grey dust, their hair and eyes a startling contrast when they took their helmets off. Charles and Hugo were covered with dust and grime and when he looked down Luc saw that he was too.

A porter and a nurse from the A&E department were waiting with a wheelchair for Bertrand, and Luc ignored his protests, motioning him into it.

'Your wife's waiting for you...' The smiling nurse ensured Bertrand's cooperation with just a few words.

'Is my mum there?' Charles asked.

'You're Charles...? Yes, your mother's there too, and so is Hugo's wife.' Now that the nurse had their attention she wasn't going to waste it. 'Come along now—we don't want to keep them waiting, do we?'

Hugo shook his hand, and Bertrand managed to signal a goodbye before the porter got the wheelchair through the doors. Luc knew that there would be no one waiting for him, and that was just the way he wanted it, even if his heart did sink a little at the thought.

Then he saw her. He hadn't wanted Pearl to wait for him; he'd hoped she'd be on her way to see Celeste right now. But still he couldn't catch his breath. She smiled, her dark eyes a blaze of warmth among the dust in her hair and on her face, and Luc found himself propelled towards her, by forces he was powerless to resist.

In the darkness of the basement, Luc had seen everything. He'd been faced with losing Pearl, and crossed every boundary, allowing himself to love her. And now he was running scared, afraid of all that might mean. How giving in to what he most wanted to do would open up so many possibilities of failure.

He didn't dare touch her. She was all that he wanted, and all that he couldn't allow himself to have. She seemed to understand that things were different now, and didn't make a move to touch him.

'Your eyes look so blue,' Pearl murmured.

'Trick of the light.' It was a lame thing to say, but she smiled anyway.

'Yes, I suppose so.'

'Guys…' Suddenly there was more than one person in the room again, and they both turned towards Maisie. 'Guys, me and the team just want to express our respect. You were both amazing.'

Pearl and Maisie's handshake turned into a hug. 'We're really grateful to all of you. Next time I'm trapped in an underground room I'll give you a call…'

Maisie chuckled. 'And next time I need a medic who doesn't mind working by torchlight, I'll give *you* a call.' She turned to Luc, giving him a firm handshake. 'Go and get those bruises looked at, tough guy.'

'Sure. Thanks for everything, tough girl.'

They watched as Maisie rejoined her team and Pearl grinned up at Luc. 'Tough *girl*?'

'I told her she was a tough guy and she made a point of correcting me.'

'Quite right. And she's right about the bruises too—you need to get that looked at. Or I'll do it...'

Luc wanted nothing more than to feel her fingers on his skin. Have Pearl tell him that he was okay, because he was beginning to hurt now. But it was time for a course correction. 'I'll go over to A&E to see how the others are doing, and get it looked at there. Are you going to call Henri and get him to pick you up?'

'I...suppose so. But I'll come over to A&E with you first.'

'Don't you want to see Celeste?'

Pearl's hand strayed to her heart. Of course she did; Luc wanted to see her too. 'Yes. I really need to hold her. But I know she's fine and that Henri and Nathalie will have been looking after her...'

Suddenly she wound her arms around him. Luc couldn't have pulled away if he'd wanted to, because he needed this hug as much as Pearl obviously did. Maybe it was permissible, after an afternoon that had tested them both to their limits, but they had to somehow find their way back to being co-parents instead of lovers.

He could feel her heart beating. Almost feel his own, which seemed intent on bursting through his ribs just to get to hers. She was as soft as new-mown hay, as strong as summer wind that carried with it the scent of flowers. Leaving her might just be the hardest thing he'd ever do, but that wasn't going to stop Luc.

But Pearl was the first to step back. 'Henri. What are you doing here?'

'What do you suppose I'm doing?' Henri was leaning in the doorway, smiling. 'As soon as they called us to let us know that the tunnellers had broken through, I came to pick you up. Are you both okay?'

'Fine. At least *I'm* fine. Luc needs to go across to A&E to get his back checked over. He says it's just a bruise, but chunks of concrete were falling from the ceiling at the time.'

Henri nodded. 'We'll wait, then?'

'No, I've a few things to do. I want to follow up on Yvette, the young woman who was injured. I'll drop in later if that's okay?'

'Of course. Whenever you like.' Henri turned to leave and Pearl shot him an imploring look.

'You will come, won't you, Luc? Text me and let me know what's happening.'

'I'll come.' There would be no time to talk at the station tomorrow, and after that it would be two weeks before he saw Pearl. And they had to somehow find their way back to a place where their relationship was safe from the fears that the past had left them with.

Nathalie had bundled Pearl upstairs as soon as she set foot inside the front door. She emerged from a hot shower to find a nightdress and dressing gown laid out on her bed, and padded downstairs to the sitting room ready to face the world again. Henri was sitting on the floor, building bricks up for Celeste to knock back down again, and he tapped the little girl on her shoulder. 'Look who's here...'

Celeste's head spun around. 'Mummy!'

Pearl sent her daughter her biggest smile, along with a two-handed wave. She'd been determined not to make a big fuss of her, in case she thought that something was wrong, but she couldn't wait to hug her.

Then Celeste pulled herself up onto her feet, taking a few steps towards her. Pearl couldn't wait any longer, and fell on her knees in front of her daughter, sweeping her up in her arms. Celeste's delighted chuckles were all she needed to hear and Pearl hugged the little girl tight as tears streamed down her cheeks.

She had to wait more than an hour before she heard the doorbell. Nathalie went to answer it, and Celeste's head turned. She ran all the way over to the door and then lost her momentum and sat down suddenly on the carpet, her arms reaching for Luc as he entered.

'Hey there, sweetheart. How was your day?' Luc scooped the little girl up in his arms, and she began to babble in reply.

'Yeah? Sounds good. I had an interesting day too. Maybe not quite as exciting as yours…' He listened to Celeste's sing-song prattle attentively, nodding her on as if he understood and was agreeing with everything she said.

'You've been keeping Uncle Henri on his toes, I hope?' He nodded to her and Celeste nodded back.

'Bye-bye.' Celeste announced her intentions, and Luc chuckled, setting her back down onto her feet.

'Okay. Bye-bye, then.' He winced as he straightened, and Henri shot him a frown.

'You've had that looked at?'

Luc nodded. 'Yep. It's just a bruise.'

'I'll get you some ice, Luc,' Nathalie offered and Luc shook his head.

'Thanks, it's okay. I'll ice it when I get home.'

Pearl would have liked him to be here tonight. To be part of this warm circle of friends and family. To be with *her*. Someone that she could curl up and go to sleep with, knowing that they were both safe and he'd be there in the morning.

'Story!' Celeste announced. She obviously had her

own ideas for Luc and it seemed that she was the only person in the room that he was unable to resist.

'You want a story?' She nodded and he followed her over to the small coffee table where Pearl had stacked her books neatly. Celeste sorted through them, giving the ones she didn't want to Luc to hold, and stopping at the book he'd bought for her, holding it to her chest.

'That one?' He tapped the cover with his finger and she nodded.

'Go and give it to Mummy, then.' He grinned, replacing the rest of the books on the table, and Celeste ignored him, pushing the book towards Luc.

'She wants Papa to read to her,' Nathalie murmured softly.

'Papa…' Celeste mimicked the word and Henri and Nathalie exchanged smiles.

Suddenly Luc's gaze found Pearl's, his eyes full of the tenderness and joy that she'd grown to love. Luc had avoided calling himself Celeste's *daddy* because he hadn't wanted to confuse her, but Celeste seemed to have come to come to a compromise of her own.

'You have time to stay and read?' Pearl asked him.

'Papa…story!' Clearly things weren't moving fast enough for Celeste, and she became more insistent.

Luc nodded, taking the book from Celeste, and she scrambled up onto the sofa, banging her hands on the cushions next to her impatiently. 'She doesn't know what that means…'

Maybe her daughter instinctively knew a bit more than everyone thought. And maybe Luc needed to learn something. 'There's only one person who can teach her what it means, Luc.'

* * *

Nathalie and Henri had left to take a walk around the garden. If Celeste wanted to cuddle up on Luc's lap, have him turn the pages of the book, then that took nothing from Pearl. Watching them together was the most complete pleasure. As if all of the disjointed pieces of her life had been put back together again.

He took his time, and when they got to the end of the book, Celeste turned the pages back to the beginning again. Halfway through, for the third time, the little girl fell asleep in his arms. Luc carried her upstairs, kissing Celeste and whispering a promise that he'd see her again soon before he laid her down in the cot.

The little girl settled back to sleep almost immediately, but Pearl sat by her cot for a while, needing some reassurance of her own. This was everything she'd come to Paris for. Celeste was making a relationship with her papa, one which had a future. Everything had worked out better than she'd dared hope, and Pearl should leave it at that. Wanting more might be considered a hunger for life, after having been trapped together in a dark place, but it might also be greed that would spoil everything.

He was standing by the open patio doors, staring out at the garden. Luc turned when he heard Pearl behind him. 'She's sleeping?'

'Yes. She's tired tonight. Nathalie took her out to the park so that they could both work off a bit of energy while they were waiting for news.'

Luc nodded. 'Thanking them enough for these last few weeks isn't going to be easy, is it?'

'No, they've set the bar pretty high. I'm hoping they'll come to London and stay with me for a few weeks, later in the summer.'

'I'm sure they will if they can. Henri's always saying he loves Paris but he misses London.' Luc smiled. 'I'm already starting to identify with that.'

She'd come here and changed everything for him. 'Do you regret it, Luc? I know that you love Celeste.'

He gave her a mystified look. 'Should I regret that? I don't. I'm so grateful for the chance to be a part of her life.' His eyes softened as he looked down at her. 'And of yours.'

It all sounded so straightforward. They wanted the same things and Pearl couldn't deny that the same chemistry still sizzled between them. It seemed one small step away from being a family, instead of just co-parents.

The feeling just wouldn't stop growing. It was as if someone had suddenly thrown back the curtains in a darkened room, and sunshine was streaming through the windows. Pearl hadn't expected this, but she could no longer deny that it was what she wanted.

'When I came to Paris, I couldn't see myself ever living anywhere but London. That's changed for me now.' Even if it still provoked a tremor of unease. The locks on her doors still meant safety. A home where she could take control of her own destiny.

His face darkened suddenly. 'What do you mean? Is this because of last night?'

'Last night was wonderful, but I felt the same as you did about it. It was something special for just us to share, but it wasn't going to work long-term. It was hard to give that up, but I could do it when I thought that it meant keeping what we have—our friendship and the chance for Celeste to have two loving parents.'

'That's how I feel about it. So what's changed?'

'This afternoon I felt… You saw me through it, Luc.

All of my fears and the times I thought we might not get out of there. Can't we see each other through becoming a real family?'

'What happens if we fail, Pearl?'

'We won't fail. Just as we didn't fail this afternoon. I know that your work here and the library are really important to you, and I won't ask you to give up your memories. But I could come to Paris, and I know that we'd be able to make things work.' Pearl was starting to feel uncomfortable now. Too needy. As if she were begging for Luc's attention and love, the way she'd begged her ex-husband. She took a breath.

Maybe she'd gone too far. Offered too much. Had she really read the signs so badly?

'It's just something I wanted to put on the table, Luc. Doesn't Celeste deserve the chance for us to be a real family?'

'I want to take it back off the table. Celeste is just a child, and it's up to us to make the kind of relationship with each other that we know is going to last. That involves boundaries and… I think it's best if I book a hotel when I come for the weekend.'

Pearl could feel her face flushing with disappointment and shame.

'You're going to make that decision for me, are you? Without even trying to explore what we might be together?' All of the decisions her ex had made for her seemed to crowd in on her, mocking everything she'd done to leave them behind.

'No, I'm making the decision for me. We thought that we could leave our own relationship to evolve but today has taught me that I can't do that. I care about you, Pearl, but I just don't see how a relationship can work between us. We're both bringing too many fears with us, and there's too much at stake to risk failing.'

It was the ultimate rejection. If Luc hadn't loved her, then she could have accepted it. But this afternoon had forced them to acknowledge something that had been staring them in the face all along. She loved Luc and she knew that he loved her. And now he was choosing to turn his back on that.

But she could hold her head high. She could preserve the one thing that she and Luc were both fully committed to, his relationship with Celeste.

'I'll see you in two weeks, then. When you come to London.'

He gave her a questioning look. 'Not tomorrow? At the station?'

'No, that's fine. Henri and Nathalie will be bringing me to Gare du Nord tomorrow and they'll come with me right up to the barrier. It'll be a lot easier that way.' There would be no goodbye kisses, no promises from Luc. They were all gone now.

'Okay. Would you mind texting me when you arrive home? Just to let me know?' Luc had clearly got the message, and was keeping to the plan. Pearl supposed that this would get easier; at least they knew now exactly where they stood.

'Yes, of course.'

'I'll be off, then, and let you get an early night. Safe journey, and I'll see you in two weeks…' Luc hesitated, and for one moment Pearl thought he had changed his mind. That the last moment had taught him that he couldn't bring himself to shatter all they had together.

But then he turned, opening the patio doors and walking across the lawn, to where Henri and Nathalie were examining the blooms on a spreading peony. Pearl stepped back from the window, but there was no need. As he took the path that led around the side of the house Luc's gaze was set straight ahead of him, never once straying in her direction.

She was crying. Silent tears, the kind she'd learned to hide during her marriage. She went to the kitchen, splashing her face with cold water and then dabbing it with a towel.

'You have said your goodbyes?' Nathalie's voice sounded behind her. She and Henri had clearly lost interest in the garden now and if Nathalie saw her tears she clearly thought they were evidence of a temporary parting.

'Yes. Luc gave Celeste a kiss and a cuddle before we put her down to sleep. We thought it was better to say goodbye now.'

Nathalie nodded in approval. 'So much nicer than doing it at the station. Are you packed for the morning?'

'There's a little more to do and I can finish off in the morning. I think I could do with an early night…'

CHAPTER FOURTEEN

HE'D HAD TO do it. That hadn't made it any easier.

Last night had been wonderful—maybe even inevitable—but neither of them had pretended that it could change anything. But today had been the kind of day that called everything into question. The only things that he had to hang on to were their own promises, and when Pearl had suggested breaking them he hadn't even allowed himself to think about it.

They had a plan, which they'd both agreed would work. An extreme situation might knock them off course for a little while, but those feelings would pass. The one thing that stayed the same was his determination to keep both Pearl and Celeste safe. Not to hurt them with wild schemes and what-ifs.

Driving was really hurting his back now, and his first priority was getting home in one piece. Luc took an easy route, without too many twists and turns, and when he got back to his apartment he made straight for the ice packs in the freezer. After half an hour the pain had numbed a little and he went into the bathroom to examine the damage. The bruise was beginning to show and, as the doctor in A&E had said, he'd be aching for a while. But there was no evidence of anything more serious.

'She'll understand.' He took the opportunity to look

himself in the eye and transmit a little advice. 'They're her decisions too. What we both wanted...'

Or maybe Pearl wouldn't. Maybe she'd seen something that he couldn't and he'd been too inflexible to listen. The thought nagged at Luc as he wandered into his bedroom.

Pearl had left the faint scent of flowers behind her, which he hadn't noticed when he'd got up this morning. Luc folded back the shutters and opened a window, but when he walked back past the bed he could still sense her fragrance. Picking up a pair of sweatpants, he walked out into the living space.

He woke, stiff and sore, on the sofa; the lights of Paris shining through the windows. Stretching painfully, he walked over to the freezer, replacing the old ice pack and getting a new one. He poured himself a glass of water and sat down on one of the high stools at the counter.

There had to be a way of working this out. Cause and effect, risk and reward. There was no question that he'd be there for Celeste, but Pearl... He had no right to risk her happiness, but he just couldn't give her up. He pulled a pad of sticky notes out of one of the kitchen drawers, making a list. Pros and cons.

That didn't really cover it; the structure was more organic than two columns. Luc decided on a separate note for each entry on the lists, sticking the notes onto an empty stretch of wall between the kitchen and living area. Moving them around, grouping them by importance...

The morning might provide an answer. Luc returned to the sofa, sitting for a while with the ice pack propped between his back and the cushions. Then fatigue began to overtake him again and he lay down, pulling the throw across him for warmth. Comfort. Whatever was going to get him through the night.

* * *

The jumble of sticky notes on the wall had grown on Saturday. On Sunday he'd reorganised and colour-coded everything. And on Monday evening he'd added a few coloured threads, connecting similar thoughts which fell into different groups. When he returned home from work on Tuesday, he sat staring at the conundrum. The matrix of ideas was beginning to look more complete, but still failing to provide any concrete answers.

A knock at the door interrupted his reverie. Henri was standing outside, a four-pack of bottled lager in his hand.

'I thought I'd pop in, and find out how things are at the library.' Henri handed him the lager, the bottles clearly straight out of a fridge and cool to the touch.

'Come in…' Luc waved him across to the sofa, which mercifully faced away from the sticky notes on the wall. Henri could have saved himself a journey and asked about the library at work, but cornering his current person of concern outside the hospital was much more his style.

Luc hurried to fetch a bottle opener and two glasses, putting them down on the coffee table between them. 'It's good of you to come. The structural engineers have been in doing a survey since Saturday and I should get their report at the end of the week. At the moment no news is good news, because they haven't found anything that urgently needs shoring up.'

Henri nodded, opening his beer. 'Must have been a shock, though. The library means…so many different things to you.'

In truth, Luc had hardly thought about it. He'd spent time there over the weekend, talking to contractors and structural experts, then found himself on the terrace re-assuring the students who'd gathered there to drink coffee and try to peer through the windows. But his heart was too numb, too broken, to properly register what was going on.

'Remember when I first showed you around the library? You'd just come back from London to take up the post of head of neurology. You know how much we've done since then. We can do this.'

Henri nodded. 'I've no doubt of it. How's Marthe doing?'

'She was there on Saturday and very upset. I told her to go home and take a few days, but she popped in to see me first thing this morning, looking much better. She's been on the library's social media page, giving updates and asking for volunteers to help tidy up once we have the all-clear to go back in there. There's been quite a bit of interest.'

'Good. That's great.' Henri was looking at him as if Luc wasn't really answering any of his questions. 'I see you've got a to-do list...' He gestured over his shoulder.

Luc took a swig of his beer. Henri must have noticed it on the way in, and if he didn't get a reaction, then maybe he'd leave it alone.

But Henri was one of the smartest people he knew, and simply ignoring what he'd said generally didn't work. He smiled amicably, getting to his feet and walking over to take a look. Henri stared for a moment and then abruptly turned away.

'Sorry. That's none of my business, is it? Although in the process of working out that it wasn't my business, I saw enough to find that I've been asking all the wrong questions.'

It was almost a relief that Henri *did* know, although he was friends with Pearl too and it put him in an awkward position. 'I asked you in, and I'm drinking your beer. Looking at the wall isn't something you need to apologise for. And yes, I'm concerned about the library, but it's not first on the list of things that are bothering me at the moment.'

Henri nodded, leaning back against the counter that separated the kitchen space from the living area. 'I'm really sorry to hear that. You both seemed to be getting on so well. Working things out.'

'We were. A little too well, perhaps. It's complicated...'

'Yes.' Henri was clearly resisting the temptation to look back at the wall. 'I can see that.'

Luc shot him a reproving look. 'You know it is, Henri. Pearl needs to feel safe. She deserves that, after all she's been through.'

Henri nodded. 'You've come through a lot too.'

'I guess... I know what it's like to lose someone, and I don't want to put either of us through that. It's different with Celeste. We're her parents and there's no question about us both being there for her. But Pearl and I—we both had a choice to make.'

'And you're not sure you made the right one?' Henri walked back to the sofa, sitting down and picking up his lager.

'I thought we did. But Pearl's questioned it, and... maybe she's right. I don't know, hence the...' Luc waved his hand towards the wall. 'I thought that if I could make sense of it all, then the answer would be obvious.'

'This isn't a version of your mind palace, is it?'

'No. My mind palaces are generally a great deal tidier. This is more like a matrix for decision making.' Or maybe it was just something to numb the pain. Writing down what he *did* know had allowed Luc to avoid thinking about all of the things he was unsure of.

Henri sipped his lager thoughtfully. Luc drank his down, and reached for a second bottle.

'Has it occurred to you that you're over-thinking this?'

Yes, it had. Luc put the bottle back on the table, deciding he didn't need any more to drink. 'What makes you say that?'

Henri puffed out a breath. 'I can't imagine the things you've both had to cope with, but what I *do* know is that you're both determined people. It strikes me that there are only two questions you need to ask yourself.'

Luc couldn't help asking. 'Which are…?'

'Do you love her? And can you commit yourself to making the relationship work?'

Was it really that simple? 'I'm going to think that over.'

'Bear in mind that your first answer might be your best.'

Luc chuckled. 'Am I to assume that Nathalie's out this evening? Since you're prowling Paris with lager and good advice.'

'Book club. She won't be home until late.'

'Stay for dinner, then. I got an extra steak on the way home, to put in the freezer, and I've a bottle of red I think you'd like…'

When they'd returned to London, Celeste had slipped back into their routine without too much trouble. Pearl, on the other hand, was finding it excruciatingly hard.

She had all that she'd hoped for. But then, she'd dared to hope for more, and losing it had brought all of the old insecurities flying back. *Did I expect too much of him? Was I too bold?*

She'd learned to think differently when she'd left her ex-husband. Encouraged by people around her, she'd spoken out and made a life for herself.

Luc had allowed Pearl a glimpse of how things should work, in a fairy-tale world and then in reality. He talked and he listened, and he'd expected her to do the same, so that they could come to an agreement. He'd asked if making love with him again had changed her mind about their relationship, but he was mistaken. It had simply reflected a process between two people who cared about each other and who valued each other's assertiveness.

But there was one thing she was definitely guilty of. Pearl hadn't thought her offer to join Luc in Paris through properly. How it might affect her career, the feeling of well-being that surrounded her in the safety of her London home. More to the point, how it might affect Celeste.

She'd thought only of Luc's love. How she and Celeste might thrive in its warmth, and how Luc might thrive in the love they had to give. Maybe he'd been right in turning her down, maybe not, but that was what he'd done. Pearl had made him choose and now she had to live with his decision.

'It's going to be fine, my love.' Celeste was fast asleep now, in her cot. 'Papa will come. He said he'd be here for you, and he will.'

Pearl could trust Luc on that score. She leaned over, putting Mr Pin-gin and Teddy within reach. 'It's not too late for you, sweet girl…'

Maybe it was for Pearl. But she would teach her daughter to be different from her, to see the mistakes she'd made and learn from them.

* * *

There was a tiredness about days that didn't have Luc in them. A grey fatigue that was weary of life and couldn't look forward to the future.

'Don't you worry about it, dear.'

Glenys Hughes had suffered a haemorrhagic stroke, caused not by a clot but by bleeding in the brain. Pearl had surgically clipped the neck of the aneurysm, and the post-operative angiogram had shown the procedure to be a success. But there was still a long road ahead.

'Worry about what, Glenys?'

Glenys frowned. She'd improved a lot in the last few days, but was still prone to losing the thread of a conversation. 'You looked a little worried.'

'Sorry. That's my resting face, I was just rereading your notes. There's nothing to be worried about there.' Pearl grinned. It was probably okay not to smile so much when she was operating, but when her patients were awake she had to make an effort.

'What do they say?'

Pearl had already told Glenys, but she went through the important parts again, remembering to smile as she did so. Encouragement was so important to stroke patients, who were struggling to relearn so much. The brain could form new connections and re-route signals through areas that had not been destroyed, but it was an exhausting process.

'The results I have from the angiogram show that the bleeding has stopped completely now. We can start working on helping you to use your hand a little better...' Pearl glanced up at the information board that was fixed to the wall beside the bed. 'I see that one of the things you'd most like to get back to doing is knitting.'

'Is that what it says? I don't think I have my proper glasses on.' Glenys's eyes had been tested and her sight was unchanged. But comprehending the shapes formed by words was going to take a little time.

'Can you see this?' Pearl patted the rows of knitting, threaded onto a pair of chunky plastic needles, which were on the table by the bed.

'Oh yes. It's a lovely colour, isn't it?'

'Gorgeous. And the wool's nice—it feels so soft.'

Glenys reached out, feeling the ball of wool. 'Yes, it does, doesn't it? My daughter got it for me and did the first few rows, but I can't seem to get around to trying it. Not with my hand the way it is.' She indicated the curled fingers on her right hand. The contraction wasn't as severe as some patients experienced, but it would still take a lot of work to restore movement and sensation enough to allow Glenys to do fine manual tasks.

'Wait till you see Jo, your physiotherapist. She has all kinds of ideas that might help. Would your daughter mind if I did a row?' It wasn't all about manual skills; hand-eye coordination played a part as well.

'Not in the slightest. I might tell her I did it. That'll cheer her up.'

Pearl laughed, picking up the knitting and shifting around so that Glenys could see what she was doing from the side that would normally face her. She formed the first stitch, and Glenys shook her head.

'Slip the first stitch, dear. I find it makes the edges a little firmer.'

That was exactly what Pearl wanted her to do. She undid the stitch and slipped it. Glenys was watching her and even though her fingers weren't responding, her hand moved in her lap along with Pearl's. 'Just give your yarn a little tug if the stitches are getting loose.' Pearl responded and Glenys nodded.

'I think I can do that. If I can get my fingers to wake up.'

'That's what we're planning on helping you with.' Pearl would make a note for Jo to speak with Glenys's daughter when she next visited, and show her how to encourage her mother. It would take time and patience, along with determination on Glenys's part...

Six beds, in the ward. Six boards, wiped clean for each new patient and then filled with their choices for care, their likes and dislikes. The things they wanted most to regain, which was such an important part of helping people with brain injuries recover. They were always different. Glenys had chosen her knitting, reading her favourite novels and being able to babysit her grandchildren again. Glenys might not be able to achieve all that she wanted, but everything here was aimed at encouraging her and showing her how best to try.

Pearl had glanced at the boards a thousand times as she talked to patients. But she'd never stopped to wonder what might be on her most-wanted list. Maybe it would be Luc's touch, or his beautiful blue eyes. The way his mind worked, his humour or his warmth. But he'd be there, along with Celeste and the family they might make. A part of her life that was worth trying her best for, even if she might not get it.

'Thanks, Glenys.'

'Oh. What for, dear?'

Pearl grinned, finishing off the row and putting the needles down, within Glenys's reach. 'Reminding me how much I like knitting...'

* * *

It had come as a surprise when Pearl had emailed him, saying she'd like some time alone to talk with him, and that she'd asked her friend Jen, from the hospital, to baby-sit on Saturday morning. Because time alone was just what Luc had wanted to suggest, but since this was his first visit he'd decided to leave the agenda to Pearl.

He'd been up early, and thought that he might doze on the train, but Luc had been counting every mile as they sped past the window. Every minute that brought him closer to her.

Luc had nothing to declare at customs. He was visit-ing friends for the weekend, with no preconceptions and no defined purpose. The only thing he was carrying that was of any value was a heart that wanted to love Pearl.

Pearl's house was in a quiet, tree-lined street, ten min-utes' walk from the underground station. As he turned into the front path, he saw a red light flicker in the cor-ner of a camera mounted high in the porch, and realised that he could be seen from inside. He smiled, wondering whether Pearl was feeling as anxious as he was.

She answered the door almost immediately. Pearl was wearing a white cotton summer dress, which emphasised the colour in her hair and eyes. Her bare feet, on the pol-ished wooden floor of the hallway, made her seem al-most sylphlike.

'You're right on time. There were no delays, I take it.' Pearl stepped back from the doorway, beckoning him inside.

'No, everything went like clockwork.' Luc saw that she automatically twisted the handle on the inside of the front door down when she closed it, and heard a multi-point locking system engage. There was an alarm console on the wall in the hall as well, but Pearl seemed to notice neither of them; all of her attention was on him.

This was her safe place. Luc knew that, but being here suddenly made him understand how important it was to her. How much of a risk she'd taken in coming to France to find him.

'I dare say you could do with some coffee...' She was padding along the bright hallway, towards the open door of the kitchen, and Pearl turned to flash him a smile.

'I'd love some, thank you.' He reached into his shoulder bag, pulling out the tightly wrapped package. 'Nathalie sent you some of the coffee that you said you liked.'

'She did? That's so nice of her. Let's have that, shall we?' She laid the package down on the kitchen worktop, opening it. 'Tell me what's been going on, Luc. Have you heard from Yvette at all?'

'I got her number from Bertrand, and went to see her. She's on the mend and getting a lot of support from her family and friends.'

'Good. That's great, she was so brave about it all, and I was hoping she wouldn't just shrug it all off, without talking about it.'

'No one's allowing her to do that. She's taking things slowly and making good progress, both mentally and physically.'

Pearl nodded, her gaze softening suddenly. 'And the library? Tell me all about that.'

'The library's closed at the moment, but we've had the structural engineer's report and the good news is that the place isn't about to fall down. There's going to be some clearing up, and it's been decided to reinforce the area where the collapse was and close it off—it's of no historical value.'

'And the undercroft? Is that all right?'

Luc nodded. 'The structural engineer was really impressed with how stable it was. He's a member of a historical buildings consortium and they've asked whether they can do an in-depth investigation down there to increase their knowledge. I have to get it rubber-stamped by the hospital board, but I've put in my own recommendation and heard informally that they're wanting to go ahead.'

Pearl was all smiles. 'That's great, Luc. You must have missed the library so much.'

Luc's first instinct was to shrug the idea off, and then he remembered what he was here for. 'I thought I would. I've had more important things on my mind, though.'

There were questions in her gaze that Pearl wasn't asking. Now that they were here, together, Luc's resolutions weren't as easy to put into practise as he'd promised himself they would be.

'We should talk, Pearl.' If he put his intentions into words then maybe the realities would come a little easier.

Pearl pressed her lips together thoughtfully. 'Do you mind? That Celeste isn't here at the moment?'

'I'm looking forward to seeing her, of course. But I came to see you too.'

Her cheeks flushed pink, and suddenly she was all motion and activity, fetching a bottle of sparkling water from the fridge, and putting coffee cups and glasses onto a tray. She added a plate of pastries, along with a wry apology that they were probably not up to Paris standards, and led him through to a light, airy sitting room.

Two small sofas stood by the open windows, and Pearl waved him towards one, sitting down opposite him on the other and pouring the coffee. The light muslin curtains, billowing in the breeze, gave a feeling that the outside was welcome inside, but carefully concealed window locks and sensors said otherwise. Keeping Pearl safe was fast becoming a different proposition.

He sipped his coffee, and waited. Pearl was clearly deciding what she wanted to say, and Luc wanted to hear it. More than anything.

'I think…' She glanced at him as if wanting permission to say what she thought, and Luc nodded her on. 'I think that we should each say what *we* want. Start from there…'

'Do you want to go first? Or shall I?' This didn't feel like a struggle anymore. Trying to do the right thing, even if it hurt.

'Will you?' Pearl shot him an entreating look, and the thought that she would rely on him for this much at least gave Luc courage.

'I love you, Pearl. I know that it won't be easy for either of us to make a new relationship, but I believe we can and I'd like to try.'

Pearl caught her breath, her hands flying to her mouth. Tears began to run down her cheeks and Luc could hardly bear to stay still, waiting for her to say something. Then Pearl took his world and tipped it upside down.

'I love you too, Luc. I believe we can as well.'

CHAPTER FIFTEEN

THIS WASN'T WHAT Pearl had been expecting. She wasn't entirely sure what she *had* expected, but it definitely wasn't this. He'd changed everything with three words. *I love you.*

And now he'd got to his feet, coming to sit with her, his arm around her shoulders. Pearl couldn't stop crying, although whether it was from happiness or fear she wasn't sure.

'This is terrifying, isn't it?'

He said all the right things. All of the things that she needed to hear if she was going to dare to love him. Pearl reached for a paper napkin from the tray, and dabbed at her eyes with it.

'Yes. It's nothing you've done, Luc… But you just seemed so sure that we couldn't make it together. That we'd hurt each other.'

'I was wrong. I tried to reason everything through but I missed one obvious thing. We couldn't choose whether or not to love each other. And if we recognise that love, then we can do anything we put our minds to. We won't fail each other, and we're not going to fail Celeste, either.'

Pearl reached for his hand, feeling his fingers curl around hers. 'I like that thought. That what's good for

Celeste is good for both of us. And that what's best for you and I is best for her. Because we're a family.'

He nodded. 'Although there may be times when I'm a little overprotective or afraid of what's coming next. I want you to tell me…'

'I can do that. If you'll tell me when I'm pushing you away. Trying not to be the person I was when I was with my ex-husband, because I know in my heart that I'm not anymore. And that you'll take care of me and love me.'

Luc smiled. 'Yeah. I can do that.' He raised her hand to his lips. 'I love you. And I'm sorry that I allowed you to leave Paris in any doubt of that.'

'You wanted the best for me and Celeste. I was falling into old habits, and accepted what you said, because I felt that you were rejecting me.'

'I'll never do that, Pearl. May I kiss you?'

Pearl loved this slow, almost formal style of foreplay, because she knew exactly where it led. Right to a place where taking what they wanted seemed the most natural and best thing in the world. But there was something she needed to do first.

'Hold that thought. And feel free to elaborate…' She leaned forward, brushing her lips against his cheek. 'I have to make a call first. I won't be long.'

Luc chuckled, nodding. 'Go. See how our girl is doing.'

When Pearl walked back into the sitting room, she had good news.

'Celeste's having a great time, playing in the garden. And before you ask, Jen and Eddie both work at the hospital. Eddie's a senior paramedic and Jen's a counsellor. They have two boys under five, and Celeste knows them well—we babysit for each other all the time.'

Luc nodded. 'I wasn't going to ask.'

Pearl sat down next to him on the sofa. 'Well, you should have done.'

He chuckled. 'Yes. I wanted to. It's not that I don't trust you.'

'I love that you care enough to want to know, Luc. And…' She put her arms around his neck, and Luc moved closer. 'I said that I'd collect her at about four o' clock. Unless you'd like to go earlier?'

'If four's good for you and Celeste, then it's good with me too.' He moved closer, his lips just a whisper away from hers. 'May I kiss you now?'

She wasn't afraid anymore. 'Yes, Luc. Please…'

Pearl had wondered whether making love with Luc could ever be as good as the last time. But it had been better.

'Have you been practising in the last two weeks?' She was curled up in his arms now.

Luc chuckled. 'No. What makes you say that?'

She kissed him. 'This time was different. Better, if that's at all possible.'

'Maybe because this is a beginning. We're not planning on making it an ending.' He shifted a little so that they were face-to-face on the pillows.

'I can't wait to find out what happens next, in this future we've created for ourselves. You can't leave the library right now…'

'And London—this house—it's your safe place. That means a lot to you.'

Pearl nodded. 'Then we'll have to find a solution. We can't go back, not now.'

He pulled her close, kissing her. 'We *won't* go back. I promise.'

They were hungry now, and they'd have to leave in an hour to fetch Celeste. They showered the scent of love-making from their bodies, and went downstairs in search of food.

'Crepes? They're quick and easy.' Luc peered over her shoulder into the refrigerator.

'Easy if you know how.' Pearl turned, kissing him. 'I'll make them.'

'You cook?'

Her question seemed to surprise Luc. 'I live alone, and I eat. That involves cooking from time to time. Why?'

'It's just something to add to my collection of things I know about you.'

He laughed. 'Okay. You can sit down and tell me what your favourite colour is…'

Halfway through the most delicious crepes that Pearl had ever tasted, he laid his fork down. 'I have an idea. What about this for a way forward?'

'Go on.'

'Suppose… Would you like to come to Paris for a year? I'd be able to set the library back on its feet, and I could take that opportunity to reorganise it—'

Pearl almost choked on the food she'd just put into her mouth. 'What? You can't do that, Luc.'

'Why not?'

'You're going to *reorganise* the library? What about all of your memories…?'

'It's about time that I stopped trying to lock them away. They need to be free. Camille was always on the move and it doesn't suit her.'

'You said her name, Luc.' He'd never done that before, always referred to 'his wife'.

He pressed his lips together. 'Do you mind?'

'The reverse. I'd like to get to know a little about her, if you feel able to tell me.'

He nodded. 'I'd like that too. What's your ex-husband's name? You never refer to him by name, either.'

Pearl felt a quiver of fear shake her. 'Why do you want to know?'

'Because I'm here with you now. I'll protect you from the fears he left behind him.'

Pearl knew that he would. That Luc could do that. 'His name is John. And I'm not going to waste my time on telling you about him.'

'That's fine. And if you do decide to come to Paris, there's something I need to give you, in return. You get to reorganise the apartment—exactly the way you want it. You wouldn't be able to practise until you were certi-fied, but you could spend a few months doing…something you've always wanted to do. Anything.'

'Your apartment's fine as it is, Luc.'

'I like it. But if you're going to live there, you might want to put a few extra locks on the doors and install an alarm system.'

Pearl chuckled. 'What, you think I'm going to lock *you* out?'

'You could, I suppose. Hopefully not for too long, Henri and Nathalie might get sick of me. My point is that you've made a safe place for yourself here. I won't take that away from you.'

'Do I get to lock you in?'

He grinned. 'Yeah. What did you have in mind? Baby-sitting duties. Cooking, maybe…'

'Sex?'

'Absolutely. Anytime you like, day or night.'

'Careful what you wish for, Luc.' Pearl had one last

request and this one was serious. 'Whenever I need a friend. Or when you need one?'

'Then especially.'

That sounded like a life. Two lives, shared. They could acknowledge the burdens they both brought with them, and find a way of moving past them.

'Okay. It's a deal, Luc.' She smiled at him holding out her hand.

He grinned, shaking his head. 'We're not going to seal our bargains like that. I have something that I'd like to give you. I know that it'll be a while before you want to talk about marriage...'

'To be honest I wouldn't know what to say, Luc. It's not that I don't love you...'

'I know. And it's fine. I want to wait until you're ready. But I do need to make you one promise, Pearl.' He took something from his pocket, holding it out for her to see. 'This is what my answer's going to be.'

The ring was beautiful, a twist of yellow and white gold strands. And Luc was holding it so that she could see something engraved inside it.

'*Yes?* That's your promise?'

'If and when you get to the point of wanting to marry me, then my answer will be yes. Always, and without hesitation.'

Pearl felt a tear run down her cheek. 'That's so... It's everything I want, Luc. For you to wait for me, and be there when I'm ready. Thank you.'

He was smiling, as if a great weight had been lifted from his shoulders. 'Would you like to wear it?'

Pearl took a breath, holding out her hand. 'I'd like you to put it on my finger. If you don't mind...'

He was on his feet, hurrying around to her side of the table. Luc fell to one knee… 'Too much?'

'No, it's just right. On this finger, please Luc.' She pointed to the ring finger of her left hand.

He was smiling as he lifted her hand to his lips. Then he slid the ring onto her finger. Pearl started to laugh with joy, kissing him.

'It's beautiful, Luc. Thank you so much. My yes ring.'

He chuckled. 'I was going to call it a promise ring. But *yes ring* is better.'

She kissed him again, feeling his limbs tremble against hers. This was a promise that neither of them were going to break.

'Shall we go and fetch our girl, Luc? So we can all be together?'

He nodded. 'Yeah. I'd really like that.'

EPILOGUE

Six months later

PEARL HAD MOVED to Paris a month later. Since then, she and Luc hadn't spent one night apart.

Not all of those nights had been magical. Celeste mostly slept through the night now, but sometimes she needed to be comforted back to sleep. Sometimes there was talking to do, things to work out between her and Luc. And there had been a few nights when fear had overwhelmed the promise of this new life. But they'd stuck together, and seen each other through the bad times.

Pearl's French needed to be of a high standard before she could practise in France, and they'd become a bilingual household. Luc spoke only French and Celeste's sponge-like ability to absorb everything going on around her meant that she understood all that her papa said to her. Pearl had to work a little harder, but afternoons spent volunteering at the library or the hospital were helping a lot.

Luc's parents had been thrilled to find out that they had a new granddaughter, and visits to London kept them in touch with family and friends there. It was a busy schedule for both of them, but it might be slowing down soon.

'Where's Celeste?' Pearl had brought Luc's cup of morning coffee up to their bedroom in the house in London.

'In her room. She and Teddy have some private business to attend to.'

Pearl laughed. 'So she told you "*Papa bye-bye*"?' Celeste had learned a lot of new words and she strung them together into short sentences now.

'Yep.' He put his hand to his heart. 'It's okay. I'm dealing with the rejection.'

'Glad to hear it.' Pearl put his coffee down on the bedside table, climbing onto the bed next to him. 'We'll both be facing a bit more of it as she starts to make her way in the world.'

Luc smiled, putting his arm around her shoulders. 'Celeste Helena Johnson Belange. It's a big name for such a little girl.'

'She's growing into it fast, Luc. And it seems only right that we should do it now, if I'm going to change my name to yours next weekend.' They were here in London to re-register Celeste's birth, with Luc's name on the certificate as her father. The three of them would be going to the registry office together this morning, and then there would be a barbeque in the afternoon. They'd be going back to Paris for their wedding next Saturday.

'I would have waited. As long as it took until you felt good about doing this.' Luc hadn't pressed Pearl, waiting for her to be comfortable with the commitments they were making. But three months ago, on a sunny Saturday afternoon, she'd asked Henri and Nathalie to baby-sit, and walked with Luc along the banks of the Seine. The marry-me ring that Pearl had given him matched her yes ring and they couldn't wait to fulfil that promise with their marriage vows.

'I know you would, but I feel good about it now and I can't wait. We're a family and it's important to me that we acknowledge that.'

'How are you feeling this morning? No morning sickness?' Pearl had shown him the positive pregnancy test a week ago, and Luc hadn't stopped smiling since.

'No, none yet. It's early days and hopefully it'll hold off until after the wedding.' She leaned over, kissing him. 'I never thought we'd get pregnant so quickly this time around.'

'Just goes to show that lightning *does* strike twice in the same place.'

'Or maybe I underestimated the effects of Paris and a French lover…'

Luc laughed. 'Don't make me choose between an understandable pride in the city of my birth and scientific fact.'

'I happen to know of a library that's full of scientific facts, and which manages to be a magical place as well.' Pearl hugged him. 'You know, of all the wonderful things we've done together, all of the pieces of magic aren't the things that mean the most to me.'

'No?' He chuckled. 'Does that mean that I have to stop trying?'

'No, and I'm not going to, either. But what makes the magic so special are the other things we do for each other. When I'm sad and confused you smile and make me a cup of tea, and let me just breathe for a while until it's all right again. When everything seems overwhelming, you remind me of all that we've achieved already.'

'And you helped me to hope and dream for the future

again. You know, the thing I'm looking forward to most today is signing my name next to yours.'

'Me too. And we'll sign our names together again, in a week's time.' Pearl let out a contented sigh.

He brushed his lips against hers. One of the small things that made the magic so exquisite. Luc chuckled as they heard Celeste's solemn goodbye, obviously aimed at Teddy and Mr Pin-gin, and she raced into the room.

'Hey, sweetheart. What's all the rush?' He leaned over, scooping the little girl up and putting her onto the bed between them. 'Don't you know that this moment is just perfect?'

* * * * *

If you enjoyed this story, check out these other great reads from Annie Claydon

Mistletoe Kiss to Heal His Heart
The Doctor's Italian Escape
The GP's Seaside Reunion
Neurosurgeon's IVF Mix-Up Miracle

All available now!

A RIVALRY
IN PARADISE

BECKY WICKS

MILLS & BOON

To the local and international NGOs who together are helping to implement sustainable waste management and plastic reduction programs in the Maldives. It's a joint effort, along with many others taking urgent climate action to ensure that the Maldives continue to stay above water, and beautiful.

CHAPTER ONE

EMILIA HELD IN a gasp of excitement as she stepped off the water taxi, holding her sun hat to her head. This was literally paradise! Looking around her at the picture-postcard scene of turquoise waves and swaying palms around the bay was so surreal. It was so flawless it seemed like make-believe… as though she'd fallen asleep in front of a screen saver during another long shift in the trauma ward and was now waking up in a dream.

Oh, Dorothy, you're not in Manhattan anymore.

The heat pressed against every part of her in a sultry greeting as the concierge, who was barefoot and so relaxed she had to wonder if he was actually awake, grinned at her from the dock, raising his hand. She smiled back, letting it sink in that this would be her home for the foreseeable future. Six months of island life stretched ahead of her like the endless horizon. This was not a dream. Finally, Emilia Sturgis had arrived!

She'd told most people she knew by now that she would be here, working at the remote island clinic for half of an entire year. Most of her friends had been happy for her, with the exception of Maxxine, her best friend, who hadn't wanted to let her go, citing that Manhattan would not be the same without her. Even though it would be, because New York didn't change for anyone. Eventually, though,

Maxxine had decided to approve it, on the condition that Emilia also took some time out from work to relax and… what was it she'd said? Do some healing?

Ugh. Why did everyone say she still needed healing? Hard work was the healer. You couldn't hear your own unhappy thoughts when you were engrossed in other people's emergencies and that was just the way she'd grown to like it. At least, that's what she'd tried to convince herself of. She hadn't had a holiday since becoming a widow. She didn't know quite how to holiday alone and who would want to come away with a grieving widow anyway? It wasn't exactly fun for the other person.

She asked about the clinic. This was one of the bigger islands, though it was still pretty small, so she hoped everyone knew where the clinic was. Sure enough, the concierge pointed to a nearby path, then offered to help with her suitcase. She waved him off. He had other guests to greet from the same taxi, ones who were actually staying at the five-star resort the island was noted for.

The Vaara Atoll Eco-Resort was pretty famous, having been the central location of a reality TV show years ago. She'd seen two episodes and then promptly switched off. Watching men and women lolling about in designer swimwear, moaning about life when they likely had nothing to moan about, was not her idea of entertainment. Her own lodgings were to be found by the Velaa Health Clinic, not too far away, if her mapping was correct.

Muttering her thanks, she pulled her sunglasses down and was off, professionalism personified in a buttoned-up blouse and long pants, striding past the tropical plants and towering palms before realising there was probably no need to rush. This wasn't rush hour and these were not the usual obstacles she met every day in Manhattan. She slowed down and tuned into the soft, relaxing sound of the crystalline water lapping gently at the shore. This really was a million miles away from the crash and roar of New York that she was used to. Well, approximately eight and a half thousand miles away, actually. Maxxine had googled it, before also searching how much flights would cost should she follow her out in a few months' time for a vacation.

Every step Emilia took along the curvy path felt like the release of a breath she'd been holding for months, even though it was hard to admit it, even to herself. Aiden would have laughed at her arrival here, and at her outfit, she mused, tugging at her suitcase as it got stuck on a protruding slab along the sandy path. He'd be shaking his head at her insistence on wearing sensible shoes, even in paradise. A twinge of memory flickered at her. Sometimes the image of him was so clear it almost seemed real. Just over three years had passed since the world went dark on her and sometimes she still woke up thinking she'd find him beside her.

She picked up her pace again. This was one of the reasons she loved and stayed in Manhattan for the most part—everything moved so fast there that she could usually outrun the memories when they threatened to take her down. Sometimes she thought she'd moved on, laughing with nice guys on nice dates, shopping for sexy underwear to make herself feel 'ready' only for it all to catch up with her unexpectedly in a torrent of guilt in a foul-smelling metro car, or on another changing room floor. She wasn't supposed to outrun it or move on, was she? He had been her everything.

She thought of Aiden practically every time she tried not to, his green eyes crinkling at the corners as he laughed at some absurd idea, the shared future they'd taken for granted, the family they'd have together as soon as she was ready. She'd wanted two children, a boy and a girl. He'd wanted three and he didn't care what, as long as they were healthy. Of course she'd kept taking her pill, putting it off, putting her work first. Other people needed her; it wasn't time to bring more life into the world. It was never the right time, until they'd run out of time altogether. His absence was still a stubborn bruise, refusing to fade, still throbbing under the weight of everything she did without him... Oh wow, look at that view!

She stopped in her tracks, yanked from her reverie by the twinkling water and the sight of two kids with bright orange snorkels splashing about ahead. Incredible. It completely stole her attention for a full two minutes, before a gush of wind threatened to knock her suitcase over into her.

Oh well, okay, maybe Maxxine was right. Perhaps this *was* going to be a great place to get her thoughts in order once and for all. There was nowhere to move very fast on a tiny island in the Maldives, nowhere to run. Stunning distractions and smiles everywhere. Maybe she really *would* do some healing here.

'Ah, there it is.' The clinic was in sight now. A modest affair to say the least, in comparison to the fancy resort. It was perched at the edge of the island and practically screamed simplicity from its thatched rooftop. She hadn't expected to see the sunburned tourists who were idling in nearby hammocks.

'First time here?' one ventured when he saw her, his voice a leisurely drawl that stretched like toffee. He was looking at her shoes in amusement. Damn, she really was overdressed, wasn't she? She noticed a bandage around his foot. Ah, he must be a patient at the clinic.

'Long-term stay,' she replied with a smile, before walking past him along another sandy walkway, intent on finding her contact, Dr Zeenath—the head of the practice. Dr

Zeenath's role extended to several other clinics on the island, so no doubt she was a busy woman, but that was why *she* was here, after all. Emilia had landed the maternity-cover role on account of her experience in upgrading medical pathways and systems, in addition to her medical skills.

It was hard to focus on one thing for more than two seconds in New York sometimes, no thanks to constant noise and bustle, but here she was distracted for very different reasons. First by the gorgeous turtle mural on the wall. Very unusual! Next by the flowers. She kept having to park her case, bend down and smell them. They were divine; she'd never seen anything like these, not even in the botanical garden.

In fact, the whole world around the clinic was a blur of colour and scent. Frangipani lingered sweetly in the air and hibiscus bloomed defiantly in every direction. Butterflies fluttered like parentheses around it all. Stunning. Her mother would be obsessed with this place already. But Emilia wasn't here to relax. It was probably going to be more like that time she'd planned a Christmas getaway to Vermont and ended up stitching an impaled hiker back together instead of sipping hot cocoa with Aiden by the fire.

A final curve brought her to the clinic door. Months of planning, and here she was. It was going to plan so far, not that much had happened. Planning was her specialty. Not having a plan was her biggest nightmare, and if her plan for this next part worked out, she'd be settled in her room within the next ten minutes and sleeping off her jet lag. But first, the formalities! Stepping inside, she fully expected to find Dr Zeenath waiting for her with her room key and a welcome guide, but…

Nothing.

The place was totally empty.

She put her suitcase by the reception desk and peeked

around it. Still no one. Not even a volunteer, which was what she'd expected. Aside from the doctor she was replacing, the rest of the staff was allegedly made up of volunteers who rotated around the islands.

'Hello?' she called out, to no one, apparently.

Gosh. This was already so different from St Catherine's Hospital in New York, where pressure and noises and squeaks and urgency chased her down every single bleachy-smelling hallway. There, her focus was purely on survival. Every decision was life or death. Here, it felt like she could pass out dead on the floor and only be discovered by that guy outside in the hammock in three days' time. There was no rush of traffic, no vibration of sirens splitting the air, just the patient rhythm of the waves murmuring unfiltered through the open windows.

The emptiness was foreign. She found her fingers tapping idly against the counter with nervous energy. She didn't really do well in the silence; it let too many thoughts creep in. A fresh frangipani decoration fell to the floor and hurriedly she picked it up.

'You must be Dr Emilia Sturgis, welcome! I'm Dr Zeenath. Welcome to paradise,' came the greeting that almost made her bump her head on her way back up.

'Thank you,' Emilia replied, turning to see the doctor in the white coat, wearing a smile that seemed to stretch across the equator.

They shook hands and exchanged a few pleasantries about her journey and her thoughts about the island so far, all while Emilia marvelled at the way the pretty dark-skinned woman leaned casually on the counter and studied her thoughtfully, like they were about to order a cocktail and talk about their exes.

'Yes, the clinic is…lovely. I particularly like the mural

outside,' she said, recounting the brightly painted wall featuring turtles and fish.

'The local kids did that. Dr Vargas encouraged them last time he was here.' Dr Zeenath headed around the reception desk and started rummaging through a drawer. And then another drawer. And then another one. It took a while before she pulled out a crumpled envelope, during which time Emilia wracked her tired mind, trying to recall who Dr Vargas was exactly. 'I hope you don't mind the heat. Or the rain. It's getting wetter all the time these days.'

Emilia offered a polite nod, her mind already spinning. 'The heat is nice,' she said weakly, taking the envelope and wondering when she would be able to sleep. Maxxine had quoted an article that called the Maldives a place where time and stress dissolved like footprints in the sand. She was determined not to dissolve along with them but already the heat was making her jet lag worse and she was starting to wonder whether anyone actually used this clinic at all.

Dr Zeenath shrugged off her white coat and to Emilia's shock, just tossed it on the reception desk, where it slid off and landed on top of the telephone behind it.

'I'll show you to your quarters first, then we can do a little tour, how's that?' she said kindly. 'We're still waiting for Dr Vargas to arrive, and maybe he'll join us.'

Then it hit her. Oh yes. Dr Alejandro Vargas. She had heard mention of the visiting physician who'd be rejoining them for the off season; some hotshot disaster relief doctor with an impressive résumé, coming back to assess the island's readiness for climate-related emergencies, among other things. She didn't know much about him but the way this woman was suddenly acting kind of flustered had her on high alert.

'You know him well?' she asked.

'Oh yes, he's very popular around here. I should think he's popular wherever he goes,' Dr Zeenath said, and her blush grew even darker, making Emilia smile. Maybe they'd hooked up or something. Oh dear. Was he the kind of man who mixed pleasure into his business and left a trail of broken hearts behind him?

Maybe it wasn't very fair to assume things, but now she'd started so…well. She couldn't imagine mixing business with pleasure but this *was* a tropical island, she supposed. People surely did. This would be interesting. She'd have to keep an eye on him. Her lead role meant he'd be called upon when required, but most of the time he'd be out and about conducting his research.

She followed Dr Zeenath along another small path obscured by more lush vegetation. The sun painted surreal patterns onto the sandy ground as it peeked through the dense canopy high above them. Birds twittered and sang gorgeous tropical songs like a serenade and for a moment she wondered why she hadn't left Manhattan and had a nature-based holiday anywhere like…ever.

Her quarters were nestled amid the greenery, a charming bungalow painted in soft coastal hues with a sweeping veranda, a hammock and a bird feeder on a tall pole in one corner. Inside, it was spacious yet cozy. A large bed dominated most of the space, draped in sheer mosquito netting and piled high with pillows. A large window overlooked the turquoise sea and she gasped audibly as she stepped closer. A real sea view. She hadn't actually imagined this, but she certainly wasn't complaining.

This was a massive contrast to the tiny Manhattan apartment she had left behind with the subletter. Nestled between two monolithic buildings on the Upper East Side, the compact one-bedroom walk-up that she'd shared with Aiden sat on the fifth floor of a red-brick building that had seen better days and hid for the most part in the shadows of its more imposing neighbours. It literally never saw the sun. She'd wanted to move after his death, away from the memories, but rent in Manhattan was so extortionate it would have cost her more to move than to stay on her fixed-rent agreement.

'Most doctors never want to leave once they see this,' Dr Zeenath commented with an amused chuckle as she watched Emilia's reaction. 'But this is all yours for the next six months.'

'I can hardly believe I'm here,' she said in awe, pressing a hand to her heart. She was surprised to find tears prickling her eyes now.

'Well, I'm very glad you are, and so will Aleja... Dr Vargas,' Dr Zeenath replied, correcting herself quickly before hoisting the suitcase onto a special stand by a rustic wardrobe. 'I hope you find it comfortable,' she added, smoothing down her dress. 'I'll leave you here to settle in. Come find me when you're ready? I'll be waiting outside for...'

'Dr Vargas, yes, I know.'

The door swung shut behind her new colleague, and the reality of where she was really sank in. Yawning, Emilia unzipped her bag and started arranging her belongings on the shelves and in the drawers, glancing at the ocean every now and then, just to check if it was actually there, casually wondering about Dr Vargas. Where had he come from? Where was his home base?

At her own home base, her view was mostly fire escapes clinging to neighbouring buildings like metallic ivy. She had to stand on the far left side of her own fire escape and crane her neck just to see the smallest sliver of nature, which was the thinnest ever slice of Central Park. Life outside had all seemed to move on without her after Aiden died, and she saw him everywhere. Yet she'd never contemplated leaving the city.

Once a New Yorker, always a New Yorker.

Until you signed a six-month contract on a remote Maldivian island, she thought with a half smile.

CHAPTER TWO

EMILIA BLINKED AT the patient chart in front of her, stifling a yawn. She was still in a losing battle with her jet lag, which had kept her awake most of the night. That and the relentless rain. She was just contemplating a third cup of hot sweet tea when a crash from the back entrance almost made her jump out of her skin. Spinning to the door, she saw rainwater pooling on the previously spotless floor, and then she saw…him.

'Sorry about that,' he said in a deep, accented voice that filled the room completely. 'The front's flooded. Again. I thought Tom was going to help fix that?'

Dr Alejandro Vargas—it had to be him—shook his head like a dog in front of her, sending droplets flying out like wet bullets from his dark curls. Emilia stood taller. She hadn't expected him to make quite such a dramatic entrance, or to make her do a double take. Make that a triple take. She realised she was staring.

Putting the chart down, she crossed her arms and frowned, watching as he peeled off his soaked jacket and draped it over a chair. Did no one use coat hooks around here? Water was dripping onto the linoleum in small, expanding puddles. A clear violation of safety protocols. She opened her mouth to comment just as Dr Zeenath rushed forward with a towel and a smile that bordered on fawning. The same smile Emilia had seen on her yesterday when she'd mentioned his name for the first time. And the second time.

'Dr Vargas! We were expecting you yesterday.' Dr Zeenath handed him the towel, her cheeks flushed.

'I've told you to call me Alejandro. Remember? Did I not say that the last time? The weather forecast did a number on me, so I caught a later flight. Did no one tell you?'

'Um…no, there was no one at the reception desk yesterday, so…'

'Well, I'm here now.' He towelled his hair briskly, then looked up, seeming to only just now register Emilia's presence. He stopped moving for a second, a look of surprise crossing his face momentarily, just as she got a clear look at his own face for the first time.

Oh, my goodness, he was handsome. She looked away quickly, feeling her cheeks heat up as his eyes raked over her. Was he here for round two of that reality TV show, filmed at the resort? The guys had all looked like this, all… massive arms and stunning muscles and gorgeous tan.

'And who is this?' he asked.

She cleared her throat, suddenly annoyed that he didn't know who she was. Hadn't he at least heard that a trauma doctor from New York would be arriving here?

'Dr Emilia Sturgis. Nice to meet you,' she said anyway before turning back to her chart, refusing to join Zeenath's welcoming committee. Whatever he looked like, whoever he was, she had actual work to do.

'Help, help!' The shout came from just outside the clinic's back door, right before a man in his forties burst through the doors, helping a struggling woman. 'Help her, please! She was stung by a jellyfish.'

Emilia moved immediately. 'Treatment bay three,' she

directed, leading the way while mentally reviewing what she knew about marine envenomation. But she wasn't alone. Alejandro was hot on her tail, grabbing a white coat and pulling it on over his wet clothes.

The monitors beeped and the rain outside lashed at the windows as he helped Emilia transfer the patient. The woman's greying face was contorted in pain, her breaths coming in shallow gasps. This did not look good at all. Quickly she administered epinephrine, all the while watching as Alejandro soothed the woman and her frantic husband and gathered supplies like he'd done this here a thousand times and hadn't literally arrived just five minutes earlier.

'BP one hundred over sixty, heart rate one-twenty and climbing,' she reported, leaning over their patient. 'Madam, I'm Dr Sturgis. We're going to help you. Can you tell me your name?'

'Pam,' she gasped. 'My God, it burns…like fire.'

'I know, but the pain will fade,' she explained calmly, but the woman's leg was already displaying the distinctive whip-like marks of tentacle contact. The angry red welts were rising on her calf, the pallor of her skin was sickly, the sweat was beading on her forehead and her hands were trembling worryingly. Classic signs of a systemic reaction. Were the waters around here really that dangerous? Emilia decided on the spot never to go in; God only knew what else was lurking in there.

Alejandro was ahead of her now, listing at least three drugs she didn't even know if the clinic possessed. 'And let's start oxygen at two litres.'

Wait, what?

Who was in charge here? She met his eyes, narrowing her own, but he didn't flinch, so she spoke, directing her words at their patient as he moved to the opposite side of the gurney, examining the sting pattern.

'Pam, I can remove any remaining tentacles and neutralise the venom. It was a blue blubber jellyfish, am I right?' she asked. 'A bluey purple colour?'

'Likely a box jellyfish, don't you think?' Alejandro followed, not looking up. 'Common in these waters this time of year.' He lowered his voice. 'We need to sort this fast, Doctor—the box jellyfish can be lethal.'

'Yes, I know.' Emilia felt herself stiffen. Who was this guy, barging in, acting all in charge? She was the lead doctor around here, not him. Maybe he was right about the box, but her jet-leg was making him even *more* annoying right now.

'I've treated a few jellyfish stings in my time...' Emilia started.

Alejandro moved in closer to the wound, then took her aside gently by the arm, cutting her off. This New Yorker, whilst undeniably attractive, seemed hell-bent on disregarding his experience and that did not sit well with him.

'I've treated hundreds of stings during relief work in coastal regions. The linear pattern of the welts is quite distinctive, Doctor. We need vinegar to deactivate nematocysts, then we'll remove any remaining tentacles, yes?'

Their patient groaned behind them. He watched Emilia check the monitors, her mind no doubt running over the chart she'd memorised prior to coming here. All these medics came in fresh off the boat, thinking they knew everything, when the truth was they usually knew nothing about these islands beyond the sunshine and sea. He had done this before, on more islands than this one. He knew what he was looking at.

To his annoyance, she took him aside again, meeting his

eyes for the first time up close. He lost his train of thought for a second. Her bright eyes were dark, intelligent and entirely too confident, but he saw a flicker of vulnerability as she studied him that made something flip in his stomach.

'Another zero-point-three of epinephrine,' she said, clearly distracted. 'And the vinegar.'

Alejandro moved swiftly, gathering hot water and cloths from the nearby cart. 'Mind if I work on the other side of the sting while you treat your side?' He hoped the question sounded innocent enough, but he was challenging her now, and he didn't even really know why. She was the lead; he was merely on call. There was something about this woman that was getting to him.

'We need to coordinate treatment here, Doctor, not divide it,' she said through gritted teeth, dampening the towels.

'Look,' he said, lowering his voice, 'I don't mean to step on any toes, but those marking patterns—'

'There's a system,' she interrupted. 'Can you check our epinephrine supply? We may need more.'

He bit back a scowl. She was probably wondering who the hell he was, questioning her methods while a patient suffered close by. Maybe he should be asking himself the same thing.

There was *definitely* something about her. Something he'd do best to ignore, he thought quickly, reminding himself of what had happened in Peru. It never ended well when women in these placements fell for him. And it *was* always them who fell. He had other things to think about.

'Is she going to be okay?' Pam's husband asked, reminding them both that he was actually there, watching from the corner. The poor woman moaned again, her face contorting. 'Please…just make it stop.'

Alejandro handed Emilia the vinegar, and she began applying it to the wound while he moved to check the patient's airway.

'Breath sounds diminished on the left side,' he noted before ushering the husband outside to wait. 'Possible pulmonary edema developing.'

Emilia seemed to register the shift in his tone. She glanced at the monitors and saw what he had already intuited. This was escalating beyond a typical reaction. She directed him to increase the oxygen and ordered an ultrasound to check for fluid in the lungs. Already her annoyance had dissipated. Maybe she was starting to be grateful that he was here, and clearly so well versed in the varied implications of jellyfish stings.

Alejandro anticipated her every need before she voiced it out loud. When the woman's saturation dropped, he had the intubation kit ready. When she called for another medication, he had already drawn it up. When she ordered ice packs for the surrounding inflammation, he pointed to where he'd already retrieved them from the freezer in the kitchen.

An hour later, Pam was doing much better. Her vitals had steadied now, and the angry red welts had begun to lose their offensive virulence. Emilia updated the chart, sneaking a glance at him, which he did not miss. Neither did he miss her eyes travelling up his tanned forearms where he'd rolled up his sleeves.

Maybe she was wondering about his scars, whether they were silver souvenirs from his disaster relief work. He hadn't exactly been living a life of comfort since his mission work had started taking him all over the world. His sister always said his work scared her, which made the guilt creep in. Even more guilt, actually…when he knew she wanted to spend more time with him. But her lifelong illnesses were the very reason he kept going. The changing climate would keep on making people sick, just like it had done to her when she was only a kid. His research could help...was *already* helping.

Alejandro found Emilia mid-yawn in the tiny kitchen area. Outside, the rain was lashing against the windows in sheets. Thunder rumbled at them, close enough to vibrate the glass. It was quite magnificent, watching the storm roll in over the ocean, even if these storms were getting worse every year.

'Tired?' he asked, making her turn from the window.

'Is it that obvious?'

The air between them seemed to thicken suddenly, and he watched her roll up her own sleeves while the coffee machine deposited steaming hot water into her cup. He leaned against the counter beside her, watching it.

'Seems like the off season is already keeping you busy. When did you arrive?'

'Yesterday, actually. Direct from New York.'

He rubbed his chin, noting the sheen of her light brown hair before it threaded into a braid over her left shoulder. 'No wonder you're tired.'

'Well, we're also understaffed,' she said, pushing a stray few strands back behind her ear. 'I heard you'd be helping for the next few months.'

He nodded, watching her squeeze out the teabag in her cup under a spoon. 'Until the rains end and the NGO needs me back in Central America. Or maybe somewhere else. I don't actually know for sure what's next.'

Her eyes flickered up to his face in interest, then refused to move. He noticed her blush slightly before she turned back to the cup. 'Central America?'

'I was doing some community training with other doctors in Guatemala. Educating locals on disaster preparedness, first aid, sustainable rebuilding practices, that kind of thing. It could be that they need me back there. It could be that they need me somewhere else.'

She nodded. 'It must be nice to be so needed in so many places, Doctor.'

'Alejandro, please,' he replied, without missing the disparagement in her tone. Was she still irritated that he'd pulled rank a little when she was the lead? He had kind of arrived unannounced earlier, much like the storm. 'Sorry for jumping in there,' he added quickly, watching her face.

She sighed. 'You know your jellyfish, Alejandro.'

'Yes, I do. But…you're in charge, Doc.'

Silence followed. Her pretty mouth twitched. 'The staff schedule is on the bulletin board,' she said a little awkwardly. 'I know you're here to work on other…projects…but if you can help out from time to time that would be great.'

'Thanks. And of course, whatever I can do.'

He reached past her for a coffee mug, the simple act becoming charged as his arm brushed the delicate curve of hers. Her skin was warm and the kind of soft that made his pulse trip unexpectedly. She smelled faintly of something herbal, maybe chamomile or eucalyptus, something calming and clean and entirely at odds with the jolt of heat flashing through his veins.

He felt her still as he leaned in, just enough to show she'd felt the connection too. That tiny flicker of awareness that existed before words or logic had a chance to interfere.

She was disarmingly beautiful. Petite but not fragile, with a quiet poise some women just wore like a perfume. He had to grip the mug a little harder than necessary to keep from doing something stupid, like grazing his fingers down the bare skin of her forearm just to see if it would spark again.

The scent of her mingled with the steam of fresh coffee.

His cologne clung stubbornly to the humid air, but now it was tinged with her too. She was a sensory contradiction he suddenly wanted to spend hours unravelling.

He caught her eyes over the rim of her cup. She was studying him now with a sort of cautious curiosity that made something primal in him stir.

'For what it's worth, you handled that flawlessly for a New Yorker. Very impressive,' he said, clearing his throat, thrown.

'For a New Yorker?' Her shoes squeaked in the silence, but she didn't throw his insult back at him. Instead, she just shook her head, biting back a smile. 'Your assistance was… helpful. She seems like she'll be okay, give or take a few more anti-inflammatories.'

Alejandro shook his head. 'I'm sure you'll monitor that closely. As we know, these toxins cause localised pain that opioids don't always touch. In Ecuador, we had a fisherman with a similar sting pattern—'

'Well, this isn't Ecuador,' Emilia cut him off, her half smile vanishing. Then she sighed again. 'Sorry…sorry. I'm really jet-lagged, honestly. But, Alejandro, anecdotal evidence doesn't override established treatment guidelines,' she added.

Just then the overhead lights flickered, once, twice, as another thunderclap shook the building and made her spin, then step backwards into him.

He caught her cup on its fall to the floor, and placed it back on the counter, grabbing a cloth and mopping the spill on the floor with his foot, all before she could say a word.

'You know, Doctor, guidelines are exactly that—they don't have to be straitjackets,' he said when the lights stabilised. 'Medicine requires adaptation, don't you think?'

'Medicine requires standard treatment protocol,' she replied, crossing her arms, clearly flustered.

'Of course, but a few…adjustments…here and there can be helpful.'

She frowned. She was extra pretty when she was being all serious like this. 'Rules exist for a reason, Dr. Vargas. They're built on evidence, not impulse. Surely you know that.'

'Alejandro,' he corrected her again, letting his gaze rove over her mouth. 'And surely you know that some of the best medical discoveries came from impulse.'

'Some of the worst medical disasters too.' She pursed her lips, as if she might possibly redirect his gaze from them. It wasn't working. Why were they arguing? How did this discussion even start?

'I should find my room and unpack,' he said finally, stepping back from what now felt like a dangerous kind of intensity with a colleague that he had not been looking to find today. Or ever. 'Seems like you have things under control. Let me know if you need me.'

'Will do,' she said. It was a lie, and he knew it. She found him far too infuriating for her jet lag to handle.

Outside, the rumble of thunder told him the storm showed no signs of abating. Neither, he suspected, would the tension that had crystallised so quickly between himself and this fascinating woman.

CHAPTER THREE

THE MORNING SUN warmed Emilia's skin instantly as she stepped onto her veranda, stretching her arms over her head with a yawn. This was definitely a world away from her fire escape in Manhattan. The golden rays made her eyes squint as her white robe fluttered against her legs in the light breeze.

If only she could capture this, she thought, to take back home. The sun shone differently here somehow, filtering through the palm fronds, dappling the decking of the veranda in light and shadows. Like a painting. If only she could transport herself here every time she felt stressed and tune back into the ocean and the trill of the brightly coloured birds who flittered around in the trees. Her bird feeder was doing its job right now, offering seeds to two common myna birds.

Paradise, she thought, letting her robe fall loose and pressing her hands to the railing, taking a deep breath of salty air and blooming hibiscus. This screen-saver reality was growing on her. In less than a week, she was already learning how to relax. Who'd have thought?

Evidently she should be getting ready for her shift. But closing her eyes, she allowed herself another moment to 'just be', as Maxxine had advised on the phone last night. She found herself smiling wider the more she concentrated on the warm sunlight seeping through her skin, relaxing into her muscles. She let her fingers run through her long dark hair, releasing it from its nighttime braid into loose waves, letting it fall over her shoulders. Paradise, she thought again. Aiden would have loved this.

Then a sound close by forced her eyes open. Out of the corner of her eye, she noticed movement. A figure on an adjacent veranda. Alejandro.

All thoughts of Aiden exited her head as fast as they'd arrived and her breath hitched as she felt her traitorous stomach flutter. She'd been getting this feeling way too often around Alejandro since day one, four days ago now. They hadn't exactly had much to do with each other, though. He'd been off interviewing people around the island as part of his research mostly, but they'd nodded in passing, and his room was right by hers, the same cabana-like structure, probably identical inside.

She took in the sight of him, his tousled dark curls catching the light, his tanned skin gleaming like some kind of burnished bronze statue. He was sitting in a hammock, and he seemed to be engrossed in some early-morning reading. His lean muscular build, which was usually hidden beneath his sensible work clothes, was on full display now, his broad shoulders tapering into a chiseled torso.

Goodness, she thought. She couldn't recall the last time she had seen a man so buff and toned. She half expected him to drop into a press-up right there on his sun-speckled decking, but maybe she'd arrived here too late for that, and his workout was already complete.

Shame, she thought, licking her lower lip, then shaking her head at herself. What on earth was she thinking?

Suddenly, Alejandro seemed to sense her presence and looked up from his book. Their eyes met for a fleeting moment before she realised her robe was undone and she was naked under it. Quickly she darted back inside her bungalow. Oh no. No, no, no!

Her heart thrashed at her ribs as she backed against the closed door. Great, had he seen that, all of it? She wasn't in the habit of getting flustered this easily—as a medical professional a naked body was perfectly normal and acceptable—but flashing a new colleague... Well, there was nothing normal or acceptable about that. How much had he actually seen?

Oh gosh. How embarrassing.

She showered quickly, trying and failing to push him from her brain, but there was something haunting about him, and something about their unexpected moment just now that haunted her too. Alejandro's piercing gaze had just made the heat rise to her cheeks, and to other places too if she was honest. How would she be able to face him today? She could only hope that their paths wouldn't cross, that he would be off somewhere else on the island, or better still, away on another island in the archipelago. Preferably a really distant one.

Of course this would happen, she thought to herself an hour later, after she'd been ushered into the small, utilitarian meeting room with Dr Zeenath and Alejandro. Its clean white walls felt stifling today, despite the cooling air conditioner and fan, but that was probably because Alejandro kept glancing at her with a look she couldn't read. It went from querying to an infuriating smirk, like he was storing up things to say as soon as they were alone. Just the thought of it was making her antsy.

'All right, team,' Dr Zeenath began, glancing between them. 'Alejandro, I know you're heading out to speak to the fishermen today, and I thought, seeing as things are quiet, you could join him, Emilia. You'll remain on call, of course?'

A silent protest bubbled in her veins, making her heart pump almost as hard as it had this morning. *I have paper-work to finish*, she intended to say. Pam, their jellyfish patient, had only been released yesterday, all well and good, thank heavens, but the excuse never left her lips.

Alejandro shot her a glance, arching an eyebrow that took her right back to her veranda, flashing him with all her nakedness. Some kind of unspoken challenge seemed to linger between them suddenly, stirring an extra helping of pure annoyance into her embarrassment. If she refused to accompany him, he would know she was mortified about this morning, and would probably conclude that she had a crush on him or something ridiculous like that…as if she had a crush. She would never allow herself to fall for a colleague, ever.

She forced a smile. 'Of course I can join you. I'd love to learn more about your work,' she heard herself say to him.

'Excellent,' Alejandro said, clapping his hands together.

Dr Zeenath made notes as he laid out the details of what they'd be doing with their day on the neighbouring island, making a point of asking a spattering of questions like 'When will you be back?' and 'How are you finding your lodgings this time?' To be fair, he answered with the kind of nonchalance that implied they hadn't had much to do with each other, not like Emilia had suspected at first.

Still, she tried to stay irked at him as he spoke, if only so as not to recall how gorgeous he'd looked all bare chested and glistening in the sun earlier, in his hammock.

The breeze picked up her long skirt and tousled the loose strands of hair that had blown from her braid as they stepped out of the clinic together. She put her sunglasses on, and Alejandro mirrored her, falling into an easy pace beside her as they headed for the dock, where a boat would be waiting for them. She had chosen a flowing linen skirt today, in a soft shade of sea foam green. It had felt like a practical choice to be worn under a lab coat with its loose fit and breathable fabric, but now that she was unexpectedly heading out and about in the sun, it retained a certain elegance, she supposed.

Why did she even care what she looked like?

'What's with the braid?' he asked suddenly, as if picking up on her sudden bout of self-consciousness. 'I notice it's kind of your look.'

She shrugged. 'It was something the other doctors with long hair did a lot in St Catherine's, and I guess it just stuck.' She held back the part about her mother braiding her hair every day before school when she was a child. Sometimes when she looked in the mirror, she saw her mother staring back at her. Not because she was dead—the church-going Miranda Sturgis was very much alive and well. It was because Emilia feared she might come off as a little too prim and proper and closed off sometimes, like her mother could be.

'St Catherine's Hospital, in New York?' Alejandro asked. 'How long were you there?'

'Too long,' she told him, picturing Aiden telling her that maybe it was time she looked for another, less busy work environment, so they could get going on starting a family. *Great, another guilt trip from my dead ex.*

Alejandro looked at her like he was expecting her to continue, but she felt herself clam up and search the horizon. It wasn't the time or place to get into all that.

Glancing at him, it was hard not to notice how good he

looked in casual clothing, which was almost as good as how he looked without his shirt on. His khaki cargo shorts showcased his toned, tanned legs, and he'd left his lightweight white linen shirt open at the collar, revealing just enough of his chest to make Emilia do a triple take on more than one occasion, noting the sprinkling of dark hairs. His dark curls were slightly tamed today, and the aviator sunglasses he wore were actually growing on her.

Looks that could undo a nun, as Maxxine had once said about a guy she'd dated.

Emilia caught herself staring again more than once as they waited for their boat by the dock. It was late to arrive, but things ran on Maldives time around here. She was already getting used to that.

Alejandro leaned against a post casually, his arms crossed over his chest as he chatted with some of the locals passing by, making them laugh with ease. It wasn't just his physical appeal that made her heart flutter in ways she hadn't experienced since Aiden; he drew people towards him like magnets. She'd known people like this before, though. Casual heartbreakers. Of course, Alejandro was just the type; why wouldn't he be? With a job like his, travelling around the world, never staying long in any one place. Even if he hadn't hooked up with Dr Zeenath, he probably had a woman in every port.

Silence fell between them as they found themselves alone, with no sight of the boat. She focused on the horizon, even as she felt his eyes land on her again.

'So, tell me,' he broke the silence with curiosity in his tone. 'What brought you to this place, Doctor? I would think New York would have kept you busy enough for a lifetime, and don't New Yorkers usually hate the silence?'

Emilia glanced at him. 'Everyone thought I needed a

break from…everything,' she said before she could think, then wondered why she hadn't just said *I've always wanted to visit the Maldives* like a normal human would. No one here on this island knew what had happened to her, only her professional history. She didn't need a pity party.

'Everything,' he echoed softly, studying her intently. For a moment, she expected him to push further. She could practically feel the weight of his eyes prying open the locked corners of her mind. 'And?'

'And what?'

'*Did* you need a break from…everything?'

'I think I did,' she answered after a moment. It was the truth, after all. He didn't have to know what constituted *everything*. 'And what about you?' she followed.

'What about me?'

'Well, where are you from? Where is home?'

He sniffed. 'I haven't been back to Venezuela in years,' he said, his gaze wandering to the water, a shadow crossing his face. 'But that's home. Is your family back in New York?'

'Not really,' she replied. 'Not anymore.'

The admission felt like a wound opening back up. She realised she could probably say something about Aiden. Maybe not that he'd made her a widow at the tender age of thirty, sticking a fork in the toaster of her—well, mainly his—family-making dreams and rendering New York an entirely different city. Maybe not that even walking the same blocks and avenues she'd walked a million times felt like being continually haunted by the ghosts of everything she'd never get to do with him again.

Argh. Even saying one small thing could lead to a sink-hole opening up, and the last thing she wanted was to drag Alejandro down into it. She shut her mouth but of course his expectant eyes were still on her.

'I wasn't actually born in New York,' she said. 'I went to med school there, got my residency and wound up staying. My parents and most of my family are in Washington. Where in Venezuela are your parents?'

She had studied Venezuela a little in her med school years, intrigued by the health care system's struggles amid all manner of political and economic upheaval. It was an entirely different world from New York and Washington, but it gave her a broader understanding of global health, something she actually did hope to continue learning about from Alejandro while he was here.

'My father passed away,' he said quietly, his gaze turning somber. 'A long time ago.'

Oh, gosh. 'I'm sorry,' she whispered, feeling her heart clench as the boat finally appeared from around the bay. She hadn't expected that answer.

Alejandro shrugged lightly. 'It's okay. It's been a while now. He died when I was young. My mother lives in Valencia now. She left with my sister, Maria, when things got really difficult in Venezuela. Maria has been asking me to visit her lately in Spain, actually.'

At the mention of his sister, a flicker of warmth sparked in his eyes.

'Maria,' Emilia repeated. 'Does she understand what you do?'

'She does, she's not that young! She's twenty-nine. I'm proud of her. We almost lost her once.'

She opened her mouth to empathise but he shook his head, as if willing the memory away, and Emilia nodded. She of all people understood the need to deflect the conversation away from personal issues. She respected that he kept the focus on the present, on his work. Just as she should.

'Are we ready?' Alejandro asked, nodding towards the

boat that was now docking at the pier. She let him guide her onto the rickety vessel, taking a wooden bench seat, feeling his knee brush hers lightly through her skirt as he sat beside her. They set off in silence once more, and yet her eyes kept drifting to him against the cerulean blue of the water. Maybe she had been too quick to dismiss Alejandro as some kind of casual, globetrotting, playboy heartbreaker. She remembered reading about the healthcare crisis and political turmoil that had plagued his home country, forcing many people to flee or face dire circumstances. It wasn't fair to label him a heartbreaker when she knew nothing about his or his family's journey.

He mentioned he had almost lost his sister once too, on top of his father dying. So, they had both lost people who were important to them.

She was just trying to banish the image of a young, shirtless Alejandro in a Venezuelan jungle waterfall from her mind when he nudged her conspiratorially.

'I'm just curious,' he murmured, so close to her ear that she felt another zing of hot adrenaline rocket up her neck. 'Do New Yorkers usually stand on the balconies of their skyscrapers, flashing their neighbours in the mornings, or is that just something they do when released onto tiny islands?'

She closed her eyes, cringing, feeling his grin even through her eyelids. 'I have no idea what you're talking about,' she managed, deciding on the spot that she was never, ever going to meet this man's gaze again.

CHAPTER FOUR

WHEN THE BOAT bumped gently against the shore of the neighbouring island, Alejandro was already over the side, landing barefoot in the warm, foamy surf. The sand shifted under his heels as he turned and extended a hand up to Emilia. Her fingers slid into his and contact was brief, but it lingered in his chest like static electricity.

She looked surprised too, and withdrew her hand, hitching up her dress. He frowned. Was she sunburned already? It was pretty hard to miss the flush now climbing the slope of her shoulders as she hitched her dress even higher and stepped lightly into the shallows beside him. She wasn't just flushed; actually, she was pink, verging on red.

'You did put sunscreen on, right?' he asked, trying to sound casual as their captain secured the boat behind them.

'Of course,' she muttered, already brushing grains of sand from her legs and slipping her shoes back on. She was proud, clearly. And stubborn as hell. It amused him more than it should have. Everything about Emilia amused him, especially the way she was pushing buttons he didn't even know he had. And he could not unsee what his eyes had seen from his veranda either…the naked curves of her incredible body in that robe, drenched in sunlight.

Good lord.

He felt bad for teasing her about it, but he hadn't been

able to help himself. Besides, she had absolutely nothing to be ashamed of.

'Which way?' she asked now, looking up at him.

He cleared his throat, starting towards the tree-lined path ahead, pointing the way. 'Down here. Not far.'

She followed, a little reluctantly, swatting at a fly. 'I didn't ask if you'd been here many times before,' she said.

He nodded. 'Lots of times.'

She muttered something under her breath that sounded a lot like *Of course you have.* It made the corner of his mouth tug up in a smile. So she still didn't know what to make of him. Fair enough. He hadn't exactly gone out of his way to explain himself when they'd met. And he'd seen that look on her face a number of times now. She thought he was reckless, impulsive. A threat to her efficiency and rule-following agenda.

Maybe he was. Maria had said the same thing. His work took him far and wide to places that weren't always as safe as it seemed here in the Maldives. It usually served him well to think on his feet. Besides, he was usually right about things.

Most of the time.

'We don't know how long we have left to enjoy these islands,' he said, the words slipping out before he could temper the weight of them in front of her. He saw Emilia glance over, a small frown between her eyes. She thought he was talking about their time together, maybe. But this wasn't about *them*.

He pulled a bottle of water from his daypack, took a long swig and let the droplets drip carelessly onto his shirt. They soaked through the fabric instantly and he could feel the sun baking the cotton against his skin, right before he caught Emilia watching him.

He handed her the bottle and she took it, seemingly grateful for the pause in the shade.

'Every day, these islanders have to watch the Maldives sink further beneath the waves,' he said. 'And it breaks my heart, Emilia.'

Her name sounded softer in his voice than he'd intended. He noticed the way she stilled, how her lips parted slightly and paused over the water bottle at the sound of it.

'I mean, we deal in facts,' he continued, noting how her reaction did something unexpected to his chest, 'but how do you measure the despair of a fisherman who has to watch his island home disappear, inch by inch? Or the divers who have to see the coral reefs bleaching into lifeless graveyards around them? I've treated children who are suffering from waterborne diseases that didn't exist here a decade ago.'

He screwed up his face. 'Sorry, I know it's depressing.'

She said nothing at first. She just listened with her eyes scanning his face like she might find the solution to it all there.

'Well, yes,' she said after a moment, 'but that's the truth of it.'

'The people of the Maldives are not responsible for this crisis,' he said, 'yet they are paying the highest price. How much longer will it be until the world really listens? Will it take until the last palm tree is swallowed by the tide? You know, sometimes I think that's the way it's going.'

Emilia's expression told him she understood.

'That's why you're here, though, Alejandro,' she said. Her voice was low, thoughtful. 'How did you get started in environmental research anyway? Wasn't studying medicine enough? I mean, I know doctors working in humanitarian aid usually do witness the aftermath of floods and droughts…'

'And landslides, and earthquakes and storms…all the nasty stuff,' he continued with a nod. 'My interest started before that, actually, when my sister got sick from something in the water. She still has asthma from it.'

The weight of memory pressed on his chest for a beat. He forced himself to keep talking.

'I did a short MPH program to better understand how the environment affects population health and took the rest from there. Why, am I making you consider it?'

She shrugged. 'I don't know.' There was a tension in her posture now, like she was still deciding whether she trusted him, and whether she could respect his methods after what he'd confessed.

But the stiffness she'd had that first day when he'd charged in, confident and…yes…probably a bit arrogant, had softened. He knew she'd hated that. She'd probably pegged him as one of those seat-of-your-pants doctors, whereas in the trauma ward, her approach was probably safer. Smarter, even. But sometimes instinct mattered more.

The dock came into view, stretching out like a jagged finger towards the sea. He squinted at the fishermen gathered ahead. Emilia tensed beside him, and he knew it wasn't just the heat. She'd caught the pungent smell of raw fish on the wind. 'It takes some getting used to,' he told her, and she smiled, clearly trying not to gag.

Emilia stayed back slightly as he approached the eldest man in the group and shook his hand.

'Can you tell me about the fish populations this year so far?' he asked in his Spanish-accented English, flipping open a small notebook. 'I was here in June. Have there been any visible changes since then? Migration? Behaviour?'

'Ah, the fish,' the skinny man in sports pants replied. 'They just don't come like they used to.'

As the old man spoke, Alejandro noticed Emilia inch closer, drawn in despite the heat and the smell and the sweat trickling down the back of her neck. Her skin was definitely turning pink. He'd have to find her some shade soon.

She contributed her own thoughts when she could, listening with that sharp intelligence he'd come to admire more than he'd expected to. She wasn't just a doctor out here on some whim, though he was itching to know more about her past and what exactly had turned her into such a control freak. She was present, and curious.

And beautiful.

Damn.

He caught her looking at him again, her eyes warm and wide behind her sunglasses, and he felt something in his chest shift. Whatever had annoyed her about him that first day…maybe it hadn't vanished entirely. But it wasn't winning anymore either.

He was in trouble.

Real trouble.

Emilia couldn't help but be fascinated by all of this. When Alejandro tried out his Dhivehi, the Maldivian language, one fisherman made a joke about his accent, which sent the group into fits of laughter, and she also felt a warmth bloom in her chest at how humbly Alejandro took the jibing.

Okay so the man was infuriating for many reasons, and he clearly had certain opinions about New York and New Yorkers that didn't always sit well, and she hadn't wanted to join this little expedition at all…but she was actually having a good time, and learning a lot too.

One of the fishermen, an older gentleman with a weathered face and bright eyes that shone at them from under a tattered baseball hat, turned to them. 'You two look like you could use a bite to eat. How about joining us for lunch?'

Emilia opened her mouth to politely decline, mentally running through her to-do list back at the clinic. She had a few new rules to implement, and instruction lists to update; and she needed to source some coat hooks, seeing as the ones she'd tried to order wouldn't arrive for eight weeks.

Before she could utter a word, though, Alejandro was already nodding his head. 'We'd be honoured,' he said, casting an encouraging glance in Emilia's direction. 'I'm ravenous!'

Okay then, it seemed they were accepting the invitation. They weren't exactly going to send two boats over to bring them back separately.

She followed Alejandro silently as they were led towards a makeshift stall, where a group of locals was cooking and eating. As they were shown their seats at a plastic cloth-covered table, the breeze blew over her, thick with the rich smell of grilled seafood and fresh herbs, not like the raw fishy smell they'd left behind them on the dock. Simple wooden benches surrounded several low tables, all of them laden with food. A real feast. It was mostly seafood that had, she presumed, been freshly caught that morning—lobster, fish, crab—grilled over coconut husks and served with local vegetables and tropical fruits.

A large pot held fluffy white rice cooked in coconut milk. It smelled delicious and was being served up steaming in coconut shells. There was even a chutney made from local mangoes, which was spicy and sweet all at once, according to the fisherman. Emilia's stomach rumbled. She hadn't even realised she was hungry until now.

The laughter and chatter around them felt as welcoming as the sound of cracking shells and sizzling pans from behind the counter. She watched as Alejandro loaded a plate

with giant prawns and started tackling a lobster with enthu-
siasm. 'What are you waiting for—get involved,' he urged
her, as she looked on in interest.

'I'm not used to this,' she admitted as she eyed the mountain of grilled lobster glistening on the platter. It was true.
She hadn't eaten out in months, aside from a pizza or a burger
with Maxxine. Especially not seafood. It had always been
too expensive in New York. And honestly, she'd never really known where to go for a good meal. Aiden had preferred
cooking at home, turning grocery runs into weekend rituals.
She, on the other hand, had always been working…grabbing
whatever was quick and cheap between hospital shifts.

Alejandro raised an eyebrow with a teasing grin, spear-
ing a lobster like he did it for a day job and sliding it onto
her plate.

'Let me guess…back in New York, it comes pre-dismem-
bered in a tiny ramekin, drowning in butter and overpriced
truffle foam?'

She laughed despite herself. 'Something like that,' she
said, taking the napkins he offered. She wasn't about to
admit that even if she had wanted to go out for lobster, she
probably couldn't have afforded it. But here with salt in
the air and all these people, including Alejandro, smiling
at her like she deserved to feast like this every day of her
life, it didn't seem to matter. She picked up a fork, wondering where to begin.

'Use your hands, it's more fun.' He grinned, his fingers
busy with his own seafood. 'Unless you really are completely averse to spontaneity, Doctor?'

She refused to let him ruffle her feathers with a comment like that. Taking a deep breath, she rolled up imaginary sleeves for his benefit and reached for the hefty claw
that lay on her plate. Then she paused, wondering again

where to start. With or without a fork, this seemed impossible. He was right; this was supposed to be chopped up already, smothered in sauce.

Seeing her dilemma, Alejandro laughed, pushing back his chair to get closer. 'Like this, see?' he said, demonstrating how to open the shellfish, his long, tanned fingers nimble and quick. He had nice hands, she mused. Big. Like his feet. What else about him was large?

Goodness, what was she thinking?

The onlookers at the table watched this little demo in amusement and she flushed as he put his hands over hers next, showing her how to crack the shell and extract the tender meat.

'Now, you try,' he encouraged, sitting back down. She could still feel the heat of his hands on hers as she did as she was told, giving Alejandro a triumphant look as she pulled out more juicy meat from the shell. In truth, she was surprising even herself now. There was no denying the satisfaction that came from mastering a new technique. Not to mention, the food was downright delicious. Much better thanks to not being smothered in a fancy sauce, she was sure.

Wiping her hands, she realised Alejandro was watching her, his eyes bright with approval—and a flash of something warmer—at her obvious enjoyment. She found herself blushing again.

'I suppose some spontaneity isn't all bad,' she conceded, tucking away a stray lock of hair that had escaped her neat braid, before taking out the hair tie and letting it fly loose. It was too breezy to contain it anyway.

'A breakthrough!' he teased, raising an imaginary glass in toast, and flicking his eyes across her long hair.

She raised her own imaginary glass, wondering if he thought her completely neurotic for the way she'd acted on the day they'd met. He didn't know how much she valued everything being predictable and reliable. There was comfort in consistency. Since Aiden had died she'd found solace in routine, all the things she could trust to stay the same. Surprises were not welcome in her life. She had never liked them, actually, not even before Aiden's death, which had come as the biggest surprise of all.

Walking back to the boat, Alejandro had half a journal of notes and Emilia had a full belly and a little sunburn, which was annoying. She had tried so hard to add enough lotion before leaving but the sun here was strong. She could feel the way Alejandro kept looking at her reddening shoulders, glancing sideways so as not to make it too obvious.

'Do you have any more sunscreen in your bag?' he finally asked, concern written all over his face.

'I do, yes, but mine appears to be ineffective.'

Stopping under a canopy of trees, Alejandro reached inside his bag and pulled out a tube of sunblock. 'Here, use mine. It's SPF fifty. You've got to have the strong stuff around here.'

'Thank you,' she said, trying not to sound too flustered as she accepted the tube from him. 'I'll need this on the boat ride back to the clinic.'

'Yes, you will.'

She squeezed some of the thick cream onto her fingers and began to tentatively rub it into her hot skin. As she tried to reach around her back, however, she couldn't quite manage it. The sunburn was worse than she'd initially thought too. Any small movement sent sharp twinges of pain through her shoulder blades. Oh dear. She was going to pay for this heavily later.

Alejandro cleared his throat lightly. 'Would you like some help?' he offered.

She turned to look at him, letting the offer hang between them in the humid air. She wasn't great at accepting help in any form. After Aiden's death she had been a mess, understandably, but she'd accepted so much help that after a while she had grown too embarrassed to ask, for fear that people might think she was taking too much. But Alejandro stepped forward through the silence and took the tube back, squeezing the white paste onto his fingers.

'Turn around,' he instructed. Then, slowly, he began applying it onto her back. He even carefully lifted the straps of her top to get it underneath them. His touch was gentle but firm enough to tell her he was serious about this task, and she did her best not to shift on her feet, which would have revealed her unease. It wasn't like she was used to being touched like this, but he was a man on a mission.

The sound of their breathing and the ocean waves crashing nearby became a soundtrack to these new sensations as his fingers traced each vertebra delicately, making sure every inch of her exposed skin received adequate protection. He was being so thorough, she thought, smiling to herself, realising she had actually closed her eyes and was fully leaning into the pleasure of his touch. Her breath caught when his knuckles grazed the skin at the edge of her bra and her eyes sprang open. She was liking this way too much now.

'Thank you,' she said, stopping him in motion by turning around. He frowned slightly, then shrugged and screwed the lid back on the tube. Had she just made things awkward? Probably. Oh, gosh.

The boat ride back to the clinic was quiet, but in a way that felt easy, like neither of them needed to fill the silence anymore. Emilia was grateful for it. Her senses were already overloaded, and far too tuned in to every shift of Alejandro's body beside her. She tried to focus on the low, steady hum of the boat's engine and the occasional cry of a sea-bird soaring overhead. She hadn't learned what any of the local birds were yet—she'd been too busy brushing up on jellyfish stings and figuring out how to order coat hooks, which had somehow shot to the top of her list. But she was pretty sure Alejandro could name every last one of them.

He didn't look at her, he just kept his gaze fixed on the horizon, like he was a thousand miles away in his brain. She found herself looking his way more than once, however. The white shirt, the wind teasing his dark curls, the aviators that made him look like he belonged out here more than on dry land. The sun was strong, but his skin didn't show a hint of sunburn, just that effortless golden glow that made her reddened bits feel worse, and the rest of her pale and awkward beside him. Why was he making her feel like this? Why was he making her feel anything at all? This was not why she'd come here!

He'd caught her off guard all day, charming the locals like he'd known them forever, making everyone laugh over lunch with that easy, irresistible humour, and then casually handing her sunscreen like he'd been looking out for her all along and had simply been waiting for the chance to assist. But every time he did something unexpected, it threw her a little more off balance.

How was she supposed to stay grounded when he kept being this version of perfect she hadn't seen coming? She was suddenly more determined than ever to dig out his flaws, just to prove to herself that he had some.

CHAPTER FIVE

THE CLINIC'S GENERATOR was acting more like an over-
worked employee today, barely keeping up with the humidity. Emilia swiped at her brow with the back of her
wrist. It had rained again overnight but somehow it felt hot-
ter than ever. She was just wishing she could escape from
the empty clinic and take another long cold shower when
the door burst open with the force of a small hurricane and
a man stumbled inside, clutching his stomach, his face a
worrying shade of grey.

Two guys flanked him, both in Maldives tourist T-shirts,
their voices tumbling over each other in a frantic rush to
tell her what had happened.

So much for a cold shower.

'It started after lunch, Doctor. He felt a bit sick, then he
started throwing up. He can't even keep water down now,'
one of them told her, pressing a hand to his sick friend's
shoulder, which only made him half topple under the pressure. Emilia was already moving.

'Get him on the table,' she instructed, rolling up her
sleeves as she assessed him quickly. His skin was clammy,
his breathing shallow. It looked like classic dehydration but
goodness, he was weak. His friend's eyes darted between
Emilia and the sweaty man, like they expected her to perform a miracle on the spot. They were understaffed right
now, as usual. She would just have to do her best.

Just as she reached for a thermometer, he walked in.
Alejandro.

She had to admit, the man had a knack for perfect timing.
She sighed to herself. She had been keeping her distance
from him a little the past few days, after that unnerving sunscreen encounter. Developing an insta-crush on anyone, let
alone an infuriating drifter on some heroic global agenda,
was not going to happen…but even she had to admit she
needed him right then.

'Food poisoning,' Alejandro declared quickly, taking one
look at the guy. She whipped her head around to find him
already snapping on a pair of gloves.

'We don't know that yet,' she said, shooting him a look
that hopefully said to back off. Okay, she was glad he'd
shown up, but could he not just remember the pecking order,
for one minute? She was the lead here. And he was always
too quick to diagnose people without adhering to protocol
or basic methods they'd both clearly studied. It was like he
couldn't help himself.

Aha, one of those flaws she'd been looking for!

Alejandro lowered his voice so only she could hear. 'He's
clammy.'

'Thanks, I have eyes,' she murmured.

'I'm betting he's eaten undercooked seafood.'

She exhaled sharply, forcing herself to focus on the patient, not the man beside her. 'We'll run a few tests before
jumping to conclusions, I think.'

He arched a brow. 'Nausea, vomiting, feverish? Looks
pretty obvious to me.'

'Or it could be something worse.' She folded her arms,
already bracing herself for the inevitable argument. 'A bac-
terial infection. An allergic reaction. Even ciguatera poisoning.'

Alejandro sighed. 'Or…it's just food poisoning. It's pretty common around here, despite the five-star buffet. People take food to their rooms…'

She gritted her teeth. He was infuriating. Infuriating and possibly right. She had seen no end of people carrying food into their hot rooms from the hotel resort over the past couple weeks, making private picnics with it in the hot sun, leaving plates unattended in the heat before going back to them, but that wasn't the point.

Their gazes locked. 'Fluids. Now, please,' she added, and he huffed the tiniest laugh for her benefit.

She gnawed on her cheek as they worked. Alejandro Vargas was all instinct and gut feeling, whereas she detested rushing in blind. He was thorough, yes, and observant, also yes, but he definitely operated differently to her. She'd spent the best part of her career on a New York trauma ward surrounded by people who all followed the exact same protocol. He had been out in the field, probably stumbling upon all kinds of scenarios that required thinking on his feet. This she knew, even understood, but it didn't make it any less frustrating to deal with.

The clinic's overhead fan spun lazily down on their silent standoff and her mind reeled. Then the patient, a wealthy businessman from Portsmouth, groaned miserably and promptly threw up on the floor.

'Oh, God… I am never eating lobster again,' he mumbled, wiping his mouth before she could even hand him a towel.

Alejandro grinned behind his hand like he'd won, and she shook her head, helping the guy off with his dirty shirt, and into a blue gown. Gradually, with some rehydration fluids in his system and the seafood now evacuated, his breathing steadied, and the pallor in his face eased up until he resembled a regular-coloured white man, albeit one who would not be enjoying much of the Vaara Atoll Eco-Resort's fresh catches for the remainder of his vacation.

As she went to the sink to wash her hands, Alejandro wiped his hands on a towel and glanced at her. 'Admit it, I was right,' he whispered.

She huffed. 'You were. Happy?'

He leaned against the counter, crossing his arms. 'You hate that I'm always right.'

'You're not always right, you're just always…here. Don't you have some coral reef to explore somewhere?'

Something flickered in his gaze. 'Just got back. I'm available just for *you* now.'

Emilia ignored the way that made her stomach tighten in anticipation. Without looking at him, she sighed. 'Let's just get through the day without another emergency, shall we?'

Alejandro grinned. 'Where's the fun in that?'

Later, when she stepped outside, the midday sun threw its harsh light across the painted mural on the wall, making the coral and turtles and darting fish shimmer like it was all actually alive. Alejandro had encouraged the kids to do this, she remembered, feeling a warm and fuzzy feeling towards him that she promptly shoved away, recalling how much of a pain in the ass he was too. Why could she not just get him out of her head?

He had left her about an hour ago, when she'd finally insisted he go be useful elsewhere, and here he was now, kneeling on the stone floor with a group of children gathered around him in the sun, their eyes all wide with wonder.

She paused just before he spotted her coming up the path. It wasn't the first time she'd caught him like this, completely absorbed in a sea of giggles and grubby hands. The local kids, most of them children of the hotel staff, flocked to him like he was some kind of sun-kissed Pied Piper sent from afar to entertain them. His hands moved in wide, animated gestures as he spoke to them all, his voice rising and falling with whatever story he was spinning now.

He was obviously in his element here, laughing, connecting, being all effortlessly magnetic in a way that she most definitely had never been, even before she'd lost Aiden. For a long moment, she just watched him, caught off guard by how easily he fit in here. How naturally he belonged. Was he like this everywhere he went?

'The ocean gives us life,' he said now as his eyes finally found hers. He was making a grand sweeping motion. 'And in return, we must all protect it.' He stood and pointed to the mural next, tracing the outline of a reef shark with his fingertip. 'Everything is connected. You, me, the fish, the sharks...'

'Not the sharks,' Emilia found herself protesting, a small smile stretching out her mouth. Everyone turned to stare at her.

'Even the sharks,' Alejandro countered, smiling back at her, and for a moment his twinkling brown eyes held hers and she momentarily forgot again just how much he had annoyed her earlier with their food-poisoning patient.

The children hung on his every word as he continued talking about an encounter with a hammerhead shark he'd had once in Indonesia, playfully imitating it zooming towards him, then darting away at the last minute. Emilia folded her arms, an eyebrow arched. She doubted much of it was true, but it didn't even matter. His captive audience totally adored him.

A little girl scrambled up and tucked herself against his side, her small fingers curling into his sleeve as she whispered a question. Alejandro bent down, murmuring something in return that made her break into peals of laughter.

Something inside Emilia twisted as she pictured Aiden with his niece, Beth. He'd been a natural with kids too. She'd had so many ideas for what she'd do with her impending motherhood role, how he would do the school runs and soccer dad stuff, how she'd bake and craft and play, just as long as they could do it all knowing her other work was done— her work at the hospital, which had, in retrospect, stolen much of her twenties and early thirties, and well…most of her life up to this point, to be perfectly honest.

And now, actually, she would probably never have the chance to be a mother. She'd squandered her prime time for getting things going, assured herself that she still had plenty of time and that she'd always have Aiden. She'd thrown herself right back into the fray after losing him too. She didn't know much about being a widow, or how to live without Aiden, but she knew how to be efficient. How to keep people alive. How to stitch up wounds and keep her emotions locked down tight.

She was good at staying in control. Alejandro was clearly good at making connections. And sometimes she hated that about him. But still, she couldn't look away. It was pure envy, she realised. She had forgotten how to be that open with people.

His shirt clung to the lines of his shoulders, damp from the heat. A stray curl fell onto his forehead as he crouched lower, his long fingers carving shapes in the sand, this time to explain how water filtered impurities. He seemed to have an absolute knack and passion for teaching. It wasn't just another way to garner admiration, like with so many other people. It made him unfairly attractive.

Another of the kids was tugging at Alejandro's hand now, pulling him into a game, pretending to swipe him with a make-believe sword. He groaned dramatically, staggering back like he'd been mortally wounded. The children all shrieked with laughter, swarming around him as he feigned defeat in the sun. Emilia huffed out a laugh despite herself.

That was a mistake, because Alejandro glanced up, catching her still watching him. His lips quirked. She should've stayed put and maintained the space between them, but instead, she moved forward, letting herself be pulled into his orbit like the kids. Stepping closer, she felt Alejandro's warm, tanned hand wrap around her wrist. Not tightly, just enough to pull her a step closer. Enough to remind her that this proximity to him was sending her heartrate to the heavens.

'So you're finally joining us, Doctor?' His voice was all smooth amusement, but there was an edge to it under the teasing, a twinkle just for her in his eyes.

'I figured someone had to make sure you weren't filling their heads with nonsense,' she shot back, folding her arms as she tilted her head towards the mural. 'What's it going to be this time? That dolphins can talk? That jellyfish are secretly plotting world domination?'

'Wait, they're not?'

'Very funny.' She glanced at the kids, now all looking up at her, and cleared her throat. 'I mean, well…we don't really know their agenda, do we? They can't speak.'

A grin flickered across his lips, but then, just as quickly, something in his expression shifted and as the children dissipated, lost in their make-believe sword game, he sank to the floor in the shade, letting his gaze drift past her.

'My sister used to love this kind of thing when she was a child. She'd never be indoors. She was like a feral cat, always slipping out for an adventure.' He smiled almost absently, like the thought had just slipped out of his mouth and now he couldn't stop more from escaping. 'She was about the same age as that one when she first got sick.' He nodded towards a girl with blonde bouncing curls, who was now chasing her friend in a fun game of tag.

Emilia nodded. She still didn't know much about Alejandro's family, except that his father had passed and his mother and sister now lived in Spain.

'Maria, right?' Emilia prompted carefully. 'Your sister's name is Maria.' She was so curious now.

Alejandro nodded, rolling the cuff of his sleeve. 'Yes, Maria. She's seven years my junior.' A pause, his eyes flicking towards the ocean in the distance. 'I told you how she got sick?'

Emilia's stomach tightened as she sank to the shady ground beside him. She couldn't imagine sitting on a floor in New York, but she was doing a lot of things here she'd never dreamed she'd be doing.

'You've mentioned something about how you almost lost her once—and a waterborne disease,' she said softly. 'But you didn't say exactly what happened.'

Alejandro exhaled through his nose, and his light dimmed just enough for her to notice.

'No one knew what was wrong at first,' he said. 'She had fevers that kept coming back, and she started losing weight fast. The doctors in Caracas ran every test they could think of, but...' He shook his head, his jaw tightening. 'They thought it was a virus. Or maybe malnutrition. Something common and treatable.'

'But it wasn't,' Emilia said.

He looked over at her, something shadowed in his eyes. 'No. It was legionnaires' disease. She got it from the local outdoor swimming pool, we think. It's not something they even tested for right away, not in those hospitals.'

Emilia's heart clenched.

'They kept missing it,' Alejandro went on, the frustration

rising in his voice. 'My father begged them to look deeper, every damn day. But no one was listening. They just kept pumping her full of fluids and vitamins, treating symptoms. By the time a private clinic finally ran the right test, the bacteria had already damaged her lungs, and her nervous system. She couldn't walk properly for a while. She still has trouble breathing sometimes.'

'I'm so sorry,' Emilia murmured. The words felt too small for the weight in his voice.

He ran a hand through his hair, staring out towards the edge of the compound. 'She's okay now. Better, I mean. But she has asthma and allergies. Her immune system's extremely fragile. She can't be out in the sun for long without getting sick, which she hates. She wanted to be outside, playing sports, doing everything. But instead...' He shrugged, his voice bitter. 'Instead, she's inside most days, watching the world through a screen.'

Emilia could feel the ache of the injustice and the helplessness behind his words.

'She's in Valencia now, like I said. And she's doing what she can. But it changed everything. Not just for her, for all of us.'

He paused, then let out a humorless laugh. 'You know the worst part? Even after we knew what it was...after we moved her out of the city...kids were still swimming in that pool, still getting sick. Nothing changed. No clean-up. No warnings. We tried to get it shut down but they wouldn't do it.'

He looked down at his hands, then back up at her, eyes dark with something like guilt. 'I drank the same water as Marie, and swam in that pool. I should have gotten sick too, but I didn't.'

'You got lucky,' Emilia said quietly.

'I would rather it had been me than her. I wanted so badly to fix it. I think I wanted to fix everything back then.'

She nodded gently, suddenly understanding a lot more about him. He still wanted to fix everything and everyone. Alejandro wasn't just a man who threw himself into his work because he loved the rush of saving lives. He was trying to make up for all the ones he couldn't save. And under it all, he carried a quiet, stubborn guilt for the fact that Maria fell ill back then instead of him. He honestly still believed he should have taken her place.

Emilia watched as his fingers flexed at his sides, like he was trying to shake off something that weighed far more than he wanted to admit. Maybe he was regretting telling her so much already, but he shouldn't.

Carefully, she nudged his arm. 'You're still trying to fix it,' she said. 'Every day. I see it.'

Alejandro's gaze flicked to hers, his expression unreadable. Then he smirked, his vulnerability retreating behind his usual bravado. 'Well, someone's got to keep you on your toes, Doctor.'

Emilia rolled her eyes. Fine, if he wanted to stay behind his shield of glib humour, she'd let him. But he'd already lowered it once, and it wasn't something she was going to forget. He'd spent years watching doctors hesitate, watching his sister waste away while they debated and deliberated, so it made sense that he'd grown into someone who acted first, fought first and considered later. It was how he'd survived what had happened to his sister, and his whole family.

Alejandro glanced at her like he was waiting for her usual sharpness, another quip in response to being kept on her toes. Instead, she just held his gaze. Then, to her own surprise, she reached out her fingers, grazing his forearm, maybe in some subconscious attempt to ground him, or to connect with him, who knew?

'So what are *you* trying to fix? Besides everything at the clinic?' His voice came at her just as she pulled her hand back again and her cheeks burned as she refocused on the kids playing. The truth was, she knew what it was like to float like that, to act like one person but feel like someone else inside. Yet telling him she was a widow at her age still felt a little…embarrassing? It wasn't her fault Aiden had died. But it always felt like it drew too much unwanted attention.

His gaze dipped to where they'd just touched as the air between them thickened. 'There's a reason you came all the way here, and it wasn't just to work somewhere so insufferably tiny and hot,' he observed. 'I see you too, you know?'

Then, a small voice shattered the moment.

'Are you two gonna keep on flirting, or are we getting back to our lessons?'

Both of them snapped their attention towards the grinning boy standing beside them. He had his hands on his hips, like he'd caught them both red-handed and was very much enjoying it. Emilia stood, flustered.

Alejandro recovered first, flashing the kid an exaggerated wink. 'Depends. You think she's impressed by me yet?'

Emilia rolled her eyes again, but the heat in her chest would not let her make light of that conversation, or that touch. Without doubt, he did see her, and she had a feeling he wasn't going to stop asking her about herself either, now that he'd started.

CHAPTER SIX

LORD ABOVE, THIS WOMAN was killing him slowly. Alejandro watched Emilia pinning her flow charts to the whiteboard. She looked particularly beautiful today, which was distracting the hell out of him, and her shoulders were decidedly less red, but he knew what was coming.

She had called a meeting in the outdoor space outside the clinic, seeing as the air conditioning unit had finally given up the ghost and was currently being fixed. The air was stifling, even at 8:00 a.m.

He sipped on his iced coffee and watched as Emilia aligned each piece of paper perfectly. He could almost hear her mind whirring as people started taking their seats in the semi-circle of wooden chairs he'd helped position about the area. They'd come from the other islands on boats, from other resorts, a crew of staff and other volunteers who somehow never seemed to be scheduled to work at the clinic... or at least rarely showed up, leaving the need for long-term resident locums like Emilia.

She looked particularly radiant in those eggshell-coloured pants and a matching blouse with her trademark braid swaying around her left shoulder like the tail of one of Maria's horses. His sister had been obsessed with those cute plastic horses as a girl. But he still found Emilia infuriating for the most part, which went some way in curbing the almost constant desire to pull on that braid, or maybe pull her pretty mouth to his and kiss her.

The thought made him smile to himself. As if he would ever do either. He'd earn himself a slap. It was pretty clear that she found him just as insufferable as ever, even though they had shared a rare moment of understanding the other day, when he'd spoken about Maria. From the way she'd acted then, it was evident that she had something going on of her own, someone she'd lost. Some other reason for being out here. Why else would she have said she'd come to get away from 'everything'.

Everyone thought I needed a break from...everything.

It sounded to him like it was more than just an urge to escape the bustle of a Manhattan trauma ward for a while, although he could well imagine the fresh hell a place like that must be on a daily basis. You couldn't pay him to do that.

The woman was an enigma for sure.

She cleared her throat at the front. 'Thank you all for coming. We'll try and make this brief. I've outlined a more streamlined response system for the clinic that I hope will help us all prevent any errors in high-pressure cases.'

Alejandro tipped back in his chair, letting the legs creak beneath him as she spoke. He liked to see how far things could bend before they broke. He didn't miss the look she'd just shot him either, like he alone provided the need for a more streamlined system around here. But she went on, and on, pointing at charts, referring to notes, even attempting to divert one of the tsunami evacuation routes so it went past the doors to the clinic.

'What if, instead of strangling ourselves with all this proposed structure, we left some room for a little flexibility?' His voice came out at her directly, warm enough, sure, but he hoped the challenge in his words was unmistakable.

Several people turned to him. He gestured loosely at the whiteboard. 'We should adapt to things in real time, don't you think, not just tick off a bunch of boxes. Life doesn't always give us time to think, Doctor.'

Would she bend? Or was she about to break?

She turned, shooting him a look that could cut glass. 'Being flexible doesn't save lives, Doctor. Being prepared does. I was hired to implement these new protocols so—'

'So no one has *any* room left to be responsive and flexible in a crisis?'

'That's not what I'm implying.'

A slow grin tugged at the corner of his mouth. There she was. Neither bending nor breaking.

'I agree we should be prepared if we're building a dam to redirect a tsunami, but in a clinic, where people stagger in at random and don't always know why they're sick, sometimes our instincts override what we've been taught. What about that guy with food poisoning who we helped the other day?' he countered. 'You were wanting to run a bunch of tests. I was getting fluids into him, watching him vomit up lobster.'

Her jaw tightened, but not before he caught the flicker of discomfort in her eyes.

'I was ruling out something more serious with the tests, as you well know,' she shot back. 'What if it had been cigua-tera poisoning? Or an allergic reaction?'

'But it wasn't.' He leaned forward, elbows on his knees, his voice dipping just enough to unsettle her composure even more. 'And that's my point. You like to control every variable, but out here? The variables laugh at your flow charts, Doctor.'

He could barely believe they were having this conversation in front of everyone, but he'd started so he may as well finish. Emilia exhaled sharply, her nostrils flaring. Oh, he was winding her up good and proper now. Her eyes screamed *Shut the hell up, stay in your lane, stop poking holes in my plans*, and the rare crack in her armour sent a thrill through him that he probably shouldn't enjoy this much. She was particularly attractive when she was pissed at him.

'This isn't about control,' she insisted, flicking her braid over her shoulder defiantly. 'I don't know how things work on your…missions, Doctor, but in the real world it's about taking responsibility. We can't afford to be reckless here, or anywhere else, for that matter.'

Alejandro let her words settle between them, watching how it made her shoulders pull even straighter. Reckless. She really thought that was what he was? He dragged a hand through his hair, letting the silence stretch before he spoke again. 'Did you ever think, Doctor, that being so rigid is just another kind of recklessness?'

That got to her. A flicker of something in her expression showed him he'd gotten under her skin, well and truly. Either way, he wasn't about to let up.

'With all due respect, all these regulations are great in textbooks. But you and I both know the real world doesn't give a damn about your perfectly laid out plans.'

Her fingers curled slightly against the table. She was either going to kill him or… Well, he wasn't entirely sure what the alternative was, but he had a few ideas. He had used up every last inch of his charm and now she was getting the rest of him. Admittedly, it wasn't the best of him. But he could hardly appreciate this strict regime she was imposing, even if it was part of the reason they'd hired her…not when he pretty much always had to work off the cuff in his job.

Some of the other attendees looked uncomfortable now, checking their phones, looking for a way out of here.

'I'd rather be thorough than gamble with someone's life,' she said curtly, glaring directly into his eyes. 'I'd have thought you'd understand that.'

He studied her, letting the moment stretch out like a rubber band. Touché. She'd just referred to Maria, and what he'd told her about the next-to-useless health care she had—or rather hadn't—received as a child. Everyone just looked confused now, but they might as well not be there. This was between himself and Emilia. There was no winning this argument, not in the way he wanted. They were two sides of the same coin with their stubbornness.

'You really don't like leaving anything to chance, do you?' he murmured anyway.

Her gaze flicked to his and she opened her mouth, but before she could retort, one of the nurses poked her head around a nearby tree, shattering the tension.

'The supply truck just arrived,' she announced. 'Thought you'd want to check inventory, Dr Sturgis? He can't stay long.'

Emilia straightened, smoothing her blouse like she could iron out whatever had just flared up between them and ruined her perfect little presentation.

'Thanks, I'm on it,' she said, already collecting her things. 'I'll leave my plan here,' she added, gesturing to her sheets of paper. 'You can all look over it at your leisure.' Then she leveled him with a look that would have chilled anyone else's bones before turning on her heel towards the clinic. He watched her go, amusement curling at the edges of his lips. Well, that was over quick. But thank God for that.

Then again, maybe he'd been a little hard on her?

She knew about Maria; he hadn't exactly held back before. Something about her presence that day, surrounded by all those happy kids, had rendered him unable to stop the memories from spilling out of him. Maybe that was why he was riling her up now. This strange new desire to be in her presence was undeniable, despite—or maybe because of—their propensity to disagree on most things, and he wasn't ready for it. Not by a long shot.

He wasn't here to get hooked on someone. Why bother when he had work to do? Important work. Everything else was just a distraction—especially a mental match like Emilia, whom he very much enjoyed sparring with as much as he enjoyed catching her half naked in a stream of morning sunshine.

He'd been imagining seeing that again. Closer up this time. With his lips on hers and his hands everywhere else.

So he'd pulled out his usual sword and fended her off.

Nice work, Alejandro, you giant ass.

The lap of the tide against the shore followed him as he strode around the bay towards the dive shop just outside the resort, rolling the stiffness from his shoulders and carrying the bag of cold beers. The meeting this morning had been a mess, which was obviously his fault. He should probably apologise to Emilia for steamrolling her like that with his usual off-putting brand of not-so-charming defiance. But he wasn't sure she'd be in the mood to hear it just yet.

She'd disappeared after those supplies had arrived and he thought he'd seen her on her veranda, talking on her phone. Probably recounting his rudeness to someone in New York, as if anyone there was likely to care. They were all rude in New York, weren't they?

He did feel a little guilty now, though.

More than a little, actually.

Tom, a longtime friend who'd come to work on the island from Canada several years ago, stood by the shop's entrance, adjusting the Reef Explorer sign that always creaked comfortingly in the sea breeze from its bronze post. Alejandro always came here when he visited the island; it was more like a second Maldives home to him at this point.

'Alejandro!' Tom called out, flashing a wide grin from under his Reef Explorer hat. 'You here to actually buy some dive gear this time, or just talk your way into borrowing mine again?'

Alejandro grinned. 'What's your policy on shamelessly taking advantage of old friends?'

Tom snorted. 'Favourable, but only because you bring beer, *old friend.*'

A flicker of movement caught Alejandro's eye as he handed the beers over. Emilia had arrived. She must have followed him here, but held back, probably wary of starting another conversation that might end badly. He cringed inwardly as she stopped a few feet away with a look on her face that could only be described as defensive disapproval.

'Sorry, I… I thought you might need this.' She handed over a large green box with a white cross on it, which Alejandro realised he had also meant to bring for the dive shop, but forgotten at the last minute. She'd come with the new medical first aid kit that had arrived on the supplies truck. The woman had done him a favour, despite him totally derailing her precious meeting before. Great. Now he felt even guiltier.

'I'm actually here on official business,' Alejandro said, throwing a glance her way. 'But now that you're here too, Dr Sturgis, you can provide your expert supervision.'

Her brow arched pointedly as she shook Tom's out-of the Eiffel Tower, with a boy on a bicycle at the front, a dog trotting beside him. When Pearl moved the slider underneath, the boy and his dog travelled from one side of the thick card page to the other.

Celeste chuckled, batting Pearl's hand away so that she could try for herself. She made the boy move back and forth across the page a few times and then Pearl encouraged her to turn to the next page, which featured the boy and his dog, standing in a flower market. Celeste tried swiping her hand across the bottom, and when that didn't work she found the button in the corner, and pressed it. A tinkling tune sounded and she leaned over, pressing her ear to the picture and chuckling.

'What a beautiful book, Luc.'

He nodded, a little awkwardly. 'I hope she likes it.' Luc seemed suddenly unsure of himself.

'Look at her face, Luc, she *loves* it,' Pearl chided him. Celeste was struggling to turn the page, and Pearl helped her with it. The next picture was of the Louvre Museum and Celeste found the slider that made the boy and his dog appear from behind the glass pyramid.

'Good. I wasn't sure what to get. I picked the one I liked the best.'

This must be hard for him. Not knowing what Celeste liked and disliked, and clearly wanting to please her. 'You're doing fine, Luc. By the way, did Henri mention dinner tonight? Nathalie told me that I should be firm and insist you come. Henri's working late and will be giving us a lift home.'

Luc chuckled. 'I took a rain check when Henri asked. I reckon it would be best to take things slowly for starters. But I'll be sure to let Nathalie know that you applied maximum pressure on her behalf if she says anything.'

He was probably right. They'd be eating after Celeste's bedtime anyway, and there was no reason for Luc to be there then. 'I appreciate that. Since I'll be here tomorrow, in my guise as fellow neurologist, then perhaps I can persuade you to come then? You could spend an hour or so with Celeste and eat with us.'

He grinned suddenly. 'Nice tactics. Nathalie will be very proud of you. I won't turn that offer down, but tell Nathalie I'll bring something for dessert.'

'Will do. I'll mention that there was no talking any sense into you...' Pearl paused as Luc's phone beeped and he took it from his pocket.

'Sorry...'

'A patient?'

Luc shook his head. 'We have a volunteer looking after the front desk this evening, and he's not sure where everything is. This won't take a minute.' He dialled a number.

'Hi, this is Luc...' He listened for a moment and then launched into a complex set of instructions in French, which seemed to include a few rights and lefts, along with several wrong turns. Finally Luc nodded. 'Yes, that's it. No problem, thanks for your help...' He ended the call and put his phone back into his pocket.

'You know where all of those books are, without even looking?' She'd recognised the names of several well-known scientific authors who wrote on a diverse range of subjects.

He smiled. 'If you promise not to laugh...'

'I'm a neurologist, with a special interest in how memory works. I won't laugh.'

'I have a mind palace, which helps me to remember the library catalogue. Since it's situated here in the library then I've been able to include pointers to where each category of books is located in real life.'

Pearl frowned, trying to get her head around the idea. 'That sounds very complicated. Wouldn't it be easier just to sit down and learn it by rote?'

'Yes and no. Because the creative part of it is that you associate things you want to remember with things that mean something to you on an emotional level. It's broadly similar to the some of the memory techniques we use with our patients, associating memories with physical objects. Pick a topic...'

'Um...pharmacology. Dermatological agents.'

He smiled. 'I'm glad to hear you're making it easy for me. That's...right at the far end of the reading room, in the gallery. Second stack. You want to check?'

Pearl glanced at Celeste, who was playing happily with her new book. 'I'll have to take your word for it for the time being. Assuming that you're right, this doesn't look quite as dramatic as it does in films.'

Luc shrugged. 'I could ham it up a bit, if it makes you feel better. But actually mind palaces date back to Ancient Greece. As I said, it's a process of associating visual clues with information you want to remember. A bit like a mnemonic is a word or letter clue.'

'Okay... And how does that work in practise?'

'We'll start with a small mind palace...'

Pearl grinned. 'Maybe a mind semi-detached. In Surrey.'

'Perfect. You're getting the idea of this—it's all a matter of imagination. You start with a room that you can visualise easily, don't tell me what it is, it's personal to you. And a list of things you want to remember.'

The image of the hotel room they'd shared floated into

her head. Pearl could almost see it, she'd thought about it so many times. 'The periodic table. I never could remember that at school.'

He took out his phone. 'Neither could I, so I'm going to look it up.' He glanced at Pearl as she raised her eyebrows. 'Mind palaces don't make your general memory any better—they're a technique of getting the most out of what you have.'

'So, start in one corner of the room, and place something there which you can associate with the first thing you want to remember. Use your emotions and your imagination, I find you can remember it better that way. First hydrogen.'

A hydrogen rainbow, reflected up onto the ceiling by the door. 'Okay.'

'Next helium. Place something that reminds you of helium in the room, next to the hydrogen. A balloon, perhaps…?'

'Hey. This is *my* mind palace…' Pearl grinned at him. A red, heart-shaped helium balloon, set free to float gently up to the ceiling, would do very well.

'That's the first two, then. Just keep adding to them, a few at a time, until you have the lot. And of course it helps to go back to the beginning every now and then, just to fix the order of things in your memory. The associations aren't so difficult if you choose them yourself.'

'And that's all there is to it? What if I run out of space in my room?'

'Then you go to the next room. Or walk out into the garden or down the street—the route you take is up to you. Before long, you'll find your "mind semi-detached" becoming a mind palace.'

'And…the library's your mind palace?'

CHAPTER SEVEN

EMILIA HUGGED THE thin beach robe around her as she stepped onto the soft sand, her bare feet sinking slightly with each step. The sand was still warm from the afternoon sun, and the calm ocean lapped at the shore in picture-perfect fashion as always, but she could hardly believe she had agreed to this.

To her right along the beach, Alejandro was assessing the horizon with its bobbing fishing boats. Ahead of them, Tom was preparing a group of divers for their sunset descent—not that it mattered what the sun was doing if you were scuba-diving, surely, she thought to herself. What did she know about diving? Even less than she knew about snorkelling, apparently.

She was still half convinced she'd made a mistake agreeing to this. The idea of slipping into such an unfamiliar world as the ocean—an entity she could not predict or control for love nor money—was unsettling to say the least. She had only agreed because she'd been cajoled into it… and because Alejandro could be very convincing when he wanted to be. But before she could dwell on it, or on the way he looked right now, bare chested in his swim shorts, her gaze caught on a figure just ahead, knee-deep in the surf, surrounded by strange rippling shadows in the shallows.

An elderly Maldivian man stood in the water, his wrinkled posture completely relaxed, his bare, wet skin shimmering in the peachy low light. Stepping closer, she realised what the rippling shadows were around him and gasped. Stingrays!

There were more than twenty, gliding and flapping around the man, their dark, sleek, flat bodies slicing through the water like silk. Absolutely dozens of them were coming in, more every second. It was like he was summoning them. Emilia stopped short, transfixed. He was feeding them? How utterly magical.

The man reached down, his fingers brushing against their smooth forms as he scattered fish from a small bucket. The stingrays crowded around him, curling and unfurling like living ribbons as they ate up his offerings, and Emilia stepped even closer, watching how their silvery wings caught the last slants of sunlight every time one broke the surface. It was incredible, like something from another world.

Alejandro let out a low whistle, announcing his arrival beside her. 'Bet you don't see that every day in New York.'

Emilia barely registered his voice. The way the stingrays were moving, so unafraid and trusting, made her pulse slow. 'How are they not—' she paused and watched as one of the creatures lifted slightly onto the man's outstretched arm '—dangerous?'

The man turned at the sound of her voice, his weathered face creased in a beatific smile. 'They know me.'

Alejandro took a step forward. 'You've been feeding them for a while, right, Manu?'

Of course, Alejandro would know him too.

Manu nodded. 'Many, many years. They come every evening, same time. They remember.'

Yet she hadn't seen this before. Most nights she spent on her veranda, making her own notes or studying other notes.

The thought that she'd been missing this sent a strange shiver down Emilia's spine. She'd never considered that animals like this, sea creatures, could be capable of something like loyalty. Of choosing to return, like clockwork dogs from the deep.

Before she could properly process it all, the man beckoned them closer, holding out the bucket to them. Alejandro took a small fish without hesitation, wading to his waist and stretching out his hand. A stingray drifted towards him and with a soft whoosh, swept the fish from his fingers.

Alejandro grinned. 'They really love these fish. Beats having to shop for themselves, huh?'

He turned to Emilia, offering her one. She hesitated. The stingrays were beautiful, but they were still wild creatures, and she'd heard about people getting stung.

Alejandro must have caught the flicker of uncertainty in her expression because he tilted his head towards the man. 'What's the trick?'

The man's eyes twinkled at her. 'No trick. Just trust them like Alejandro did. Trust yourself.'

Emilia exhaled, steeling herself. She took the fish and held it out with her fingers hardly skimming the surface. For a breathless moment, nothing happened. But then, as if sensing her hesitation, one of the stingrays glided forward. It didn't snatch from her or jolt at all. It simply took the fish gently and glided away again.

Exhilaration shot through her. She was waist-deep in the water now. Her robe was soaked already and without thinking she took it off and tossed it backwards onto the dry sand. She glanced at Alejandro and to her surprise, he wasn't watching the stingrays anymore. He was watching her.

Warmth curled in her stomach as the old man straightened, waggling his empty bucket at the horizon as the stingrays disappeared as quickly as they'd arrived.

'The sun is setting. Good time to go in.'

Alejandro grabbed their masks and snorkels from the sand and returned with that knowing glint in his eyes. He held out a set. 'Ready, Doctor?'

She squared her shoulders and slipped the plastic thing over her face. 'I suppose I really don't have a choice now, do I?'

Alejandro's grin was all slow-burning mischief as he reached up to adjust the strap for her, his fingers brushing the nape of her neck. Gently, he moved her braid aside, and the touch sent another unexpected shiver right down her spine, straight to her core. His hands lingered just a second too long as he tightened the strap around her head, eyes locked on hers.

'You always have a choice,' he said softly. 'You just happened to make the right one.'

Oh, good lord.

The water was soft, wrapping around her like a second skin or watery blanket as she floated just beneath the surface with the snorkel in her mouth. It was quite surprising, actually, how…well…peaceful it was. She had expected to feel exposed, she supposed, maybe a little or a lot uneasy. But with Alejandro beside her, guiding her with gestures and finger pointing, the fear she'd braced herself for never came. Instead, she only felt awe.

Beneath them, the crystal-clear ocean came alive. Clusters of coral in impossible colours stretched out like miniature cities just half a metre below them as they drifted with the gentle current. Schools of bright yellow fish darted around them in synchronised chaos, flicking between the rocks, almost teasing them into following. Deeper below, she could see Tom leading a group of divers, their bubbles drifting lazily towards the surface. And wait. Was that a small shark?

Her eyes widened behind her mask. But Alejandro grinned around his snorkel and she knew from that expression alone that she was quite safe. She noticed the black tip on its tail. Ah, a harmless one.

Alejandro swam ahead, gesturing for her to follow. He pointed to a parrotfish, which she recognised from a photo in the dive shop. Its scales shimmered like it had stolen sunlight and swam down here with it—if only she had thought to invest in an underwater camera. To think, some coral no longer looked like this. Some coral was bleached and dying. It broke her heart, there was so much life down here depending on it.

A clownfish peeked at her, swimming up from the delicate anemone, and she laughed as it darted back between its swaying tendrils. Every time Alejandro pointed at something else he thought she should see, she caught the child-like excitement in his eyes. He looked like he belonged in this world, and he loved sharing it. God help her, it was so, so, so hot.

His quick wit, his relentless teasing, the way he managed to infuriate her and amuse her in equal measure… This man was going to be the death of her. She'd been spending so much time so far resenting his looseness, his absolute refusal to adhere to things she deemed imperative. But here, watching him move with absolute ease and joy in the water, she saw it for what it was. He wasn't careless. He was free.

For the first time in a long time, she felt a little bit free too. It had been years since she'd let herself feel this free. She had actively been choosing to wallow in the guilt of trying to enjoy a life without Aiden. What kind of a life was that? Probably not the kind of life Aiden would have wanted for her, if she was being totally honest with herself.

Alejandro glanced back, checking on her, giving her the thumbs up. She could not ignore the way his muscles looked under the water, the way the water slicked over his skin, highlighting the lean, toned cut of his torso. The way he moved with such effortless power wasn't helping her heart rate around him. Objectively, he was a beautiful man. She wasn't blind. But it wasn't his body that unsettled her the most, oh no. She wasn't in control around him. She certainly couldn't control the way she was starting to feel.

She went up for air, steadying herself in the setting sun. *It's just the environment*, she told herself. *Not him as a person.*

But then, when he reached out, offering his hand to guide her over a narrow stretch of sharp coral reef, she took it without thinking.

Okay then. Maybe the environment wasn't the only thing making her heart thrum. She would have to rein it in, though. Developing feelings for a colleague was a very bad idea, especially a reckless one who didn't seem to stay in one place for very long. Restoring the reef was admirable. She could understand why he was so passionate about that, and maybe she would get in on that project while she was here, in whatever capacity they could use her…but they had absolutely nothing in common except this island. She was a New Yorker and he was a man of the world.

She would just have to look and not touch, she decided.

Just then, a muffled noise sounded through the water. Emilia turned her head, her heart hammering at her ribs as a sudden flurry of movement erupted below. The group of divers had been exploring a cluster of coral, but one of them was thrashing now. Even from a distance she saw the way his limbs had started jerking. It sent a bolt of alarm right through her. Something was wrong.

Alejandro saw it too. He tapped her arm, then pointed down before surfacing. Emilia kicked up, ripping off her mask as soon as they broke through.

'Something's happened to that diver,' she gasped, breathless from the exertion.

Alejandro was already scanning the water. A second later, Tom surfaced, dragging one of the divers with him.

'He's not breathing right!' Tom shouted. 'Something spooked him, he shot up too fast!'

Alejandro swore, his limbs already thrashing towards the beach. 'Get him to the shore, now!'

Emilia and Alejandro both helped haul the diver's unresponsive body onto a paddleboard, thanks to a guy who was paddling nearby. Every second counted as they made for the beach.

As soon as they reached the shallows, Alejandro heaved the man onto the sand, flipping him onto his back. The diver was middle-aged. His face had gone pale and his lips were tinged with an ominous shade of blue. His wetsuit clung to his chest, rising and falling in erratic, shallow breaths.

'Emilia, airway!' Alejandro barked.

She was already moving, tilting the diver's head back, checking his breathing. Too rapid. His chest was barely rising. She pressed her fingers against his neck. 'Pulse is weak.'

'Damn,' Alejandro muttered, scanning the dive shop. 'We need oxygen, but this place barely has a functioning first-aid kit.'

'Yes, it does. Remember—I delivered that thing myself, just now! Tom, go grab it!'

Tom blinked at her for one second, then sped into action, coming back with the O2-rated aluminum cylinder she'd ordered. It was 100 percent medical-grade oxygen. She'd been stunned that the hotel had not provided any to the dive shop in case of a situation exactly like this.

Emilia secured the mask over the diver's face. 'Come on,' she murmured, watching for any change, her own pulse thrumming in her ears. She was shivering now in her swim-wear. The sun had all but disappeared into the horizon and she had no idea where her robe or sandals had gone.

The diver groaned weakly, his body shuddering as his breaths stuttered. It was helping a little but...

'He's going into shock,' Alejandro warned. 'We need to get him to the clinic before he deteriorates. We don't have time to wait for an evacuation.'

He was right. With Tom's help, and as a crowd of concerned locals and tourists looked on in concern, they loaded the man onto a makeshift stretcher, keeping him breathing the oxygen. Luckily, the clinic was only just up the beach. That was one good thing about being on a small island, at least.

Inside, she slid on some shoes in the doorway that were definitely not hers but which went some way in helping her not to slip on the shiny floor.

'Put him on his side,' she ordered in the treatment bay. If he was on his way towards an arterial gas embolism, they needed to keep the bubbles from reaching his brain.

Alejandro knew the drill and maneuvered him gently. A nurse who'd been covering for Emilia at late notice rushed over with another oxygen tank, and Emilia wasted no time in adjusting the flow. After a minute the diver's breathing steadied slightly, but he was still in danger.

'He needs a hyperbaric chamber,' she said. 'But until transport gets here—'

'Start an IV, keep him stable,' Alejandro cut in.

Emilia started a line, trying to keep her hands from shaking in the newly fixed air conditioning, which was chilling her damp, bare skin. Alejandro, also still in just his swim shorts, monitored vitals, adjusting the air, all the while murmuring reassurances to the semi-conscious diver. She kept stealing glances as they worked, watching how Alejandro checked the man's pupils, his jaw tight with concentration. He was good under pressure—more than good. He was calm, decisive and maddeningly competent. He'd fit right into a New York trauma ward, she thought, as if he'd ever willingly step foot into one.

'Breathing is still irregular,' he muttered.

'The sooner we get him into the chamber, the better his chances,' Emilia agreed.

As if on cue, Tom burst through the door. 'Evac boat's here!'

As the medical team took over, Emilia exhaled in relief, hugging her arms around herself for a second. Her adrenaline was still surging, and Alejandro was quick to locate a blanket, which he draped around her exposed shoulders. The clinic was suddenly still. It was just the two of them now. Everyone else had hurried outside.

Alejandro turned to her, rubbing a hand over his damp hair as he let himself flop into a swivel chair. 'Not bad for an inflexible control freak.'

She let out a breathless laugh, shaking her head. 'Not bad for a reckless improviser.'

Their eyes met, and he wheeled the chair closer, taking her hand, holding it steady. 'Seriously, Emilia. If you hadn't thought to order that extra oxygen for the surf shop...'

'I know,' she agreed and nodded.

They didn't need to discuss it. It was clear he knew what she'd done, and how her preparedness had possibly saved that diver. The electricity buzzed between them, thrumming through her exhaustion and this time Emilia didn't shove it away.

'I don't know about you,' she said on a sigh. 'But I need a cocktail.'

CHAPTER EIGHT

ALEJANDRO LED THE way along the beach to the resort. The stunning open-air restaurant beckoned them with mellow jazz music, the low hum of diners chatting and flickering candlelight. The tables were all set up like something from a dream around the infinity pool, and the scene helped to banish the last of the adrenaline that was still coursing through her veins.

They had stopped to quickly shower and change. Alejandro had been faster. He was already there, waiting for her on his veranda, when she emerged from her room wearing a sundress. She hadn't bothered braiding her hair again, so it hung long and loose around her shoulders. She didn't miss the double take he gave her, or how her pulse skidded when he saw the appreciation in his eyes, but she reminded herself that he was just a colleague and this was just a casual drink, even though he looked more handsome than ever in another casual, loose-fitting linen shirt, the remnants of the day's sun splayed across his cheekbones.

In the five-star Vaara Atoll Eco-Resort, however, nothing felt as casual.

Glass lanterns flickered on each table for an extra romantic touch, throwing sultry golden halos onto the crisp white tablecloths. Breathing in deep, she inhaled the rumble-inducing scent of grilled meat and seafood, but jasmine and incense lingered in the balmy air too. This was no cheap beach affair; this was the ultimate in fine dining. Even if she'd be avoiding the seafood, just in case.

A few other couples were tucking into exotic dishes around them, but as they settled into a table near the edge, where the pool's glassy surface caught the moon's reflection, Emilia felt a lot like they were on a date. She hadn't ever been anywhere as romantic as this, not even with Aiden. The stars above were impossibly bright now, twinkling in their constellations across the black velvet sky. She felt something inside her core unclench.

Was it the setting? Or him?

Was she really still asking herself this question?

Alejandro rolled his shoulders and tilted his head back, visibly relaxing. 'Hell of a night,' he said, picking up a menu.

Emilia hummed in agreement, scanning the screen of her phone for an update on the diver. 'No news yet,' she frowned, setting it down again.

'He'll be okay,' Alejandro said, fixing his steady gaze on hers. 'And you had a lot to do with that.'

She nodded, wishing his eyes didn't seem to see straight through her. 'I guess my affinity for organisation is paying off around here, bit by bit.'

'It would seem so.' He smirked.

A waiter arrived and placed two chilled glasses of white wine down in front of them. She hadn't wanted a cocktail after all, not once he'd suggested an imported Italian Pinot Bianco. Well, why not? Alejandro was right; it had been a hell of a night. They clinked their glasses together without a word and Emilia took a sip, enjoying the crisp, cool liquid as it slid down her throat.

'Right then,' Alejandro said, settling back into his chair. He flashed her a soft, disarming smile that immediately put her on alert. 'Now that we're no longer dragging half-conscious divers out of the ocean, tell me something, Dr Sturgis.'

She arched an eyebrow. 'Something specific, Dr Vargas, or should I just start listing random medical trivia?'

His mouth twitched as he twirled the stem of his glass between his fingers. 'I mean this in the nicest possible way. But why are you such a control freak?'

The teasing lilt in his voice softened his question, but Emilia still felt something inside her stiffen. She wasn't exactly used to people observing, let alone pointing out, her flaws with such abandon. Alejandro must have noticed her tense up, because his smile faded slightly as she exhaled long and hard, rolling the base of her wine glass between her hands. She wet her lips, staring at the reflection of the moon on the swimming pool.

'My husband, Aiden…he died three years ago.' The words still felt foreign on her tongue, even after all this time. 'Car accident. It was so cliché—a rainy night, and he was coming back from working upstate at a conference. So sudden. So random. One second he was here, the next…' She snapped her fingers lightly. 'Gone.'

Alejandro's expression faltered for a second, but his gaze didn't waver from her face. He reached a hand across the table and placed it on top of hers. It gave her the courage to continue and she swallowed, pushing past the tightness in her throat.

'I hate the thought of people disappearing on me. I like to know what I'm doing, and where, and with who.' She shrugged softly. 'Maybe I hold on too tight to things that make sense to me. Because… Well, if anything else goes wrong, I need to know I did everything I could to prevent it.'

Alejandro exhaled, raking a hand through his damp hair.

'Holy crap, Emilia.' His voice was low, rougher than before. 'I had no idea.'

She offered him a small, tight smile, her eyes flitting to the blackened ocean. 'I don't exactly bring it up in casual conversation.'

And she still hadn't told him all of it. The guilt she carried around. That she was supposed to have been at the conference too, but had decided at the last minute not to go. She'd stayed at work, as usual. That Aiden had badly wanted children, and she'd kept putting him off, thinking they had all the time in the world.

For a long moment, the night and the restaurant seemed to press in around her like a vice. Then, he spoke again. 'Well, look, I know it might be tough for you to believe, but I'm not perfect either.' He traced the rim of his glass with a fingertip. 'I don't hold on too tight to people or places, or protocols... I don't hold on at all.'

Emilia moved her chair closer to the table, waiting.

'I had an ex-girlfriend on a stint in Cusco,' he continued, sitting back in his chair and signalling for more wine. 'She wanted me to stop putting my work first. Thought she could shape me into someone I wasn't if she just kept telling me where I was going wrong.' He huffed a quiet laugh, shaking his head. 'I didn't realise how much I resented her asking me to stay until I was already on the runway. Haven't been back to Peru since.'

He met her gaze. Something like defiance flared from the depths of his dark eyes. 'I haven't let anyone get close enough to try and stop me doing what I need to do, and I can't say I'm always proud of it. I've hurt people.'

She frowned. 'But...what do you need to do?'

He scoffed an incredulous laugh. 'What?'

She leaned closer. 'What do you still need to do? I mean,

there are endless projects, endless NGO's. I know you want justice for your sister but couldn't you instead just… I don't know, spend more time with her? Life is short, you know.'

He studied her lips as she said it, and Emilia waited while her words sank in. He looked at her like he'd never contemplated how life could actually be much simpler, if he just decided that was how it should be.

She could see it now—though she still hardly knew him, she supposed—how he was always the one to crack a joke first, the one to tease and deflect. Never the one to dig too deep. Not until now anyway, until this conversation. It wasn't just charm or defiance. It was his own brand of protective armour. Not so different from her own, actually. Only he was out to save the world on behalf of his sister, who probably just missed her big brother while he was doing it, and she herself was…running away from the guilt of wanting to move on.

But what a fool she'd be to make the same mistake as that woman in Cusco, she thought as she studied his lips in return. If she started anything at all, she'd fall for him without question. And then inevitably she'd lose him too. She knew it because he shook his head again, and emptied his wine glass, and then said, 'It's not that simple. I have a hand in so many projects now, so many places. I don't like to leave things unfinished.'

She pursed her lips and lifted her glass to be refilled, then held it between them. 'To seeing the real you,' she said lightly, arching a brow at him in a vague effort to seem nonchalant and mysterious, even while her mind was reeling. It seemed like he left a lot of things unfinished simply because he was always zooming around the world.

Alejandro studied her for a beat before clinking his glass against hers. 'To seeing the real you,' he said.

She took a sip of wine, noting the warmth that was swirling in her chest. Okay, so they were very, very different people—that much she had established—but this was all so amazing. The stars, the ocean, the soft glow of the lanterns, the wine. The fact that for the first time in a long time she had told someone else about her struggles after losing Aiden.

It wasn't just Alejandro making her feel so…free.

Liar, her inner voice laughed. It definitely was.

Most of the conversation over dinner centred around his work, thank goodness. She was able to relax and enjoy herself as he talked about his relief work with the NGO in Guatemala and pretty much every other corner of the world. He steered away from talking about Cusco, which intrigued her. Although Emilia listened intently, her eyes never leaving his animated face as he described all the crazy things he'd done, like living in bamboo huts in remote villages in Laos, taking day-long boat rides through the Amazon to set up remote emergency clinics in the rainforest and being lowered from the sky to treat a family injured by a flood who'd climbed to their rooftop in Bangladesh. What a life.

Despite the kind of intense situations he was describing so vividly, he made her laugh so hard at certain points too, like when he told her about a not-so-fun encounter with toothbrush-stealing monkeys in Brazil. He was throwing a light on parts of the world she had never known about!

In return, she gave him an abridged version of her own life: her childhood in suburban Washington, her early fascination with medicine and her subsequent decision to pursue surgical techniques, and how she'd ended up working at New York's top medical centre…which was where she'd met Aiden, though she only mentioned that briefly.

In comparison, she felt she'd lived a pretty boring life,

but Alejandro seemed genuinely interested in her stories about the crazy-paced city of New York. He threw in a couple of trademark jabs about New Yorkers, which was likely based on him never even having been there…and insisting he never would, but he didn't mention Aiden again. In turn, she didn't ask about his ex in Cusco, even though she was burning to know more, suddenly.

Their meal stretched into the early hours until they were the last two people in the restaurant. Emilia hadn't realised how much time had passed until she noticed the tired staff hovering, trying not to look like they wanted them gone. Alejandro checked his phone for any updates on the diver. Finding none, he stood up from the table and offered her his hand.

'Walk with me?' he asked. She barely hesitated before graciously accepting his hand.

The night was warm and not too muggy for once, and the smell of jasmine followed them as they left the restaurant and took off their shoes, both letting their bare feet sink into the cool sand. Being barefoot was quickly becoming her preference. The rhythmic hush of the waves filled the silence between them, and this time, it felt more like a comfortable silence, one that didn't need to be filled. They had been speaking for hours, after all.

The path ahead was illuminated by the stars. The island was quieter now. Most of the resort guests had retreated to their bungalows, leaving only the distant sound of laughter from the beach bar and the occasional flicker of lamplight from private decks spread out on stilts across the lagoon.

Emilia glanced sideways at him, catching him doing the same to her. She hadn't expected to reveal so much tonight. And she hadn't expected Alejandro to reciprocate. And yet, here they were. It felt as though their defences had been cracked a bit. All her edges were a little softer than before in his company. Maybe it was good to talk about Aiden. If only the man she was talking to about him wasn't the finest specimen of untouchable masculinity she'd ever laid eyes on.

Alejandro nudged her lightly with his shoulder. 'You okay?'

She forced a small smile. 'I'm great. Just thinking.'

'Dangerous habit.' His voice was teasing, but his gaze lingered on her a moment too long again before he turned his eyes back to the ocean.

'Look,' he said, gesturing up ahead.

Emilia followed his gaze and gasped. The wet sand at the water's edge just ahead was…glowing.

What? Walking just behind him, she could see it shimmering with an eerie, electric-blue light. It was like the stars had fallen from the sky and scattered across the shore, lighting it all up. Every gentle wave was sending the most incredible glowing tendrils up onto the beach before retreating, leaving a glittering trail in its wake.

'What…what is that?' she breathed, utterly mesmerised.

Alejandro's lips curved. 'The sea of stars,' he said, pressing a hand to her arm, then urging her forward into the surf. 'Bioluminescent plankton. They react to movement, so every wave, every footstep, it all lights up, see?'

Emilia stepped closer, watching in awe as the soft glow swept around her ankles, flickering brightly with every ripple of water. The shallows around the entire lagoon seemed to be pulsing with an otherworldly luminescence suddenly, like something out of a dream. It was hypnotic and impossibly beautiful. She remembered seeing this on a nature show once, but had completely forgotten about it until now.

Alejandro crouched down, running his fingers through the surf. 'It's even more incredible underwater,' he said, looking up at her. 'Snorkelling in it feels like you're swimming through stardust.'

'I can imagine!'

'And diving?' His grin widened. 'That's next level. You move and the light just explodes around you. Like being in space.'

She smiled at the excitement in his voice, the genuine wonder. It was rubbing off on her already, this love for the ocean and its secrets, the way it could turn something as simple as a wave into something so magical. She really didn't spend enough time in nature, she realised. She would do it more often when she got home. Or maybe she would just leave New York altogether.

The thought shocked her for a second. What?

'You should try it with me,' he added, standing and brushing his hands off. 'Try diving one time. You trust me, don't you?'

The question caught her off guard. He asked it casually but as his eyes met hers in the moonlight, she saw the hope there. She did trust him. That was the problem.

Her heart beat wildly as the glowing ocean cast its strange, shifting patterns over his face, highlighting the sharp cut of his jaw, the warmth in his deep brown eyes. She was getting to like his eyes a little too much. The moment seemed to pull taut between them, and for one wild, reckless second as his eyes glazed over, she wanted to yell *Hell yes* and close the distance.

She wanted to kiss him so much, to just be wild and free like he was. And she could tell by that look in his eyes that he wanted to kiss her too. But then reality crashed back in like a bull had come charging up the beach.

She was losing her mind.

She had just told him she was a grieving widow. She'd

literally just confessed how terrified she was of losing people, how she was guilty of holding on too tight. And he... he had told her he didn't hold on at all. That he didn't ever let people get close.

What was she doing?

Emilia tore her gaze away, turning sharply back towards the beach path. 'We should get back,' she said.

A pause. Then...

'Right.' Alejandro's tone was unreadable.

They walked the rest of the way in silence and by the time they reached their quarters, the tension was heavy in the air again. She knew they both felt it.

Pausing at the bottom of her steps, she told him, 'Thank you for a wonderful night. The meal was incredible.'

'Goodnight,' he said, just as politely. Then he hesitated in the sand, glancing at her as if considering saying something else. But he didn't. And neither did she.

Instead, Emilia stepped inside her bungalow, closing the door behind her before she could look at him for one moment longer and change her mind.

CHAPTER NINE

ALEJANDRO BRACED HIMSELF as their small boat rocked violently against the churning water. The sky had changed in a matter of minutes on their trip across to the neighbouring island and now the approaching storm looked like demons in the sky, darkening the clouds to an ominous steel colour. If he was honest, it was making him feel a little ill.

'Are you okay?' Emilia asked him in concern.

'No problem,' he replied on autopilot. It wouldn't do to admit he was feeling quite seasick, especially not to his colleague, and especially not when he'd spent the majority of last night waxing lyrical about his crazy outdoor adventures. 'It'll pass,' he said, and she nodded, though her eyes narrowed and he knew she'd be watching him.

Not that she hadn't been watching him since this morning anyway, he thought, since even before Dr Zeenath sent them both out on this mission to deliver supplies to the community centre and treat whichever local residents might need their help.

He adjusted his grip on the crate he was guarding, casting another glance at Emilia beside him. She was holding on tight to another box. Her posture was rigid, and her eyes seemed locked on the dock ahead suddenly, as if she could make them reach it faster with willpower alone.

Their conversation from dinner still lingered in his mind. It had done so all night, since that awkward goodbye. He couldn't think what he had done or said to cause that. He'd been wracking his brains. One minute they'd been paddling in the bioluminescence and he'd been asking her to dive, and the next, she'd clammed up. Maybe he'd talked too much, tried too hard to push her out of her comfort zone. It was still tough to imagine what she'd gone through.

The way her voice had tightened when she spoke of her late husband still haunted him. The way her fingers had curled around her glass like she was holding on for dear life. He hadn't expected that. And he couldn't have prepared for the sudden weight in his own chest when he realised just how much she must carry with her, every single day. How could she not?

The boat jolted as they hit the dock. He jumped down first, reaching back instinctively to help steady Emilia. She didn't take his hand, of course. Stubborn as always. Instead, she climbed out on her own, landing on the shore with a slight stumble before taking the box of supplies and starting out on the narrow path that led to the village's modest community centre. He arranged for their boat to come back later and set off after her.

Wind lashed through his hair as they stepped inside the community centre. The air was suffocatingly thick with humidity as he dropped the crate and looked around. It had a weird, fusty smell, like no one had been inside for weeks. The old wooden shutters rattled in protest against the gusts outside, the rain picked up in intensity and he had a sinking feeling that they wouldn't be leaving anytime soon. He doubted many of the locals who'd been expecting them would even be able to make it here either.

'This is…rustic,' Emilia said, swiping her brow between pulling out bottles and tools from her box. She was wearing khaki shorts today, and a white shirt. Strangely, he had dressed more or less the same. He unloaded the portable diagnostic unit, but he'd barely plugged it in before a loud pop and a flash of bright sparks made him leap backwards. He almost landed on top of Emilia. Oh, man.

The portable diagnostic unit let out a pitiful whine before its screen flickered and died in front of them. He shook it, but nothing happened. 'Damn it, that's our newest piece of kit,' he muttered, yanking his hand back. The acrid scent of fried circuits swirled around them, making them both bat the stench away.

'We don't have time to fix it,' Emilia said, her sleeves already rolled up. 'We'll have to make do.'

He ran a hand through his damp hair, exhaling sharply, biting his tongue. The community centre was sparsely equipped as it was. They only sent someone from the clinic over once a month. Luckily, they had most of what they needed to run working desks with centrifuge, blood analysis, urinalysis and a blood bank for lab tests.

Emilia worked quickly alongside him, unloading and setting up. There was no hesitation in her, he noticed, though she did look tired. Maybe she'd had trouble sleeping too, after that big meal. And that big conversation.

Alejandro watched her as he set up a station. He hadn't had a dinner date like that in a long time, not since he'd first met Rosa on the first night of that NGO placement in Cusco. Nurse Rosa, with the fiery eyes and a heart as big as the Andes. He shook his head free of the memory. He hadn't thought about Rosa in months before last night, but now he was remembering more than he cared to. Maybe because Emilia reminded him of her a little. They were both petite, both dark-haired and spirited, and both had dedicated their lives to medicine.

But at least a widow with her heart still fixed on her late

husband wouldn't try to force him into staying where he didn't want to stay, he thought, before realising he was still staring at her, still imagining what would have happened if he'd kissed her last night on the beach.

She looked up to find him watching her. Damn it. But then came the wailing from outside.

Emilia was already moving towards the door. They emerged into a blast of heavy rain to find a local woman clutching a small child with a face as pale as the sheets he was wrapped in.

Alejandro's pulse jumped. The boy's small body was limp, head lolling against his mother's shoulder. His skin was clammy and his breathing was far too shallow for his liking.

Emilia was already moving. 'How long has he been like this?'

'Since this morning,' the mother said, her voice tight with panic. 'He got worse so fast. I wasn't going to bother you, and with the storm… I think it's dengue.'

'You did the right thing,' they said together. How long had it taken her to trudge here? Already, there were already several people lining up outside. They'd all braved the weather. They would need to see to all of them, but this kid came first.

Alejandro exchanged a glance with Emilia. The fever, the lethargy, the rapid breathing definitely all fit the dengue profile. But they needed confirmation.

Emilia was already on it, of course, her fingers pressing gently against the child's wrist. 'Did you give him aspirin or ibuprofen at home?' she asked the mother.

'No,' the woman whispered, clutching her son tighter. 'Only paracetamol.'

Alejandro reached for the boy's arm, pushing back the rain-soaked sleeve. 'Look at this.'

Tiny red dots freckled the skin. A clear sign of capillary

fragility. Emilia cursed under her breath, nodding. 'That's dengue, all right.'

Alejandro exhaled, already switching gears. 'We need to get fluids in him before this gets worse.'

'I'll start hydration and monitoring. You prep an anti-pyretic,' Emilia ordered before hurrying back to the people waiting outside. 'Please, we'll see everyone, but we need to focus on this little one first.'

At least the porch was sheltered along one side from the lashing rain currently hammering the front door.

Alejandro crouched beside the cot, holding a new mask in place over the boy's face, and his fingers brushed against Emilia's as she checked his pulse again. Rain ran in rivulets down her temple, stray hairs stuck to her cheek. She looked fierce and determined. Not a hint of the vulnerability he'd seen last night.

The memory of her voice from dinner resurfaced as they waited for the boy's breathing to stabilise: *I hate the thought of people disappearing on me...*

Disappearing on people was what he did best. He was a pro at it by now. He owed it to Maria not to get distracted, though, not while he was walking the earth and capable of helping those in need. He couldn't have helped her. He'd been too young and clueless. He should have been the one to get sick, not her. But at least, in being strong and capable, he could do his best to keep others safe and healthy. And that required him moving, always, to wherever he was needed. Nothing would ever take him to New York—a concrete jungle where everyone already had it all. Another reason why he'd never kiss Emilia.

Good. He needed to keep on finding reasons.

The storm raged against the thin walls, but it wasn't too long before the child stirred. Alejandro breathed a sigh of relief as his eyelids fluttered open for a brief second before closing again.

'Come on, kid,' Alejandro muttered under his breath. 'You're doing so good.'

Emilia's fingers brushed his accidentally as she checked his pulse. 'It's much stronger now,' she said.

He glanced at her, catching the equal relief in her eyes. They were in this together, but he thought of Rosa again, all the times during those intense few months in Peru when it had been just the two of them, with their team scattered or stuck in various other places. If he'd known then how hard Rosa would fall for him, maybe he wouldn't have made his move. He knew he'd broken her heart when he left, making her yet another casualty of his relentless pursuit of purpose over personal happiness. He'd have to live with that forever, but he could hardly change now.

The minutes stretched. The wind screamed outside. And then, finally, the child took a deeper breath. His chest rose, slower but steadier, and his eyes stayed open. The fever wasn't gone completely, but it had abated considerably and the worst was definitely over. His mother choked on a sob, clutching at Emilia's arm. 'He's...he's better?'

Alejandro nodded, removing the oxygen mask carefully. 'He's not out of the woods, but he's responding well. We'll keep monitoring him.'

Emilia squeezed the woman's hand. 'He's a fighter. He just needs rest.'

The exhausted mother exhaled a broken, grateful breath, and Alejandro did the same with his back turned. That had been a tough one. Almost as tough as dealing with that diver. And now, more people were crowded at the doorway, the rain lashing against them, soaking their clothes. The word had spread. It was going to be a long afternoon.

He tried to ignore the ache setting into his bones as they moved from one patient to the next. First, a deep cut from a fishing accident, no thanks to the wind that had thrown the man overboard onto a sharp motor. A feverish elderly man, a pregnant woman. Each case was different but each one pulled them deeper into the emerging night, and the whole time, the weather continued to get worse outside.

Soon it was twilight. He was just passing Emilia yet another bottle of water when a loud rumble of thunder tore through the walls, rattling the old light fixtures overhead again. Then, total darkness swallowed them. For a second, there was only the sound of the storm and the palm fronds thrashing the building. Then came a few frightened murmurs from the villagers. The power was out again.

Alejandro reached for the flashlight on the supply table, flicking it on. It was going to be near impossible to work like this. Thankfully, they only had a few patients left to see, and nothing too urgent, but still, this was not ideal.

'Generator?' Emilia asked.

'No backup,' one of the locals said grimly. 'It went out last time we lost power.'

Alejandro pulled his phone from his pocket. No signal. But as he turned, it buzzed in his palm and a call came through from their boat's captain.

'We can't get back in this storm, Dr Vargas. You'll have to wait it out.'

Alejandro swallowed back a curse. He had expected as much, but where on earth would they go now? They were stranded. He turned to Emilia, who had already pieced their predicament together from the look on his face. She didn't say anything at first. She just pressed her lips together, nodding once.

'We'll manage,' she said, as if this was simply another

problem she could solve without much difficulty. 'We'll find a hotel.'

He snorted. 'This island has no hotel, Emilia, no tourist facilities. There's only the fishing village.'

'Oh.' She looked around her and he did the same, eyeing up a pile of towels and blankets in the dim light. 'I guess we could just stay in here then,' she shouted over another crash of thunder.

He nodded, but already it sounded less than appealing. They were both still damp, and hot, and hungry. And he needed a proper night's rest after barely sleeping at all last night.

One of the village women—an older lady called Mariyam, whom they'd just treated for a minor burn injury on her arm— stepped forward. 'You have helped our people all day. You can't stay here in the dark with the storm so strong like this. Come with me. You can come to my home.'

Alejandro exchanged a glance with Emilia. He knew full well that neither of them particularly wanted to impose on this lovely lady, as she also needed rest for that burn on her arm. But the rain was relentless and they didn't have much of a choice at this point.

'Are you sure? That's very kind of you.'

'Come,' the woman insisted, her voice firm as she took Emilia's hand. 'You need food. And rest.'

Alejandro sighed, scrubbing a hand through his damp hair. He could hardly disagree with that. Besides, there was no way out of this one. 'We'll come back as soon as it gets light in the morning,' he said, promising the same thing to the rest of the people they hadn't seen yet.

Then, taking the flashlight with him, he closed the door behind the last person and followed Mariyam and Emilia out into the rain.

CHAPTER TEN

THIS WAS A modest home, Emilia thought. Very cute. Almost unintentionally boho chic. Woven mats covered the cement floor, and the furniture consisted of a low wooden table and scatter cushions. A single armchair had clearly seen many years of use, but it looked so comfortable it made her yawn. She was exhausted, and so was Alejandro. He'd looked tired since this morning and she wondered if he also had a restless night after their dinner together. They'd barely had time to talk today…not that that was a bad thing. She was here to work, after all.

Near the back, a curtain billowed in the wind, revealing a tiny bedroom that looked barely big enough for a bed and a small chest. A second door led to a simple bathroom. She wondered momentarily where they would sleep but figured she could curl up on the scatter cushions if Alejandro took the chair.

Mariyam had offered to make them dinner. Emilia didn't miss the way the kind woman winced when she tried to stir the pot over the small gas burner. Emilia had personally tended to the burn on her arm, which was wrapped in clean cloth now. Emilia had seen enough injuries to know it must be very painful.

'You shouldn't be cooking,' she said gently, getting to

her feet and leaving Alejandro checking his phone, despite the fact there was no signal. 'Let me.'

Mariyam looked uncertain at first, but she soon relented with a tired smile. 'If you don't mind, thank you.'

Emilia shook her head; of course she didn't mind. She never dreamed she'd get the chance to cook in a proper local's Maldivian kitchen. A shelf along one wall held a selection of mismatched dishes, a few tubs and packets of spices and several battered cooking pots. She took stock of what little Mariyam had…a bit of tuna, some coconut, white onions, red chillies, garlic and curry leaves. There were fresh limes on the windowsill too, and a pot of rice already simmering. They were simple ingredients, but there was definitely enough here to make something delicious.

She worked quickly, frying the onions and tuna in the coconut oil, then adding just enough spice to give it some heat. Alejandro leaned against the door frame, watching her in curiosity.

'So the doctor can cook,' he mused.

'You sound surprised,' she replied, stirring the rice without looking at him.

He chuckled and it curled around her ears, low and warm like the steam from the pot, and without another word he moved to help, slicing limes. He did it with such casual flair, it was clear that he wasn't completely useless in a kitchen either.

'So, the nomad can cook too?' she teased, acutely aware of his closeness in the small kitchen.

He shrugged. 'I enjoy it when I get to do it,' he said.

She was quiet for a second, thinking of all the questions she now had for him, especially after last night. It was still painful remembering the awkward way she'd said goodnight. 'Did you cook much with your ex, in Peru?' she asked. 'What was her name again?'

He bit back a smile. They both knew he hadn't shared her name.

'Rosa,' he replied. 'And yes, sometimes. We were on a three-month stint with a base camp and a working kitchen. The team would have a schedule for meal prep. It was never anything too fancy, not like Mama would make at home.'

'Oh really, what would your mama make?' she asked. And while they somehow agreed on what to make together without a single argument, he told her all about some of the Venezuelan dishes he'd grown up with. He described them so well she could almost taste them: *arepas* stuffed with shredded meat and cheese; *cachapas*, which were sweet-corn pancakes; and a special kind of cheese stick wrapped in dough and deep-fried to perfection.

The way his eyes lit up when he spoke about his mother's cooking really touched her. She imagined him as a boy, helping her out in the kitchen or eagerly pestering her to put one of those meals in front of him and his sister. She wanted to ask about Maria too, and his stint in Peru, and how serious he and Rosa had actually been before he decided to leave and never return, but she also didn't want to darken the moment.

'So how does someone who basically grew up on cheese get to look like you?' she asked instead, before realising she had pretty much just admitted how devastatingly hot she found him.

She was still flushing into the pot of rice when he replied, 'I could ask the same about a woman who lives on bagels and hot dogs from roadside carts. Isn't that what you New Yorkers eat?'

She laughed to herself, glad he had kept things light.

'Pretty much,' she said. 'But I don't see too much food when I'm working sixteen-hour shifts in a trauma ward.'

He put his knife down, turning to her. 'Are you serious?' She shrugged.

'Emilia, that's no way to live. Food is life. Sixteen-hour shifts are death.'

She laughed, until she realised he was serious, and even sad on her behalf. Before coming to the Maldives she had never even thought about using her skills another way. The days at St Catherine's had stretched into months, then years, and despite Aiden's concerns about her mental well-being she had never found the time to contemplate doing anything different.

'I guess I thought I'd have to slow down when I got pregnant,' she admitted into the silence. 'It just never happened.'

'You didn't slow down when you got pregnant?'

'No… I just never got pregnant.'

He nodded without looking at her. Then without warning, he placed a warm hand over hers and squeezed it. 'I'm so sorry for what you lost.'

She was so tired that just the gesture and his sentiments made her sigh heavily out loud and she had to blink back tears. Oh lord, she was an emotional wreck. Thankfully, she managed to hide them and busy herself getting the plates out.

When the food was finally prepared, they all sat together on the floor, sharing the dishes in the glow of one single oil lamp. The storm clattered the tin roof outside, and the wind was still howling like wolves against the walls, but inside it was quite cosy and Mariyam hummed her approval as she ate, nodding appreciatively at Emilia.

'You will make someone a very lucky husband,' she said

with a knowing smile. Then she looked between them suggestively. 'Maybe you, huh, Dr Alejandro?'

Emilia nearly choked on a mouthful of rice. Alejandro coughed into his glass of water. Mariyam only laughed, getting up to fetch three fresh coconuts from a woven basket in the corner. She refused Alejandro when he offered to help and deftly sliced the tops off them herself with nothing but a small knife, despite her lack of mobility.

'You must drink,' she said. 'Good for strength.'

Emilia sipped from the coconut shell, beyond grateful for the cool, sweet taste on top of all this delicious food and hospitality, but the woman's comment played over in her mind. She had already made someone a lucky husband once, and she would not be making that mistake again. There was far too much risk involved, too many uncontrollable variables. But every time Alejandro sneaked a glance at her she felt like his eyes were burning holes through her clothes and she might spontaneously combust at any moment. Getting married again was one thing; she'd never do it. But…a night of fun?

Eventually, Mariyam gestured towards the bedroom. 'You must rest, both of you.'

'Oh, we can just sleep on the floor,' Emilia said quickly. 'We don't want to take your room.'

Mariyam waved her off. 'Nonsense. You are guests. And the bed is big enough for two. The shower is just through there.'

Emilia opened her mouth to protest, but Alejandro, on the way back from stacking dishes, gave her a look that clearly said *Just go with it*.

She swallowed hard. Fine. She knew this woman wanted to help them, as they had helped the village today. They couldn't very well insult her by refusing. So she mumbled a thank you instead.

The bedroom was small, just like the rest of the house, and the bed barely fit inside it. It was meant for one person. Maybe one and a half. Definitely not two. Emilia stood at the door as Mariyam bustled back into the kitchen, acutely aware of Alejandro just behind her.

'Well,' he said, his voice laced with amusement now. 'This will be cosy.'

She shot him a warning look, grabbing a spare blanket and folding it down the middle of the bed. 'We'll sleep like this,' she muttered. 'Your side is there. My side is here.'

He smirked. 'Of course.'

'I'm serious.'

'You're always very serious.'

Then, to her absolute horror, he reached for the hem of his damp shirt and peeled it over his head in one smooth motion. 'I'll take the first shower if that's okay?'

Emilia turned away so fast she nearly tripped over her own feet. She busied herself with her bag, trying not to think about the fact that Alejandro was currently stripping down behind her, but then—

The sound of a belt unbuckling. The rustle of fabric. She squeezed her eyes shut. A few seconds later, the bathroom door creaked open.

'There's no lock on the door, and it doesn't seem to shut,' he said, his voice rough from the adjoined room. 'Try not to look.'

'As if I would!' she sputtered, but suddenly it was taking all her strength not to turn around and face the open door.

She sank onto the bed, pulling a pillow up to her chest. The sound of the running water was barely audible against the rain outside but the steam crept through into the bedroom, along with the milky floral scent of the soap, and she groaned as she turned just a fraction and caught the briefest glimpse of a bare butt cheek just behind the steamed-up glass cubicle.

Oh my…

She snapped her head away again, heart hammering. She shouldn't, but… Well, he would never know.

No. She pulled the pillow over her head and tuned into the sound of the rain. She shouldn't and she wouldn't. But the smell of the soap and the feel of the steam around her was intoxicating. Just one more peek. A little one.

Her eyes locked onto Alejandro's muscular back instantly through the cloudy steamed glass. Oh God. His wet skin was positively glowing under the dim bathroom bulbs and she found herself with her mouth slightly open, transfixed, watching him massage his scalp with big hands, tracing the rivulets of water coursing down his back.

How does a man get so impossibly gorgeous?

Running her tongue over her lips, her mind flooded with an onslaught of thoughts and images that by all rights should be forbidden. What might she do if she allowed herself to step into that bathroom now? If she was a brave, fearless, spontaneous woman instead of a chicken?

Forcing her eyes away again, she felt the blush creeping up her cheeks as she chastised herself for such an invasion of privacy.

Wrong, wrong, wrong, Emilia, he asked you not to look!

She squeezed her eyes shut as a dip in the volume of the rain allowed the sound of the creaking shower taps to reach her ears. He was done. She pictured him stepping out of it, towelling himself off, pulling on a dry shirt that Maryam had left out, all the time willing herself to resist yet another peek. He would definitely see her if she looked now.

Before long the bed creaked under his weight as he settled back in beside her. She swallowed a silent groan from the back of her throat. Lord…this was even worse. Now she could breathe in the freshly cleaned, delicious scent of him and feel the warmth radiating into her from his muscles. Already he was taking up most of the space, but he couldn't help it. Her flimsy makeshift blanket wall was pointless in such a small bed.

'Your turn,' he said, his voice husky.

Nods being inconsequential in the dimly lit room, she forced herself to reply verbally through the lump in her throat. 'Okay.'

Sure enough, the door wouldn't budge. She turned back into the bedroom. He was lying facing the opposing wall, like the gentleman he was.

'I'm not looking at you,' he said anyway, as if sensing her eyes on his back. 'Just get on with it.'

She cringed. 'Okay,' she said again, mentally scolding herself for making such a big deal of this. He was just a man after all—an incredibly attractive, kind and charismatic man—but still just a man. And a doctor no less, who'd seen more than his fair share of bodies in all shapes and sizes. Just because she'd been unable to resist looking at his, why would he want to look at hers?

Mind you, he had already seen hers, she reminded herself, cringing yet again.

When she was done, Emilia changed into a clean shirt that was soft but far too big on her. The hem brushed against her bare thighs as she hesitated in the doorway.

Alejandro was still lying on his side in the bed. The thin sheet barely covered his lower half and left the broad, tanned expanse of his bare back exposed. Even in the dim light, she could make out his muscles shifting with each steady breath. His skin was tanned and smooth and begging to be traced with her fingers, but she wouldn't. She would never!

She swallowed and forced herself to move, slipping beneath the sheet as carefully as she could. The bed was too small. Way too small. No matter how she positioned herself, she was acutely aware of how close he was. His warmth radiated towards her, and despite the pull of it she made do with curling herself into as tight a ball as possible, trying to create even an inch more space.

The mattress dipped as Alejandro shifted. Then, just as she thought she was in the clear, he rolled onto his back with a deep sigh.

'Good God,' he muttered, his voice coming at her rough with lack of sleep. 'I swear I've slept next to sheep who are less skittish than you.'

Emilia froze. 'I… What?'

His eyes stayed closed, even as he tilted his head towards her from his pillow. 'Would you prefer I took the floor?'

'No,' she muttered, her cheeks burning hot. 'I was just trying to…'

'Relax?' He let out a quiet laugh. 'Feels like you're about to start bouncing off the walls.'

She exhaled sharply, realising he was teasing her. 'I was trying not to kick you, actually.'

'How considerate.'

His voice was thick with amusement and despite herself, Emilia found her lips twitching. 'Sorry, go back to sleep, I'll try and keep still.'

'It'll be a miracle, truly.'

The rain continued drumming softer now against the roof, and soon Alejandro's breathing evened out again. She sighed, finally allowing herself to settle properly against the mattress. She stared at the ceiling, a smile still tugging at her lips, until she drifted off into a deep, dreamy sleep.

CHAPTER ELEVEN

HEAT. THAT WAS the first thing she noticed. A delicious, solid warmth pressed all the way along her back. A heavy weight draped possessively over her hips.

It took a few seconds for her mind to catch up, but when it did, Emilia's breath caught in the morning light and she cursed internally at this…well…this problem.

Alejandro was wrapped snugly around her. His hot chest was firm against her back, one arm slung around her middle, his legs tangled with hers. He was spooning her completely, him the biggest spoon she'd ever imagined possible. She could feel the slow rise and fall of his breathing, the heat of his skin against her own. His scent, still clean and fresh from last night's shower, wrapped deliciously around her senses.

His grip tightened as he breathed out sleepily against her neck, and panic flared in her chest. Carefully, she started inching away, but the moment she did, Alejandro let out a soft groan and promptly pulled her back against him.

Emilia's heart pounded. She was trapped like this! But then again, she didn't hate it. For a brief, thrilling moment that soon slid into a good twenty minutes or so, she didn't move an inch. It was only when Mariyam peeked her head around the door with a tray of steaming coffee cups that Alejandro extracted his limbs from around her, mumbling incoherently. He sat up, looking back at her over his shoulder in mild confusion. She immediately pretended she had only just woken up too, blinking, rubbing her eyes with a yawn for good effect.

'Good morning,' she said, and he nodded, dragging a hand sleepily through his hair, mirroring her yawn.

Taking the coffee gratefully, she decided on the spot that she would never admit she'd caught him holding her like that. Never. She'd be too embarrassed. He would ask her why she didn't wake him up!

But she wouldn't forget it easily either. It had felt so nice, waking up in the arms of a man. It was something she hadn't realised she'd been missing quite so much.

Back in the community centre, they saw to the patients they hadn't gotten around to treating the night before, and thankfully the storm had passed. The sky was blue again now, and sunshine flooded in brightly through the windows. Alejandro seemed to be treading lightly around her, though. Did he know he'd spooned her in his sleep? Was he actively avoiding talking about it? It didn't seem like him to be embarrassed about something like that. He'd make a joke about it if he remembered, surely?

Honestly, this was getting silly. She literally couldn't decide if she was relieved or disappointed that he wasn't saying anything about it.

Soon they only had a few more chores to do before the boat was due to collect them.

'Shipments are here,' Alejandro announced suddenly, breaking the silence. He picked up a clipboard from the windowsill and started checking off what was being delivered, leaving her to start checking off another batch. Outside, the sun's rays bounced like lightning bolts off the wet ground, blinding her. Alejandro seemed to notice that she couldn't find her sunglasses. He handed her his aviators without a word, then gestured for her to follow him to the truck.

The physical exertion of unloading the supplies and carrying them inside helped distract her from the odd aura surrounding them, and she was more than thankful for it. He looked like he'd spent a lifetime lifting heavy items, but she tried to keep her eyes on the job and not on his muscles. Soon though, the sweat was sticking to the back of her neck. His aviators were slipping down her nose. Lifting boxes and sorting supplies in such stonking heat wasn't exactly regular practice in the trauma ward.

Alejandro seemed just as hot but decidedly unbothered, like sleeping in a cramped bed with someone pressed against him all night before performing midday manual labour didn't faze him at all. She, on the other hand, had spent the entire morning trying not to think about the way she had woken up wrapped in his arms. The feel of his body pressed against hers. The weight of his legs tangled with hers. The way his breath had been warm against her neck. And yet despite her best efforts, it kept creeping back into her mind along with something even worse.

A memory. A very clear memory. She hadn't meant to look last night. Truly. But she'd seen him through the steam.

Bare. Golden skinned. A body carved by some clearly excellent genetics and years of working outdoors, trekking, building, lifting, all taut muscles and broad shoulders, tapering down into the narrow definition of his hips. And lower…

Emilia clenched her jaw. *God help me.*

'Let's take a break,' Alejandro suggested, placing the last box on a stack, then swiping the sweat that trickled down his temples.

Emilia stretched out her stiff shoulders. She was definitely feeling the effects of having slept in that cramped tiny bed. It had crossed her mind that her mouth had betrayed her in her sleep. Sometimes she got quite vocal if she slept on her back. Gosh, if he'd heard her talking in her sleep, talking about Aiden, or him...

There had been more than one interesting dream involving Alejandro recently.

'The boat isn't coming for us for another hour,' he said, casting his eyes across the calm lagoon and the ocean beyond. 'We've seen all our patients for today. I don't know about you but I'm dying to get in that water.'

Emilia hesitated, putting her final box down beside his. 'We need to carry all our stuff back to the dock first.'

'We'll do that for you,' a voice piped up behind them. A few of the local volunteers were offering to help all they could, which was great, even though it wasn't exactly their fault that they couldn't have made it yesterday.

'Thanks so much, guys,' he said before turning to her. 'Swim?' he prompted again. 'Maybe just a paddle, huh?'

How could she refuse? In minutes she was following Alejandro back the way they'd come yesterday before the storm, to the beautiful bay where their boat was due to arrive, and he was peeling off his shirt, tossing it aside, rolling up the bottom of his khaki pants. Then he seemed to think better of it and started unzipping them. She looked away, but there was a gentle laughter in his voice when he turned back.

'Haven't you seen it all before, anyway, Doctor?' he teased. 'You couldn't help yourself last night, could you?'

What?

Emilia swivelled her head up to face him, but he was already striding away from her, revealing that taut round ass for a fleeting moment before striding waist deep into the water. How did he know? How…?

Oh Lord, so embarrassing. He must have seen her peeking last night. She hugged her knees to herself on the sand, cursing him and herself under her breath as he waded out more and then dunked under the water, emerging with tantalising droplets sparkling a path down his muscular frame. Then he started doing laps, one arm over the other, cutting through the water like a shark.

This silly, one-sided attraction was doing her no good. But she also needed to know what he'd just meant, exactly. Did he know for certain she'd sneaked a peek? Did he remember the spooning? It would do her no good to know. Clearly there was no benefit to having this information; it would only haunt her. But even so, she still needed to ask him. Getting to her feet, she waded into the surf, keeping an eye on his every move. As long as she was able to see him, even though she didn't want to see too much, as long as he was safe, as long as nothing happened while he was…

She shook her head. She was haunted, all right. Haunted by everything Aiden had left her with, a sense of panic every time someone she cared about stepped or swam out of her line of vision. Great.

'Sure you don't want to come in?' he called now, from ten metres out, and she groaned. She was roasting. Of course she did, but she wasn't going to. She didn't have a bathing suit with her.

'I'm fine,' she called back, putting a hand above her eyes to shield the sun and spotting the boat on the horizon, just coming around the bay.

'Just a little one,' he called back.

'I don't have a bathing suit!'

'I've seen it all before, remember,' he hollered. 'Your veranda…the morning sunshine…'

'Stop it, come back, the boat is coming!'

The little blue motor boat was getting closer now, zipping through the water towards them, but he didn't seem to see it.

'The boat, Alejandro!' she yelled again, but he was already swimming out further. Her heart clenched as she watched him disappearing deeper into the turquoise waters without a care in the world. Just the sight of him getting farther away from her and closer to the approaching boat was enough to make her heart jump to her throat.

'Dr Vargas!' she yelled again, her voice echoing out around the bay. Still, he didn't respond, his muscular form cutting through the water at a speed that only amplified her utter terror. He was far too close to the boat; what if he got caught under it? What if the driver didn't see him… like the driver of the other car that night, which allegedly hadn't seen the red light before he'd rammed through it, straight into Aiden…

She started pacing up and down the sandy shore, trying to keep her eyes trained on his retreating form, ignoring the hot sun streaming down on her. The boat was almost here. The driver gave her a wave and a grin from under his wide-brimmed straw hat and sunglasses as he cut the engine. Bobbing closer, he started securing the boat to a post, and frustrated, Emilia turned back to the shimmering water, the exact spot where Alejandro had been just moments before. But he wasn't there now.

She waded in, right up to her waist, not caring now if her clothes were soaking.

'Alejandro!' she called again, even louder this time. She thought she might actually be sick. What if he'd swum under the motor and been sliced to pieces? What if a friendly blacktip shark had turned evil and pulled him out to the depths?

'Did you see him?' she asked the guy on the boat, but he just shrugged and swigged from a bottle of water, then took a seat and pulled out his phone. Not a care in the world. Her heart was a wreck in her throat.

Then, just like that, a head bobbed up from right behind the boat. Emilia gaped at him, then promptly collapsed into the water as her knees gave way underneath her. He was perfectly fine; of course he was. He was grinning, curse him, his dark hair slicked back from his face. He looked absolutely nothing like a man who had almost given someone a heart attack! In fact, he looked like he'd just been reborn from the sea itself, damn him.

He was safe! Of course he was safe; he was perfectly used to these environments, and he'd only gone for a swim! But in a flash his grin disappeared as he eyed her. Wading towards her, his face showed nothing but confusion now as he reached out his arms to pull her up. She collapsed against him, horrified to find she was about to cry!

'I thought you weren't coming in,' he growled. His husky voice vibrated against her ear and right through her as she bit on the inside of her cheeks. It catapulted her straight back to this morning when she'd woken up completely entangled in these same powerful arms. It flooded her senses. She pulled away abruptly as a surge of irritation and embarrassment scorched through her veins, turning to wade back to the shore.

Alejandro followed, pulling on his pants and shirt quickly while her back was turned. She risked a glance over her shoulder and met his worried eyes. He was concerned about her now. Great. He probably thought she was a complete neurotic nightmare.

'You okay? What happened?'

She pushed her hair from her face, as if she might regain some semblance of her dignity. The volunteers were coming up the beach with the items they'd brought over yesterday, loading them onto the boat. Her clothes were soaked through and so was her underwear, not that it wouldn't dry in minutes but still. She'd made an idiot of herself.

'Sorry,' she said to him quickly. 'I couldn't see you for a minute there.'

'I'm fine.' He put a hand to his sparkling chest in the shirt he'd left unbuttoned. 'Look. I'm in one piece.'

She waited for more from him, a wisecrack, something about needing to see him naked maybe, but Alejandro didn't say anything more. Instead, he offered his hand to help her onto the boat.

When she hesitated at first he didn't lower it, and finally she placed her hand in his. Sitting on the wooden bench she squinted at the horizon and forced herself to breathe as Alejandro climbed in after her, saying goodbye and thanks to the volunteers before signalling to their driver to leave. Soon the boat was slicing through the turquoise blue. Neither of them spoke a word.

Emilia stared at the distant line where the sea met the sky. The wind tugged at the loose strands of her hair, drying the damp fabric clinging to her skin while she thought about what to say. She should definitely say something. Explain herself. Apologise for overreacting. But where would she even start? Would she tell him she'd frozen in fear because for a split second she thought she'd lost him like she'd lost Aiden? She barely knew this man and yet the idea of something happening to him had left her totally paralysed with terror.

None of this was normal, she thought, clenching her fists

in her lap. If he saw, Alejandro didn't press her. He didn't try to demand an explanation for whatever the hell had just happened. He just…watched her. And somehow, his silent understanding unraveled her even more.

CHAPTER TWELVE

ALEJANDRO WAS TRYING his best to steady the fidgety fisherman's hand. The burly guy in the shirt full of holes kept on moving, which wasn't helping him or Emilia to treat him. She was prepping him for stitches, and Alejandro tried not to look at her while she was so deep in concentration, her trademark braid swept over her shoulder and her lips set in a hard line. Instead, he studied the flyer taped to the wall.

It was pretty fancy. All midnight-blue hues and gold trim with the resort's stylised logo—a silhouette of a manta ray— hovering subtly in the bottom corner. The elegant script on the front read: 'Vaara Atoll Eco-Resort presents "An Evening Under the Stars"'.

That's right, the fund-raiser gala event was in a matter of weeks. He'd completely forgotten about that.

It was no secret that the resort had been instrumental in funding the clinic's establishment. They had long ago recognised the need for quality health care for their guests, as well as for the local islanders who made their livelihood here. Since long before he'd been coming to the island himself, an annual fund-raising gala had become a bit of a tradition, hosted every year at one of the sprawling pavilions that jutted out over the lagoon. Resort guests and patrons were always invited to partake in an extra-luxurious evening of indulgence while hopefully contributing generously towards expanding health care services on the islands.

He rather enjoyed such events, if only for the chance to mingle and appreciate those people who helped to keep the doors open around here. He had a lot of research to share already: the climate studies were going well, even if they showed an alarming rise in rain and storms for this time of year and a consequential effect on marine life. It was his worry, as it was in every place he chose to move his self-appointed mission further, that water tests would show higher levels of pathogens than the year before.

He held the fisherman's hand steady as Emilia worked, but his mind was a thousand miles away. He could still hear the beeping machines, the doctors whispering behind curtains, the way their mother had clutched his hand, completely beside herself when they'd realised they couldn't help Maria.

Ever since then, water wasn't just water, not to him. It was a living thing. Both a carrier of life and, if neglected, a slow and silent killer. He couldn't have saved Maria from legionnaires' but he could try to save others now. Most people had no idea what tiny shifts in climate could do to the fragile ecosystems around them…to the children who played in stagnant public pools and algae-riddled lagoons, to the fish they ate.

His latest findings showed increasing salinity shifts in the shallows, stress in coral health and elevated fecal indicators in water runoff post-storm. That, coupled with the influx of new infrastructure on the islands, was a ticking time bomb. This event was a perfect chance to make sure someone was listening…and this year, Emilia would also see that a fancy gala at a five-star resort was more than just a chance for guests to flaunt their designer gowns. She would see how they put their wealth to good use; contributing towards maintaining and expanding a medical facility that provided critical care for people living and working in such remote surroundings. He'd be her date, of course.

If only he could get around to asking her.

His mind kept drifting back to the other day when he'd woken up with his arms around her. What a predicament. He'd just lain there watching the early sun play in her hair, wondering how best to extricate his limbs from their tangle with hers without raising the alarm. Then, of course, he'd decided not to move at all, to let her think he was still asleep, even when he'd felt her stirring. It had been an accident, after all, so why make a big deal out of it? He hadn't meant to end up like that; the bed was tiny, and he was big… and she was decidedly nice to hold onto.

Had she felt the way his heart had drummed through his chest, right into her warm back?

'Hold still,' Emilia instructed now. The fisherman nodded, his eyes darting to the instruments they'd laid out on the tray, like the very sight of them was frightening despite a life spent slicing fish to pieces with tools of his own. Some people did not handle the sight of blood well.

The man winced as she dabbed antiseptic onto his wound, but Emilia seemed to ground him at least. She was so admired here already, he thought to himself. All the locals knew who she was. They asked after her when he met them on his trips around the islands. She was always composed, even in the face of a crisis. Well…except for when she thought he'd been swept away on the tide and drowned. There hadn't even been a tide in the shallow lagoon the other day, but she'd acted like he'd emerged from a tsunami unscathed. He could still see the terror on her face if he closed his eyes.

'Almost there,' Emilia told their wriggly patient, stitching carefully around the wound. Alejandro held the man's wrist, glancing at the clock. He was due an afternoon off and was already looking forward to a cold beer and a few hours of reading in his hammock.

He couldn't help keep stealing glances at her face, wondering if he should bring up that night dive again. She would probably refuse. And he shouldn't ask anyway; it would only make him want to do things he shouldn't want to be doing. At least the gala would be safe. They'd be surrounded by other people. He wouldn't be tempted to kiss her in front of such a high-brow audience.

Over the past few days, he'd been moving between the neighbouring islands, focused on his research. But no matter how far he went, his thoughts kept circling back to Emilia, whose moods were as unpredictable as the tides. She must have been haunted by her late-husband's death. A car accident, she'd said. She hadn't elaborated. But she had said 'I hate the thought of people disappearing on me.' And he had unwittingly fed into that fear somehow, going off for a swim where she couldn't see him.

The fisherman winced again, pulling Alejandro's attention back to the present. 'And we're done,' Emilia assured him. But just as she was about to continue, no doubt with her instructions to keep his hand dry, a nurse burst into the room, interrupting the moment.

'Dr Sturgis, Alejandro, we need your assistance with another patient.'

Alejandro barely had time to exchange a look with Emilia before the nurse continued. 'There's a woman in labour at the far end of the island. She's alone, no one can get to her fast enough on the roads right now, not by car. They're sending a team from the mainland by boat but it'll take a while.'

Alejandro was already moving, grabbing up his bag and shrugging out of his white coat. 'I'll take my scooter.'

'No, I'll go,' Emilia cut in, standing up and pulling off her own white coat, revealing a sensible long blue skirt and white shirt. 'It's my duty. You have an afternoon off, don't you?'

He raised an eyebrow. She knew his schedule? 'You know how to ride a scooter?' he asked instead.

She hesitated. 'Not exactly.'

He huffed a laugh, making for the door, touching a hand lightly to the small of her back. 'Then we'll both go. Let's move.'

The sun was a brutal fireball on his shoulders as they sped down the dusty track. He would take the dirt road to the edge of the bush around the resort, and then a secret path that only the locals knew about. Emilia's arms tightened around his waist as the road grew a bit bumpier and he steered them through clusters of palm trees and over uneven ground. He could feel the press of her fingers against his stomach through his shirt, her breath hot against his shoulder.

Focus, Alejandro.

'She's alone?' Emilia shouted over the roar of the engine.

'She must be terrified,' he called back. He'd gotten more details as they'd packed a bag and he'd quickly located another helmet for Emilia. 'Her husband's out fishing. No signal. She managed three seconds on the call to the clinic before the line went dead.'

Emilia cursed under her breath and he had to bite back a smile. She might be new to island life, but she was already in it, heart and soul. She knew how casually confident people could be around here, often to their detriment. He could almost hear her thinking *Who on earth would go out fishing, knowing their wife might go into labour at any second?* But some of these locals had no choice; they had contracts with suppliers who demanded results.

Sand kicked up around them as Alejandro swerved past potholes, dodging the odd roaming goat and weaving around lounging lizards and slow-moving bicycles. He was going as fast as he could, considering, and he swore he could feel Emilia's pulse racing against his back.

She was good under pressure, though. He admired that about her, how she swept her own grievances aside to get the job done. He brought his own guilt into everything; he couldn't help it. Sometimes he thought he wouldn't recognise himself or his life without it. It kept him focused, kept him on the move. It kept him striving to be the person who made the difference.

All the more reason to get his head on straight with regards to Emilia, he thought. She was getting too deep under his skin.

They skidded to a stop outside a small, stilted house, and straight away as he cut the engine, the sound of laboured cries broke his heart. Before he could even flip the stand, Emilia was already springing off the bike, and running towards the sound with her helmet still on.

CHAPTER THIRTEEN

THE AIR INSIDE the house was thick with heat and sweat and seawater. The woman lay moaning on a set of grey cushions that constituted a couch on the floor, clutching her swollen belly and a cellphone. Around her roughly fifteen cats were loitering, looking on in interest. This was some kind of sanctuary for cats by the looks of it. Instantly Alejandro's skin itched. Allergies. Damn. He would just have to cope. The woman's breaths were coming in hot, short, desperate pants and Emilia was already kneeling beside her, her bag open.

'Alejandro, get me some towels and water, please. This baby wants out pretty badly.'

He nodded, slipping into action as she asked, 'How far apart are the contractions?'

The woman groaned, gripping her own knees. 'Very close. I need my husband!'

He came back with some towels as requested, eyeing up one particularly large grey cat who was flicking its tail in his direction from a nearby bookcase. 'I'm afraid your husband probably won't make it back in time,' he told her, clearing his throat. Already the tickle felt like something he wanted to shove a fist down his throat to scratch.

A thin and scrawny cat with yellow expectant eyes had crept closer now too, sniffing at the damp towels near his knee. He tensed, shifting slightly, right as another ginger cat hopped onto a rickety wooden shelf beside him.

Emilia was frowning at him. 'Everything okay, Doctor?'

He nodded stiffly, but his skin had begun to prickle everywhere by now. It always started like this, subtle at first, then debilitating. He had nothing on him to treat this, but he had to focus. This baby was coming now.

Emilia wiped the woman's forehead with a damp cloth. 'Deep breaths. You're doing amazing.'

The woman whimpered, clenching her hands into fists, and Alejandro took over mopping her brow as Emilia did her best to reassure her. 'With the next contraction, I need you to push,' she said, and he clamped his mouth shut, trying desperately not to sneeze.

The air was thick with the unmistakable musk of feline now and his reaction to it was not getting any more manageable. The cats were everywhere, like word had spread that their mistress was in distress and they wanted to protect her. There were more cats than he could count, perched on the wooden beams, curled up in corners, slinking under the battered table against the wall. One particularly bold one was licking its paws, throwing him the side-eye.

He held his breath as a scream ripped through the room. The baby was crowning. Emilia counted softly, encouraging her as Alejandro wrinkled his nose, curbing another sneeze.

'One more push,' Emilia urged, looking at him and raising her eyebrows. She'd noticed he was suffering now. He ignored her. This was embarrassing.

Soon after another scream, a piercing wail filled the room. Emilia and he worked quickly, clearing the baby girl's airways, wrapping her in a blanket, and he watched Emilia pass the tiny, wriggling form to the exhausted woman, who let out a shaky sob. For a moment he clean forgot his allergies as he saw the look of awe in Emilia's eyes and heard her soft sigh. There was a kind of longing about her that he recognised. He'd seen it before in women he'd dated, when they talked about wanting a family. It had always made him want to run a mile. Now for some reason, he was envisioning Emilia as a mother. She'd make such a good one.

Emilia's hand pressed against the woman's belly. Her expression tightened. 'Alejandro.'

His heart kicked as he curbed yet another sneeze. The ginger cat was too close now, sniffing his arm like it was some kind of snack. 'What?'

'There's another one.'

The mother groaned. He could see her body already tensing with another contraction. Swearing under his breath, he repositioned himself. Twins—of course it would be twins right now, just when he was about to pass out and die, covered in cat hair.

'All right,' Emilia soothed, taking the first baby from her mother's arms and passing her to him quickly. 'We're going to have to do this all over again, Mama. Are you ready?'

This time, it was faster. Within minutes, a second cry joined the first.

'A boy,' he breathed, wrapping the newborn up before placing him beside his sister. Relief rushed through him, along with the need for another sneeze as the mother sagged back, exhausted but beaming. Emilia sat back on her heels, her eyes meeting his as she handed the lady some water, preparing for the delivery of the afterbirth.

Alejandro swallowed hard, rubbing his nose against his sleeve. No way was he sneezing in the middle of this. Once the afterbirth arrived, this woman would need to go to the clinic and be checked over thoroughly, as would the twins. They needed all the hands they could get.

'Here,' Emilia said, tossing him a fresh towel. 'You're sweating.'

The miracle of birth wasn't exactly why his pulse was jumping right now, but he took it with a nod, resisting the urge to rub at his madly itching eyes.

The woman reached up and clasped Emilia's wrist. 'Thank you,' she panted. 'So much. Both of you.'

Alejandro forced himself to smile. 'It was all you,' he said, his voice coming out hoarser than intended. He cleared his throat, but it only seemed to make things worse.

Emilia frowned at him. 'Wait a second—'

A sudden, sharp tickle clawed up his sinuses. He turned away just in time. '*Atishoo!*' The sneeze bent him forward, shaking his whole frame. Then another. And another.

'Oh dear...' Emilia trailed off, taking in his red-rimmed eyes and the way he was now backing up like the cats had transformed into a wild pack of tigers out to kill. He excused himself and hurried for the door, and several cats followed.

'Oh no, poor you,' Emilia said slowly. 'You're allergic.'

'I'm fine,' he muttered, but his voice sounded as choked as his lungs were getting.

'You're not fine,' she countered. She looked entirely too amused as yet another sneeze tore through him.

One of the larger cats, clearly unimpressed by his sudden outburst, flicked its tail against his ankle as it trotted past into the sunshine. Alejandro swore under his breath and took another step onto the porch.

Emilia followed him outside. 'Why didn't you just say you were allergic to cats?'

He shot her a glare as he dabbed at his nose. 'I didn't know I'd be walking into a cat sanctuary, did I? I just— *atishoo!*—seem to physically reject them.'

'Clearly.' She bit her lip, trying to suppress a laugh, but

the new mother was chuckling behind them now too despite the events that had just occurred, cuddling her newborns against her chest. Even the cats seemed smug about his misery.

'You should go, get something for that,' Emilia advised. 'I'll stay here with them till we can all get transported back to the clinic. They'll need to check Mom and the twins over properly.'

Alejandro sighed, already planning how quickly he could get back via the scooter and dunk his head in ice water.

'The boat shouldn't be long,' she said. 'The crew know where we are.' She was still watching him with that teasing glint in her eye and he had the sinking feeling she would never let him live this one down.

'Go ahead,' he said dryly. 'Get it out of your system.'

Emilia just smiled. 'Go on, sneezy. Go get more fresh air before you go into anaphylactic shock.'

Alejandro groaned, swiping at his nose as another cat slunk past his legs. He didn't have a choice. When he looked up from pulling on his helmet, she had a different look on her face, one of concern.

'You'll be okay, riding back in your state?'

He narrowed his eyes. 'I'll be perfectly fine as soon as I get away from those cats—don't you worry about me.'

'I'm not... Well, okay, fine, I worry.' Her eyes shot to his, searching, and his stomach tightened as he started the bike. He knew that look. She was worried, which surely meant she genuinely cared about him. What was he supposed to do with that knowledge? He cared too, what she thought, what she did, but he wasn't here to entertain thoughts like that.

'I'll come and find you later,' she said, running a hand over her braid, still scanning his eyes.

He adjusted the bike mirror and sniffed, forcing himself

not to blow his nose too hard in front of her. She wouldn't care if he did. She was too kind and understanding, despite her teasing. Another thing that was so great about her. God, this was dangerous. She was getting attached and if he wasn't careful, she would fall for him. The way things were going, if he gave her even a fraction of what she could be starting to crave—what he'd caught himself craving too, all the damn time—she wouldn't let him go.

And, more importantly, what if he didn't want her to?

The thought punched through him as she took a step closer to the bike, ignoring a ginger cat as it curled around her ankles. He watched her fumble for another tissue. What would happen if they hadn't just delivered twins, and if he wasn't on the verge of breaking out in hives thanks to a humiliating cat allergy? He'd stop halfway home in a pretty spot he knew, and then he'd give in and finally kiss her. But then he'd probably regret it.

If he let this happen, everything he'd worked so hard for would go down the drain. Maria's situation had already cost him and the family too much. Her suffering, the months in that hospital bed, the way she still winced when she thought no one was watching—it had all shaped him into who he was. He had sworn a thousand times that he would never be the kind of man who let emotions cloud his judgement. He had a plan. He was proud to have such self-discipline. Emilia was a detour he could not afford to take.

'You take care of her,' he said stiffly, looking over her shoulder to the woman cuddling her babies inside the house. 'I'll take care of me.'

Then, with another loud sneeze that he simply couldn't hold in a second longer, he turned and sped away.

CHAPTER FOURTEEN

PUSHING HER SUNGLASSES onto her forehead, Emilia made her way down the narrow path towards the beach to the meditative sound of the waves. But even that didn't stop the electric bolt that powered up her heart as she spotted Alejandro and Tom working together on the dive shack deck. Alejandro was bent over a pile of masks, cleaning off the salt water, and Tom was chatting away. Every now and then he would laugh out loud at something Alejandro said.

She could hardly help the nervous energy now. She hadn't seen him since this afternoon, right before he'd sped off on the scooter in the middle of another sneezing fit, and he hadn't seemed too interested in her finding him later either. He was probably embarrassed. She hadn't laughed too much at his plight, had she? Either way, it was like her body had decided she wasn't allowed to just exist around him without stirring up something deep in the pit of her stomach that she hadn't felt since she'd first started dating Aiden.

That thought alone made her want to walk…no, run… far, far away, where Alejandro's rejection and indifference couldn't touch her, but in the same breath it made her want to get closer, fool that she was!

'Emilia!' Tom called out, waving her over. 'When are you doing the fun dive with us?'

She walked up to them, clasping her sweet, fresh coconut

between two hands. Tom looked as if he truly expected her to take the plunge, but the idea of submerging herself in the ocean's depths still made her stomach twist into Manhattan-sized knots. She did not belong under water. Her feet were fine on the ground, thank you very much. Sure, she had come to terms with the basics in the daylight—the water was beautiful, calming and as seductive as the desire for another illicit night with Alejandro's arms around her—but the idea of diving into the deep, dark unknown at night still made her uneasy.

'Maybe a night snorkel first,' she said, stealing a glance at Alejandro over her coconut before taking a sip that drew his eyes right to her mouth. 'I don't think I'm ready for the full dive yet.'

Alejandro's lips curled into a knowing smile. She caught his eyes dipping to her cleavage in her loose white cotton dress before he dragged them away and cleared his throat. 'Maybe you should snorkel with Tom,' he said, more coolly than she'd been expecting. 'You seem to fear the ocean more than you let on, Doctor.'

Ouch. His words stung like a baby jellyfish—what on earth had brought on that dig? It sounded a lot like he'd completely retracted his initial offer. What had she done? Maybe his ego was bruised after she'd laughed at his allergy earlier. Oops.

'Maybe,' she said with a forced laugh. But she didn't feel amused at all. 'How are you feeling now?' she asked Alejandro. He barely looked up from his box of masks before moving along to a row of tanks, which he proceeded to test for air, one by one.

'All better now,' he said. 'Took some antihistamines and felt good as new. I hear our mother and babies are resting under supervision at the clinic.'

'They're purrrr-fectly fine,' she said, and waited for his chuckle. It never came.

Awkward.

'Can we take a walk?' she asked him, before she could think better of it. He looked at her from his crouch over a tank, his dark eyes filling with curiosity before he nodded and stood, brushing the sand from his hands.

They walked away from the resort, along the beach. The guy who fed the stingrays was there already, chopping up fish for the feast he'd be giving them at sunset. Already the late-afternoon sun was casting its long, spindly shadows across the fine white sand and the cool breeze off the water was a relief on her warm skin. They didn't speak at first. The space between them felt heavy, like a storm was brewing. It was as though they were both too aware now of all the unspoken things swirling between them, but neither of them wanted to speak up.

She should just be brave and say something; at least make a joke about waking up in each other's arms that time. Only that didn't seem funny either. There was nothing funny about the way she was starting to crave this man's attention and company.

'So, the gala,' she said eventually, breaking the silence. 'One of the volunteers was just talking about it. Sounds pretty fancy.'

He nodded, looking down at the sand, pressing his hands in his pockets. 'Big event. Lots of people. It'll be good for the clinic.'

'Are you looking forward to it?' she asked, keeping her tone casual, even though she was more than curious as to whether he'd invited anyone. They were allowed plus ones, even though that mostly applied to the local staff and not the foreign workers, who usually travelled alone.

'I suppose,' he said, his gaze briefly flicking over to hers. 'I'm not really one for the spotlight, but it's important. Did you know it's hosted by Aurora Starr herself?'

She nodded. Aurora Starr owned one of the most luxurious villas at the resort, which people said she loved more than her Hollywood movie career. Her love for the Maldives had been cemented on a movie shoot here years ago, and that had led to her becoming deeply involved with various community projects.

Wait a minute. 'Do you actually know her?' she asked him.

'Sure, I've met her. She's been coming down here for years now,' he continued. 'After she visited the clinic and saw the work that had been put into it, she started to help raise funds for it. She has a good heart, that woman.'

Emilia nodded, picturing her. Aurora Starr was a real icon; her films were blockbusters and her weekends were spent on magazine shoots and TV sets with her multi-millionaire real-estate-mogul husband. But she championed education for underprivileged children, worked tirelessly for animal rights and now it seemed she was also passionate about supporting clinics like the one they were working at. And soon she'd get to meet her.

For a second she was quite star-struck. She could only imagine what it would be like to converse with such a woman. Would they discuss medicine? Humanitarian work? Or would they simply have a laugh whilst stealing glances at Alejandro looking hot in an expensive suit? No straight woman with a pulse would be able to resist doing that.

She realised Alejandro was watching her and her bubble burst. Ever since she'd arrived, things between them had been so…complicated. She just couldn't avoid it anymore. It was eating at her.

'Look,' she started. 'I owe you an apology.'

He stopped walking, turning to look at her.

'I… When you disappeared in the water the other day, I freaked out,' she continued, struggling to get the words out. 'I know you saw it. I shouldn't have. I know I overreacted. But…' She swallowed, taking a breath. 'It reminded me too much of losing Aiden, how quickly it all happened.'

Alejandro turned towards her fully, his face softening. 'You don't have to explain,' he said gently. 'I get it. I shouldn't have made that jab just now, about you being afraid of the ocean. Forgive me.'

'No, I—' She paused, shaking her head. 'I need to say it. It's just… I've been carrying it around for so long, Alejandro. The guilt. Knowing that I should've been there with Aiden. I feel like I could have said something when you told me you felt the same, about your sister getting sick instead of you but…'

'Hold on. Wait? How could you have been there with your husband when it happened? Wasn't he on the way back from a work thing?'

She hugged her arms around herself, fixing her gaze on the ocean. The sun was starting to sink now, turning the sky a fiery orange.

'I was supposed to go to the conference too,' she said, swallowing back her emotions. 'I decided against it at the last minute. We actually had a fight about it. He'd booked me into the hotel he was staying at, along with spa treatments and a five-star steakhouse dinner. It was meant to be a romantic break. But I was working late on the ward and couldn't get out to meet him before he left. He ended up going without me and calling me from the car. I'll never forget how upset he sounded. He said I always put my work first. We didn't speak the whole time he was there—he wouldn't take my calls.'

She realised she had dropped to the sand, and Alejandro had sat beside her. 'He was right, I did always put my work first,' she said, hugging her knees. 'We could have started trying for a family sooner if I hadn't been working round the clock. We could have done so many things. He was gone before I even had a chance to say sorry, or goodbye.'

Alejandro was watching her. The intensity in his eyes when she turned her head made her breath catch.

'I'm so sorry,' he said softly, shuffling a little closer to her in the sand. 'For what you went through. I know it's not the same, but... I can understand why you'd fear losing someone else, Emilia.'

She nodded, her chest tight, grateful for his understanding. 'Thank you,' she whispered. It felt good to get it out. She hadn't admitted her raging guilt to many people. Only to Maxxine, who always told her what she thought she needed to hear.

Alejandro reached for her hand without a word. He didn't speak for a while. They just watched the sun sink hand in hand, and she allowed herself to just breathe.

'You know, Doctor, maybe you and I aren't so different, always putting our work first,' he said after a while, nudging her shoulder with his, still holding her hand. 'Carrying all that guilt around like an overstuffed suitcase too. It hasn't helped me much, and it hasn't helped you either, by the sounds of it.'

She sighed, letting her head fall lightly against his shoulder. 'You can say it helps me be a paranoid control freak, if you like.'

'I would never say that to your face,' he dead-panned, and she laughed. It felt so good to laugh, and it had cleared the tension in the air for now, at least. 'You know what, Emilia,' he added, leaning slightly closer to her ear. Suddenly, she was acutely aware of how his warm and steady fingers were still wrapped around hers, like he wasn't quite ready to let go either. His grip tightened slightly as he pulled her gently back to her feet to face him.

'What?' she breathed as she found herself face-to-face with his broad chest, tilting her head up. Her pulse had revved right up again. The beach had all but disappeared. She swallowed, trying to steady herself, but her body refused to obey. Her heartbeat drummed in her ears as his all-knowing brown eyes locked onto hers like he was about to say something that would unravel her entirely. His gaze flickered down to her lips and it was all she could do to keep from leaning forward. She might fall into him if she wasn't careful.

'We should do it, Emilia.'

Her breath caught. Time? The world around them seemed to slow. The island sounds dimmed and faded away as everything else narrowed down to him. She looked at his pink, inviting lips as the air between them pulsed, thick with expectation.

'We should…do what?' she whispered, though she already knew. She shouldn't do it. She'd only regret it. But screw it, what was one kiss?

His lips parted, his words cutting through the silence, low and raspy, and decidedly not what she was expecting. 'We should do our night-snorkelling expedition. Right now.'

Oh.

She opened her mouth to respond, but no words came out. All she could do was stare at him, knowing her body was betraying her. She was already leaning in, for goodness' sake, tilting at an angle like she was expecting his kiss. How mortifying. Quickly she dropped his hand, then turned away.

'I thought you said I should do that with Tom.'

'I changed my mind,' he said simply, and started back down the beach.

CHAPTER FIFTEEN

THE WATER GLITTERED with surface stars as Emilia stepped into the shallows. Tom had lent them snorkels and masks and Alejandro was already knee-deep ahead of her with the moonlight falling deliciously across his shoulders. 'Are you ready?' he called back to her.

She nodded, but obviously she couldn't completely hide her trepidation. Whatever it was about their conversation that had eased the tension between them she was grateful for, but with her two feet in the ocean, not even the outline of this man's incredible body three steps ahead could calm her racing heart. If anything, he was adding to it. She could still picture him disappearing into the unknown and almost giving her a heart attack. And just now, he had almost kissed her; she was sure of it. And she had almost kissed him back. The temptation to close the distance had been completely overwhelming and, if she was honest, her head was still swimming from it.

Thank goodness they hadn't kissed! That would have only deepened her impossible crush, and he was not the kind of man she should be going around kissing, anyway. A vagabond bachelor, albeit one with a steady paycheck and a heart of gold, who apparently carried just as much pain and guilt around in his suitcase as she did.

'Come in deeper,' he said now, turning over his shoulder

when he realised she hadn't moved. She was still watching the moonlight playing in his hair. Shaking her head, she waded in further, feeling the coolness of the ocean rising until it lapped at her waist, until she felt completely immersed in the night, in the ocean and also, as she fixed her eyes on the water glistening off his body, in Alejandro. She tried to steady herself, pushing the panic down into her feet, lodged in the sand, but with him so close, every breath felt heavy.

'You're almost there.'

His voice and encouragement sent a shiver across her skin. The bioluminescence below them lit up the water with an amazing show of tiny blue fireworks that seemed to dance and shimmer around them, casting them both in an otherworldly glow. This was utterly breathtaking to witness in person, up close. She had seen it from the shore before, but nothing had prepared her for the wonder and beauty of standing among it and watching it react to her movements in person.

'Look at that,' she whispered, completely awestruck. 'I feel like I'm in the sky and the world just turned upside down.'

'Exactly,' he said, as his gaze burned into her, taking a slow step towards her, and then another, the water rippling around them. The bioluminescence followed his every move, swirling around him, creating a halo of light as he reached out.

'It's my favourite thing about the water. All water,' he murmured, his voice so close to her ear that it sent a ripple of shivers up her arms and through her chest.

It was impossible to focus on anything now, except her heart pounding, and the way his hand was lingering near hers. She had wanted this, and she'd even wanted him to kiss her. But now these sparks were crackling between them, she wasn't sure if she was ready. Why was she even feeling this way so soon after losing Aiden—what would Aiden think? Would he really want her to feel this way with someone else?

The water seemed wrapped around her like a blazing blue blanket as she followed his lead and pulled her mask over her face. She felt so fragile and vulnerable in this environment and yet there was something totally intoxicating about the whole thing. Emilia turned her face towards him with her mask on. Their noses nearly brushed, they were so close, and he laughed but didn't move away. She couldn't remember the last time she had felt so out of control, so dangerously aware of every movement someone made.

'Are you ready for a trip into space?' he asked, his lips curling into a teasing smile. The heat in his voice made her skin flush.

'I think so,' she replied. Her voice came out almost shaky, though she wasn't sure at this point if it was the ocean or him that was making her feel this way. Both, probably. She moved back a little, but before she could dwell on what she was even doing out here, he dunked under the water, and not wanting to get left behind, she followed him. Instantly, she was immersed in another world.

The water around them was alive with colour, the light shimmering as their bodies moved through it. All she could hear was the water in her ears as she followed his form, gliding through the stars. They were two astronauts in a totally foreign world of light, and she had never been so enchanted in her life!

His hand drifted closer beneath the water, brushing against hers again, just as she surfaced for air. This time, she didn't flinch or pull away. She let the contact linger and leaned into the way her whole body lit up, nerve by nerve, cell by cell. The heat in his gaze, the way he was looking at her like she was the only thing in the world worth watching despite the glittering water—she would never forget this as long as she lived. Her breath caught as he moved in closer with the water glowing around them like a million fireflies trapped in a tide. It truly felt like something dormant inside her was flickering to life among these stars.

'You don't have to be afraid of the water, Emilia,' he muttered. 'Or me.'

The words sank straight through her. Her heart stuttered in her chest.

'I'm not afraid of you,' she whispered.

It wasn't a lie. Not really. She wasn't afraid of him. She was afraid of what she felt when he touched her, when he looked at her like this. Like he saw everything she'd tried to bury but didn't want to run from it, or from her. She was afraid she was falling for him harder than she'd ever fallen for her late husband...

He took a slow step forward, and now their legs brushed underwater too, bare skin against bare skin.

'Maybe I'm a little afraid of you,' he said, almost growling. 'I wasn't going to do this. I wasn't going to give in.'

She gasped softly, her pulse skyrocketing as the turquoise sparks danced across his shoulders, illuminating the lines of his face and the sharp cut of his jaw as he removed his mask.

'Neither was I,' she managed, taking off her own mask, looping it around her wrist.

His hand slid from hers, quickly finding her hip beneath the surface, anchoring her. 'Do you want me to stop?' he asked her.

She didn't answer. Her body did the speaking for her instead as she leaned in, powerless to resist this man for one second longer.

And then he kissed her.

God, he kissed her!

It wasn't gentle either. It wasn't slow. It was pure hunger after weeks of tension and near misses and long hot days of the stifling heat fizzing and steaming between them. This one kiss had all of it exploding in one fiery moment as his mouth claimed hers and she melted into him, letting her hands slide up to his shoulders, gripping tight as the water churned softly around them. He pulled her closer, one arm circling her waist, holding them chest to chest.

Her body was fire and ice. Hot where he touched, cold where he hadn't yet. She let the kiss deepen and felt the ache inside her uncoil from its painful grip. All she cared about now in this moment was the press of his lips on hers, the stroke of his tongue, his hand splayed across her back.

Maybe it was okay to feel like a wanted woman with someone else, someone who made her feel alive. She was still alive, and she'd never had more proof of it than now.

When he finally pulled back just a fraction, she stayed there with her forehead to his, trying not to laugh with the thrill of it. The night shimmered around them. There were stars above and stars below them, and stars in her eyes, probably.

He smiled slightly, pulling her closer by the hips again, sending a thrill right to her core that made her moan softly.

'Was that actually something spontaneous and un-planned, Doctor?'

She shook her head, her heart thundering, her lips tingling, letting her fingers thread through the wet hair at the back of his head. 'It was definitely something uncontrollable,' she admitted. 'But you know what? I don't really care.'

For the first time in a long time, as Emilia went in for another kiss, she really meant it.

CHAPTER SIXTEEN

THE DAYS MELTED together after that. Emilia woke up every morning with sand still in her hair and salt on her skin, her cheeks sore from smiling and her heart so full she sometimes wondered if it might burst. How could this romantic fairy tale be her real life? Even on the rainy days, when the weather was so awful she couldn't leave the clinic, she found herself humming happy songs, and calling Maxxine to inform her friend just how much healing she was doing over here in the Maldives.

Alejandro was very good at appearing with secret little gifts, which he'd present her with completely at random. Already, she had a cute collection of shells that he'd given different human names to. He was still deeply engrossed in his research, but whenever he was with her—in the clinic with his sleeves rolled up and his brows furrowed in concentration, on his veranda, typing away on his laptop, on the beach with his shirt unbuttoned, salt clinging to his chest as he carried the dive gear with Tom—he would glance her way and shoot her a look that seemed to tell her he didn't even need the sun to light up his world when she was in it. She would steal looks at him too, every single chance she got, and wrap her arms around him, wishing she could bottle his scent.

But they hadn't slept together yet.

This restraint was surprising, even to her, given how every single one of his kisses still felt like it might tip her over the edge. But there was a mutual understanding between them that this wasn't a thing to be rushed. Their hearts were still bruised in places. They were learning from each other slowly and leaving nothing out. And, for now, that felt like enough.

Most nights, they'd walk barefoot to the edge of the island, where the palms leaned low over the lagoon and the world felt quieter. Sometimes they'd cruise out in Tom's little motorboat, watching a visiting pod of dolphins perform their somersaults over the water. Sometimes he'd coax her out for a moonlight swim, his hands on her hips under the surface, whispering teasing comments into her ear that would make her either laugh out loud or wrap her legs around him and kiss him. Those moments burned into her soul like little gifts that could never be taken back; things she would remember after she'd returned to New York. Things she would remember her entire life.

The island had noticed them. Of course it had. Everyone knew. Even Dr Zeenath, who at first had seemed a little jealous, if she was honest, giving her a touch of the cold shoulder. But it had soon passed. The volunteers would throw them knowing smiles, and her coconut dealer had taken to whistling whenever he passed them. Even the children had started calling Alejandro *dhoani bey*—which meant 'boat boy'—whenever he showed up at the bay, because he always appeared to be taking Emilia somewhere these days.

The breeze seemed to carry his scent right to her nostrils, even when he wasn't there. She found herself laughing more easily, dancing on her veranda when no one was watching, humming whether she was flicking through her book or administering a vaccine. Everything felt lighter and richer, almost like she was living someone else's life. The bougainvillea bloomed brighter now. The ocean shimmered more vividly than it had before, and she didn't care if she was imagining it.

Still, there were fleeting moments when the air shifted and she caught a shadow behind Alejandro's eyes, or when her own breath would catch, remembering the life she would have to go back to when this was over. Unless she made some serious changes. She found herself thinking about it more and more; could she really leave New York? Sublet her place and pack another bag, go on a longer adventure? Maybe she would run into him somewhere, sometime. That wouldn't be so terrible. It wasn't like he would ever come to New York. The way he seemed to talk about the ocean and water and nature... New York had none of that. A thought that made her increasingly quite sad.

Alejandro never pushed her for her thoughts, and she didn't pry into his either. They both let the shadows pass like clouds over the sun. It was easier, she thought, not to talk about it.

One night, they set up dinner under the stars on the beach, away from the resort and its wandering tourists. The table was really nothing more than a plank of driftwood that Alejandro had balanced on top of two mango crates. She'd sourced two candles from the hotel staff that she'd left flickering in jars. Alejandro had bought fresh tuna earlier that day on the way back from one of his research trips, and they grilled it over a fire and ate with their fingers, cracking up when the wind picked up and blew rice off their plates and the passing crabs stopped to inspect it.

Alejandro reached for her across the table, letting his thumb brush a stray grain of rice from her cheek. His hand lingered and she leaned into it, feeling so blissfully happy that the words just tumbled out of her mouth: 'You know, you really do make this place feel like home, Alejandro.'

He didn't answer straight away. He just looked at her for a long, long moment, like he was memorising the width of her eyelashes or something, and she panicked. Why on earth had she just said that? She hadn't meant that at all—had she?

Alejandro just smiled. 'You feel like home, Emilia,' he murmured, making her breath catch.

The silence that followed was full of a million other things that she still didn't know how to say, or even what to do with. Home? They were talking about home already.

She tore her eyes away as the guilt crashed over her. Aiden had been home, and Aiden was gone. Hadn't she told herself a zillion times that she would never again put herself in the position where her 'home' could fall to pieces around her? She could never be home to anyone else either, especially not a man who spent his life living out of a suitcase. But this was all so nice. So comforting, and romantic. It was hard not to get carried away. In the heat of every magical moment she wanted to ask whether he might consider coming to New York to visit her when this was over. Even just for a few days?

But she didn't say it. It would be ridiculous to say that. He wasn't her home, and he never would be. He was a wanderer, and she had roots. She might dream about packing up for good but she couldn't really do it...could she? And what would be the point of him even visiting her anyway when he'd only leave again and leave her missing him?

Yet even with the walls she still kept up, Emilia knew very well what was happening. She was falling for Alejandro—deeply, unexpectedly and in that quiet, dangerous way that crept up on you when you weren't looking. Maybe that was why they hadn't slept together yet. Maybe that was why neither of them had pushed for it. They both knew that once they did, there'd be no pretending that this was still something light and inconsequential. No going back to the way things were. As long as they were both careful not to cross that final line, she would still have a foothold in her old…well, normal life. She could tell herself she was just passing through, still the woman who had built a life and home somewhere else, who didn't belong on a sun-drenched island with a man who looked at her like she was a whole new beginning.

All she had to do was resist, remember…remind herself over and over and over again that this was just some fun. She was usually so good at staying in control. Why should now be any different? Just because night after night his sandy fingers found hers, and his voice in her ear set her nerves on fire, and his eyes pulled her closer and deeper with every conversation, it did not mean she had to give up all control and sleep with the guy.

CHAPTER SEVENTEEN

ALEJANDRO PULLED AT the collar of his linen blazer, eyeing the enormous overwater villa where the gala was already in full swing. The laughter was already spilling from it, and the music drifted on the warm breeze around his ears as he stepped onto the jetty. The lights from the Vaara Atoll Eco-Resort's restaurant, where he and Emilia had spent that long evening not so long ago, glittered beyond it, golden and inviting against an inky-blue sky.

Everything, from the lagoon beneath them to the soft jazz humming through the speakers, was designed to dazzle at this annual event. The whole place smelled of money, he thought, and coral-safe sunscreen and designer perfume. It should've felt foreign and fake, especially here on a relatively small Maldivian island, but even the clinking crystal glasses faded away when he saw her.

Emilia stepped onto the deck ahead of him, and for a second, the world went still. Wow. The woman had outdone herself tonight. Her dress was a deep teal colour, all silky and cut low in the back. It clung like it had been made just for her sensational figure and he dragged a hand through his hair, muttering a reminder to keep his hands to himself tonight.

The braid was gone. Instead, her hair was swept up on top, loose tendrils curling softly around her face. Her lips had been painted a colour he wanted very badly to taste. Alejandro couldn't keep his eyes off her. He'd seen her flushed from the sun, laughing in the bioluminescence, and just yesterday inland on the neighbouring island, knee-deep in muddy pond water helping a villager with a broken ankle. She was beautiful to him in any situation. But this version of Emilia? Well, she was stealing his breath right out from his body.

Catching him looking at her, her smile flickered into a slightly sheepish look before she straightened, seeming to remember he found her utterly irresistible. She held his gaze with a confidence he'd only seen bloom over the last few weeks and something tugged hard in his chest…the same calling he'd been feeling for weeks and pushing away.

They hadn't slept together.

Not yet. God, he wanted to. But he'd been holding back, just like she had. The heat between them was a constant ache under his skin but it wasn't just the desire to feel her naked body pressed against him that was burning him from the inside out. It was more now. A lot more. And maybe that was the problem.

He'd been meaning to tell her about the prospective transfer. The NGO had called him last week. They wanted him in Madagascar next, not Central America. In two weeks' time no less. He should have known it; the projects and their placements filled up fast, and they needed him to confirm his place on this one as soon as possible. A new reef restoration project needed a lead—urgent, understaffed, high-impact. It sounded right up his street and would also give him time to reflect on his research here in the Maldives before he was due to present it.

He hadn't said yes. Not yet. But the decision was clawing at him. He knew he had to tell her, but it would break the spell they were both under and he wasn't quite ready for that yet.

'Wow,' he murmured as he reached her. 'You look…'

She tilted her head. 'Is that the start of a compliment, Doctor, or is your brain short-circuiting?'

He chuckled. 'A little of both. You look beautiful tonight, Emilia.'

'Why, thank you, Alejandro. You don't look so bad yourself,' she said, trailing her eyes across his jacket and up to his mouth.

He could see how hard she was restraining herself from kissing him right now, and he felt exactly the same. She went to loop her arm through his as they stepped into the villa, but then seemed to think better of it and dropped it. People on the island knew something was going on, obviously, but a lot of these new people didn't, and he'd already told her he had worked with some of them before in various corners of the world. Some of them knew his past too…his propensity for hooking up with women and then leaving. He didn't want them thinking Emilia was just another one of them, because she wasn't.

Although he would have to leave her soon, he remembered, adjusting his collar again. Just like he'd left the others. There were things to do that were far more important than anything his stupid heart might start to want. This was getting far too complicated.

A string quartet was playing softly in the background of the lavish villa. Waiters floated by with silver trays full of drinks and Emilia looked up at the impressive vaulted ceilings before resting her gaze on the guest of honour. At the far end of the room, Aurora Starr was already holding court. Platinum blonde today, dripping in sequins, the glamorous fund-raiser and former movie star turned marine advocate saw him and waved him over with a glass of rosé swishing in her hand.

'Alejandro!' she called as he approached, leaning in to kiss both his cheeks. 'And you must be Emilia. I've heard so much about you from the staff at the clinic.'

Emilia smiled politely, doing her best to hide how starstruck she clearly was. 'Oh…all good things, I hope?'

'Oh, darling, only the juiciest.' Aurora winked and turned back to Alejandro. 'So, listen, I just wrapped on this little Netflix docudrama in the Seychelles, and we're premiering it next month. You have to come. Maybe bring that friend of yours, what's his name? The one from Panama with the sea turtle tattoos?'

'Leo,' Alejandro said with a nod. 'He's still in Bocas del Toro, I think.'

'Ugh. Lucky man. Speaking of turtles, are you still talking to that marine biologist? What was her name…? Leila? You two were very friendly the last time I saw you on the Manta Project.' She winked at him, and he felt Emilia stiffen slightly beside him. Just the subtlest shift in her graceful poise, but enough that he noticed. He always noticed her.

'That was a long time ago,' he said, brushing off her words. 'A long time before I even came here.' She was talking about an affair he'd had before…well, before the affair he'd had with Rosa in Cusco.

Aurora nodded, clearly unfazed, then moved on to small talk before turning and starting to schmooze another cluster of guests.

Alejandro leaned close to Emilia. 'She's…a little much sometimes,' he said apologetically. 'She had a thing with Leo from Panama. Her husband doesn't know, of course.'

Emilia turned to him. 'She couldn't even remember his name was Leo!'

He shrugged. That was Aurora all over, but Emilia was frowning now. 'Was she telling the truth?'

He hesitated. 'About Leila? Yes. It was nothing serious, though.'

She nodded, lips pressed together, her gaze flickering out over the water where the horizon twinkled.

'It's never anything serious with your lot, though, is it?' she said lightly, but her voice had that tight edge to it. The one she used when she was really wanting to say something else.

He ran a hand through his hair. This was getting more than awkward already. 'My lot?'

'You…you nomads, always moving from place to place. You're not even that different to Aurora with the things you've seen and the places you've been.'

He stepped closer, brushing her hand with his, waving away a waiter. 'That's not exactly who I am anymore.'

She sniffed. 'You don't have to justify it. I know this is nothing serious, Alejandro, you're a free agent. Go where you like, be with whoever you want to be with. It's what you've always done, isn't it?'

Alejandro felt his jaw ticking side to side. 'Emilia, we're talking about something that happened over a year ago… Is that really what you think I'm all about?'

She looked away and he watched the breeze tug at the loose strands of hair around her face. 'I don't know, but I think this is exactly what we agreed it would be.'

He stepped in front of her, forcing her eyes back to his. She was riling him up now. 'Did we agree, though? Or did we both just decide not to ask too many questions because we were afraid of the answers?'

She blinked, her glossy lips parting slightly. Then she closed her eyes and sighed at him. 'Don't do that.'

'Do what?'

'Make this out to be something it's not.'

He dropped his voice, eyes darting to the nearest cluster of guests. 'I'm not making anything up, Emilia. Every time you so much as look at me, I feel like I've done something right for once in my life. But you're still in love with your husband, aren't you?'

She swallowed hard and looked away, while he instantly regretted his words. That was a low blow. She wasn't still in love with him; she was trying to move on, maybe even with him, and he was freaking out and pushing her away.

'This has nothing to do with Aiden,' she said tightly.

'I know that… I'm sorry…'

'You think I don't lie awake at night wondering what we're doing, Alejandro?' she went on, her words rushing now, shaky. 'Of course I do. But you don't talk about the future. You don't make any promises. You don't ask me about what's meant to happen next. We haven't even…'

'Made love, I know.'

Made love? What the hell had made him say it like that?

She studied the art on the wall. Alejandro looked down at her while the truth pressed against the inside of his ribs like it was begging to be set free. Madagascar. He hadn't told her, but he couldn't tell her here.

Instead, he said quietly, 'Maybe I'm a little concerned that if I make love to you, I will never want to stop.'

She gave an indignant snort for good measure but her cheeks had reddened again. He pressed a hand to her forearm. 'And maybe I'm also concerned that if I start talking about the future, I'll lose what I have with you right now.'

She let out a short humourless laugh this time. 'Concerned, are you? I think it's more a case of you deciding to just enjoy the present until it's convenient to leave. Like you did with Leila, and with your girlfriend in Cusco, and God knows how many more…'

'That's not fair.'

'No, what's not fair is that I finally feel something real for the first time in years, and I know I'm just another island on your map. A brief stopover, isn't that right?'

Her voice cracked and something inside him fractured. He hadn't been expecting so much passion to flare up like this in a crowded room. Or to want to stay and iron things out. Usually, he'd be long gone at the slightest hint of confrontation with a woman who was asking too much from him. But Emilia wasn't asking too much. She wasn't asking anything, really. And it was making him want her even more.

'You're not a stopover,' he said, stepping closer. 'How can you think that, Emilia?'

'Then what am I?'

He opened his mouth but the words wouldn't come. He wanted to tell her about the call. About Madagascar. About how the moment the offer came through, he'd looked out at the ocean and felt…nothing. Just a hollow ache in his chest that told him the life he'd built around moving on to place after place might not fit quite as comfortably anymore. But he owed it to his sister. He couldn't just give up on his work and mission because his stupid heart had become anchored to this amazing woman who lived in New York City of all places. What the hell would he do there? This wasn't something that was ever going to last. It didn't matter how good it felt being with her right now.

'You're looking at me like you're already sorry,' she said again, softer now, eyes narrowed.

'I'm not sorry,' he muttered roughly. 'I'm just trying to figure out how the hell I ended up caring this much.'

Her breath hitched. Behind them, Aurora laughed too loudly. A cork popped. At the far end of the villa the band was starting a slow dance. He reached for her hand again. This time, she let him take it and he drew her close—to hell with what anyone thought.

'I don't know what comes next,' he said finally. 'I really don't. But I'm here with you now. Can that be enough for tonight?'

She didn't answer right away. She just looked at him with those wide, searching eyes and on the sidelines he felt other eyes on them, Aurora's included. He was pretty sure that any second now, Emilia was going to walk away and leave him standing here humiliated, but she didn't.

'Okay,' she whispered, letting him lead her onto the dance floor, where he looped his arms around her and breathed into her hair, and prayed it could be enough for them just to hold each other, just to know that this was something. But the secret he carried twisted even tighter in his chest as they danced. Madagascar wasn't going away. And neither was the clock ticking on whatever this something was between them.

CHAPTER EIGHTEEN

THE MUSIC WAS just winding down when a scream carved the night in two and made them spring apart. A woman had collapsed near the buffet table, loudly sending a tray of plates to the floor on the way down. Her mouth was open in a silent gasp, and her hands started clawing at her throat. Her husband, or whoever the guy was who'd appeared at her side, grabbed her shoulders, shouting for help as chaos erupted around the villa.

'What on earth…?' Aurora looked horrified, leaping forward to help them clear some space around her.

'Anaphylaxis?' Alejandro said, dropping to his knees beside her.

Emilia nodded, bunching up her dress as she knelt down next to him. 'Check her bag!'

He knew what she meant and he yanked the woman's purse open, his fingers diving past lipstick, lady products and tissues, looking for an EpiPen and thankfully finding one.

Emilia was tilting the woman's head back already, checking her airway. 'Oh boy. I see massive swelling…her tongue too.'

Alejandro uncapped the EpiPen and jabbed it into the woman's thigh. 'One dose in. Time?'

'Marking now. Nineteen forty-seven,' Emilia said. 'Pulse rapid. Respirations shallow. Chest and neck…'

He moved fast for the mask, grabbing the emergency kit from its place on the wall of the villa, calling for a transfer boat. When he returned, Emilia was gently rolling the woman to her side. The crowd had gathered too. Some of the women were crying, and someone else hurried to his side with towels and water.

'Have we got a central line port in the kit?' He felt along the woman's neck, and tried to keep his cool as the sobbing from one of the traumatised bystanders increased a notch.

'Is she going to die?' one woman whispered dramatically to her friend.

Frowning, he tuned them all out. They didn't matter, not even the photographer who was covering the event mattered, even though he was documenting the whole damn thing. What was wrong with people? At least in Madagascar there wouldn't be all this drama; he'd be remote. Based on a campsite. Living in a tent.

Far away from Emilia.

He looked at her now, but she was entirely focused in extracting the port from the first aid kit. He would miss this look on her face. He'd miss all of her. She wasn't a stopover. At least, he hadn't intended for her to become one, but he could hardly help the way he felt.

He slid the needle home and secured the port, calling for a pulse check.

'Still rapid. BP is dropping. Ninety-two over fifty-eight. Come on, come on…'

The woman's lips were a dusky blue now, and her chest rose shallowly as Alejandro checked her pupils. She was still reactive.

'You're okay. Just hang in there,' he soothed using one

hand to steady the woman's jaw and the other to adjust the mask seal.

This woman must not have known there was seafood in the dish; reactions this severe didn't sneak up on a person. They slammed in like a storm and knocked you for six, a bit like his unfortunate lifelong cat allergy, although this was far worse. His reaction gave him itchy hives and misery and, as with the last incident at the cat sanctuary delivering those twin babies with Emilia, a ton of embarrassment. Hers was threatening to steal her consciousness, maybe even her life, God forbid.

Two volunteer staff from the clinic were at the scene now in their fancy attire. The emergency transport boat was almost here. The woman's husband knelt nearby, and he noticed his trembling hands.

'She'll be okay,' he told him firmly. 'She's stable now. We've got her.'

Five minutes passed. Then ten. Slowly the woman's colour began to return to her lips and cheeks. Her pulse steadied. The wheezing in her lungs softened too, but when her eyes fluttered open she was still barely able to focus. Emilia reached for her hand as she blinked and a tear slid down her cheek. She mouthed her thanks, and it was only then that Emilia seemed to notice her dress had a little rip in it from where it must have snagged on something as they worked.

When the ambulance boat finally pulled away with the woman and her husband on board, Alejandro let out a long breath that had been taking up his entire body and sat back on his heels. His shirt was damp with sweat. His knees ached. He felt like he'd been pulled through a wringer.

Aurora handed him a chilled glass of wine and he refused it. He refused everything offered to him, and instead took himself outside, where he sat on the sand, gathering himself together. What a night! First, that dispute with Emilia and now this. Maybe he should just go to Madagascar as soon as possible, get away from all of this.

Emilia soon found him. She sat next to him in the sand, also catching her breath. Her tight updo had loosened. A few strands of her hair now stuck to her temple. She was the most beautiful thing he'd ever seen. Hell, forget Madagascar. Maybe he should never leave here. Feeling this torn was new to him; what the hell was he doing?

He turned to face her. 'Emilia…'

She shook her head. 'I'm exhausted.'

He nodded, clamping his mouth shut again. So was he. 'Then let's get out of here,' he said.

They walked silently, the sound of the band's music slowly fading behind them. By the time they reached the path to their lodgings, their side of the island was quiet, which went some way towards soothing his aching brain, but their argument still lingered in the air, along with his secret.

In Emilia's room, Alejandro stood just inside the doorway. The ocean glowed faintly through the window. He didn't miss the way her hands shook as she slipped off her shoes. He should just get it out. Tell her.

'Emilia…'

'I'm sorry about tonight,' she said, sitting down on the edge of the bed with a deep sigh. 'I don't want to argue with you, it's stupid, Alejandro. Life is so short, and precious. Just being here with you now is enough.'

He studied her from the doorway for a long time. Was it enough, though?

'Get some sleep,' he told her, though his feet wouldn't seem to move and take him back to his own room. Her fingers found the rip in her dress and she sighed again, shaking her head. Then she met his eyes, oceans full of longing that turned his stomach and set his heart pounding in his chest. Just being here wasn't enough for either of them, and they both knew it.

'I don't know if I can sleep after that.'

'Me neither.' Alejandro stepped forward, then sat on the bed beside her. Gently he took her face in his hands, traced her lips with his thumb, and kissed her. It was the kind of kiss that confused the hell out of him because he'd never done any of this to win her, or claim her, not really. He'd done it because she deserved to feel held and safe, and alive. And because in her own way, she made him feel seen and safe, and alive too. But just like dancing with her wasn't enough, kissing her wasn't enough. It would never be enough.

They didn't speak as their clothes fell away, or as her hands explored the muscles of his back, or as her breath caught when he lifted her onto the bed, moving slowly, making sure she really wanted this too.

Her body rose to meet his, just like it had been waiting all this time. To hell with over-thinking, and over-complicating everything. They fit perfectly together…her sighs against his skin, his mouth on hers. When he finally moved inside her and her hands clamped down on his shoulders, he knew that if this was a mistake, he was done with caring about it, and Emilia didn't seem to care much anymore either. It was a choice they were both making.

But she doesn't know you're leaving sooner than planned… It's not the time to bring it up.

After, as they lay tangled in the silence, the surf crashing faintly outside, Emilia turned her head towards him on the pillow. 'I didn't mean for this to happen tonight, you know that, don't you?'

He smiled. 'All I know is that I know when you're lying.'

She smacked his chest lightly, then rested her cheek there. He could joke all he liked but they both knew by now that this was something different. It couldn't exactly be denied at this point.

Neither of them moved for a long time. The sounds of the night wrapped around them in the dark and as the rain started speckling the roof, for once Alejandro didn't think about what came next or where he was supposed to be headed. He only thought about Emilia.

CHAPTER NINETEEN

EMILIA SAT ALONE on the edge of the jetty, watching the water glimmering gold beneath the sinking sun. The sky was all coral and flames and several people were snorkelling. Fishing boats bobbed gently. It used to feel like a wonderful dream, like a fairy godmother had whisked her away from New York to start a better life, but now…

Nine days.

It had only been nine days since the first time she and Alejandro had made love, but it felt a lot like the sky had turned upside down. If she closed her eyes she could still be back in that bed, the first morning after the night they'd spent making love, when she'd sighed in his arms and he'd pulled her close and picked right back up where they'd left off. She hadn't thought further than the door to the veranda then, but maybe she should have.

She pulled her knees to her chest, feeling the cool cotton of her linen trousers brushing against her bare, tanned arms. She should be working now, charting those follow-ups from the clinic, replying to that message from the nearby island that was asking about their upcoming supplies. But here she was. She couldn't believe what she had just overheard.

But then again, she could.

Her focus had splintered days ago because despite their

new closeness over the last nine days, she'd felt Alejandro slipping away.

It hadn't been abrupt. At first, it was just the little things. A kiss that didn't linger as long as it used to. A comment that felt too careful, like he was choosing his words so as not to ruffle any feathers. He still touched her in the mornings or after long shifts at the clinic, in the quiet of his room when the rest of the island had gone to sleep. But it was different now. It felt a lot like he was pulling away and holding her hand at the same time.

And now, she was doing the same. She was also creating distance on purpose because *she* didn't want to ruffle any feathers. He wasn't hers any more than she was his. She was dancing a stupid dance of pretend indifference and it was getting more than uncomfortable at this point!

She'd caught him, more than once, staring off into the lagoon with that same restless look he wore when something heavy was on his mind. Like the horizon whispered to him more sweetly than any woman ever could. Like the stillness made him nervous. Of course, she knew that look. She'd seen it before, on Aiden's face.

Her late husband had that same spark. That same ache for more. The difference was, Aiden had taken her with him, across countries and continents, to far-flung conferences, making even those into romantic dates. And she'd mostly put her work first. Until his body had been pulled from the wreckage of that car and she'd had to accept that their last silly argument had literally been their last, she hadn't even realised how her chance at motherhood and adventure might have been slipping away from right underneath her nose.

She'd sworn to herself then…no more putting her work first. But she had done it anyway. Because what other choice was there? How else was she supposed to numb the pain?

And then Alejandro had smiled at her that first day in the clinic with those ridiculous sparkling eyes and mussed-up hair, and he'd challenged her. Made her angry, ignited something long dead, then charmed her completely and kissed her like he meant it. For a while she'd let herself forget that good things didn't always last. She'd let herself wonder if maybe she could find a way to go with him. Wherever he wanted her to go!

Buried in his arms it felt like anything was possible, until he started closing off yet again.

By midweek, she'd buried herself in the clinic. Long days turned into longer nights. Inventory needed restocking. The solar generator had a fault she couldn't fix. A family from a nearby island came in with a fever that wouldn't break.

Alejandro offered help where he could, but she started turning him down. Not coldly. Just enough that he felt it. Just enough that she could convince herself she was pulling away before he could.

When he came by the clinic one evening with his shirt all damp from a dive, asking if she wanted to watch the turtles hatch with him under the full moon, she'd forced a smile and refused.

'I'd like the chance to talk too, Emilia,' he said.

'Can't. Got to sort the meds log. It's overdue.'

He hesitated then, looking at her carefully, obviously about to say something more, but she hadn't waited. 'Better go.'

She still hated herself for the way his face closed off, but the fear had taken hold of her heart, just like it always did.

The night after that, she didn't go back to her room until late, so he wouldn't have the chance to come knocking. Instead, she slept for a while in the bunk behind the consultation room, avoiding the way her heart cracked a bit more whenever she spotted a reminder of him: His favourite mug by the kettle, his notes on a whiteboard about the reef's recovery. Gosh, she was in far too deep.

She tried to tell herself that this was better. Safer. It was easier to breathe when she wasn't constantly waiting for the other shoe to drop, but her lungs still burned.

And then came tonight.

The clinic was locked up. She was thinking maybe they should talk, get whatever this was or wasn't out in the open. It wasn't fair on either of them to be playing this silly game, and all because they were scared of a few real feelings. She was heading back to her room when she heard his voice. Calm and controlled, but muffled.

He was on his veranda, half shadowed, pacing.

'Yes, you're right. Madagascar does make sense. I'll wrap things up here in the next few days.'

The world tipped sideways. Emilia froze, then quickly dipped into the shadows of a nearby tree as he paused. 'No, I haven't told them yet.'

Her heart thudded against her ribs. What? Who was he talking to?

'It's complicated,' he continued. 'But I won't leave the foundation in a mess...'

Emilia turned back on herself and walked away before she could hear any more. She didn't cry. She just moved like she was walking through water. Every step felt heavier than the last until she found herself here on the jetty, hugging her knees, watching the sky turn darker by the second.

Rain was coming. And he was going. Of course he was. So much for her not being another stopover. She fiddled with her loose hair, braiding it absently. She hadn't braided it for a while, loving the feel of it loose. A sign of becoming less rigid and more like the free-spirited Emilia she *wanted* to be.

What did it matter now?

Maybe he'd known this for weeks. Maybe he'd meant to tell her and just hadn't found the right moment. Or maybe he had tried to talk—several times, on reflection—but she hadn't let him. She had been too terrified of this exact moment.

It didn't matter anymore. She'd let herself believe for a fleeting second that things might be different with Alejandro. That a man who'd spent his life chasing the horizon might actually want to stop and stay a while with her. That she might actually find love again, when in reality, all it did was leave a sting in its wake that she definitely did not need, not after Aiden. Hadn't she learned anything from losing him? Nothing this good was ever going to last. She'd walked headfirst into this, but what had she expected? That this magical daydream could last forever?

She was still cursing her own misfortune when she heard him come up behind her. Had he come to look for her?

Instead of pausing and letting him sit beside her, she stood, flustered, just as the thunder cracked the sky. Then, not really stopping to think about what the heck she was doing, she stripped off her clothes down to her swimsuit and leaped from the jetty.

She swam around the bay, eventually pulling herself out of the water under a stormy sky. He was right behind her but she couldn't face him, not after what she'd heard, not knowing he'd probably been keeping this information from her for weeks, all while they'd been sleeping together. How dare he?

She stalked ahead along the beach path in her violet swimsuit, pretending she couldn't hear Alejandro behind her. But she could. She could hear every scuff of his flip-flops in the sand and every breath he took as got closer, and it made her heart pound. He'd probably seen her leaving the shadows around their rooms just now and decided that now was the time to talk. Well, it was too late.

'Emilia, slow down,' he called. But she couldn't slow down. If she slowed down, she might stop altogether. She might turn around and do something stupid like forgive him, or worse, kiss him. And right now, she needed distance.

The breeze whipped her hair around her face as she forged her way to where the path disappeared and gave way to rocks. The sea churned ahead of her under the darkening sky, and as the first sting of rain slapped her skin, she growled to herself, barely even feeling it. She only felt mad.

Alejandro caught up to her, grabbing her arm gently but firmly. Damn it, she couldn't get away from him now if she tried, the island was just too damn small!

'Enough, Emilia!' he snapped. 'We need to talk.'

She ripped her arm free, whirling on him. 'About what exactly, Alejandro? About how you never intended to tell me you were leaving? About how this was just a pit stop before you ran off to save someone else, somewhere else? What's in Madagascar? Or should I ask, *who* is in Madagascar?'

His face tightened. His hair was messy from the wind, his unbuttoned shirt flapping about. God, he looked good. Better than good, as usual, and she hated him for it.

'You knew what this was,' he said. 'You knew from the start I wasn't staying here forever.'

'Yes, but I didn't know you'd make me want you to stay,' she hissed at him before she could stop herself.

The words hung there between them as Alejandro dragged a hand through his hair. 'Emilia, I never lied to you. You're the one who's making this into more than it was supposed to be.'

Ouch.

Her stomach twisted, white-hot. 'Oh, so now it's my fault I fell for you?'

His mouth opened, then shut again. Rain was hitting her harder now, already plastering her hair to her face, but she barely noticed.

'I care about you,' he said finally, his voice rough. 'But I can't stay. And I can't be what you need.'

She let out a laugh. 'You think I need saving?' she snapped. 'I'm not some broken little bird you need to patch up before you fly yourself off to the next crisis, Alejandro. I didn't ask you to stick around anywhere with me. I just thought—' She cut herself off, swallowing down the emotion that was clawing its way up her throat. 'It doesn't matter. You're right. I have been making this into more than it was supposed to be.'

His face twisted as the thunder cracked loudly overhead, making the sand vibrate under her feet. What was this? What were they doing to each other? Even now, through her pain and fury, all she wanted was to bury herself in his arms, but he was leaving, so she couldn't, and she most definitely would not admit how he was tearing her to pieces right now.

'I have had the time of my life with you,' he ground out, stepping closer, his forehead nearly touching hers, his breath ragged. 'But I'm not built to stay anywhere, or with anyone, for long, Emilia. I thought maybe I was, when you and I got close but…'

'Don't even say it,' she huffed, humiliated. Hot tears clouded her vision. 'You don't have to say it. We should never have started this.'

Alejandro's face crumpled for a half second…so fast she almost missed it. Then he stepped back, putting two feet of agonising space between them. It was quiet now, except for the rain and the rising roar of the waves.

'You deserve better than me—you deserve more than a man who just…disappears,' he said, voice hoarse.

'Oh please. I already lost someone I loved. I already know how to survive being the one who's left behind. Losing you won't be any different, Alejandro.'

There, she'd said it.

She might as well have lashed out with her hand from the look on his face. But she'd lied to him; it would be different. She already knew that. It would be worse, because this time, she wasn't losing someone to fate or bad luck. This time, he was choosing to leave her, to resume the nomadic existence that she had no part in. And he hadn't even told her he was planning on going. He'd just waited for her to overhear.

Another crack of thunder split the air. The rain was soaking them both to the bone by now and Alejandro looked wrecked.

'I'll see if I can get out of here earlier,' he mumbled, balling his fits to his sides. 'Goodbye, Emilia.'

She didn't answer him. What was there left to say? She just watched him turn and walk away, his broad shoulders disappearing into the sheets of rain.

CHAPTER TWENTY

THE STORM SPLINTERED the night just as he turned back, but he had already lost sight of her.

Alejandro barely made it ten paces back down the sand when the first gust hit with enough force to send him staggering forward. Holy crap, this was unlike anything they'd ever experienced here before. He had heard on the radio that there was a big one coming, but already the palm fronds were bending so low to the earth he thought they might snap.

He pushed forward, noticing how they were bowing ever lower beneath every sudden howl of wind. Rain lashed sideways at him in sheets, flattening the already soaking landscape, like the island was punishing him for his own cowardice and stupidity. Why had he said all that? Why had he told Emilia that she was the one making this into more than it was supposed to be? He hadn't meant to be so…callous. It was self-preservation, obviously.

He froze, his breath catching in his throat. He'd meant to go back to his room, to let the air cool his temper, to lick the fresh wounds she'd left with her own words about not needing him, not missing him once he was gone, but something twisted in the atmosphere. A deep, reverberating sound carried across the island like thunder rolling over metal and straight into his ears. The ominous sound of something cracking and splintering made his heart sink.

It was coming from the direction of the resort.

And then he heard the screams.

Alejandro turned on instinct, shaking off his flip-flops and bolting barefoot across the squelching sand towards the source. From the south side of the atoll, past the line of overwater villas, he saw it—two of the huts were now tilting sideways on their stilts, battered by rising waves and a freak surge that had come out of nowhere.

Shouts cut across the night. He made out a child's terrified cry, and then a woman's voice yelling someone's name.

'Hold on.'

He sprinted as fast as his legs would let him in the wind, and it fought him every step of the way, dragging at his wet shirt, pushing him back, but he kept on going. He splashed through rising seawater and eventually reached the path that led to the villas, stopping short just as one of them—a new-build suite with a glass-bottomed floor—tilted with a loud groan. Part of it cracked away and collapsed into the water. His hands found his head in horror.

'No, God...'

Two people were in the water. He could see them flailing even from here. One of them was clinging desperately to the edge of some broken decking, and the other one was bobbing on the surface of the black lagoon several metres away.

'Hold on!' he repeated, though he was certain no one could hear him over the wind and rain.

So he yanked off his shirt and dived straight into the turbulent washing machine. The swirling mess of broken wood and debris rose up to meet him like a thousand knives intent on slashing his skin, and his sister's face flashed into his mind among the dead fish. His shoulder clipped something extra sharp as he plunged downward, but he ignored it, kicking hard towards the figure that was now slipping under.

It was a boy. Around ten, maybe twelve, already coughing up water, his eyes wide and terrified. He thought he'd seen him around the island.

Alejandro grabbed him around the chest and pushed upward, breaking the surface as a new wave slammed into them and his sister's face flashed at him again from out of nowhere, almost like she was telling him something from across the miles. The salt stung his eyes. His lungs burned. But he kept them both afloat somehow, kicking towards the half-submerged deck.

'Help!' he shouted over and over. 'Somebody!'

And then, like a miracle, Emilia was there.

She reached over the broken edge of the walkway, her eyes wild and panicked, her loose hair completely hair drenched. She was still only wearing that swimsuit. Quickly she extended a length of rope. Someone must have brought it from the storage hut.

Her voice was steady despite the chaos all around them, and the lash of the wind and the rain. 'Pass me the boy first!'

He didn't question her but merely obeyed, and he was surprised when it took every ounce of his strength. Battling all the debris in the water had taken it out of him.

Emilia pulled the child out of his arms like he weighed nothing, dragging him up with two volunteers who had appeared beside her now. Alejandro scrambled after them, coughing. Blood was slicking his arm where the debris had sliced him but he couldn't afford to let it slow him down.

'There's another one,' he gasped. 'Still in the water. She's clinging to the far post.'

'I'll go,' Emilia said immediately, tying her hair back. 'You're bleeding.'

'I'm fine.'

'No, you're not.'

Another scream made his heart lurch into his throat. They both looked up quickly, just in time to see another section of walkway break loose right in front of them under the pressure of all the water and wind. The boy shrieked.

Alejandro caught her wrist. 'We go together,' he said, and she didn't refuse. She was all business now, like their argument had already been forgotten.

They leaped together this time, pushing through the churning sea, reaching the woman in seconds. Her arm was badly cut, but thankfully she was conscious. Alejandro held her upright while Emilia checked the bleeding as best she could. And then all three of them were hauled back to what remained of the decking by another team of brave locals and volunteers. He hated to admit it but he couldn't imagine what might have happened if they hadn't.

'Are you okay?' he whispered, unable to stop his hand reaching for hers. She was cold, and shivering. But she yanked her hand back and avoided his eyes. She was only concerned about the boy.

By the time they got the woman into the clinic, the rain had turned to needles and the entire south side of the resort was pretty much underwater. Several of the locals were fighting back tears, and even Emilia gave a little gasp when the power went out.

'The generators will kick in,' he told her, and sure enough, three seconds later they did.

Through it all, Emilia didn't speak to him again. Not once. They moved around each other doing what needed to be done like the professionals they were, but every glance seemed to burn with the remnants of that stupid argument, which certainly had not been forgotten, much as he hoped it might be. It was all so stupid… Of course she meant more to him than a casual fling or stopover, but his sister…his work. He had panicked!

All of it sat there in the silence between them, which was getting so loud he could barely think.

Emilia stitched the injured woman's arm while he checked the boy for concussion. She didn't glance at him. Not even when he reached for a fresh towel and brushed against her shoulder. Not even when he whispered 'Careful' as she shifted to avoid a trailing IV cable.

He wanted to say something. Anything. But what?

You were right? *I was going to leave without saying goodbye*?

A sudden crack outside had them both running to the doorway.

The lagoon had risen even higher now. Lights blinked out one by one across the horizon. A boat had broken from its mooring and smashed against the far wall of the dive centre. There were locals out in it now, trying to recover it, the idiots, and Alejandro swore under his breath.

'I'll go,' he said, already moving. 'Tom might need me.'

Emilia stopped him with a hand to his chest.

'Don't,' she said, her eyes finally meeting his. 'Please. They've got it, Alejandro. Look, there's a few of them out there. You are needed here, for when the injured start coming in.'

Their eyes locked, and in that moment a thousand unsaid things seemed to wash into the space between them. Alejandro saw exactly what she was saying without words, what she couldn't bring herself to actually utter. She didn't want him out of her sight. Not because this stupid rift between them had been miraculously healed and not because she had decided to offer him forgiveness, but because the thought of him vanishing into danger cut too deep for her.

Her fury earlier hadn't just been about his silence; it had been about how she'd found out, about being blindsided again, abandoned without warning.

The weight of it crashed over him like a second storm. God, how could he have been so blind and ignorant? He'd thought he had been sparing her pain by keeping his impending departure quiet, but in truth, he'd only reopened old, still-raw wounds. She'd trusted him and he'd only gone and betrayed that trust. He'd totally freaked out in secret, knowing that against his better judgement he was changing. Because of Emilia, some things about his life were going to *have* to change. Instead of dealing with all that like a man, he'd panicked and pushed her away. He'd made the call, accepted the position, told her he was going to expedite his departure.

Idiot.

He didn't deserve her loyalty, or her bravery. But he wasn't going to stand by while some avoidable tragedy happened in the water, not when he was an expert swimmer and there were volunteer medics around the clinic to help her. She would understand eventually, because he planned to tell her exactly what she meant to him, but right now, there was no time.

'I'm sorry,' he told her wild eyes instead. Then he flung open the door and sprinted back out into the storm.

CHAPTER TWENTY-ONE

THE STORM HOWLED like a wounded beast outside the clinic, battering the shutters, screaming through every crack in the building. The power was still out. The generators had given up, too. The candles and battery-powered lanterns they'd scrambled together were throwing eerie dancing shadows on the walls, stretching Emilia's already frayed nerves to the edge.

Where was he?

She moved from one patient to the next, doing her best to calm her whirring thoughts. First the triage, then the clean, stitch, bandage, reassess, start over again. A few other volunteers were helping out, and between them they had things mostly covered, but she was still beyond mad that Alejandro had gone out there. And more than a tiny bit scared.

A tourist who'd crawled in with a gash across her thigh screamed as Emilia cleaned the wound, but she didn't flinch. Her hands were moving as steadily as usual, or so she thought. Her voice came out as calm as if she were operating on a cloud, but her insides were utter chaos because he was gone, and there was still no sign of him. She kept glancing up at the door as if he might suddenly walk in, but he didn't.

She cursed him under her breath. He just couldn't help himself, could he? The man had a switch in him that flipped every time disaster struck. While others ran for shelter, he ran right into the eye of it every time, like he had something to prove, the stubborn idiot.

'Hold that there,' Emilia muttered to one of the resort staff who'd come to help, placing their hand firmly on a bleeding shoulder wound before moving on to the next patient. 'Keep pressure on it, okay?'

The next man on the table had a broken arm, and his bone had come clean through the skin. She didn't even stop to flinch. She set it efficiently, ignoring the wet heat sliding down her cheeks until she realised she was actually crying. And not for this poor man.

'Doctor?' someone said gently behind her. It was one of the new volunteers who'd barely been on the island a week.

'What?' she barked too sharp. Then she exhaled and softened her voice again, reaching for the calm she didn't feel. 'Sorry. What is it?'

'They think two men were pulled under when the railing collapsed. A boat capsized…they found one body. The other's still missing.'

Emilia's lungs froze. Her hands did too, mid-suture, mid-thought, mid-everything. She didn't want to ask. She didn't want to hear the name, but she knew it was him.

She just knew.

Alejandro.

He was the kind of man who would give his life to save someone else's without blinking. And now, she was certain that's exactly what he'd gone and done. Oh God…

Okay…it might not be him.

Don't panic.

How the hell am I supposed to not panic?

The air rushed out of her lungs in a stuttering gasp. She squeezed her eyes shut and did her best to swallow the urge to wail without causing her patient any alarm. She even forced herself to keep stitching. This was what she did, what New York City expected of her. Only now she wasn't there. All of New York had been washed out of her weeks ago, replaced with this place, and...him.

If her patient noticed her shaking hands, he didn't mention it and she was grateful. She kept on stitching, trying to hate Alejandro for being the kind of man who seemed to thrive on vanishing into chaos. And even worse, he knew very well what losing someone had done to her once, and he'd just walked out into the storm anyway. The man had just proved how little he cared about her, as if he hadn't given her enough proof earlier! How could she want someone who'd put her through this again?

She didn't want him and she sure as hell didn't need him.

The lie shattered inside her like glass.

She did want him. Because she loved him. Fiercely. Stupidly. With all of her heart. And now it was probably too late to ever tell him.

The wind shrieked louder, lifting a loose corner of the roof in the far wing. Water started to pour down the wall, soaking one of the beds. Someone screamed. Another patient moaned in pain. A child got up and clung to her leg, whimpering for his mother.

Emilia knelt down, holding the child close, whispering that everything was going to be perfectly fine, even as her own voice cracked in her throat. The clinic was full of people in pain. She had no time to break down, but her heart, God, her heart was in pieces.

If he was gone...if she was never to see Alejandro again... if the last words she ever said to him had been spoken in anger, she couldn't bear it. Not again. She'd argued with Aiden before he—

No.

She just had to keep moving. Keep treating people who came in. Keep on breathing. What else could she do?

Another hour passed. Then another. The rain didn't let up. Throughout the night, they treated the injured. A dislocated shoulder, then an awful suspected fracture and dozens of cuts and bruises, too many to count in the end. The radios were down. The only news from outside came in trickles from people who stopped in as they ran from one end of the island to the next, scouring the debris where they could reach it over the floodwaters.

No one had seen Alejandro since he left. No one. He really was gone.

Pain. That was the first thing Alejandro felt as he came to. He winced at the searing bolt that shot down his ribs and through his left leg, and pressed his hands to his throbbing temple, feeling the rough burn of salt on his skin.

Then came the light. Too much of it. Blinding, brilliant, golden light. It made no sense.

He groaned, blinking against the blazing sun as the world slowly came back into focus. A stretch of white sand. Broken palm fronds scattered like bones. The lap of gentle waves against the shore.

He was alive. Somehow. And the storm was over. But where was he?

Sitting up, he realised he was shirtless and his shoulder and leg hurt like hell. Oh yes. He'd knocked his shoulder yesterday diving into the floodwaters, pulling that boy out. The boy was okay. But his leg…his leg was not okay. How had that happened? He couldn't even remember.

He rubbed his eyes as his sister's face flashed into his

brain, quickly followed by Emilia's. Was Emilia okay? Where was she?

He caught something moving in the corner of his eye. Men. They were all wearing orange vests, jogging down the beach to reach him, yelling and waving their arms. In seconds he heard the drone of a helicopter circling above them.

'Hey! You! You okay over here?' someone yelled.

Hands were on him seconds later, checking his pulse, lifting his head, sliding something under his body. He tried to speak, to ask what the hell was going on, but his throat was raw and his lips were cracked. The words just wouldn't leave his mouth. Damn, he must be busted up pretty bad. He could barely get his thoughts straight, he was so dehydrated.

'Just hang on,' a voice said, confirming his thoughts. 'We've got you. You're gonna be fine, bud.'

Before he knew it, he was in the helicopter. Then he was coming to again with the beeping of a heart monitor in his ear, and the pungent smell of antiseptic wafting uncomfortably up his nostrils. He winced as a needle slid into his upper thigh, and registered that he was in a hospital somewhere getting help, at least. Then he passed out again.

He drifted in and out for hours, maybe even days. It was hard to tell. Everything blurred together in a fog of painkillers, whispered voices, squeaky wheels on shiny floors and the occasional sharp jab of a regretful memory. The wave that had knocked him off the pier the second he reached it to go after the floating dive equipment, the desperate kicks to reach the surface from underneath the rubble, the drag of the current pulling him under again and again. The argument with Emilia.

Wow. Tough night by anyone's standards.

And Tom. Where was Tom?

When the nurse finally told him one of the men hadn't made it, his stomach twisted into knots. No, please...not Tom.

'Was it...the guy with me?' His voice came out hoarse, barely there at all. 'Tall, dark hair?'

The nurse shook her head gently. 'No. A local fisherman. They pulled your friend in earlier. He's recovering.'

Alejandro closed his eyes, feeling the relief loosening the knot in his stomach. Tom was safe, thank God. But still, the guilt settled like lead on his shoulders. One man hadn't made it. One life had been lost while he'd clung to that driftwood and let the sea decide if he himself deserved to live.

The words he'd exchanged with Emilia on the beach kept coming back to him, like his own memory was desperate to punish him for what he'd said, and what he hadn't said too. He was confined to bed for three whole days. The bruises on his ribs ran deep, his busted leg was wrapped from ankle to thigh and he couldn't walk beyond the bathroom without pain clawing through him. He asked about the island and the clinic, and Emilia. But no one had answers. No one even seemed to know who she was, and the island's cell tower had been toppled in the storm, so there was still no signal, no way of reaching her, if she was even still there.

So he waited. Day after day. Listening for her footsteps. Watching the door, hoping for a miracle that never came.

Maybe she didn't care anymore. Maybe she hadn't even bothered trying to find him. Maybe she thought he was dead and was doing her best to move on. Maybe she was relieved to be rid of him one way or another. He'd told her he was leaving anyway. He'd been a total ass.

The ache in his chest was worse than the pain in his leg, and worse than all the bruises. He'd never had this much time to simply sit and think before and it was killing him.

But then, on the fourth afternoon, just as the sun began

its slow slide towards the horizon, he looked up from an old tattered thriller novel, and there she was.

Emilia was standing in the doorway, looking at him in pity. Her hair was back in its braid, although looser than usual, and despite the dark circles under her eyes she was a thousand times more beautiful in this moment than she'd ever been.

He tried to sit up. 'Emilia…'

She held up a hand, stepping towards him tentatively. 'Don't. You'll tear something.'

The tears in her eyes nearly broke him. 'I thought…' He struggled to find the words. 'How did you know I was here?'

'I didn't know anything until this morning,' she whispered, stepping closer. 'I didn't even know they'd sent anyone to the mainland, Alejandro. The phones were down…'

'I know.'

'I thought you were dead,' she managed. The words came out choked. 'They told me two men drowned, and I thought…' She faced away from him, gripping the edge of the bed so hard that her knuckles whitened.

He reached for her, ignoring the pain in his ribs. 'You came.'

'Of course I came,' she said, her voice fierce now. 'The second I found out, I got on the first boat. Do you have any idea what you put me through, you reckless idiot?'

A smile tugged at his lips. 'I could ask you the same thing. I thought you'd be glad to be rid of me.'

She shook her head. 'I watched you dive into that water without thinking twice. I watched you risk yourself for people you don't even know and I hated you for it, Alejandro, but only because I was so worried.'

'I know why you were worried,' he said.

'You have to forgive me for making you believe I didn't

care about you. I care too much, that's the problem. I don't want to lose you to Madagascar, or anywhere else. I know that's selfish, and I know you need to do what you need to do, but...'

A stray tear slunk down her cheek before she swiped at it with the back of her hand. 'But I need you alive, okay? Even if that's all you are to me. I needed to see you one last time to know you're okay and to tell you... I don't want us to part on bad terms, or make you feel guilty in any way. I'm... I'm going to be fine without you, eventually. If anything, you've shown me a different way to live. I've been thinking I might even leave New York.'

'Oh, really?' This was news to him, but already his head was spinning. 'Where would you go?'

She shrugged. 'I don't know. Anywhere. I want to keep shaking things up. I've been stagnant for way too long. Maybe a nomad's life wouldn't be too terrible for a while.'

'Wait a minute, hold on,' he said, wrapping his fingers tighter around her hand. Already, it sounded like she was moving on and making plans that didn't involve him, and the thought was suddenly debilitating. 'Are you seriously saying you're thinking about moving around the world, just as I'm thinking about staying in one place?'

She opened her mouth to speak, but closed it again. She tried again. 'One place?' She swiped at another tear, staring at their fingers with confusion written all over her tired face. 'What are you saying? Which place?'

'I don't know. I don't care,' he growled, struggling to sit up again despite her telling him not to. 'That's redundant. I thought I'd never get the chance to say this,' he murmured. 'But I love you, Emilia. I love you. And if you ever let me walk into a storm like that again without telling you that, I swear to God I'll...' He paused, shocked for a moment by the look on her face. 'I'll… I forgot what I was going to say. You are distractingly beautiful, do you know that?'

She frowned at him, a smile playing on her lips. 'Are you high on meds right now?'

He laughed, drawing her hand to his lips and kissing her fingers. 'Maybe, but it's true. I don't need to keep moving, at least not as much as I have been. I don't need to prove anything more to myself or my family. I mean…look at me. Look where running off into the line of fire has gotten me lately. I almost lost you, and my leg.'

She winced. 'How is your leg?'

'I'll need physio for a few months,' he sighed. 'I'll be off it for a while too. I'll be looking for a nurse, maybe a private one.' He drew her even closer, this time bringing his lips to hers. 'Do you know any?'

Emilia leaned down and pressed her forehead to his, her breath warm against his skin. 'Absolutely not. You'd be a nightmare patient. And I don't mix business with pleasure. Besides, who knows where I'll be? If you're not going to Madagascar, they'll need someone else. Maybe I should go in your place?'

'You're killing me.'

She smirked. 'I hope not, because I love you.'

'Say it again.'

'I hope not.'

'The other part.'

'I love you?'

'I love you too.'

Emilia laughed through her tears, and then she kissed him. It was a kiss that promised something he didn't even have the words for, but it was definitely something worth staying still for. Wherever he ended up resting and healing his damn leg, he already knew it wasn't going to be very far from Emilia.

Two Years Later—Valencia, Spain

'Emilia, more sangria for you? Or are you pretending to be responsible again?'

Maria's voice carried from the terrace table, teasing her, and Emilia smiled and lifted her glass. 'I was pretending,' she called back with a grin. 'Top me up, please, girl! Or should I say *llenar mi vaso*?'

Alejandro's sister grinned and poured the red wine concoction generously into her glass, the fruits inside jingling against the ice in the late-afternoon sun. Beyond them, the rooftops of Valencia glowed impressively golden as she'd come to love them on their frequent visits. Swifts darted through the sky above them, slicing between the lemon trees and wrought iron balconies. It was a scene straight out of a painting, or a dream, she mused. Mind you, her life felt like a dream sometimes, these days.

'Your Spanish is actually getting decent,' Alejandro murmured beside her, brushing a hand along her bare knee under the table.

'That's what cultural immersion does,' Emilia said, feigning smugness. 'A year in Guatemala, half a year coming here more regularly and now I can order wine and negotiate a local ambulance. Are you proud of me?'

'You know I am. You know how to flirt too.'

'Hmm,' she turned to him, eyes dancing. 'I can do that in a hundred languages, because it doesn't take any words.'

Alejandro's smirk faltered for half a beat. She caught it.

'What?' she asked.

'Nothing.' He leaned in, kissed her cheek. 'Just loving you for being you.'

Suspicious, she thought, and not for the first time today. He was being very sweet but also more than a little sneaky. 'You know what, I have the strangest suspicion…'

'*Atishoo!*' His sneeze completely stole the words from her mouth, just as she noticed the skinny white cat slinking around the table leg. Leaping from his chair, Alejandro all but sprinted towards the house, mumbling something about fetching the antihistamines he had clearly forgotten to take this morning.

A lucky escape, she thought, exchanging an amused smile with Maria. Much to Alejandro's dismay, his sister had refused to get rid of her beloved cat, Maestro, even when they announced they'd be spending more time with the family in Spain.

She'd noticed it all week though, this secrecy. The way Alejandro kept checking his pocket when he thought she wasn't looking, the way he whispered with Maria and clammed up the second Emilia walked into a room. Once, she'd even caught him rehearsing something in the mirror, his expression the perfect blend of agony and vulnerability. She'd pretended not to see, of course, but her heart had stumbled and leaped like a frog to places her mind had not been ready to visit! Surely not...this thing between them was still so new. Wasn't it?

But then again, maybe it wasn't anymore. It was just that their relationship always felt that way—so fresh and new!

Ever since her contract at the clinic had ended and she'd taken him back to New York, which before had been all grief and ghosts to her after Aiden, everything had changed. He hadn't wanted to go at first. He'd insisted his leg would finish healing better somewhere quieter and warmer and less—what was it he'd said?—less rude. But she'd needed it. She had needed the closure before they could start something new together. She had unfinished business at the hospital, ties to untangle, patients and staff to say goodbye to.

And he'd come for her. She'd told him she would make it worth his while.

During those weeks in Manhattan, she'd shown him her favourite hidden bookshop in the West Village, the diner with the pancakes the size of his head, the rooftop where she used to cry and now just watched the city lights blinking like distant galaxies, feeling nothing but gratitude. They'd walked slowly through Central Park, his leg still dragging a little like the three-legged dog she'd come to know out on its daily walk with its owner, keeping her arm around his waist. He'd teased her for being a New Yorker who still got excited by the squirrels. She'd fallen for him even more because of the way he saw her world, and the way he saw her, unfiltered.

Alejandro had made New York feel new again. He'd made it feel like home again. Not a shrine to Aiden and most definitely not a place of endings. It was a place of beginnings, instead. And when they'd left, having packed up her apartment and rented it out and bought two one-way tickets to Guatemala to start their NGO work, it had felt right. Like they were moving forward together. It was the plan she had needed, with enough freedom and spontaneity to make Alejandro satisfied.

Still, she hadn't expected…well, this. Not yet. But with every nervous glance from his direction, every barely hidden grin at his sister, it became harder to deny. Something was coming. She could hardly finish her sangria now. Her heart was in her throat.

'So,' Maria interjected now, clapping her hands together as Alejandro took his seat, giving the cat the side eye. 'Are you two heading back to Guatemala after this? Or making Spain home for a bit longer? Oh, please, say Spain!'

Emilia looked at him, her jitters momentarily forgotten.

'Guatemala again,' he said. 'For now. The project's expanding. We're training more midwives in remote areas and setting up a new mobile clinic.'

'And he's on a new water quality and access project,' she added proudly.

Alejandro was studying contamination levels in rivers and wells over there in parts of the Maya Biosphere Reserve, helping the locals set up rainwater collection systems while also researching the impact of climate change on local water cycles. It was always going to be his passion and she loved him more for it, especially when she saw her pride echoed in Maria's eyes.

'I've rented my place in New York indefinitely now,' she added, shrugging. 'Guess I'm not done running after this lunatic just yet.'

'I think it's me who's running after *you* these days,' Alejandro said, and she watched him reach for a slice of orange, popping it into his mouth and grinning. She felt her heart resume its weird irregular beat. Maybe she was imagining that he was hiding something?

No.

No way, she knew him too well!

Later, as the sun bled out into a beautiful burnt-orange dusk, Alejandro tugged her away from the terrace and his sister and her new boyfriend, and down the winding cobblestone alley at the back of the house.

'Where are we going?' Emilia asked, laughing.

'You'll see.'

They climbed a narrow staircase between the ancient walls that he hadn't shown her before and on the way up, she felt the nervousness settle in her stomach all over again. At the top, she gasped before the breath lodged in her throat.

The rooftop was empty except for a single table, two chairs and a view that stole whatever was left of her breath straight from her lungs. The Mediterranean shimmered and blinked at them in the distance, the last light of day twinkling orange over its surface.

'Wow,' she whispered.

He pulled her close, holding her for a long moment in silence, and strangely she felt a tear prickle in the corner of her eye. He was always surprising her with new things, even in places she thought she knew.

'Two years ago,' he said finally as her arms came up around his shoulders, 'I thought I was going to die in that storm.'

She looked up and touched his jaw gently. 'Yes, so did I, but you didn't.'

'No. I didn't. Because life clearly had other plans for me. One of them, I think, was you, Doctor.'

She blinked, her heart jumping into her throat again. 'You say the sweetest things.'

'I'm making up for all the times I didn't.' He took her hands, his brave mask slipping a little in a way that only she would have seen. Then, very slowly, he sank to one knee, reached into his pocket and pulled out a small velvet box. That was it. She was fully crying now, swiping at her face.

'I knew it,' she mumbled, staring in wonder at the simple ring, which was catching the last rays of sun, making it look like it had been crafted with fire.

'You knew it?'

'Never mind.'

She would let him have this moment. This utterly perfect moment.

It was gold, she realised. A single sapphire in the centre. She'd stopped to look at this very ring in the window of Tiffany's some time ago, and then when he'd caught her, pretended she hadn't been looking at it at all. That had been a *long* time ago, actually. Had he bought it then, in preparation? Had he been planning to ask her this since New York?

'Emilia,' he said quietly, forcing her frenzied thoughts back into focus, 'I have followed you across continents, into storms, into chaos and calm and parks, and even Macy's Day parades, and… I love you through all of it. And I want to keep loving you for the rest of our lives. Will you do me the immense honour of keeping my wild nomad ways in check forever, and marrying me?'

Time stopped completely. If there were any other sounds from below on the street she didn't hear them.

'I love your wild nomad ways,' she admitted, blinking back her tears. She couldn't believe she hadn't seen this coming, and then had absolutely seen this coming, all in the same day. Was this real life?

Then, with so many tears in her eyes that she could barely see, she dropped to her knees too and kissed him hard.

'Yes,' she breathed. 'Yes. A thousand times yes, I will marry you, Alejandro.'

'And have my babies?'

'However many you want, whenever you want.'

The city seemed to breathe out around them suddenly, like it had also been holding its breath for this magical moment. The hum of life below rushed back, the clang of dishes in a nearby restaurant, the flutter of pigeons, the soft strum of a guitar. Then, as if summoned by something completely divine, the church bells chimed the hour from around the block. She laughed through the tears in her eyes.

'Did you plan that?'

He only smiled, his eyes never leaving hers. Maybe he *had* planned it. She wouldn't put it past him.

On a rooftop in Valencia, wrapped in the most stunning golden light she'd seen since the Maldives, locked in the arms of the man who'd taught her how to live again, Emilia found herself letting go of everything she'd carried around with her for years, this time completely. If it had all been squeezed into a suitcase, she was now tossing it off the side of the building—all the grief, all the guilt, all the fear of loving someone who might one day leave her heartbroken and alone. It all wafted away on the breeze and disappeared into the sunset.

Here, with Alejandro, who was steady and brave and impossibly hers, she felt safe and whole, and she knew she always would. She wasn't looking back in fear anymore, only forward with the kind of excitement and lust for life that she hoped very soon to pass on to their children.

* * * * *

If you enjoyed this story, check out these other great reads from Becky Wicks

Christmas with Her Rival
A Daddy for Her Babies
From a Fling to a Family
Nurse's Keralan Temptation

All available now!

MILLS & BOON ®

THE PARAMEDIC ROOMMATE PACT
JC Harroway

'Sometimes life doesn't make much sense,' he said, his gaze lingering on her mouth for a few exhilarating seconds during which Kaia became increasingly convinced that he wanted her too.

'It makes no sense to me that a guy would walk away from you.'

A thrilling gasp sounded in her head. 'You're just saying that because you're my friend,' she pointed out, almost from habit, clinging to her last shred of willpower.

Their jokes often bordered on flirtation. But Levi's expression wasn't friendly. It was intense and searing and raging with need.

'I *am* your friend,' he confirmed, the look on his face and the few cryptic words he'd spoken, flooding her pelvis with liquid heat that slid down her legs so she feared she might actually collapse.

Drunk on the excitement pounding through her body but safe in the knowledge that he cared about her, that she trusted him, she slowly raised her hands to his shoulders.

'Well on that note, happy birthday,' she whispered.

She rose onto the tips of her toes and pressed her lips to his. Brief. Forbidden. And so tempting she couldn't breathe.

Continue reading

THE PARAMEDIC ROOMMATE PACT
JC Harroway

Available next month
millsandboon.co.uk

COMING SOON!

We really hope you enjoyed reading this book.
If you're looking for more romance
be sure to head to the shops when
new books are available on

Thursday 26th February

To see which titles are coming soon, please visit

millsandboon.co.uk/nextmonth

MILLS & BOON

LET'S TALK

Romance

For exclusive extracts, competitions and special offers, find us online:

- **f** MillsandBoon
- **X** @MillsandBoon
- **◎** @MillsandBoonUK
- **♪** @MillsandBoonUK

Get in touch on 01413 063 232